DRAGON TEETH

Also by E. Howard Hunt

UNDERCOVER: MEMOIRS OF AN AMERICAN SECRET AGENT
THE BERLIN ENDING
THE HARGRAVE DECEPTION
THE KREMLIN CONSPIRACY
THE GAZA INTERCEPT
THE DUBLIN AFFAIR
MURDER IN STATE
THE SANKOV CONFESSION
EVIL TIME
BODY COUNT
CHINESE RED
THE PARIS EDGE

Jack Novak Series:

COZUMEL
GUADALAJARA
MAZATLÁN
IXTAPA
ISLAMORADA
IZMIR

DRAGON TEETH

A NOVEL BY

E. Howard Hunt

DONALD I. FINE BOOKS

Donald I. Fine Books
Published by the Penguin Group
Penguin Books USA Inc., 375 Hudson Street,
New York, New York 10014, U.S.A.
Penguin Books Ltd, 27 Wrights Lane,
London W8 5TZ, England
Penguin Books Australia Ltd, Ringwood,
Victoria, Australia
Penguin Books Canada Ltd, 10 Alcorn Avenue,
Toronto, Ontario, Canada M4V 3B2
Penguin Books (N.Z.) Ltd, 182–190 Wairau Road,
Auckland 10, New Zealand

Penguin Books Ltd, Registered Offices:
Harmondsworth, Middlesex, England

First published by Donald I. Fine Books,
an imprint of Penguin Books USA Inc.

First Printing, May, 1997
1 3 5 7 9 10 8 6 4 2

LIBRARY OF CONGRESS CATALOGING-IN-PUBLICATION DATA
Hunt, E. Howard (Everette Howard).
Dragon teeth / E. Howard Hunt.
p.   cm.
ISBN 1-55611-523-7 (acid-free paper)
I. Title.
PS3515.U5425D73   1997
813'.54—dc21   96-50132
                                    CIP

Printed in the United States of America
Set in 11.5/14 Bodoni Book

This book is for Laura, with love.

Set round with brambles
Lies the Chin-Ling dragon
Guardian of the Five Celestial Lakes.

His sleep is open-eyed
His teeth dark-stained with
Blood of a thousand warriors
Who dared challenge his repose.

Lin Tu-li
A.D. 462

Prologue

"THE PRISONER WILL RISE!"

As he heard the harsh voice of the Chief Judge, the blindfolded prisoner felt guards' hands grip his armpits. Roughly he was hauled to his feet, steadied against the wave of fainting weakness that washed his body. Cords bound his wrists together; rope hobbled his ankles. Despite the old quilted Mao uniform the prisoner felt chilled to the bone.

"Prisoner, you have been charged and found guilty of high crimes," the Chief Judge continued. "Espionage against the People's Republic of China; criminal conversation with antisocial elements; fomenting rebellion against the People's Republic of China; circulating subversive materials designed to undermine the authority of the State; attempted subversion of prison guards."

The words barely penetrated the pounding in his head, but he had heard them many times before during exhausting interrogations. He was familiar with them and inwardly conceded that some were true.

His mind, drifting reflectively, refocused as the judge cleared his throat. It's coming now, the prisoner thought, and his muscles tightened. A secret verdict delivered in a closed courtroom. No foreign observers to report the outcome of his capture, no friends present.

"Because you have refused to reveal the identities of your fellow conspirators and spymasters, and in view of your failure to show repentance for your evil deeds, it is the judgment of this People's Court that you be imprisoned for a term of eleven years. During which time—"

Eleven years! A death sentence . . .

"—you will be offered opportunities for confession and ideological rehabilitation. The prisoner is advised to take advantage of these opportunities, to repent and show by word and deed that he is ready to become an obedient and useful member of Communist society." Throat clearing. "Only thus can the prisoner mitigate his sentence. Guards, remove the prisoner!"

His stomach churned, bitter bile flooded his throat. As his knees buckled only the guards' firm grip kept him upright. They dragged him until he was able to shuffle in his hobbled fashion, rope-soled straw slippers rasping on the roughness of the floor.

Eleven years!

As his mind began to recover from the impact of the judge's words, the prisoner compared his sentence to Wang Dan's—four years for a key organizer of the Tiananmen protests; Ren Wanding—seven years; five years to Academician Bao Zunxin for circulating an anti-Deng petition; student leader Guo Haifeng, four years . . . no announced sentences as heavy as his own.

But as his guards dragged him down unseen steps into the warmth of brief sunlight, the prisoner reflected that of them all, he alone had been charged with espionage.

Guards fitted him into the seat so that he rode between them as the clanging vehicle bumped over cobbled streets. Hundreds, maybe thousands of Chinese would hear and see his passage, but without pause or lifted eyes. In their circumscribed lives it was not prudent to take open notice of transported prisoners; much less so to mention such a happening to family or friends.

As his vehicle sped past cook stalls and open-air markets, the prisoner could smell the deliciousness of roasting pork and steaming vegetables, and his mouth watered uncontrollably.

Forcing his senses from the savory scents, the prisoner turned his mind back to his arrest, secret trial, and equally secret imprisonment in some Chinese Chateau d'If.

If only the Western press had been permitted to learn of his arrest and trial . . . some international human rights organization could have intervened, perhaps gained him a lesser sentence. But China was untouched by human rights concerns, indifferent to the pleas of foreigners. What outrage had erupted at the Tiananmen Square massacres diminished in following months because the West wanted business as usual with the PRC, the People's Republic of China.

So the West would not help him.

Zenmo ban? What to do?

The vehicle braked to a jerky stop. The prisoner was hauled out and hustled up a flight of steps. Metal gates clanked open, then shut behind him. He was propelled down a corridor familiar from its unclean smells, heard his cell door groan open.

They pushed him against the wall while they undid his bonds, removed the blindfold, and shoved him into his cell. The door clanged shut, the ancient lock turned and for a moment there was silence.

Then a guard snickered, "Eleven years, eh? Prisoner, you'll never leave." Their footsteps rasped the flooring like stiff brooms.

Only then did the prisoner open his eyes. He did so slowly, carefully, shielding his vision with one hand, peering slit-eyed lest a blaze of light sear his pupils. But, no, the ceiling bulb was off. A special favor? Or had the block guard forgotten to turn it on?

For a while he stood in the center of the cell that measured three meters by four, and flexed his arm and shoulder muscles, did knee bends to restore sluggish circulation. His straw mattress lay on the floor, the night-soil bucket as distant as possible. He sat down on the mattress and bowed his head between his knees.

Before accepting the mission, he remembered, he had understood its potential dangers, but only intellectually. His mind hadn't confronted the hazards of arrest and prison. He had thought he could bring it off unscathed.

Always the optimist, he berated himself. Worse, a fool.

He sat motionless while his mind reprised the circumstances of his mission and the sickening shock of arrest. As he had a thousand times he tried to find one point, one mindless mistake that had slid him deep into a Dantesque hell, but was unable to fault his performance. From beginning to end it had been flawless.

Leaving the inevitable conclusion that since ruin had not been self-inflicted he had somewhere, somehow, been betrayed.

Opening his eyes, the prisoner stared at the iron-grill door, saw that his bonds had been left just outside. Soundlessly, he moved to the grill and listened, then managed to peer in each direction. Nothing. No one. He had to act now. *Now,* before the sweeper-trusty took away the cords. Stretching his arm through the grill he grasped and scooped them into his cell. Hurriedly he inserted his prizes into the mattress straw, deep, deeper, then sat on the mattress again.

They were his only tools, those lengths of cord and rope. With them he could fashion a garrote for a guard or—and now his mind embraced the other possibility—a hanging noose for himself.

Death was the ultimate surrender, he understood that. Just as he knew without qualification that he could never survive eleven years. Still, the Central leadership was old, aging, ill, if you believed what you heard. New leadership might grant amnesty to the Wangs and Haifengs of Tiananmen Square . . . and himself.

No, not himself, not the hated spy. No leadership could free him to tell the world all that occurred. Face would be lost, trade treaties endangered.

With leaden claws the realization gripped him that to save his life he had to escape. Failing that, the prisoner's friend: the noose.

By one means or another he resolved to cheat his captors of their cruel triumph. Not today, not tomorrow, but soon—before he was too weak to fight and travel. Before hunger and sensory deprivation disoriented his mind, making him incapable of logical thought.

Soon.

Automatically, he rose at the sound of the rice cart making its creaking progress down the corridor. Other prisoners yelled and chanted, beat wooden spoons against their bars. The prisoner stood close to the grill and took the half-filled wooden bowl as it was handed to him. He ate voraciously, licking up the last grain of soggy rice before surrendering the bowl to the sour-faced trusty.

Turning back to his mattress the prisoner belched. His shrunken stomach was filled. *Chi baole.* New life seemed to throb through his veins.

He must not give in to despondency, he told himself. Instead, he must employ the hours to fashion a plan, a scheme to make him free again.

Cholera. Everyone dreaded cholera. Infected prisoners were quickly removed. Could he feign cholera? What were the symptoms? Diarrhea. He could induce diarrhea by swallowing pulverized straw. Then when they moved him to the clinic . . .

It was a chance worth taking.

For a time he reviewed the idea, but broke off as he heard a muffled tapping that came from the water pipe running through the cells. Alert, he listened to the tapped-out Morse: dot, dash, dash, pause, three dashes . . . converting the long, cautious message to: *Wo shi yi ge xue sheng.* I am a student.

He breathed in relief, having heard that statement often enough in the world of light and wind. But was this student also an informer? Slowly he tapped back: *xie xie* (thank you) and *dui bu qi* (sorry). A noncommittal reply for which he could not be penalized even though communication between prisoners was forbidden. Guards knew it went on but were too lazy or indifferent to prevent it entirely.

There was time, time ahead, to ask more of the student-prisoner, and when the initiator did not tap again, he lay back on the mattress and closed his eyes. To think.

Think.

Before the shielded light came on the prisoner relieved himself in the slop bucket and positioned it near the bars for collection. His daily contribution, he reflected, helped fertilize rice paddies flooded by the Yong Ding River and worked by communes around the outskirts of Beijing. Unwillingly, he increased the seasonal harvest of rice. Rice he might someday be fed.

But he could not last through another harvest, could not survive. Hopeless, he had to generate his own hope however illusory it might prove . . .

Down the corridor a prisoner lifted his hoarse voice to chant:

> Red is the east, rises the sun.
> China has brought forth a Mao Tse-tung.
> For the people's happiness he works,
> *Hu er hai ya,*
> He's the people's liberator . . .

And oppressor, the prisoner thought. And if not all Chinese misery over the decades since Mao proclaimed the Great October Revolution could be blamed on the Great Helmsman, most of it was his doing. The anonymous voice continued:

Chairman Mao loves the people.
Chairman Mao, he is our guide.

Grunting a contained protest, the prisoner stretched out on his mattress, wondering how best to employ the treasures it contained.

PART
ONE

One

I**T WAS A LITTLE** after five when Mark Brand darkened his computer monitor, removed tinted lenses, and massaged his eyes.

Leaving the module, he cleared his desktop, sorting papers into their respective folders, each one overprinted with the red *Galaxy* indicator, which was not a Federal sensitivity classification but internal to the GlobEco Foundation, where Brand was known as a senior researcher on Mainland China.

While Brand was returning work folders to his combination safe, Abby Wainwright—his secretarial assistant—entered his office and glanced briefly around. "Anything else, Mr. Brand?"

"Nothing, thanks." He spun the safe dial, noticing that she was already gloved and carrying a small rolled umbrella against Washington's unpredictable spring showers. Cocktail frock, a brighter shade of lipstick, and spike-heeled patent leather shoes. "Weekend plans?" he asked.

"At the moment, no." She smiled fleetingly. "But TGIF, and one can hope."

"See you Monday." He went back to his desk and checked his appointment calendar thinking that Mrs.—no, she preferred the ambiguous Ms. since a long-ago divorce—Wainwright was prepared to enter the Friday night singles fray in a city where unmarried women outnumbered eligible men two to one. Or was it three to two? Depended on the columnist you read.

His immediate engagements were two: an hour's workout at his fitness club, then dinner with Nina Kenton in her penthouse overlooking the Department of State. Brand had been "seeing" Nina for three months, having met her at a Georgetown dinner party soon after her move from La Jolla/Santa Barbara. At forty-seven, Brand had been widowed more than twenty years, whereas Nina at forty-odd had won a lucrative divorce action less than two years ago. "Bernie," she'd remarked soon after meeting Brand, "should have realized I'd be watching him with falcon eyes. After all, a man intelligent enough to amass all those millions from something as risky as real estate should have assessed the risks of setting up his poopsie in Beverly Hills, where I have so many watchful friends." She smiled her lynx smile at a noncommittal Brand.

Turning off his desk lamp, Brand reflected that money aside, there was little difference between Abby and Nina. Both were divorcées on the prowl for suitable males in a game where truth was an early victim if it figured at all.

Nina admitted to a son in his late teens, whom she described as "sensitive and frail." Euphemisms for what? Sexual ambiguity? Brand was unconcerned over Gareth's persuasions, for he had no intention of becoming the lad's stepfather.

But reflecting on Nina's son reminded Brand of a third commitment to honor: a periodic call to his son, Peter, who was twenty-four, an Arts graduate of the University of Virginia and a junior-level manager at a bank specializing in Asian investments. To spare his son embarrassment Brand planned to raise the subject of Peter's financial needs and respond positively. Unless you were part of the banking hierarchy, salaries were subsistence level, or less. And not long ago Peter had moved from a small Georgetown apartment to a larger and more expensive one in the gentrified yuppiedom east of DuPont Circle, where fortunes had been made rehabilitating run-down row dwellings and carving them into upscale apartments.

Brand scratched the side of his chin. Must shave before dinner.

And Peter had a roommate now, a Chinese girl described as an exchange student who overstayed her visa and was granted work papers after the dissident turmoil, repressions, and massacres in Peking.

No, *Beijing* now—ever since Mao in his paternal xenophobia had imposed *pinyin* to supplant the Wade-Giles transliteration system that had served all parties well for generations. The old system, of course, was Western and so intolerable to custodians of the New Truth, the New Ways.

Brand frowned. His Chinese had been learned from the lips of his amah, calligraphy in Taiwan schools, where his widowed father had placed him after their hurried flight from the Communist takeover on the Mainland.

Well, he thought, as a sovereign nation and a world power the People's Republic of China had every right to spell as it chose, but the revisions grated him as they still irritated his father.

After an automatic surface check to make sure nothing sensitive had been left out of the safe, Brand left his office and walked down the marble-floored hall to the curving staircase that gave out on the large, Roman-style lobby.

The mansion had been built in the twenties by a Kansan who made his fortune supplying beef to AEF doughboys fighting in France and Belgium. After a term as governor, the profiteer had appointed himself to a vacant Senate seat and commissioned the mansion to herald the glories of his native state. His wife and three daughters hired speech tutors and suppressed their Kansan accents. And thanks to the Senator's influential associates, the entire family was admitted to the select circle that formed Miss Ball's Dancing Classes, then the apogee of Capital social distinction. But after two terms the Senator had been defeated, and though he retained the honorific "Senator," the old man and his wife found their social magnetism diminishing with each passing year. Their married daughters had dispersed to Seattle, Dallas, and Palm Beach and seldom visited their parents' manse. Alone together, as World War Two began and servants vanished, the elderly couple found maintaining the property too burdensome and gladly accepted a purchase offer by some alphabet agency needing space for rapid wartime expansion. From remaining friends the couple heard of all-night activity in the unmarked building that had been their home; of men and women in uniform and mufti who came and went, many of distinctively foreign appearance. A disquieting change.

At war's end the former owners passed into the gardens of eternal rest, and the once distinguished mansion passed to the asset disposal column of the General Services Administration. After three years disuse the property was acquired and managed by a trust that comprised friends of William Donovan and James Forrestal. The corporation was registered in Delaware and Curaçao, and its relationships with successive lessors, and their activities, were hidden behind corporate veils.

GlobEco was the current occupant, an unobtrusive, unpublicized think tank openly dedicated to global ecological concerns. As such, it attracted little notice from neighbors or high-profile think tanks like Rand and Brookings that made up Washington's burgeoning intellectual community and provided employment for out-of-office politicians.

Brand reflected on these origins as he passed the desk of a security officer who wore a gray whipcord suit, not the usual blue uniform and badges of rental guards. That difference, Brand knew, was to enhance the civilian image of GlobEco to outside visitors, although the security officer was unobtrusively armed. That precaution had become SOP when, soon after GlobEco occupied the building, an assault team entered unopposed and sacked much of the intricate computer network before Metro Police killed the intruders. Their corpses bore no ID and could not be interrogated, so their sponsor remained officially unknown, although some good guesses could be made as to the country responsible.

Brand went down the steps of the massive gray-stone building and walked around to the rear parking area, where he slipped into his BMW sedan and drove on S Street to his fitness club on Connecticut near the Mayflower Hotel.

For an hour he strained muscles against Nautilus equipment, took a cold plunge and a hot shower before shaving in the locker room. The mirrored face was more angular than oval, chin slightly cleft, gray eyes, and thick gray hair touched with white. An inch over six feet tall, his body was well muscled, husky chest tapering into a thirty-four-inch waist and flat, hard abdomen. Thighs and calves firm from weights and running. Weight seldom varied from an even one-eighty.

Brand applied aftershave to his face, antiperspirant to his armpits, and dressed before driving out Connecticut Avenue and over Rock Creek Park to Cathedral Avenue opposite the National Zoological Park.

From his parking slot under the apartment building Brand rode the elevator to the sixth floor and entered his apartment. After turning on lights he checked his answering machine for messages. Nina Kenton's voice purred: "Just to remind, darling—expecting you at eight. Seems ages since we were together. Miss you." End of message.

It was nice to be missed, Brand thought, but it hadn't been "ages" since they were together; only Wednesday evening they'd dined at Le Pierrot and returned to her penthouse for the rest of the night.

As Brand loosened his tie he considered the ardor of Nina's lovemaking; it was innovative and exhausting, as though fueled by the anger of a betrayed wife, and only occasionally tender.

He had occupied the same two-bedroom apartment for nearly ten years. Like GlobEco's mansion the Towers had been constructed after the First World War, with high ceilings, spacious rooms, and thick walls. His library held built-in bookshelves; what spaces there were displayed Chinese curios and antiques collected by himself and his father. His furnishings were Chinese rosewood rubbed and burnished with beeswax until it glowed softly in the light. The walls were hung with good ancestral and illustrative scrolls, many from Nanking, others by Hsian and Chengtu artisans. Here and there were enamel Palace vases and cloisonné jars, a reclining dragon of white jade, bronze deer and tigers, gold-leaf sconces, a coromandel cabinet, enameled display plates, and before the fireplace a thick silk-wool rug of Chinese design. His father, Dr. Simon Brand, had no need of them in the Appalachian cabin where he lived in semiretirement, ministering to the medical needs of remote mountain dwellers. Two years ago, Brand recalled, he had installed a Sanyo high-fidelity system in that cabin, and supplied CDs and tapes so his father could listen to the symphonies and operas he adored. To Brand it was a lonely life, but it suited his father and Brand knew it was useless to suggest anything resembling change.

The Rolodex supplied his son's phone number at the new P Street apartment, and Brand punched it in. By now, he thought, Peter should be home from the office and having cocktails with his girlfriend, Hsiao La-li, who transcribed her name as Lally.

When she answered, Brand identified himself and asked if Peter was there.

"No, Mr. Brand, I'm afraid he's not."

"Will you ask him to call me? I'll be here until a little before eight."

She hesitated and when she spoke Brand detected a tremor in her voice. "I thought you knew Peter is away."

"Away? When will he be back?"

"I—I wish I knew. He phoned from Hong Kong two weeks ago and I've heard nothing since."

"I didn't know he was traveling—not like him to leave without telling me." Not like Peter at all. Suddenly Brand felt apprehensive. "A business trip?"

"Oh, yes," she said quickly, "but it came up suddenly and then he was gone."

Brand breathed deeply. "Would you mind letting me know as soon as you hear from him?"

"I'll be glad to, sir. And I hope it's soon."

"So do I. Well, thank you, La-li. *Zai Jian.*"

"*Zai Jian,* sir," she responded, and Brand hung up.

Hong Kong business? Why hadn't the firm sent a senior partner to handle whatever needed to be transacted? True, Peter spoke Chinese, but so did more senior members of the firm. Still, why get alarmed? Entrusting a financial mission to Peter suggested the approval of his superiors and potential advancement. La-li knew so little that Brand decided to call Peter's office on Monday to get a fix on his son's return.

He made a note of it on his calendar pad and berated himself for not following up earlier. Last week and the week before he had left messages on Peter's machine, and their going unanswered should have alerted him to his son's absence. Damn it! Why hadn't Peter told him? Show of independence? What *was* it with Peter's generation, anyway?

Well, few answers to that. Brand went to his bedroom and turned on CNN for a summary of the day's news. Another revolt in Suriname, oil spill in Boston harbor, plane crash in Alaska . . . he left the set on as he undressed and selected fresh clothing from the walk-in closet.

Later, as he drove down to Nina's place, Brand found his mind dwelling on Peter's absence. He had raised his son as best he could and they had always been close—or so Brand thought. Raised him with the same care and affection his own widowed father had shown him all those years, and believed the rearing successful. At least Peter hadn't entered the drug scene at Charlottesville or become a political activist like his anti-establishment mother, so Brand felt he hadn't done too badly. Hell, he'd done well by any standard.

At Nina's condominium Brand turned into the visitor parking area, identified himself to the lobby security guard, and rode to the penthouse.

Nina greeted him in a flowing blue hostess gown, kissed his cheek, and asked if he preferred wine or something stronger.

"Walker Black," he said, and poured it over ice.

"Don't deaden your taste buds, dear. Dover sole is on the menu, okay?"

"Okay." He nodded, and told her of Peter's unexpected absence.

Shrugging, Nina said, "Oh, I shouldn't worry if I were you. Weeks, sometimes months, go by before Gareth reveals his whereabouts, and nothing really bad has ever happened to him." She sipped Chardonnay and smiled encouragingly. "Is Peter very much like you?"

"Maybe—hard to say. I know him better than I know myself. He'd have to give you that answer."

"And will—one day soon." She took his hand and led him to a sofa aligned with the fireplace. Gas flames flickered around artificial logs giving a warm, homey touch to the elaborately decorated room. A room that implicitly demonstrated how imaginatively a large amount of money could be spent with results that were as tasteful as they were comfortable. The firelight seemed to gild Nina's perfect features. Blond hair carefully coiffed, high cheekbones, soft blue eyes, snub nose, and resolute chin. One California female who hadn't destroyed her skin with long hours on beaches and tennis courts.

"You know," she said offhandedly, "over the months we've been together—and I've enjoyed every moment, Mark, believe me—but when I think of you—which is disturbingly often—I realize how little I really know about you, your life before we met."

He sipped his drink and set it on the long, glass-topped coffee table. "Haven't concealed anything on purpose," he lied, "just that those things seemed unimportant."

"Oh, no. I find you a truly remarkable man and so I wonder what made you what you are."

Might as well get it over with, he thought. Once done, no more questioning.

"I was born in western China—Kunming, Yunnan-fu—during World War Two. My father was a medical missionary—more medical than missionary—who had been sent to Peking but left when Japanese troops came in. The Kuomintang government resettled in Chungking, but Dad disliked Chiang's gang and went down to Kunming, where there was a big Flying Tigers base. He treated shot-up pilots and Yunnanese Chinese, and when my mother wasn't helping him and treating the ill and wounded, she spread Christian word among Buddhists and other heathen." Brand smiled. "The word *remarkable* applies to her far more than to me, and I wish I'd known her."

"Oh—you didn't?"

"I was two when she flew over the Hump to Calcutta to bring back medicines. On the return flight her plane crashed on some Himalayan peak—a frequent occurrence those days."

"I'm sorry, Mark."

"So am I. Well, we stayed in Kunming until '49 when the Communists conquered the Mainland, then went to Taiwan in the flood of Nationalist refugees." He reached for his drink and sipped lengthily. "We're qualified refugees, no question, Dad and I."

She nodded understandingly. "You two went through a lot, Mark. Is your father well? Do you see him?"

"He's aging well—seventy-five now and active. Cares for himself and those who need his help." Brand paused. "His whole life has been spent helping people, can't expect him to stop now."

"And being active is bound to prolong his life." She rose, and left briefly to refill her glass. Returning, she asked, "So what about you? Where did you go to school and so forth?" She resumed her place beside him and closed one hand around his.

"Oh, there were schools on Taiwan for foreigners," Brand replied, "and I must have gone to most of them. Then Dad was given home leave and took me to Philadelphia. I was twelve when he put me in Chestnut Hill, and after he returned to Taiwan I was the loneliest boy in Pennsylvania. But I learned American games and American English, and every summer I'd visit Dad on Taiwan or he'd come to Philadelphia, where his church mission was." He thought nostalgically of the incomparable joy of reunion with his father. "I went to Haverford," he continued, "because it was a good school, and a missionary's son didn't have to pay full tuition. Dad helped as much as he could and I worked as many jobs as I could find, so I made out. Chapel choir, waiting tables, selling subscriptions, landscaping and mowing athletic fields . . . anything and everything to earn money."

"Girls?"

"I dated girls who'd settle for a Coke and a movie, maybe a hot dog, but for Main Line young ladies that was pretty restrictive. Then I met Sela Wayburn at a Bryn Mawr dance." He stopped at a memory grown painful.

"Sela?"

"Her baby version of Selina stayed with her. Anyway, we dated, went steady even though her father didn't exactly approve of me. He was an Episcopalian bishop, High Church, with money, social position, and community esteem. Sela said she didn't care for those things, and the night I graduated from Haverford she agreed to marry me. I'd won a graduate fellowship at Penn—where Dad went to med school—and with my stipend and her trust fund we lived as well as most graduate students do. Peter was born shortly after I got my Master's, and we went to Taiwan on a Rockefeller Fellowship." Brand breathed deeply. "I was studying the sociological impact on Taiwanese aborigines of Nationalist dominance, preparing for my doctorate. But Sela hated living there; didn't speak the language, didn't like the people, and sympathized with the Mainland Communists."

"She did? But how could she, knowing the terrible things they did?"

"Maybe she was just bored with me, I don't know. Anyway, she went back to the States—to visit her family, she said—and never returned."

"Just abandoned you and Peter?"

Brand drank again and replenished his glass. "Like me, Peter had an amah who loved and cared for him so he wasn't wounded by his mother's desertion. Not then. That came years later."

"And your wife? What happened to her?"

"When she'd been gone more than a year her mother phoned to say Sela had been killed in a tragic accident, no details. Before the funeral I found out considerably more. My wife had joined a gang of Maoist terrorists. Four of them were making bombs in a Newark hideaway when there was an explosion. Three killed, one blinded and defaced. Sela died with her companions. The Newark Four." He drank quickly. "When I went back to Taiwan the project I'd undertaken seemed trivial against the realities of what was taking place around the world—war in Vietnam, turmoil at home and in Palestine, repressions on the Mainland, Soviet challenges . . . I realized I'd been encapsulated in something of interest only to other scholars, so when I got an offer from a Taipeh-based Navy group I accepted. They needed Chinese translators, interpreters, and document analysts, and for the first time in my life I began earning a decent salary." Brand chose not to reveal that it wasn't really Navy but a CIA Station because of what it could suggest about his current work.

Nina's face was pale. "Sela—what a horrible way to die."

"Had the grace of immediacy, no lingering on in a ruined life. Often wondered how Peter and I would have handled such a situation."

"Manfully, I'm sure." She hesitated. "How did Peter take her death?"

"For years he understood that she had been killed in an industrial accident—at her workplace—and he accepted that. But leave it to the old Bishop, a true limousine liberal, to tell his only grandson—my son Peter—that his mother died a martyr in the fight against imperialism." His voice thickened. "Died making weapons to fight the just cause for humanity . . . the cause she believed in. Damn him for that!" His shaking hand made the ice chime against the crystal glass. Setting it down he said, "Sorry."

"Oh, Mark, *I'm* sorry I asked. So sorry." Her cheek pressed his. "You liked working for the Navy?"

"Taiwan was okay," he admitted, "but after the freedom I'd known there Washington took a lot of adjustment. I stayed with the Department as long as I could, then moved over to GlobEco."

"Where you do—what?"

"Help put together worldwide ecological studies which the Foundation sells to clients."

"I'm intrigued. What sort of clients?"

"Oh, the Pentagon, State, agribusinesses, petroleum companies, mining consortiums, lumbering firms, foreign governments—Brazil for one, where the Amazonian rain forest is being destroyed."

"And you have no particular interest in China?"

"Right now I'm interested in a particular area of the Mainland, the Kunlun mountain range."

"Never heard of it."

"Not a household name, though it could be. The range is a thousand miles long and forms a natural barrier between northern Tibet and Sinkiang's Tarim Basin. It rises in a vast barren region that's largely inaccessible and uninhabited except for a few nomadic tribes." The same region where China's unacknowledged missile silos had been concealed until recent satellite thermal-enhanced imagery found them out.

"Why would anyone be interested in your Kunlun mountains?"

"The range may hold unbelievable amounts of iron and other ores. The range itself is igneous rock, the ore-bearing kind. The plains from which it rises are mostly sedimentary deposits that blew and wasted away leaving the much harder ridge exposed. The plains may cover enormous petroleum deposits but until test borings are made, the type of deep shales can't be known."

"And China's rulers aren't about to let anyone start drilling."

"Hardly." He finished his drink, hand steady again. "So much for Kunlun's geology. More wine?"

"At dinner. Which, by the way, seems to be ready."

As Brand walked her to the table he felt tremendous relief at having appeased her curiosity. He had let her draw it out of him in a natural way so that she had no reason to suspect he had glossed over some parts, and been less than forthcoming with others. Now that Nina had his legend she was free to retell it to her friends, and he hoped she would. Coming from a presumed lover, the tale would gain credibility with every telling.

THEIR REPAST AT A TABLE seating twenty-two was prepared by Nina's favorite restaurant, Dominique, and served by Nicolas, a captain of waiters in frock coat and white tie. It commenced with *petite marmite* and *escargots de bourgogne*. The entrée *sole Normande* was accompanied by *artichaut vinaigrette* and *pommes rissolées*. For dessert, *soufflé vanille* accompanied by a light pear liqueur. Dinner wines, Château Clemens, a white Bordeaux, and Puligny-Montrachet, a white Bourgogne.

Patting his stomach, Chinese style, Brand said, "Glad I didn't dull my taste buds, or I couldn't have enjoyed it as much as I did."

With a smile and a nod at Nicolas, Nina rose, aided by the captain who murmured, "Always a pleasure to be of service, madame."

She took Brand's arm and they walked to the fireplace coffee table where Nicolas had set out cognac and liqueurs. "Something?" Brand inquired.

"Not at the moment, but do have a brandy."

While Brand was warming the snifter Nicolas brought in a gadroon coffee tray with demitasses and filled them. "Anything else, madame?"

"Thank you, no. Oh, you might bring in the Pommery and glasses."

"Of course." He disappeared, and after sitting near Nina, Brand dribbled a teaspoon of cognac into his small cup, then tasted appreciatively. "Nothing like a *fine café* after a hard day's work."

"Mark—I can't imagine you doing a hard day's work. Is GlobEco really that demanding?"

"At times." He sipped again. The Colombian grind was her own mix of body and flavor. "Most people would find it dull."

"But rewarding."

"To me it is. Will you dine with me a week from tonight?"

"With pleasure. Chinese, I hope."

"Only cuisine I know." He poured more coffee into their cups.

She pointed a remote control at a barely visible CD player and presently music surrounded them from concealed speakers. "Chopin," she said archly.

"Prelude in E-flat Major."

"Mark, Mark," she said despairingly, "you know absolutely everything. How am I ever going to surprise you?"

"Oh, you have. By sharing part of your life with me."

"The meaningful part, the most important part."

"I know," he said quietly, and kissed her cheek as Nicolas placed a champagne bucket and chilled glasses on the table.

After a discreet cough the waiter said, "The cleanup crew will arrive at ten in the morning if that is satisfactory?"

"Quite," she said dismissively. "Thank you, Nicolas."

"Good night, madame, m'sieu." He withdrew as quietly as he had come.

Nina nuzzled Brand's chin and murmured, "How refreshing not to be served by a pimply-faced youth in a stained tie who introduces himself as Freddy and says he's the waitperson and what'll you have for drinks."

Brand laughed. "Yeah, refreshing is the word." Carefully, he filled their tulip glasses, and Nina touched hers to his.

"Won't be long before they'll be introducing customers to chefs, salad boys, and dishwashers, God forbid."

Brand chuckled. "Little hard on the restaurant trade, aren't you?"

"Deservedly." She sipped champagne.

After a taste of the chill, bubbly wine, Brand said, "And sharp on social distinctions."

"Dear—money gives one that privilege. Now, bring the bucket as we repair to the lady's chamber."

* * *

FOR A WHILE THEY soaked in Nina's gold-flecked Jacuzzi, enjoying bodily relaxation and the exhilaration of champagne. Touches became more frequent, then boldly purposeful, and soon she was astride his thighs, kissing and tonguing his open mouth while her hips moved rhythmically until she gasped and moaned, clinging hard to his shoulders as they climaxed together.

Later they dried each other, and as Brand raised his arms above his head she touched a place just below the hairline of his left armpit. "What an unusual tattoo. Green. Looks Oriental."

"A souvenir of my youth in Taiwan."

"Hmm. Looks like a telephone pole about to topple. What is it?"

"Ideograph: *Fang-tse.*"

She continued drying his chest. "Meaning?"

"It's the ideograph for house, or sometimes heaven. It conveys the idea of a closed society." He began drying her back. "Identifies me as a member of a particular Chinese clan."

"You mean, like a family?" She giggled. "Tong? Chinese Mafia?"

"I suppose. My father belonged to it—still does, actually—and after I'd saved a Chinese schoolmate from drowning he allowed me to be inducted into the tong, as you call it."

"I see. Oh, *don't* tickle, please! The boy you saved was a member?"

"His father." Brand inserted the fluffy towel between her thighs and frictioned gently.

"Lecher," she breathed and held him close. "That's fun, but let's not waste it here. To bed, love. All pleasure should be shared."

Kneeling on the bed, thighs apart, she reached back and with one finger touched her anus. "Here," she said huskily. "Do me here."

As Brand hesitated, she said more urgently, "I don't have AIDS, if that's on your mind."

"Don't want to hurt you," he temporized, staring at the corrugated rosette so lewdly displayed.

"Hurt me? Bernie's favorite nook—called it his Glory Hole. Jelly's in the drawer, so bugger me while I'm hot and horny."

"Another time," Brand told her and entered her vagina, penetrating gently until her muscles relaxed and penetration was complete.

Groaning, Nina began thrusting backward, exposing and then concealing his shaft until their bodies were slamming together. "Can't . . . wait," she husked. "Come, you bastard, fuck me, make me feel it. Ah, Jesus, I love it so."

The tight, milking contractions of her cunt excited him, and presently he exploded deep within her core. Nina began trembling and shaking as she climaxed, beating her fists on the bed, uttering inchoate sounds while Brand's hands gripped her pelvis to press her buttocks close and give her full measure.

When her body was quiet they lay spoon-fashion on their sides. Breathing shallowed, and sleep enveloped them in a warm, dark cloud.

IN PETER BRAND'S APARTMENT a meeting was under way. La-li had volunteered the premises to eighteen young Mainlanders, dressed in jeans, T-shirts, and denim jackets. Sipping strong Henan tea they spoke in Shanghaiese, Fukienese, Cantonese, and Mandarin, exchanging news from China and debating the possibility of return. Five had actually been in Tiananmen Square when government troops and tanks moved in. One, a dour-faced youth, said, "Never happen. Not until that senile old Central Committee dies off. Only then can we return."

"Or the gang's overthrown," added a girl who bore a truncheon's keloid scar above her left eye.

"We tried that," a young man reminded them, and fingered wispy chin whiskers. "Nearly wiped us out. Which is what they're determined to do." He was a graduate student in computer science at Howard University. "Me, I'm resigned to a long stay in this country—as we all should be."

"No, never," protested a young pre-med student from Lanchou. "I can't settle for that. For every one of us they kill or imprison, there are a hundred thousand others to fill in."

"Doing what?" inquired the scarred girl. "Printing leaflets and passing them around? Painting wall slogans? Holding meetings like this? Good for morale maybe, but ineffectual. Totally ineffectual." She turned to their hostess. "And what do you hear from friend Peter?"

La-li's gaze lowered. "Nothing, I'm afraid. Not since his call from Hong Kong."

"Are you worried?"

"Not much," she lied, "though I'm sorry he went off as he did."

The computer scientist nodded understandingly. "He's an American with an American passport—what can happen to him?"

La-li shrugged and said nothing. But she thought, Something bad, really bad can happen to him, and I'm afraid. Really afraid. I'm sorry I let him go.

Unknown to most of the others in the room La-li was one of a three-member cell that maintained contact with fellow dissidents in Beijing, Nanking, and Shanghai. Through trainmen traveling daily from Kowloon to the border at Lo Wu, letters, leaflets, and currency were smuggled into the People's Republic of China; occasionally a junk crewman or airline stewardess would help, but La-li realized it was only a trickle instead of the necessary flood.

More tea was poured, sweet buns passed around, and as refugee talk died away the scarred girl began singing the dissidents' song "Hope Rises in the East":

> Let hope rise in the East,
> Like sunlight, covering our
> Land from Shangdong
> To Sinkiang.

The others joined enthusiastically in the second verse:

> Our fertile land,
> Our Middle Kingdom
> Will be cleansed by
> The crystal waters of Truth.
> Then happiness and peace
> Will reign forever.

When the last notes died away the young people shook hands and bowed to each other and went their separate ways.

La-li placed teacups in the dishwasher and stored uneaten buns in the refrigerator, then went to the bed she shared with Peter Brand.

It was bad enough to miss him, she thought as she turned off the light, but fearing for his safety was almost more than she could bear.

*   *   *

Mark Brand spent Saturday morning at his office, going over the latest computer imagery that had arrived via the National Reconnaissance Office link. Work was proceeding rapidly on a new silo complex, and Brand wondered whether its missiles, when installed, would be targeted at the U.S. or Russia, and whether this intelligence would be shared with the Confederation of Independent States. That was a policy decision, not his. Brand was responsible for Mainland target selection and updating, a job made easier by the Chinese decision to work at night, when heat from digging machinery, earth-moving equipment, and human bodies was readily detectable by the Gorgon geo-synchronous satellite and flashed to the Taiwan installation every hour.

In a few more months, Brand mused, the ChiComs would have ICBM parity with CIS, then what would happen? Somewhere in the bowels of State, the Pentagon, and the CIA rested a contingency plan approved by the highest authority—the President. Brand was a contributor to the China portion of that plan, having collated All-Source Intelligence in preparing his estimate. And as usual he had argued heatedly with Darman Gerold, the Agency's Far East Chief, over Brand's suggestion that the Chinese were preparing for a preemptive missile strike. In the end, Gerold had altered Brand's "probable" to "possible," and Brand felt he could live with that; at least he was on record as what Gerold laughingly called a "doomsayer," though if Doomsday came records wouldn't matter.

As Brand gathered up his working papers he reflected that he and Darman Gerold went back in time together; too damn far back, ten years to be exact. And he remembered the first time Gerold had come to the Taipeh compound on a familiarization tour of the Far East. Darman Gerold of the Arrow Collar profile, the face so unlined as to suggest collagen smoothing. Flesh so pinkly delicate that Gerold hid it from the sun under broad-brimmed hats and long-sleeved shirts. His black hair (retouched?) was combed straight back with a razor-thin part in a style affected by Ramon Novarro in the days when Astoria was the film capital of the world and Hollywood a vast stretch of citrus groves.

Gerold would have been, Brand mused, a boy not good at games, a boy who hung back and malingered to avoid the rough-and-tumble of contact sports and employed his crafty brain to suck up to masters and gain their approbation.

Long out of St. George's, two decades out of Harvard Law, and a total novice to the profession of Intelligence. But ignorance, Brand reflected, had never been a barrier to Agency admission; not as long as you were well connected at the White House or the Agency. *Guanxi.* And Gerold had been an Assistant Special Counsel to the President, then a National Security Council factotum before coming to CIA's Office of Legal Affairs.

To Brand, Darman Gerold had always seemed restless and dissatisfied in whatever position he held, always on the move toward something better. His first wife, who came from a wealthy Portland family, divorced him to marry an Italian banker. The Gerold son and daughter were notorious for high-powered cars and equally high-powered drugs, witless vandalism, and bizarre political causes. Gerold's present wife, Pauline, was a widow from Upperville, even wealthier than Gerold's first, and a pedigreed member of Virginia's horsey gentry.

Brand remembered how Gerold tired of Agency legal chores and maneuvered a lateral transfer to Operations. After completing training at the Farm, Gerold wangled a two-year tour in Singapore, where the real work was handled by London's Special Branch. Field-qualified, Gerold's Old Boy seniors found him ready to assume senior supervisory responsibilities in Far East Ops.

What a farce, Brand thought, and remembered the incident that had determined the course of their relationship thereafter.

He had been driving Gerold from the compound to Pei-tou on Taipeh's outskirts for steam massage by the blind women and men who worked in the spa. Gerold, who professed himself a China expert (based on three cruise-ship visits to Hong Kong), pointed to a string of objects in a vegetable stall and asked if they were garlic. "No, Darman," Brand had replied disgustedly, "they're lichee nuts," and Gerold's face had flushed even pinker before it turned away.

Since then they had been tacit antagonists, and when Gerold became Far East Chief he had forced Brand out of the field, out of Operations, and suggested he'd be happier at the deep-cover installation called GlobEco.

That was true, Brand mused, for he had seen the futility of launching agents by boat and plane into the Chinese Mainland, or sending

Legal Travelers to their deaths. Denied Area ops for HumInt (Intelligence from Human sources) seemed beyond the Agency's capability, and he was close to agreeing with a notorious former Director that satellite reconnaissance was the ultimate answer to collection.

He locked his safe and left the building, thinking as he often did that even satellites were not immune to neutralization. With more advanced Western-built computers the ChiComs could shoot down Gorgon and its replacements and those hi-tech computers would have been sold to China for cash or easy credit terms, so frantic was the West to profit from ChiCom trade.

Driving down Connecticut toward Georgetown, Brand reflected that he was probably well out of Operations and their inevitable disappointments. At first he had resisted the insularity of GlobEco, then gradually concluded that his work filled an otherwise unfillable void. His annual contract paid double his Agency earnings, and occasional trips back to Taiwan refreshed him by renewing contact with his roots.

But with every plus came a minus, and Brand's was the bi-monthly meeting with Darman Gerold, for what Gerold called an "overview" of GlobEco activities. Both were members of a small M Street club, and when Brand entered the basement grill he found a dozen members watching baseball on a TV screen. None of them would be caught dead or alive at a ballpark rubbing shoulders with sweaty, beer-guzzling, hot dog-munching fans of America's pastime. Nor would Darman Gerold, who Brand saw at a corner table, cocktail glass in hand as though posed for a "GQ" ad against the grill's paneled walls.

He was wearing a gray three-piece sharkskin suit tailored at McIntosh's in Hong Kong, teal blue poplin shirt with white spread collar and French cuffs from John Stone's estimable Jermyn Street establishment. From a gold vest chain depended a small ivory pig, silent symbol of Harvard snobbery. For Gerold was a lover of the label and a displayer of the expensive ones he wore.

Brand drew back the other captain's chair and sat down. "Drink?" Gerold inquired with studied casualness, beckoned to a waiter, and looked pointedly at his watch. "Think this'll take long, Mark?"

"I'm ready to leave now."

Gerold smiled his reptilian smile while Brand asked for Walker Black on the rocks.

"So," Gerold began, "how're things going?"

Brand shrugged. "Same as usual. Product consumers satisfied?"

"They say. But they always want more. Nature of the business."

And Darman Gerold was now a certified expert on "the business." Languidly, Brand thought, Gerold lifted glass to lips and sipped before asking, "Anything new?"

"Silo complex proceeding rather rapidly, I'd say."

"Based on . . . ?"

"Comparison with older installations. Some concrete mixers have been withdrawn, suggesting pouring's finished at some silos."

"Some?"

"Three." He took his drink from the waiter's tray. "Thanks, Ned."

"Leaving . . . ?"

"Eighteen by last count."

"Which was when?"

"About an hour ago."

"You do stay current, don't you?"

"What I'm paid for." He sipped gratefully.

Gerold helped himself to a basket of pretzel sticks and chewed while Brand savored his drink. After a roar from the baseball watchers Gerold said, "How's company morale?"

"Far as I know, okay."

"Yours?"

"Passable."

"Go off to Taiwan whenever you want, Mark. Write your own ticket."

Brand nodded.

Gerold leaned forward. "Anything on Chinese intentions?"

"You know the Central Committee doesn't confide in me, nor the Politburo. We've got what Gorgon supplies, that's it."

"So we still need HumInt."

"Were it possible."

"Hmmm. Tom Gray's about to retire. Think there's a place for him with your outfit?"

"Might be." Gray was an old-timer and like Gerold a Harvard alumnus. But unlike Gerold, Gray had spent years in foreign operations and knew how to prepare an intelligible report.

"You resist the idea?"

Brand shook his head. "I was just wondering where a vacancy might exist. Monday I'll check with Personnel."

"Do that, will you, and let me know."

Brand nodded, thinking it wouldn't be easy for Tommy to shift from ops mode to analytical; hadn't been easy for him.

"So," Gerold inquired, moving the emptied glass with one finger, "what else?"

"I'd like a favor, Darman. Put my son Peter on the travel watchlist, will you? He went off to Hong Kong on banking business and hasn't been heard from."

Gerold's eyebrows lifted. "Worried?"

"I worry as a father when my son's out of touch. Don't you?"

"Depends whose son." His smile was very faint. "Maybe Peter's caught up in the carnal pleasures of Wanchai."

"Doubt it. A man would have to be pretty hard up to screw those wasted whores. Anyway, Peter lives with a girlfriend."

"Chinese, yes?"

Brand couldn't conceal surprise that brought from Gerold a condescending grin. "Sure, we still keep up with the contacts of our valued employees."

"Including family."

"Of course."

"I don't particularly care for that, Darman."

"Comes with the territory."

Brand grunted. "Where have I heard that before?" and drained his glass. "So, be a good fellow, will you? Get Peter's name watchlisted."

"Said I would," Gerold replied surlily, and rose from his chair. "Chit's signed. And, Mark—do keep an eye on Korea. *Ciao.*"

"*Zai Jian.*"

Brand breathed relievedly as he watched Gerold walk from the grill. He left the table, seeing a third-base runner steal home to the loud approval of clubmates, and walked along a corridor to the telephones near the facilities.

Before dialing, Brand wondered what he was to make of Darman's throwaway admonition. The Korean Peninsula was a big territory, though Darman probably referred to the North, where a half-acknowledged nuclear missile program had long been under way. But the NKs wouldn't fire missiles unless their Chinese Big Brothers approved. So—? It occurred to Brand that Darman was being purposely enigmatic—to give him some puzzled moments. Angrily he thought, the son of a bitch succeeded. Then he dialed and heard La-li pick up after the third ring. She said she hadn't yet heard from Peter. "Isn't like him, is it, sir?"

"Not like him at all. Tell you what, Monday I'll ask his office what the story is and let you know."

"Oh, I'll appreciate that, Mr. Brand. Thank you."

"And you'll let me know of any contact from Peter."

"Immediately. Are—are you worried, sir?"

"Not yet. We'll stay in touch."

From Georgetown he drove back to his apartment and read mail, paid bills, and placed a call to his father that went unanswered. Probably out stitching up an axe wound, Brand thought and retired to his bedroom for a nap. Before falling asleep, Brand found himself hoping that Nina had been truthful in saying she didn't have AIDS.

IN THE EVENING he took Nina to National Theater where a revival of *Fiddler* was playing—Topol having rejoined the cast in his original role. Then paella supper at El Bodegon and on to bed, chez Nina.

Toward noon Brand left Washington for a horse show and dressage exhibition at Warrenton, Nina having declined on the excuse of probable poor weather.

She was soaking in a bubble bath, foam to her chin, when the telephone rang. She blew foam from one hand and took the gilded receiver from the wall. "Yes?"

"How did it go?"

She sighed. "I finally got him talking about himself."

"And?"

"He stayed with his cover legend. Totally."

"Shit!"

"Not a nice word, *mon cher*."

"But applicable, sweetheart." The male voice pronounced it "shweetheart" à la Bogart, and Nina thought, what a coarse man. "So, tell me," the voice went on, "there has to be *some* take. We didn't set you up like an empress just so you could fuck his balls dry."

"Actually," she said in a steely voice, "he's got the endurance of a teenager and a bagful of Oriental tricks. *I'm* the one who gets exhausted, and every orifice aches."

"Poor you," the voice mocked, "now let's get back to business. Uh—he's not around, is he?"

"Now you ask. No, he's off with the horsey set miles away. He failed to mention his father's wartime OSS connection, and said he'd worked for a Navy group on Taiwan. He didn't mention the insurance payout when his wife was killed, or the trust that passed to him and Peter when old Bishop Wayburn kicked off. More or less describes himself in academic terms. Oh, one thing, he said he's working on the geology of the Kunlun mountain range."

"Kunlun?"

"China, old dear, where else? Says it's got lots of goodies like iron and petroleum, but I think that's just bullshit."

"Ummm. Maybe worth checking out. Kunlun, eh? Could be significant."

Her eyes rolled upward and she stared at the ceiling. What an oaf! "Something else, since you're so damn curious—his son went off to Hong Kong a while back and hasn't been heard from. He's worried."

"Yeah? Kid's probably fucking every ivory figurine who'll spread for him."

"How charmingly you put it. Clean up your act when you talk with me, you bastard!"

Long chuckle. "Thought that'd get a rise from you. No harm meant. Ah—think he's bribable?"

"Doubt it. He's got money, and as a missionary's son he's frugal."

"So what's the long term? Will he ever confide in you? Tell you what he really does?"

She was silent while she considered. Then, "What do you want me to say? If I say no, all this is over." She gazed possessively around the tiled room with its gold-plated taps and faucets, the form-fitting French bidet. "If I say yes and nothing happens you'll hold me accountable." She paused. "Won't you?"

"Any chance of an honest answer?"

"Slim."

"If necessary, would you marry him?"

"Listen, he is one great hunk and I'd marry him even if it weren't— as you put it—necessary."

"Now that's an interesting revelation. Ah, just don't get so hooked on him you blab the setup, okay? Do that, babe, and the penalties could be extreme."

"Don't call me babe!" she yelled, but the line had gone dead. Slowly she replaced the receiver and slid down into the foam. How long, she wondered, could she keep stringing Brand along? Not that it was objectionable, in truth it was enjoyable. All of it.

The pit of her stomach warmed and she felt a familiar needing deep between her loins. How was it that just thinking of Mark Brand's strong body could make her juices flow?

Two

The offices of Asian Investment Ltd. occupied a handsome old four-story red brick house on New Hampshire Avenue near Washington Circle. Mark Brand arrived promptly for his ten-thirty appointment, and after identifying himself to the Eurasian receptionist waited in a lacquered chair until Peter's supervisor, Paul Kremers, appeared. Brand rose, and they shook hands. "What can I do for you, Mr. Brand?" Kremers inquired. He was a short, slightly built man in his mid-forties, with unkempt black hair and thick, steel-rimmed lenses; a tic tugged his left eye. "We're very satisfied with Peter's work—he may have told you." Both eyes blinked rapidly, and Brand thought that in another setting Kremers's rumpled clothing and hand-washing would cast him as an unsuccessful accountant.

"I'm glad to hear it." Brand cleared his throat. "I'm not spying on my son, not checking up on him, but I understand he went to Hong Kong on company business."

Kremers nodded. "That's so. Normally we'd have sent a more expe-

rienced man—myself for instance—but I've not been feeling well—
liver, you know—and so it was decided to see how well Peter handled
things." The tic was working overtime.

Brand said, "I see. And could you give me an idea when he'll be
back?"

"Afraid not. He was to explore a certain situation—pardon me if I
withhold business details—and then, of course, return." His smile was
bleak as an undertaker's and equally insincere.

"Do you know the hotel where he's staying?"

Kremers shrugged. "I suppose we won't know until his expense
account comes in. But I rather assume he booked into the Hilton or the
Furama." The upper lip rose and his nose wrinkled unattractively. "Possibly the Mandarin. We like our associates to travel first class. Good for
their morale, you know, and in the end it's the client who pays."

"I understand. I'd like to contact my son, so perhaps you'd let me
know who it was he's seeing? Save me the trouble of phoning all those
hotels."

Kremers glanced nervously at the receptionist and motioned Brand
toward the room's far corner. "This is all very delicate and confidential,
you do understand?"

"Whatever you say," Brand was beginning to feel apprehensive.
"No problem."

"No. No, of course not." Nose twitched like a rabbit's. "The individual in question does not reside or work in the Crown Colony, he is a
resident on the Mainland, no way to contact him at all. No, not at all, I'm
afraid."

Brand frowned. "Then how was Peter to contact him?"

"Oh, it's the other way 'round. When he arrived from the Mainland—coming when he could, as it were—he was to contact Peter."

Brand felt like shaking the little man. "How could he contact Peter
if you can't? I don't understand."

"Oh, it's really very simple, Mr. Brand—and please don't become
upset, loud voices are not at all the thing here, not the custom at all." He
swallowed and his Adam's apple bobbed. "The visitor—if I may so refer
to the arrival—was to leave a message for Peter at a certain place. Then
Peter would know how to get in touch with him," he finished trium-
phantly. "You see? It is quite a logical arrangement, arrived at to protect
the visitor."

"Protect him from what?"

Kremers licked his lips. "Persons, I suppose, who have interests contrary to the visitor's."

"Tells me nothing," Brand said roughly. "Now, before I lose patience, please identify the 'certain place' and the visitor."

Kremers swallowed, and when he spoke his voice was lower. "The desk of the American Club in Hong Kong. Peter was to inquire daily for messages. As to the, ah, visitor"—he spread his hands and smiled helplessly—"that is indeed a private business matter, fully confidential, you understand."

"No," said Brand, "I don't fully understand." His hand closed over Kremers's and squeezed until the banker winced in pain. "The visitor's name, please." He squeezed tighter while Kremers's free hand clawed at Brand's powerful grip.

"Lok Chong Liu," he gasped.

"Fine. Good. You're getting the idea." Brand slightly eased pressure. "And what is Lok's position on the Mainland?"

"A trade official from Jiangxi Province. Very senior. *The* senior trade official. Please release my hand." Brand did so and Kremers rubbed and flexed the fingers.

"A trade matter?"

With a resentful look, Kremers nodded. "Seeking credits for a tourism project."

"Which you are prepared to grant?"

"Depending on Peter's report. I must say I don't at all like what you just did to me. Not one bit."

"Keep it to yourself," Brand advised, "and don't take it out on my son. Lok Chong Liu, eh?" He took a business card from his billfold and placed it in Kremers's undamaged hand. "Anything from Peter, you tell me. Then I won't have to bother you again." His gaze lowered to Kremers's reddened hand. "Better that way, don't you think?"

"Oh, yes, better. Much better. I'll be sure to tell you just as soon as I have any word."

"Appreciate it." Brand turned to leave.

Behind him Kremers said, "You're concerned about your son, aren't you?"

"I think we both should be." In the vestibule he opened the outer door, whose upper half was glass-etched with Victorian curlicues. A fine old house, solid. He wondered if Paul Kremers was solid, too.

At Washington Circle Brand entered a pharmacy and used the coin phone to call Peter's apartment, not really expecting La-li to answer since it was a workday and she had a job somewhere. But she answered in a choked voice and gasped when Brand gave his name. "I have some information," he told her, "but first, have you heard from Peter?"

"No. Nothing."

"Ummm. Well, I've just talked to his employer, and—"

"—Mr. Brand, it's better if you can come here," she interrupted.

"Phone tapped?" he asked half jocularly.

"It's—no—I'm not feeling very well. Do you mind?"

"What's your street number? I'm not used to it yet."

She gave it to him and asked that he ring four times.

At the apartment he rang the bell as requested and in a few moments La-li let him in. She was wearing a green terry-cloth bathrobe and floppy slippers. Her face was pale. Brand said, "You're not feeling well?"

"I wasn't up to working today."

He followed her to a large, worn sofa probably bought third-, or fourthhand, wondering if the girl had flu or perhaps cramps. He remembered Sela's monthly difficulties, until she became pregnant with Peter.

Holding herself in a contained fashion, La-li said, "You have some information? I'm so glad, Mr. Brand, I've been really worried, and—"

"Easy," he cautioned, "just bits and pieces. Peter's office doesn't know where he's staying—or says they don't. One of Hong Kong's better hotels was the best they could do." Her face looked drawn, dark circles under her eyes. "But he was to be contacted," Brand went on, "through the American Club."

"Contacted? By who?"

"Some fellow from the Mainland, Jiangxi, who didn't want his presence—" He broke off as she leaned forward, cupped a hand over her mouth, and fled. From where he sat Brand could hear the sounds of vomiting. Sela all over again, vomiting every morning while—Oh, Christ, he thought, the girl is pregnant. No wonder she's worried about Peter.

Tap water running, more retching sounds, and after a while La-li reappeared. Brand rose, circled her shoulders with one arm, and said quietly, "How long?"

"How—?" Her upturned face betrayed nothing.

"How long have you known you were pregnant?"

Turning from him she burst into tears, curled on the sofa, and sobbed brokenly. When sobs subsided Brand touched her cheek. "La-li, look at me. It's not the end of the world. Does Peter know?"

She shook her head violently. "I only knew last week, because of this, this morning sickness."

"That's what it's called." He sat beside her and held her hand. She tried tugging it free but Brand held it firmly.

La-li looked away. "You want me to abort, don't you?"

"No. No, I don't. In fact, I'll do everything I can to make sure the baby is born healthy and on time." He felt a surge of emotion he had not experienced since Sela had told him she'd conceived. Poor La-li, he thought, alone in a foreign land, expecting her man's father to make her abort . . .

"You'll help me?" She brushed aside tears.

"Of course. This is a family matter now, don't you see? And we both want Peter back." Her upper body relaxed into the shelter of his arm. Hello, Granddad, he said to himself, it's time you did something for someone other than yourself. "Anything you learn," he said, "could be of value. I have contacts here and there. I'll start by phoning the American Club, try the major hotels. We're sure to come up with something." He paused. "If we work together."

"Yes, yes, we will." She shivered as though swept by a sudden chill.

"Are—are you all right?"

"I won't throw up again . . . it's when I think of Peter. I miss him terribly. I love him . . ." Her voice trailed away.

"So do I. For many years he was all I had, La-li. Now I have you . . . and the baby."

That brought more tears. Brand gave her his handkerchief and while she was dabbing her eyes he said, "Your doctor confirmed pregnancy?"

"I didn't go to a doctor. I took a test you buy at a drugstore."

"But you have a doctor?"

"I've seen one at the free clinic, but that was for cold and fever."

"Peter can afford doctors."

"I—I just didn't want to bother him, sir. I can take care of myself."

How Oriental, he reflected. Leave the male undisturbed while the female serves his necessities and whims. "All right," he said, "we'll get you a good OB, best in the District, and you go see him. He'll bill me." He looked around the scantily furnished room. Its size and fresh paint were all he could see to recommend it. "Tell me if you need anything. Anything at all." He got out his billfold. "Money?"

"Oh, no, Peter left house money, and I have what I make."

"But you'll tell me . . ."

She nodded, and again tears welled in her eyes. "I'm so grateful, sir."

"Well, first thing, let's do away with sir and Mr. I'm Mark from now on. Okay?"

"Okay."

"And Peter will be overjoyed when he learns he's fathering a child." Brand smiled. "Especially by so beautiful a wife."

She managed a brief smile. "Thank you."

"Mark."

"Yes. Thank you, Mark."

He could think of nothing else to say. His daughter-in-law-to-be was a healthy young woman who would bear this child and then another. The knowledge of things to come suddenly was filling an unacknowledged void in his life. Again, after so long alone, he had a family.

And his father, too. Simon would be happy.

Great-grandfather Simon, Brand thought, would spoil Peter's baby as he spoiled me, his son. Tonight he would phone his father, maybe drive up later in the week. After Peter was found.

Brand went to the telephone table and looked up his internist's office. The medical receptionist gave Brand their referral recommendation and Brand copied it down. To La-li he said, "Dr. Edward Carpenter, 1608 K Street. I want you to call for an appointment. Today."

"I will."

"Don't walk that distance, take a cab."

She nodded dutifully.

"And call me whenever you want—for any reason."

"You're wonderful," she said simply, and bowed her head.

Brand kissed the crown of her jet-black hair. "You're bearing my blood, daughter. While Peter's away I'll care for you."

Walking toward DuPont Circle for a taxi, Brand sensed new interest in his surroundings. Grass and budding leaves seemed greener, flower beds deeper-hued. A cardinal flashed from one tree to another; had its plumage always been so brilliantly crimson? Suddenly he felt close to La-li, closer than he had ever imagined. A feeling of protectiveness suffused him. Getting sentimental? he asked himself, and answered, When was I not?

All right. Today there were developments, some negative, some indeterminate, one sublimely wonderful, and it was barely noon in Washington. In Hong Kong, the early hours of another day. A good time to canvass hotels for Peter's registration. And the American Club would have an all-night duty clerk.

In his office he told Abby Wainwright what he wanted done, closed the door, and took work materials from his safe.

Brand arranged them on his desk and activated his terminal for the morning's satellite feed from the National Reconnaissance Office. As his computer came on-line, Brand reflected that NRO had been established by CIA in the aftermath of the Cuban Missile Crisis, but after a turf battle with NASA the Air Force had assumed overall control.

He remembered Darman Gerold's Saturday throwaway line: Keep an eye on Korea. Was the Harvard puke serious, or exercising the snide one-upmanship he was notorious for. Hell, Korea had been static for years, and he was plenty occupied keeping an eye on those parts of China with ICBM sites. Screw Darman, the old lichee nut expert. *Garlic,* Mark?

After a while his secretary brought in a tray bearing soup, a rare roast beef sandwich, pickles, and strong coffee. After setting it down, she said, "Negatives from the Mandarin, the Furama, and the Hilton. The American Club clerk said Peter wasn't a member and knew nothing about him. However"—she drew in a deep breath—"the Cathay clerk ran Peter's name through the reservation computer and told me Peter had been there for three nights, then left."

"Three nights, when? Where did he go?" Brand sat forward eagerly. First trace of his son.

"Two weeks ago. The clerk had no idea where the guest went after leaving the hotel."

"Damn!" Brand bit down on his pencil eraser. "Kai Tak airport? Star Ferry? Railway station? He didn't come home, where the hell is he?" Irresponsible father-to-be.

"Shall I try the airlines out of Hong Kong?"

"Please do. Those dates will help. Thank you, Abby, thank you *very* much."

He tried concentrating on NRO's feed, but it was futile. Finally, he drank coffee—cold as the soup. Had no stomach for a sandwich, and recognized the clutch of stress.

"No airline's record, sir." Abby Wainwright; hadn't realized she'd entered.

"Well, thanks, anyway." He slumped in his chair dispiritedly. Wasn't like Peter to go off on his own without leaving word—he wasn't an impulse traveler. Peter made careful plans. Boat to Taiwan? Possible, but why? Peter hadn't been there in years, said the pervasive scent of camphor caused allergic reaction, made it hard to breathe . . . No, not Taiwan, where Sela had abandoned them for the heady conspiracies of terrorism.

By now the Asian watchlists might have come up with something. Should he phone a reminder to Darman, or wait for his call? *Would* Darman call? Had he bothered to issue the notice?

Undecided, Brand stared at the phone. While he was staring at it the phone began to ring.

Three

"MARK BRAND?" THE VOICE was low, with a suggestion of hoarseness.

"I'm Brand. Who's calling?"

"You've been asking about your son."

"Who is this?" Fully alert, Brand gripped the receiver.

"Unimportant. What's important is I can give you information."

"I'm listening."

"And perhaps taping this call. That would not be in my interest, yours, or your son's. So if you want information you will meet me."

"Tell me where Peter is—tell me now."

"Inadvisable, for the reason given." The voice had developed a confident harmonic. "Eight o'clock, foot of Wisconsin Avenue under the freeway."

"That parking area by the river?"

"Exactly."

"How will I know you?"

"I'll know *you.*" Click, disconnect. The line hummed.

Slowly Brand lowered the receiver, feeling a chill of fear for Peter's safety. Had his son been kidnapped? Held for ransom? He'd pay his last penny to bring Peter home.

Eight o'clock. How did the caller know he was trying to locate Peter? Who was he? What information did he have? And why the secret meeting?

Should he tell La-li? Kremers? No, not until there was something to tell.

His palms were clammy. He dried them on a handkerchief and gulped water from his desk carafe. Five hours to the meeting. How could he bridge them? What did parents do in hostage situations? Call the police? FBI? No, nothing solid to tell them. But, after the meeting . . .

Who was the caller? Some lackey of Kremers's taking cruel revenge for his humiliation? Possible, though the banker hadn't seemed the type to take reprisal.

Thoughts whirled. The new factor, Peter possibly endangered, made him nauseous. Brand swallowed more water, pushed the glass aside. Closing his eyes, he tried to organize his thoughts, decide what to do.

Simple. He'd meet the unknown contact under the Whitehurst Freeway. At eight o'clock.

He'd be there.

* * *

AT THE FITNESS CLUB Brand worked the weight machines vigorously, even viciously, to sublimate his fears for Peter. An observant instructor said, "Hey, take it easy, huh? You'll pull the damn machine apart," and handed Brand a towel. "How many sets've you done?"

"Lost count." Brand dried his dripping face and throat.

"You're not a kid, y'know, so gentle down, willya? We don't wanta lose a member."

Brand managed a smile. "You're right." Leaving the machine, he headed for the shower, then sat on a sauna bench spilling water over heated stones, inhaling cleansing steam.

Finally able to relax, Brand let his mind drift back over the years to his childhood and adolescence, years when Dr. Simon Brand had been both father and mother to him. Letting him watch simple surgeries, learn the cures for fever and the bites of animals and insects. How to sterilize and bandage, identify and use the fortifying herbs, barks, and plants that abounded on Taiwan. Making kites of rice paper, flour paste, and string. Brand remembered his father patiently showing him how to make a bow from cherry wood, fire-harden arrow tips as did the aborigines. His father taught him the songs of wild birds, the lonely whistle of a hawk, how to cup his hands and call down geese and ducks. To pry the shells of abalone from tidal rocks and tenderize the meat . . . so many things.

And not least, to learn the arts of kung fu in classes with boys his own strength and age. Cheng Ziang the Manchurian was his instructor, a man whose wife and baby Dr. Simon had saved when both were at the point of death . . .

With Peter, Brand had shared less exotic things: fishing for trout and bass and salmon; shooting skeet and ducks; helping the boy earn Boy Scout badges. Hoping to make his son as self-reliant as he had become under his father's kindly tutelage.

His thoughts were interrupted by the entrance of a paunchy man who sat in a sauna corner and tossed water on the stones to bring up clouds of steam. They nodded at each other through masking vapor, and Brand reflected that this man could be his unknown caller.

Why the damn secrecy? he wondered. Why meet in darkness to convey a few sentences that would inform him, lighten his concern? He was troubled by the conspiratorial nature of the contact though he doubted he would face personal danger. More likely the contact had information to sell and wanted to remain anonymous.

But who would have such information? Some local Chinese with lines back to Hong Kong? A fellow employee of Peter's bank seemed the likeliest possibility. And I'll pay him, Brand thought. Gladly.

The least likely being a subordinate of Gerold's who was willing to sell what Gerold was withholding: a travel trace from watchlisting Peter's name.

Two more men entered the sauna, and Brand decided the wooden enclosure was getting too crowded. He emptied a dipper of cold water over his head, left the steam-choked atmosphere, and plunged into the icy pool.

The shock cleared his head and he began to feel optimistic about the meeting's outcome.

Before eight Brand drove over M Street to Wisconsin and turned down the hill. On a Monday night there was plenty of space in the parking area, and he guided the BMW to a place under a light where it could be easily seen. Above, traffic hummed along the freeway, the Potomac River glinted dully, and beyond it Brand could make out the darker line of the Virginia shore.

Eight o'clock. He got out of the car and stood beside it, arms folded. Waiting. Tentacles of mist reached toward him from the river. The air held a stench of decay and exhaust fumes; odors from the old cement plant permeated the raw earth underfoot. He heard the screeching jets of a plane rising from National Airport to pass overhead and fade in the northern distance. No cars had entered the area since his arrival. Monday night was a quiet one in Georgetown after the weekend's exuberance along the M Street strip.

Minutes dragged on. Where was the contact? Was he coming, or was this a probe?

"Good evening, Mr. Brand." The voice came from behind him. Brand turned and saw a man standing in shadows a dozen feet away. The man's hat was pulled low on his forehead, the lapels of his outer coat shielding his face to the eyes.

"You have information about my son? Where is he?"

"Patience, please. How much cash have you?"

"A hundred, maybe more." He reached for his billfold. "Is Peter alive?"

"Alive, yes. Toss me your billfold."

Brand skimmed it across his car's roof and the man picked it up. After extracting the currency the man tossed back the billfold. "Do you know why your son went to Hong Kong?"

"On business for the bank he works for. So I was told."

"Accurate as far as it goes, Mr. Brand. I doubt it has ever occurred to you that Peter had additional business there."

"What kind of business?"

"Heroin. Cocaine."

Brand shook his head. "Impossible."

"What every parent believes—until the truth comes out. Unfortunately for both of you, Peter's plan was to bring heroin to this country, enough to make him wealthy."

"I don't believe it. Even were it true, where is my son?" His voice hardened. Unseen, his hands clenched into fists. "Where's Peter?"

"Macao."

"Macao? Why?"

"He went there to buy heroin. The seller betrayed him, and Peter was arrested."

Brand's throat tightened, went dry. He knew something of the Portuguese, the Macaoese and their brutality. "In prison?"

"Jail. But release is still possible. Such things are negotiable."

"I see. How much to free him?"

"A sum has been suggested. Ten thousand dollars key money."

"Paid to you?"

"As facilitator."

"And how do you know all this?"

"I have—contacts."

"Ah." Ten thousand was insignificant—*if* it freed Peter. But—"I don't know your cultural background," Brand said harshly, "but mine says the sinner pays for his sin. If Peter's become a drug dealer he pays the price."

"Twenty years hard labor?"

"It'll be a learning experience."

There was a long silence before the man said, "Five thousand, then. Surely not too much for your son's release."

"Tell you what, Jethro," Brand said coldly, "I'll pay a thousand for the name of Peter's jail—and yours." *Fuck this extortionist*, he thought. *I'll go to Macao, hire the island's best lawyer, and get my son back. Pay key money direct, not through any middleman. If that's what he is.* "Well?"

"Such a hard, unfeeling father. That's a bargain I can't accept. Not without consulting my, ah, principals. And my name is not Jethro."

"We'll start with that. Show me ID."

"Not so fast, Mr. Brand. I can't agree to that."

"No deal then. Macao is a small place."

"With many cells—and dungeons."

"Not too many. My offer stands. Think it over, Jethro." He paused. "Twenty-four hours."

"Very little time," the man objected, "and *don't* call me Jethro."

"Time enough to contact your principals."

"Perhaps. Why does my name concern you?"

"If I got to Macao and find you've lied I'll want to locate you fast."

Silence. Then the stranger spoke, "Why go to Macao? Why take the trouble, when everything can be arranged between us?"

"You've got till tomorrow night, Jethro. After that no deal at all."

Across the space between them the man's rage exploded. *"Stop calling me Jethro!* You doubt my bona fides?"

"Haven't seen any. As to your story, it's unsupported." And easy to fabricate, Brand thought, by anyone who knew of Peter's absence, my inquiries. Adding to easy bucks.

As he opened the car door the other man shouted, *"You* think it over."

"I have," Brand snapped and started the engine. He spun the car and headlights caught the coated figure running toward the river. It dodged between girders, among scattered cars, and on impulse Brand floored the accelerator. The BMW shot forward in pursuit, Brand steering around obstacles until the coated figure began dodging left and right trying to avoid the relentless headlights. Still running, the figure glanced back and tripped on a low pile of scrap metal. Brand braked hard and vaulted at the man who was trying to rise, knocking him backward. The hat rolled away as the head slammed a rusted metal plate, and the body went limp.

Brand straddled it, brushing aside coat lapels to see—an Oriental face. Long, coal-black hair, dusky skin but for a whitened scar that ran from left eye to ear. Brand searched for a billfold, found three bus tokens and a hundred twelve dollars in currency that he pocketed.

He slapped the man's face and in Chinese spat, "Wake up, get up!"

Eyes opened, rolled fearfully, the body struggled beneath Brand's heavier weight. "Now, my friend," Brand said coldly, "who are you, and where did you get your information?"

White teeth glinted as lips drew back. The head shook wildly, negatively. Brand thumbled a neck nerve and the man screamed shrilly. "That's a sample," Brand snarled. "Who's your source? Your principal?" His hand reached for the thin neck and gripped it.

"Wait, wait—my girlfriend told me you were asking about your son."

"Who's your girlfriend?"

"She works at Asian Investments—receptionist." Perspiration beaded the man's forehead.

"And she put you up to this—extortion?"

"No—no, she knows nothing. She mentioned your circumstances. I—I need money, I decided to get it from you."

"Try working," Brand snapped.

"No papers," the voice said sullenly. "I came as a student, visa expired. Can't go back to China."

Hundreds, maybe thousands like him, Brand thought, and felt an unexpected surge of pity. But he said, "Then you'd rather not explain this to the police."

"Please . . . please, no."

"We'll see. My son is not a drug trafficker?"

"No—I know nothing of that, made it up."

"And he's not in Macao?"

"Maybe. I don't know where he is."

"What's you name?"

Tongue flicked out, wetting dry lips. "Feng Wah."

From behind Brand heard an oncoming vehicle, and got up, not wanting to be mistaken for a mugger. Slowly Feng Wah sat up, rubbed the back of his head, got to his feet, and looked for his hat.

"Tell your girlfriend to keep her company's business to herself."

"Yes, yes," the voice hissed. Hat replaced, the man stood up, stark in the oncoming headlights.

"Go home," Brand advised. "Crime's not for you." He walked back to his car and reversed it to back into a clearing where he could turn around. As he drove slowly away he saw a man and woman leave their car and walk toward the hill. Brand felt drained, disgusted.

He was halfway to his apartment before he remembered his Saturday commitment to Darman Gerold. Monday had passed and he hadn't phoned Tommy Gray.

In his apartment, Brand downed a double shot of Walker Black and dissected the mini-conspiracy that was to have separated him from his money without rejoining him with his son. Now, he reflected glumly, he had nowhere to turn. Unless the Agency watchlist turned up a usable clue.

Four

Thomas Appleton Gray II—tall, thin, with unkempt graying hair, bushy eyebrows, and almost bloodless lips—faced Brand across a table in the dining room of Gray's downtown club, one that collected academics, astronomers, mathematicians, and assorted eccentrics. The high ceilings were darkened from decades of tobacco smoke, wall varnish cracked with age, but the Logos held a deserved reputation for a kitchen that specialized in Chesapeake Bay seafood. Before ordering from the menu Brand had drunk two rye Manhattans, and Gray three iced vodkas. Despite his host's Agency and age seniority Brand found Tommy deferential. Gray's fingers trembled noticeably as he lighted a cigarette. "Glad you found time to see me, Mark," he said, exhaling smoke.

"Sorry I didn't give you more notice. How soon are you retiring?"

"Papers are in, I can leave anytime."

Brand nodded. "I want to be blunt, Tom. Darman asked me to find a place for you at GlobEco. At the time I resented it, but on reflection I think I can accommodate him, and you."

Gray's impassive face twitched into a half smile. "Good news."

"If we can get a few things straight. You had trouble with Darman?"

Gray shrugged. "Personality clash. You didn't get along with him, either."

"True. But I wasn't at Harvard with him, you were."

"Barely. I was three years ahead of him and in a different club. He was a figure around the Yard." Gray dropped ash into a small porcelain tray that bore the club's green logo.

"Personality clash—or professional disagreement?"

"The latter."

Brand eyed him. "Specifically?"

"You know what he's like, Mark, a kibitzer, always poking around, rephrasing estimates, making absurd operational suggestions." He breathed deeply, stubbed out his cigarette. "Finally told him to stay out of my office unless invited in."

"And that did it?"

"Well, it gave point to an accumulation of things over the years."

"What kind of operational suggestions?"

"Send in a hit team to assassinate Kim il-Jung, for one. Dispatch agents by submarine to report on Shanghai harbor . . ." His eyes narrowed in thought. "Bomb the Beijing building where the Central Committee meets . . . I got tired of it all, blocked most of his crap from my mind." He managed a smile. "I have that facility."

"Lucky you." Brand waited while the waiter served shrimp cocktails and moved away. "How's your health?"

"Okay, I guess. I drink and smoke too much—as you may have noticed—but that's because of my wife. Lila has multiple sclerosis."

"Tom, I'm sorry."

"Yeah, me, too." He lighted another cigarette, glanced at his shrimp cocktail, and stubbed it out. "In one way we're lucky, no money problem. And the Agency's health plan takes care of medical bills." Brand nodded, remembering that Gray's wife had come from a prominent banking family in Portland. Tommy's family was in Northwest shipping and lumber. No money problems there.

"So why do you want to keep working?" Brand asked as he dipped shrimp into red cocktail sauce.

"To keep my mind occupied. Something new like GlobEco would be a challenge. I'd be busy, not brooding over life's inequities."

"Have you got Gorgon clearance?"

"Recently. Until then I never knew where that good targeting stuff came from; didn't realize you were in charge." He picked up a small fork and stabbed a shrimp. "Word in the halls is Seth Williamson runs GlobEco."

"That's for external consumption," Brand told him. "Seth signs the checks but we're organized on regional breakdowns. I'm in charge of Far East which mostly means China."

"So you still butt heads with Charmin' Darman."

"Now and then," Brand conceded. "Incidentally, Darman said I should keep an eye on Korea. Any particular reason I should?" As chief of Far East Operations Tommy ought to know.

"He was probably thinking of political stability, or instability. Those Seoul demonstrations forever on TV—students with stones, riot police with tear gas, clubs, shields, and water wagons."

"Inspired by the North?"

"Some of it, sure. But the kids embrace anarchy the way ours embrace dope. And there's the unification idea, Korea all one country again. Kim's son ruling the whole peninsula, of course backed by nuke missiles."

"None of that's new."

"No, it isn't. So I don't know what was on Darman's weasley mind." He speared a shrimp, munched, and swallowed. "Could be throwing you a curve, Mark, just to make you uneasy. Like him."

"Reasonable," Mark agreed as the waiter showed Tommy a dripping bottle of white wine and began uncorking it. "Or one of Darman's transient enthusiasms."

"Yeah," said Tommy sourly, "the instant enthusiast for anything unusual. Enthusiasms he drops with the speed of acquisition after impracticalities are explained to him." He sampled the wine, nodded, and the waiter filled Brand's glass. "Of course, it was too often left to me to explain those impracticalities because Darman's acolytes only grinned and praised their boss."

Brand smiled. "Whatever else Darman learned at Harvard he has an amazing ability to recruit supporters."

"By perks and promotions. Like the wine?"

"Excellent. California?"

"Sonoma. Not a wine snob, are you?"

"Not recently." Brand sipped again. The cold dryness tingled his tongue. French might possibly be better—at three times the cost. "I'd like you at GlobEco as soon as you can comfortably arrange it."

"Right away?"

"Sooner the better." He sipped again and set down the glass, stem between two fingers. "Darman said he'd watchlist my son's name. Has he?"

"Peter S. Brand? Your son, eh?" He leaned forward, dabbed a napkin to his mouth. "I wondered about that when the name came through. What's it about, Mark?"

Brand told him what he had learned, including last night's encounter under the freeway, and waited for Gray's reaction. When the older man spoke, he said, "Without prying, is Peter in some kind of trouble?"

"None I know of. But his girlfriend's distraught, and I'm plenty worried. Unless answers come soon I may do some field reconnaissance on my own. Which is why I'd like you briefed and in place at GlobEco."

"I see. How about Monday?"

"Friday would be better."

"Okay. Friday."

"The Admin people will check you in, give you the security drill, handle paperwork, where you want salary sent, so on." He let Tommy refill his glass.

"Were you born on Taiwan, Mark?"

"Kunming. But I spent a lot of years in Taipei. School, academic research, and the old Navy group. It's familiar territory."

"Ever want to go back?"

"Occasionally, but there's not much left for me. Memories, I guess."

"Hmm. As I recollect, you had a Chinese girlfriend there—after your wife died."

"Chen Ling-mei. Probably should have married her, but I didn't. Her father had been museum curator in Beijing, brought her to Taiwan when Chiang's gang decamped. I had academic dealings with the old man, met his daughter." Over the years Brand had made himself forget Ling-mei, who had succored him through the aftermath of Sela's death.

"Is she . . . still there?"

"Apparently not. Years ago I went to the house but there was another family, and at the Antiquities Museum another curator, who said his predecessor had died." He shrugged. "So much for memories." But he could never forget her tiny budlike breasts, the beguiling curvatures of her loins, and the wisps of dark silk that fringed her sex. So soft, so pliant, so loving, so loyal . . . Where is she now? he wondered, and forced his mind back to his host.

"So you raised Peter by yourself," Gray said.

"Aside from boarding school and college."

"He wasn't interested in the Agency?"

"I squelched any latent interest, told him to work in the real world."

"Good advice," Gray pronounced and added more wine to his glass as the waiter delivered plates of broiled rockfish. "He would have found it far less interesting than when I joined. Or you, Mark."

Brand grunted. "Sending agents into the Mainland meat grinder wasn't exactly interesting, Tommy. It was sickening."

Gray nodded forcefully. "Kept doing it because it had always been done that way, and Darman Gerold still thinks it's the way to go." He sighed. "Every time he'd run another infiltration project past me I'd shoot it down. Remind him there was an NSC order against it. Not because infiltration was provably unproductive, but because Sino-American détente is not to be risked. Then I'd remind Darman of the old Legal Traveler program and suggest his scouts recruit businessmen willing to look around and report back." He separated bones from fillet. "Darman wanted me to spot bodies but I said I was too busy and lacked his range of contacts. That flattered him and he'd go away—until next time."

"You played him like a Stradivarius," Brand said admiringly. "I should have used honey with Darman, not vinegar."

"Yeah, he's the kind of simpleton who loves flattery. Sometimes I thought I laid it on too thick but he couldn't get enough." He chewed and swallowed a mouthful, washed it down with wine. "And the rumor is he may be our next DCI."

The thought appalled Brand. Shaking his head he said, "Darman probably started the rumor."

"Sure. Early positioning for the directorship. After a run of incompetent DCIs, maybe the White House will appoint someone from the Agency, on the theory he knows the business."

"Then they better bypass Gerold."

"But will they?" He chewed and swallowed in silence. Brand did the same before changing the subject. "Still live in Cleveland Park?"

"Yeah, same old roomy frame house I've had for twenty years. Too comfortable to sell, too old to fix up. And I'm glad I didn't because now I can bus to GlobEco and not have to drive over to Langley every day. You know what that's like on a rainy day. Murder." He sipped and his expression grew reflective. "Lila loves the old place, Mark. I fixed up a first-floor bedroom so she doesn't have to climb stairs. We've got a cook-maid, and a nurse visits two or three times a week, so . . ." His voice trailed off as his head lowered.

To break his mood Brand said, "The Paladar satellite covers all Korea, shows NK troop movements, that sort of thing. So you might want to pay some attention to Paladar product in case Darman bugs you about Korea."

"Will do." His head lifted slowly and Brand saw that his eyes had reddened.

"If you can find time before Friday I'd like to show you through the building, introduce you around, figure out your title for personnel listing. It's all pretty relaxed, none of Langley's hierarchy bullshit."

"That'll be a relief." He blinked and twirled his glass between thumb and forefinger. "If Darman ever comes up for Senate confirmation there's one part of his background he won't want to surface."

"What's that?"

"Well, since we have basically the same attitude toward our leader I'll pass along a story Lila told me a long time ago." He paused, eyeing Brand. "Ever meet his first wife, Susan?"

Brand nodded and Tommy continued. "Suzie and Lila were schoolmates in Portland; Lila was a bridesmaid when Suzie married Darman, so they knew each other pretty well. Intimately. Suzie decided they'd spend the first part of their honeymoon at her family's lodge in the high country near Bennett Pass, an isolated place where they could be together." He drew in a deep breath. "Know anything about Darman's mother?"

"Not really. His father was an investment banker with Morgan."

"Right. Big bucks. And he married a showgirl, Amy something, who was much, much younger. Darman was their only child, and by the time Suzie and Darman got married his mother, Amy, was maybe forty-four or -five. And according to Suzie, still quite attractive."

Brand wondered what Tommy was leading up to but said nothing. Tommy sipped water and cleared his throat. "Suzie and Darman spent their first married night at the lodge alone. Next evening, along about cocktail time, Amy drove up saying she wanted to see them again before returning to Boston. Suzie hadn't expected the intrusion but played the gracious hostess. A lot of champagne was consumed by the three of them, and when it got late Suzie suggested Amy stay over to avoid night driving on mountain roads. And Amy had drunk too much to drive safely." He shook his head. "Plot thickens, eh?"

"Plot?"

"Bear with me, Mark. And I ought to explain that Suzie Gerold told Lila the story over mucho drinks at the country club."

"So—what happened?"

Tommy frowned. "After Suzie had washed the dinner dishes she found her husband and his mother in bed together."

"Jesus! You're kidding?"

"Incest isn't a kidding matter where I come from. Yeah, Suzie said Amy and Darman were getting it on, going all out. She yelled at them and Amy yelled back that Darman was her kid and she'd fuck him any time she wanted, said Suzie was a Gerold now and better get used to it."

"Unbelievable!"

"Yeah. *The Honeymooners* without Ralph Kramden. X-rated." He smiled. "My wife believed Suzie and I believed my wife."

"So what did Suzie do?"

"Got the hell out. Drove back to Portland and hid out in a hotel. Darman found her a couple of days later, promised it wouldn't happen again, and persuaded Suzie to stay with him."

Brand grunted. "If all that happened, then Darman's what a lot of people have called him."

"Yeah, a motherfucker." He stretched back in his chair. "Couple of years later Amy got herself killed waterskiing off Cannes, so Suzie didn't have that problem anymore. By then she'd had a couple of kids and eventually they were divorced. But it's quite a story, eh? I've never told anyone but you."

"Does Darman know you know?"

"He might surmise something, knowing how close Suzie and Lila were. Hell, maybe he eased me over to GlobEco to keep me quiet."

Brand considered the implications before asking, "Suppose Darman gets the DCI nomination?"

Tommy shrugged. "I'd tell the story to someone on the Senate committee—a staffer who'd pass word along. What would you do, Mark?"

"I'm not sure. But I don't want Darman as DCI."

"So we'll cross that bridge when we get to it. None of it is provable, of course, but it's salacious enough to attract a lot of interest." He extended his hand across the table. "You're a considerate man, Mark, and I'm lucky to be joining you." They shook hands, and when they parted in the club parking lot Gray said, "Mark, I've been frank with you, now you be frank with me."

"What is it?"

Gray looked back at the building's weathered granite. "Anything about your job you don't like?"

"Yeah, it's inside the Beltway."

"So we have to tough it out with the President." And as they moved toward their cars Gray said, "I hope you locate Peter soon, Mark. I know how worrisome a thing like that can be. I had to search Soho and Venice West for two of mine but they're okay now, thank God."

Brand drove toward his office, dismayed by Tommy's revelation. Was it possible? Had Darman's bride interrupted mom and her kid fucking up a storm in the honeymoon cabin? Possible but not provable. Distasteful at best. And it disturbed him that Tommy had known about Ling-mei. Was their old love affair office gossip? Why had Tommy asked about her? Clearly he was out of line, Brand thought, and felt a flush of resentment. Then on impulse he changed course and headed for Peter's apartment.

BRAND RANG THE DOORBELL five times, and was turning away when La-li opened the door. Her face was drawn, making her eyes seem unusually large. Her hair was disarranged, and she seemed to lean on the door-jamb for support. Anxiously, Brand touched her shoulder. "You don't look well. Have you—?"

"It's this belly-sickness."

"Can't the obstetrician give you something . . . ?"

She sighed as Brand came in. "My appointment is next week. Until then—" She shrugged resignedly, then her face brightened. "You've heard from Peter?"

"No. I wanted to ask you the same thing."

He saw her lips tremble before her face turned from him. Brand took her arm and led her to the sofa. "I'm trying not to cry," she quavered. "Trying very hard. But I feel so alone—never so alone before."

"You're *not* alone, La-li," Brand said. "There's me, and your friends."

"Oh, yes, my friends." Her mouth twisted. "Chinese students, some with papers, most without, always looking for work to earn money, fill rice bowls. Peter and I, we fed the really destitute but we couldn't care for them all."

Brand went to the kitchen, boiled water, and made a pot of herbal tea. When he brought it back in two cups he said, "So Peter knew some of these student friends."

After sipping, she nodded. "He had great sympathy for them, and our movement."

"The dissident movement?"

Again she nodded. "Hope of returning to a free China is what keeps them alive. We're exiles, Mr. Brand—"

"Mark."

"—and no matter how hospitable America is we don't belong here."

"But with the baby and Peter you'll belong here. Truly belong, La-li." It distressed him to think of Peter and his grandchild living on the Mainland, however remote that possibility.

"Perhaps," she said diffidently and sipped from her cup. "I suppose exiles everywhere always plot to overthrow the government they fled from, but I can hardly bear to listen to my friends plotting and planning. I don't want to see more martyrs; we've seen quite enough martyrs in Tiananmen Square alone."

"Yes, it's foolish to confront an implacable armed force with sticks and stones. Guns always win."

"As Chairman Mao said. But they make much of what happened in East Europe, Rumania, Germany, Hungary . . ."

"Where circumstances were quite different."

"Yes, but they won't be convinced. They print leaflets, collect a bit of money in Chinatown, and try to get it to the Mainland . . . but it's all so impractical, so futile." She looked away, isolated by sorrow.

"Do you know a Chinese student, Feng Wah? Long hair, facial scar?"

She nodded. "He comes around now and then. Why?"

Brand described Feng Wah's extortion attempt and La-li's expression was horrified. "How could he *dare* to do that? How could he take advantage of us? Oh, that's so disgraceful—did you tell the police?"

"No. But if he tries again . . ."

"He deserved a good beating, and I'll never give him food again."

"I'm sure he was desperate, probably hungry, or—"

"No excuse," she said firmly. "What he did was criminal and reflects on all of us. I think I should tell the others."

"I've punished him enough."

She shrugged. "Very well—but if you change your mind . . ."

"I'll let you know."

She sighed. "Feng Wah was studying chemistry; even today he'd have a good job in China if he weren't a dissident. Here he's—nothing."

"He ought to get his papers in order," Brand counseled. "Maybe your friends could advise him, help him through the maze."

"We've tried but he doesn't trust America, thinks he'll be sent back to Shanghai and prison. He's blind about it, and deaf."

"Well, those who won't be helped can't be helped." Brand glanced at his watch. He should be in his office for a meeting with NRO. And he needed to brief Personnel on Tommy Gray's hiring.

"Mark," she began hesitantly, "isn't there any way you can find out about Peter? Where he is?"

"Has to be, but I haven't figured it yet. So don't worry, okay? It takes two weeks for a letter from Hong Kong to get here."

"But he could call."

"Yes," Brand conceded, "he could do that." How to keep up her spirits when his own were reaching rock-bottom? "Do you need anything?"

"No, thanks. I'm going to try to go back to work tomorrow. I've only vomited twice today."

He kissed her forehead and thought that she was a resolute young

Chinese woman, in that respect not unlike his Ling-mei of so long ago, though not nearly as beautiful. "I'm thinking of visiting my father soon," he told her. "He's old and I haven't seen him in too long. You'll meet one day and you'll like each other."

"I'm sure of it." She rose and walked beside him to the door.

"I'll call," he assured her, squeezed her hand, and left.

Driving back to his office, Brand wondered how involved Peter had become with the dissident students. Had Peter allowed himself to be manipulated into some foolish and possibly dangerous action on their behalf? No, Peter's judgment was too good for that, and La-li had said nothing to indicate it. So, don't buy trouble in advance, he told himself. Any day now the Agency's watchlisting could give him the answers he needed.

Beijing

The prisoner had become aware of movement in and out of the prison. He could hear dragging and scuffling, yelled protests, the sound of beatings, cries, and whimpers, and from arrivals learned of more dissident trials and sentences. Information was whispered in relays along the corridor, one cell to another, passed surreptitiously on scraps of paper. Now that the most prominent dissidents had been tried, the sentences of lesser figures averaged around four years. Less than half of mine, the prisoner thought bitterly, and wondered if anyone in the West was aware of his harsh treatment.

Never fat, the prisoner could now count his ribs at a glance. Two daily bowls of rice or rice gruel with an occasional bit of pork tendon kept him alive but without strength. He hoarded energy by lying on his mattress most of the time. The cords were still secreted beneath him, but so far he had not been able to devise a means of using them to escape. That did not mean, he told himself, that there would never be an opportunity. He gave the guards no trouble, spoke only when told to, and avoided complaining, though he had asked to have his skull shaved after the mass of lice became intolerable. Fleas he could capture and crush between fingernails though their bites often woke him from sleep.

The only relief from confinement was a weekly cold shower. Then he could soap swollen flea bites and gain some surcease—until in his cell again more fleas erupted from his mattress.

Only that morning he had seen a corpse dragged down the corridor. Welts on the body and blood on its face contradicted the guards' story that the inmate had died of heart failure. Probably the man had been beaten until his heart gave out.

The prisoner shivered and drew his knees against his skinny chest. Whatever the provocations, he must avoid suffering that wretched prisoner's fate.

The post-Mao China, he reflected, was little different from the cruel years when the Great Helmsman ordered its destiny.

Five

BECAUSE BRAND DECIDED to visit his father, he advanced his dinner date with Nina to Wednesday and visited Chinese grocery stores of F Street before going home. There he soaked bok choy, bean sprouts, red and green peppers, snow peas, veined shrimp and sliced chicken breasts and pork loin, and marinated the meat in soy sauce. He chopped water chestnuts, bamboo shoots, garlic, and spring onions, then got out two Taiwanese woks and seasoned them with safflower oil. While chilling a bottle of Chinese rice wine, Brand shaved, showered, and changed into fresh clothing. He treated himself to a half tumbler of iced Walker Black and watched evening TV news until the doorman announced Nina's arrival.

She wore a low-cut cocktail dress of shimmering black material, a string of pearls, and a large marquise-cut emerald. Her hair was swept back in a coif he had not seen before, and as they kissed he said, "I'm glad you were free tonight."

"Mark—when am I not free for you?" She returned his kiss, tracing his lips with the point of her tongue. "I've really been looking forward to this. Imagine, a man who can actually cook!"

He smiled as he led her to the sofa. "What it really means is that I was brought up among household servants."

"Well, I suppose that's one interpretation." Languidly she fingered her pearls. "So, tell me—where will you be on Friday? Some mysterious trip for GlobEco?"

"Nothing mysterious. It's past due time for a visit with my father." He made her a vodka martini and speared a pearl onion that he handed to her.

"Cheers," she said and sipped lightly. "To your safe return from the mountains."

"And to my son's return." He lifted his highball glass.

"Of course—how thoughtless of me." Her eyes narrowed. "Any news of Peter?"

"Nothing," he said, "but I tell myself he's grown now and I shouldn't worry too much. When he gets back he'll have a perfectly reasonable explanation."

"That's one difference between your son and mine. Gareth seldom bothers to explain his absences. So—I simply stopped worrying." She shrugged. "What else could I do?"

"If I had an answer to that I'd apply it to myself." Moodily, he drank, savored the rich, full taste of the liquor.

"If there is anything, anything at all I can do to help, you'd let me know?"

"Of course. How hungry are you?"

"Moderately."

"A Chinese meal takes a lot of time in preparation, but very little for cooking."

"Then let's enjoy drinks now, dine whenever the mood comes over us."

Brand put on a CD and background music flowed through concealed speakers. Ronstadt and Riddle. After her second vodka Nina said, "You know, we've never danced. Shall we?" Rising, she glided into his arms and presently Brand felt the thrust of her pelvis as they moved together. She pressed her breasts to his chest and began undulating her loins in a way that soon excited him. "Oh, Mark," she murmured throatily, "you're such a magnetic man I can't help wanting you. It's been so long since you were in me." She rolled down her dress top exposing her breasts. As he touched them she whispered, "A quickie now?"

"Mmmm." He nuzzled her nipples.

"But we mustn't crush my dress." She wriggled her skirt upward around her hips. No panties. Under the soft light her blond patch glistened moistly. "Turn around," he ordered, "bend over."

Elbows on the sofa, cheek pressed against the cushion, she swayed her bottom lewdly. No cellulite. Brand stroked her buns before parting them, then entered. "Oh, God," she breathed, "how I've needed you," and uttered no more words. Brand heard hoarse exclamations, muffled cries, as he gripped her hips and took her.

Later, she watched him at the woks, used chopsticks clumsily until he provided a fork, and vowed she'd never dined more regally.

In the morning they showered together, made love, and while Brand packed an overnight bag Nina called a taxi and left.

BRAND TOOK I-95 to the Baltimore Beltway and picked up Route 83 north of the city. He drove to York and Harrisburg and followed the rain-swollen Susquehanna until a branch formed the Juniata, where the Blue Mountains became the Appalachians. Through Millerstown and Mifflintown, then a two-lane blacktop to McAlisterville. Just outside town he turned onto a farm road that coiled upward through forests of tall pine and deciduous trees in early leaf, alders and birch, whose white bark shimmered in the midday sun.

A rural mailbox lettered BRAND marked the steep, rough access road to his father's cabin, and as Brand drove into the clearing he saw his father's battered pickup parked beside a venerable chestnut tree, one of whose major limbs had been splintered by lightning. Surrounding the log-faced cabin were pink and violet azaleas, dogwood, and mayberry growing in indiscriminate profusion. Dr. Brand was fond of flowering shrubbery, Brand reflected, but left gardening to the whims of nature.

The air was clear and pure, breeze whispered through tall pines, gently swaying their tops. In a cherry tree a male cardinal shifted branches and proudly preened his crimson plumage.

Brand carried his bag toward the porch and heard his father bellow, "Come in, be with you shortly!" He went through the screen door into a large, high-ceilinged room that was floored in random-width oak. Indian rugs were scattered across the worn and polished floor, and at the room's far end a screen divider concealed Simon Brand's surgery. Brand dropped his bag beside the massive stone fireplace and helped himself to scotch from the antique breakfront.

Chinese scrolls hung from the smoothed log walls, unpainted shelves were crowded with Chinese bric-a-brac, much of which Brand remembered from his youth. Yellow and green jade figurines, bronze horses, dog, and birds, a porcelain fish bowl, cloisonné pots and vases, and an intricately carved rosewood Quan Yin statuette. Other shelves were jammed with books in Chinese and English, medical texts, pharmacology, Victorian novels, dictionaries in a variety of languages, Churchill's memoirs . . .

Limping, a whiskery young man in boots and hiking garb emerged from behind the screen, followed by Brand's father. The patient shouldered a rucksack and said, "How much do I owe you, Doctor?"

"I dunno—how much can you afford?"

"Will five be okay?"

"Make it three." He handed his patient a small packet of pills. "One every four hours the next two days. Plenty of liquid to purge infection, and favor that foot. No more infected blisters."

The patient counted out three dollars and handed them to the physician. "I was lucky I found you," he said.

"You were at that. Well, that's what I'm here for—to treat strays and unfortunates. Pass the word along the Trail."

"I will, Doctor, and thanks."

"You take it easy now. Can you get back on the Trail?"

"Sure, I've got my compass."

"Don't lose it. And watch out for copperheads, they'll be out sunning today. Since snowmelt I've treated three bites and I'm out of antidote." With that warning he watched the hiker leave, then strode to Brand and hugged his son ferociously.

Dr. Simon Brand was a tall, burly man with powerful shoulders and hair so white and thick it resembled a powdered wig. His leathery face was lined and open. Alert gray eyes studied his son from beneath bushy eyebrows. Releasing Brand, he said, "It's been a long time, son. I'd begun to think I was by way of being forgotten."

"Never."

He smiled broadly. "Then sit and tell me your troubles." He extracted granny glasses from the pocket of his worn denim shirt and peered at his wristwatch. "By four the fish will be feeding again. Until then we do as we choose." Noticing Brand's glass, he said, "I'll join you," and poured liquor at the cabinet. Returning to the big timbered sofa he touched his glass to Brand's and drank. "How was the drive?"

"Good. I like the countryside in spring."

"So do I. Plus winter, summer, and fall." He smiled and drank again, then his expression turned serious. "Peter's missing, eh? What's that mean? Lost? Misplaced? Stolen?"

"Don't know." Brand related all he had found out, after which his father brought over the Old Grouse bottle and replenished their glasses. "Honkers is big now, a real city where a man can get lost with ease." He eyed his son. "You thinking of looking it over?"

"Considering. But I want your advice."

"Hmmm. That girl of his—La-li—holding anything back?"

"Not sure . . . Why should she?"

"You tell me, I haven't met her."

"Her friends are mainly dissident students like herself."

"Plotters? Philosophers? Activists?"

"All of that, I'd think. One of them was the renegade who tried to extort me. They're all on hard times."

"That's the exile story. You were too young when we reached Taiwan to remember those Nat exiles. Broke, scared, and still under the thumb of Chancre Jack."

Brand chuckled at Generalissimo Chiang Kai-shek's wartime moniker. As a boy he had been warned never to utter it.

"Is La-li deep into exile politics?"

"Don't think so. She goes along to get along."

"And Peter?"

"Probably no more than a sympathizer."

"Let's hope," he sighed. "And your own life, Mark? Got a lady friend?"

Brand nodded. "A sunny Californian from the Santa Monica-Beverly Hills axis. Divorced. Fortyish. Nina Kenton. Blond."

"Natural?"

"Provably."

His father smiled. "Good. I don't trust a woman who travels under false colors."

"You don't like women, period."

"Ho-*ho!* What your ancient father does is no business of his son's."

"You mean—even up here in the wilderness . . . ?"

"My missionary days are far behind me, lad, so there's no conflict of interest. Got to have someone to wash clothes, iron shirts, scrape skillets, don't I? Let's leave that subject, and you tell me how your work goes."

"It's productive."

"I didn't think you'd adapt well after Field Ops."

"I manage." Except for intolerable assholes like Darman Gerold, he thought. "And I've taken on Tommy Gray. Did you know him? He had the old Navy compound for a tour."

"Name only. Hundreds, thousands, passed through before I left Taipei. Wartime Kunming we were smaller—a few score brave lads and ancillaries, no more."

"Ever hear from old Mainland contacts?"

"Maybe once a year I get a card, but writing back would endanger them." He shrugged. "Mao's long gone, the Gang of Four disgraced, but it's still Revolutionary China. Hard to get in, harder to get out." He removed his spectacles and polished them absently on his shirt. "The old Kuomintang retinue's dead, fossilized, or fled to Honkers, Manila, or Japan—wherever there was money to be made. Thieves for the most part. Stole from their own troops and expected them to fight Chu Teh's Fourth Route Army." He shook his head disgustedly. "I saw it all, Mark, and the memories aren't good."

"No. Anything to eat around here?"

"Nothing but venison stew, oven bread, and apple cider. Suit you?"

"Always has."

"Dinner depends on what we hook and land. Oh, I fished Beaverkill opening day, got three rainbows and a dolly. Ate two on the spot and brought the others back for me and, ah, my lady friend."

"Who shall remain nameless."

"Who shall remain nameless. They come and go, y'know, on to better things, or back to their families. The mountain way."

"Which is just to your taste."

Nodding, he beckoned Brand into the country-style kitchen, where he heated stew in a large cast-iron pot, warmed an uncut loaf in the oven, and made a crisp salad from wild edibles seasoned with lemon juice and pepper. The ingredients Brand recognized were myrtle sedge, arrowleaf, wintercress, wild mustard, and wild leek. His father was an indomitable forager for foods nature provided.

"You squeeze the cider yourself?" Brand asked as he sipped the cold, tangy beverage.

"Naw, a kid comes up to do it, picks the apples, too. But I make the cherry wine, can't corrupt the local youth."

"And you treat wayfarers pretty well. At three bucks a pop you'll never get rich."

"Don't want to. I make enough to pay for medicine and magazines, but the best part is Internal Revenue lost track of me when I moved here from Alaska. Now I don't report nothin'."

"A true mountain man," Brand said approvingly. "If you saw what taxes go for around Washington you'd defect to Tibet."

After lunch Dr. Brand rinsed dishes and they turned in for midafternoon naps. At four they gathered tackle and made their way over the hill behind the cabin and down the other side to a rocky stream in the valley, Brand bottling some unwary grasshoppers along the way. While his father bent on a bucktail fly, Brand hooked a struggling grasshopper and laid it upstream, reeling as it drifted past. From a quiet pool beside the riffles a fighter erupted. Brand sank the hook, played the trout for a while before netting it, and then his father cast the fly. Action came faster to the doctor, and as Brand reached for his net he noticed a doe and her camouflaged fawn observing them from the hillside.

By five they had extracted six keepers from the stream, gutted and cleaned them in its chill water, and made their way back over the hillside.

As they approached the rear of the cabin Brand noticed a large brown bearskin pegged to the side. "When did you take up blood sport?" he asked.

"Sport? That fellow was a rogue. Killed my dog, Lancelot, and tried gnawing through the back door. Had to do away with him," he said huffily as though his principles had been challenged. "Still, braised bear paws are a delicacy, I have to admit. And if you're wondering about the venison, a patient brought me two quarters and a loin last winter.

Barter works for folks who don't have much cash and are too proud for welfare. Like Depression times when I was a kid."

Brand examined the curing pelt carefully. Its claws were larger than his little finger. "No bullet holes, Dad. You shoot him in the mouth?"

"Not that good a shot, not with these old eyes. No, I boiled down copperhead venom and tipped a bunch of darts, not knowing what they'd be used for. Cut a blowpipe from PVC and when Mr. Bear came battering at my door I puffed a couple down his throat. By the time I got the door open he was in bear heaven."

"Leave it to you."

"No, I just thought back to our Taiwan aborigines, the way they tip arrows with *habu* venom." He shrugged. "Nothing to it."

Before they went in Brand noticed sprigs and bunches of herbals drying under the eaves. Dandelion greens, witch hazel, red sage, feltwort, horehound, wild ginger, and digitalis, medicinals his father knew how to prepare and administer to patients leery of chemical remedies.

In the kitchen they iced the trout and Brand helped his father lay kindling and logs in the great fireplace. He produced wine from his bag and set two whites on ice beside the trout, decanted a Bordeaux, and opened the Harvey's cream sherry.

Until it was time to grill the trout they sipped sherry and snacked on mountain-made cheese. And while arrowhead tubers and wild asparagus were boiling, Dr. Brand reminisced about wartime OSS operations from Kunming against the occupying Japanese. "Our lightly wounded we usually got back," he told Brand, "but others were never seen again. We trained a Nat parachute battalion and I set a lot of broken legs and ankles. Kids came down rigid, couldn't get them to flex legs landing, they were too scared." He glanced at Brand. "You trained at Bragg, didn't you? Landing at sea level's a lot softer than hitting at six thousand feet where the air's thin."

"Yeah. And twenty years later we were still shoving young Nats out of planes over the Mainland. A few made it back, but damn few."

"The Commies organized the Mainland pretty fast, Mark, knowing they had to control the countryside, unlike the Japs who settled for towns and villages. Our teams flowed around them like water, hit rails and bridges, troop convoys . . . quite a war, Mark. Detachment 202 did its share of killing and destruction." He sighed. "You still working on the China problem?"

"Targeting missile sites."

"Away from Langley. Whoever thought up that one did a good day's work. You staying with it forever?"

"I've been thinking of going into some kind of business involving the Orient—with Peter."

"Sounds good. First you have to get him back."

Brand felt a chill of apprehension. "That's right, I have to get him back."

BRAND'S SLEEP WAS INTERRUPTED by the noisy arrival of a truck, pounding at the front door. He heard his father talking with someone, and came out to see Simon pulling on clothing. "Anything I can do?" Brand asked sleepily.

"Not unless you're prepared to handle a breech delivery. Mrs. McIlhenny's having a hard time, her husband says. He'll take me and bring me back, so go back to sleep. See you for breakfast." He grabbed a large black medical bag and was off. Brand heard the truck rattle down the bouldered road until its chuffing faded in the night.

Two-fifteen by the mantel clock. The fire was mostly embers, the big room chill. Brand dropped kindling on the embers, added two split logs, and poured himself a double scotch, sipping while flames gained into a blaze. He stretched out on the sofa and thought that it had been a wonderful day with his father—all of them were, had been since his earliest childhood. Peter should have shared their day, he told himself; he hadn't seen enough of his son in recent years, and he didn't want Peter to slip away into marriage and fatherhood until Peter got to know his grandfather better. The Beaverkill on opening day, grouse and pheasant in the nearby valleys; outings that accumulated into what was now termed bonding—blood ties enhanced by affection. Peter deserved it all.

How had the years gone by? he asked himself, and realized they were grouped in geographic segments: Beijing, Taiwan, Seoul, Philadelphia, Taiwan, Washington. He seldom thought of Sela, dead now twenty years. She had betrayed him and their son and he felt no shred of sorrow for her fate, no obligation to her memory. Had he loved her? he wondered. Had she loved him? That they'd mated and produced a child proved nothing save that they had coupled one night when she had not troubled with her diaphragm.

Since then he had known dozens of women, he reflected, but the memory of none lingered with him as that of Chen Ling-mei. Why had he failed to marry her? He could no longer recall distinctly the stresses he had been under at the time. Or had he never seriously considered her as wife? Perhaps he'd felt her father would disapprove his daughter marrying a Da Bi Zi, a big nose. He had foregone milk and cheese to rid his body of those foreign odors Orientals found objectionable, not wanting to inflict his body stench on—what had she been? Mistress? Lover? Concubine? He couldn't categorize, never had, didn't want to after so many years away. And perhaps he could never have seen her as she saw herself—through Oriental eyes, refracted by the prism of Chinese custom. Still, but for texture of skin, the eyelids' epithelial fold he was as Chinese as she. China born and educated, China acculturated . . .

How had she fared over the distant, irrecoverable years? Was she well? The mother of children? Wife of a man her equal in descent and culture?

How strange that Gray had mentioned her, revived dormant memory. Why had Tommy done it? Gerold would have brought up Ling-mei's name to embarrass him, but Tommy was a different sort not given to put-downs.

Brand decided that Taiwan Station Security had noted the relationship in his 201 file, where it was available to be read by anyone with access. And Sela's explosive fate hadn't aided his career, Brand was sure. He'd been too beguiled to take much notice of Sela's SDS connection, her unbounded admiration for "El Ché," thinking those predilections a phase on the road to political maturity. But how wrong he'd been. My wife, the urban guerrilla, he thought bitterly, got up, and added more Grouse to his glass.

The fire had overcome the room's night mountain chill. Brand stared at the dancing flames and realized that he missed an open fireplace. He would inherit the cabin, but he could not contemplate his father's death without sadness. For then he would be alone in the world, his son, wife, and grandchild living lives of their own.

Should he marry Nina Kenton? They seemed to share a group of values and she was certainly sexually exciting. Well, Sela had been, too, though after Peter was born her interest dwindled to zero without apology or explanation.

But why marry? he asked himself. Nina had never suggested it, and she was available without that binding formality. That she was anal-erotic wasn't a drawback; options enhanced excitement. Besides, he and Peter would be forming a business venture, and he'd be too involved to pay proper attention to a bride. So, let it go, he decided; if not Nina, then someone else—in time. Maybe.

He was too comfortable on the sofa to replenish his empty glass. The flames were gradually dying, and for a while Brand thought of his father working with all his skill to save two human lives. On Taiwan Brand had seen the doctor deliver babies, aided by a Chinese nurse or two, often in straw hovels that lacked even rudimentary sanitation, and he had been as impressed by the mothers' stoicism as by his father's calm efficiency. Brand remembered the first time he had seen a baby's head emerge from a woman's loins, bloody and slimy, the sight making him vomit uncontrollably. After that incident the doctor had explained how babies were conceived, and told Brand that a man should bear responsibility for what his pecker produced. It was a lesson Brand remembered through adolescence and college, and passed on to his son. Peter, he was confident, would marry La-li when he returned.

He considered appropriate wedding presents, finally deciding to ask the couple what they needed most or wanted. That was the best solution.

As the flames dwindled, Brand turned his face away and in near darkness fell asleep.

He woke to the smell of coffee and frying bacon, sat up, and rubbed his eyes. His father was in the kitchen still wearing the clothing he had left in. "Morning, Mark, how'd you sleep?"

"Little stiff, but otherwise okay." He took a coffee mug from his father and sipped; the real thing. "Mother and child doing well?"

"Yeah, but he was a reluctant little fellow, fought being turned but I finally persuaded him." He smiled tiredly, and Brand saw circles under his eyes. "Parents didn't want circumcision, they belong to some Jew-hating evangelical cult, so after I warned about phimosis Mike McIlhenny brought me back."

"How long ago?"

"Maybe an hour." He turned the crisping bacon. "Flapjacks?"

"Absolutely."

"Take a wake-up shower and I'll have everything ready."

Before showering, Mark shaved, then got into clean clothing. The bacon was shed-cured and sliced thick, country style; pancakes scratch-made from biscuit flour, and syrup boiled from the sap of mountain maples.

As they ate, Brand's father said, "I know you worry about my isolation here, but I don't want you to. My patients are friends and I have everything a man could want. I'm lucky, too, at an age when most physicians would be withering in their Florida condos I can still practice medicine. I wouldn't want to leave."

"I don't exactly worry," Brand hedged, "but I'm concerned something could happen, and there's no other doctor around."

"True, but unless I'm knocked flat by paralysis I can medicate myself. And if I'm paralyzed I don't want to live. Bear that in mind, Mark, and honor my wishes."

"I will," he promised.

"And next time you come bring Peter. I want to hear about the girl bearing his child and his family plans." He forked another pancake onto his plate. "You're starting a business with him, you said."

"I want to but not right away." He poured more coffee. "Still have Mainland contacts?"

His father shook his head. "Don't think so. Old Chang-ko went to Peru about ten years ago and established a string of *chifas* around Lima. Big Chinese colony in Lima, Japanese, too. He's done very well, but I don't think you want to get into the Chinese grocery and restaurant business."

"How about our Taiwan 'brothers'?"

"The Fang-tse clan? I suppose the oldsters are still around, but the ones you were initiated with took off for Honkers." He frowned. "Reports have it they formed a criminal group smuggling narcotics and extorting businesses." He paused. "It's also said they bring out ancient artifacts from diggings in northern Xanshi, sell them in Honkers for incredible prices. Oh, your blood brothers are doing well, but on the far side of the law."

"If I look for Peter in Hong Kong," Brand mused, "they could help me."

Dr. Brand nodded. "Honor-bound."

"How could I make contact?"

His father sighed. "Cruise the Wanchai bars. Ask for Eddie Wong, Sammy Lu, Tommy Ning—in Honkers they use Western names."

Brand repeated them, said, "Eddie was the natural leader."

"When you weren't around. More bacon?"

"Can't resist."

"Take back a slab; I can get plenty more."

"Let me pay you," Brand offered.

"Trade for the wine."

So, after breakfast they said good-byes, and as Brand drove away he wondered, as he always did on parting, if he would ever again see his father alive.

BY DRIVING SLIGHTLY ABOVE the speed limit, Brand reached Washington in under four hours and was in his office before Tommy Gray arrived for briefing and introductions.

Brand placed a call to La-li, who said there'd still been no word from Peter. Brand tried to soothe her melancholy with limited success. Probably, he thought, as he ended the call, because his own spirits were so low.

Gray came in, they shook hands, and as Tommy pulled up a chair he said, "I checked the watchlists yesterday—negative for Peter. Sorry, Mark, but I know one thing, your son can't just disappear."

"In Hong Kong he can—anyone can," Brand said morosely.

Gray shook out a cigarette, hesitated. "May I?"

"It's your life."

After exhaling, Gray asked, "Any chance Peter would be traveling under an alias?"

"There's a chance, but I can't think why. He'd need false documentation, where would he get it?"

Gray grunted. "Both my kids had false docs when I found them; there's a regular underground for SS cards, birth certificates, and so on. The Agency isn't the only source of false ID, any connected kid can get them." He paused. "Or steal them."

"I suppose," Brand remarked, "but Peter was never part of that scene. And he was traveling legitimately, no need to conceal identity."

Gray stretched back in his chair, exhaled smoke toward the ceiling. "Suppose Peter decided he wanted a look at the Mainland—where you were born—takes the Lo Wu train through the New Territories and walks across the river bridge. There'd be no record of frontier crossing by him or anyone else. Every day hundreds travel that way between Hong Kong and Canton for shopping, business . . . Not like the old days, Mark."

For a while Brand considered Gray's hypothesis. Finally he roused himself to say, "It's a possibility, Tommy, and I see only one way of checking it out."

"You mean—go there."

Brand nodded. "So let's get you briefed and ready to take my place. You've seen Personnel?"

"Right."

"Salary okay?"

"More than generous, Mark. Midnight ended my Agency years except for continuing clearances. Gorgon, Keyhole, Atomic, Sideslip—the works."

Brand unlocked his safe and brought out a thick *Galaxy* folder. "While you're absorbing this I'll bring the NRO feed on-line; after that I'll show you how it's done." After activating the computer and accessing the secure link he turned to Gray. "I'd like you here through the weekend, Tommy. There's a lot to show you before I'll be able to get away."

Gray sat forward. "Then you've decided to go."

"Unless Peter shows up damn soon."

Six

Nina Kenton was enjoying a long, elaborate luncheon at a small French restaurant in Alexandria's Old Town. Her companion was a lean, swarthy man whose table manners she found detestable. But she kept aversion to herself in the interests of rapport. Her contact was paying for their three-figure meal as he paid her living expenses, and though she wondered initially what happened to the fragments of information she provided, she had decided it was prudent never to actually inquire.

"Sometime, John," she said over her second champagne cocktail, "you must tell me how you happened to choose me—unless it's some sort of trade secret."

He stirred ice in his vodka glass with an index finger, then eyed her. "Actually, Nina, it *is* a trade secret, one I'll have to keep from you. Just as you keep secrets from others. Like Mark Brand."

"I see," she said coldly.

"Not entirely. The group that employs me—and you—is extraordinarily well informed about well-placed, attractive Americans who, shall I say, customarily live beyond their means. Or in some cases face financial disaster." He drank noisily from his glass.

"Industrial espionage?"

"For conversational purposes," he said with a nod, "though it's not a term I would choose." Abruptly he switched subjects and his tone became businesslike. "My people vetted what you told me about Brand's interest in the Kunlun mountain range—Western China—and found that it does contain mineral deposits, though in quantities that have never been determined. And there are probably petroleum deposits in the Kunlun region, but the area is inaccessible to extractive industry." He paused. "What does that suggest to you?"

Calmly she said, "Either Mark lied to me, or his GlobEco group is on to something your people haven't been clever enough to notice."

His eyelids blinked rapidly. "Or a cover story for distractive purposes. Can you find out what company contracted with GlobEco for a Kunlun survey?"

"Maybe."

"Nina—listen to me. Listen hard. Find out the name of that company. If you can't, you're not as clever as I've been led to believe."

"Perhaps not, John, though I wouldn't want to hear that assessment from you." She sipped delicately from her glass, noticed the waiter approaching with their Chesapeake Bay oysters.

After the waiter left, she said, "I do know that Mark may be planning a trip to China."

"China? Really?"

"Well, Hong Kong. His son went there, you know, and no word since."

John thumbed the point of his chin. "I don't want Brand going to the Mainland."

"Why shouldn't he—if it involves the Kunlun mountains?"

"Because the Chinese might decide to keep him in China."

"Oh? Why would they want to do that?"

"Because Chinese have long memories, and they will remember he worked against them for years from Taiwan. They might even assume he was still working for the CIA."

"Umm. You should lower your voice when speaking those magic letters. Do you think he is?"

"Not really my concern, dear. But if he mentions a continuing connection I'd want to be the first to hear."

"Of course." She squeezed a few lemon drops over an oyster and swallowed it, closing her eyes as though to prolong the pleasure. "You don't want him on the Mainland," she said after a while.

"That's what I said." John was having difficulty anchoring a large oyster to his small fork.

"And how is he to be prevented from going?"

"That, dear lady, will be your challenge." He gulped down the oyster, ran the back of one hand over his lips. Really, the man could be nauseating.

"How much do you not want him on the Mainland?" she purred.

His eyes narrowed before he spoke. "Could be worth a bonus, Nina."

"How exciting," she breathed with a little-girl moue. "Quite by chance I was in Rosenberg's—only yesterday—and found myself infatuated by a full-length stone marten. It was just my size and I could hardly bear to take it off."

John grimaced. "One step at a time, eh? Let's consider Hong Kong—why don't you accompany Brand?"

"I think that could be managed—paying my own way, of course, with a suite at the Peninsula for effect."

"Keeping him off the Mainland would be worth it," he said reflectively.

She smiled, showing small, perfect teeth. "And in the event he won't be dissuaded?"

"Then he might have to be destroyed."

AFTER A VIGOROUS WORKOUT at his fitness club Brand stopped at the Nanking Restaurant where he ordered a lavish meal for later delivery at Peter's apartment. From there he went to his own place, checked phone messages, and shed his travel clothing. While soaking in the tub Brand reflected that Tommy would perform adequately once he learned the techniques of evaluating high-resolution photo interpretation. The transition from positive ops to estimates was bound to be frustrating—as Brand had found five years before, when he'd allowed Darman Gerold to banish him to GlobEco. Any career agent-runner was bound to prefer ground observation to satellite intelligence, until persuaded that Gorgon did it faster, better, and without loss of life.

Gorgon's relays could predict Chinese strike-readiness if that was the Chinese plan. What it couldn't predict—and here one had to rely on human-source intelligence—was Chinese *intentions*. But no one yet had been able to infiltrate an agent into the Central Committee, where strategic decisions were made.

His son, Brand mused, would have been an ideal candidate to carry on the pure essence of intelligence work. Peter was cool under pressure, organized, thought logically, and was effective with people. All essential qualities for an agent or agent-handler. But Peter, he reminded himself, is no more able than I to suffer fools and display a calm demeanor. Inevitably he would have been sanctioned for frankness and his career shortstopped before it was well begun.

So, I'm glad I discouraged Peter from applying. Banking is safer if less exciting, and when our joint business is successful, he'll be able to devise his own rewards.

By contrast, Darman Gerold was of a species Brand was unable fully to understand. Grabbing for power, manipulating people to his own advantage, always reaching toward the next pinnacle . . . Had those traits not been visible to his superiors? Brand wondered. Were all of them so vulnerable to Gerold's servile flattery that they failed to discern the manipulative man behind the smiling mask? Men at the top were paid to make hard judgments, but in the case of Darman Gerold they utterly failed.

As the tub drained Brand dried himself and decided that he thought too often of Gerold and must end the practice before dislike became obsession. He had other things, worthwhile matters, to occupy his mind: his son, La-li, and their unborn child foremost among them.

Brand dressed and drove to Peter's apartment, where he was relieved to find his future daughter-in-law looking less wan and in somewhat better spirits.

After the Nanking's delivery arrived, La-li said she wasn't sure how much she could eat but agreed to try. She made tea and set the table, Brand noticing that she brought out cheap Chinese bowls for their servings. It distressed him that his son had not provided better utensils for home use, and Brand decided to upgrade them himself.

Seated across from him, La-li poured rice wine into small porcelain cups, and they *gan-peied* together. She managed to get down sweet-and-sour soup, but hesitated before picking up chopsticks. "I'll see how this settles," she said, and sat back, watching as Brand helped himself to shrimp and thin-sliced beef in oyster sauce, *lo mein* noodles and almond chicken. "Peter always likes chicken with Chinese vegetables," she said in a low voice. Then, "Oh, how I wish he were here!" And burst into tears.

Brand left his chair to console her. "I wish so, too," he said quietly, "but we have to carry on—for now."

"But how long? How much longer?" she wailed while Brand held her trembling shoulders.

After her sobs subsided Brand resumed his chair and took up his chopsticks. "It's hard, I know," he said, "hard for us both, but I don't think anything bad can have happened." He chewed thoughtfully. "So if there's no word over the weekend I'll go to Hong Kong, pick up the trail. Tell me—is there anything you can think of that would help? Anything I ought to know?"

Her gaze lowered. "What—what do you mean?"

"I don't know—anything at all, La-li. Like, who was he supposed to meet in Hong Kong? The contact arrangements seem, well, unusual."

"The bank said that?"

He nodded. "Did Peter tell you anything?"

"Oh, sir," she blurted suddenly, "you think I'm holding something back."

"Are you, La-li? If you are, now's the time to tell me."

Tears rolled down her cheeks. After dabbing at them with her napkin she said, "Peter was helping us, a small thing, not dangerous . . ."

"Who's 'us'? Your students?"

Silently she nodded, dried her eyes again as Brand felt anger rise. "Helping how?"

"Taking money . . . leaflets to a Mainland contact who was meeting him in Hong Kong."

"Hong Kong, not the Mainland, you're sure?"

"Oh, yes, sir. I would never have him go to the Mainland. So there was no danger to him."

Brand laid down his chopsticks and sat back, grappling with this new factor. After a while he asked, "Did Peter make delivery?"

"I—I don't know. I think so. If the contact came to meet him," she said defensively. "At Peter's hotel."

"Not the American Club, his hotel. The Cathay."

"His hotel, yes."

"Whose idea was it, La-li, making Peter a courier?"

"The—our group," she faltered. "Peter said he was willing, glad to help."

"Who in your group?"

"Yu Min-sheng. It was Yu's contact."

Brand repeated the name. "I want to talk to Yu. Can you get him here?"

"He's—they say he went to Vancouver where he has family."

"When did he go?"

"Soon after Peter left." Her hands were clenching and un-clenching, the small knuckles reminding Brand of his amah's bound foot. "Did Peter leave anything here? An appointment book? Diary?"

La-li rose and went to a scarred, student-size desk, brought back a pocket notebook. Wordlessly she gave it to Brand. Appetite destroyed, Brand scanned the pages, noting that the final entry had been made three weeks ago—Peter's departure time from Dulles airport, and below it: HK—Cathay. Feng Lu-chih.

"Is this Feng the Mainland contact?"

"A dissident, yes," she said listlessly.

"Wish you'd told me before," he said. "Now I'm really concerned." The notebook's last page showed half a dozen phone numbers—in Peter's hand. Brand closed the notebook and pocketed it. He'd call those numbers after anger diminished. He felt like shaking the girl. "How much money was Peter taking?"

"All we could collect. Eight hundred and forty dollars."

"And leaflets."

She nodded.

Brand said, "I'd give many times eight hundred dollars to have Peter here right now." He pushed back his chair. "Anything else I should know?"

Slowly she shook her head.

"Don't ever hold out on me," he told her. "Understand?"

"I understand, sir." Tears welled in her eyes. "I'm so sorry."

Bending over, Brand kissed her forehead. "Let's try not to worry," he said in a gentler voice and went out to his car.

In his apartment Brand opened Peter's notebook at his desk and scanned the telephone numbers. Five were D.C. local; the sixth had a 703 prefix—northern Virginia. Then 555-2369. Aloud, Brand repeated the numbers and memory stirred. It was a long time ago but if he was right . . .

He licked dry lips and picked up the receiver, punched in the numbers. He counted the rings: one, two . . . was it possible? Three, four . . . after five there should be a response if—

A disembodied computerized voice said, "After the tone leave your name and telephone number. You will be contacted as soon as possible."

Clenching the receiver, Brand waited, heard the recorder beep, and said, "My name is Mark Brand. My son, Peter S. Brand, traveled to Hong Kong three weeks ago and has not been heard from. I have reason to believe you were involved in his travel and I strongly suggest you come clean with me." He paused. "Before I go public."

Leaving the desk, he put ice cubes in a glass and filled it with scotch. After a long pull he thought that if his memory was accurate there should be a response. Five rings before the machine cut in, that was the remembered drill.

The number was one provided agents who could not call headquarters directly for security reasons. That Peter had the restricted, special-purpose number chilled Brand, for there could be only one explanation: His son had been conducting Agency business in Hong Kong and risking all the dangers covert work entailed.

Drinking steadily, Brand waited until midnight before staggering off to bed. He was wakened by the insistent ringing of his bedside phone. Fumbling for it, he saw the glowing numbers on his alarm clock: three-nineteen.

"Mr. Brand?" Male voice.

"I'm Brand."

"Sir, I'm responding to your inquiry."

"Well?"

"Obviously this isn't something for the telephone. Someone will contact you tomorrow."

"When?"

"When it's convenient for you."

His mouth was fuzzy, tasted like a blackboard eraser, his head throbbed. Nine o'clock? No, later. "Ten," he said. "Who's coming?"

A pause before the voice replied. "He'll identify himself as Arthur."

Obviously a work name. "I'll be expecting answers," Brand said heavily. "He'd better have them."

"You will be told as much as possible."

"That may not be enough," Brand said, and heard the line go dead.

He lay back and stared up at the dark ceiling. "Those bastards," he muttered, and thought how cynical and unforgivable it was that the

Agency had co-opted his son for a mission, sent an untrained novice on a potentially hazardous op.

Made Peter a Legal Traveler.

Seven

BEFORE THE AGENCY REP arrived Brand drank black coffee, ingested B1 pills, and subjected himself to hot and cold showers. Shaving, he noticed that his eyes were red-veined and puffy. He seldom got drunk but when he did the penalty was severe.

"Arthur" was a well-dressed man in his mid-thirties, probably case-officer level, Brand surmised as he poured coffee with unsteady hands. Seating himself, he said, "Where's my son?"

"Before answering I'd like to know how you learned of his Agency connection."

"Peter left the contact number. I remembered it. And I'm surprised it's still active."

"There are field people we can't recontact to notify of change. It's their lifeline, Mr. Brand. You understand that."

"Where is Peter?"

"We're not sure."

Brand sat back. "Let's summarize: Peter went to Hong Kong on business for his bank. You piggybacked and persuaded him to do a job for you. What was it?"

"A simple task—service a drop."

Brand's eyes narrowed. "If the drop was in Hong Kong the Base could service it. Where?"

Arthur licked his lips. "Canton."

"Canton," Brand repeated. "Peter went there?"

"Apparently he did," the man said uncomfortably. "The Base sent over a backup and found the drop empty."

"So, what's the operational assumption?"

Arthur looked away. "Apparently he was picked up, sir. For interrogation."

"Logical assumption." He felt sick to the point of nausea. "Nothing in the Canton or Beijing papers?"

"Nothing. Or Chinese radio."

Brand grimaced. "And because Peter isn't a trained agent with inside knowledge he can't tell interrogators what they want to know."

Arthur said nothing.

"Was Peter paid?"

Arthur swallowed. "He was given five hundred dollars—he didn't want money for himself; he said he'd give it to some Chinese students. Dissidents."

"So it was to be a quick, one-day in-and-out, right?"

"Right."

"Well, it's been a lot longer than one day, Arthur. What's being done to retrieve my son?"

After hesitating Arthur said, "Right now the nets are trying to locate him. Once we know that we can do other things."

"Like what? Diplomatic protest? Trade back a ChiCom agent?"

"A diplomatic note seems the best bet. The Chinese don't trade back their agents, they ignore them, cut them off."

"Diplomacy, eh? Does State know the problem?"

"They have general awareness."

"Specifically, who has this general awareness?"

"Irving Chenow."

"Assistant Secretary for Far Eastern Affairs."

"You know him?" Arthur looked apprehensive.

"Dealt with him—not a gung ho type. Who else at State?"

"Win Hilyard, China Desk."

"And that's it? How about the Agency? Who authorized involving my son in this nonsensical op? Aside from you?"

"The Section Chief—Applegate," he said reluctantly.

Brand grunted. "For sending Peter I ought to kick his butt." A thought occurred to him. "Darman Gerold?"

"I can't say how much Mr. Gerold knows."

"Can't say—or won't?"

"I just don't know."

"Then I'll ask him."

"Could you hold off, sir? A few days and we may have more information than we do," Arthur pleaded.

"Today's Saturday. Gerold will be at his country place until Monday. If I don't have positive news from you by noon Monday I'll be asking why he allowed Peter to be co-opted, and what's being done to get him back. So, between now and then I suggest you come up with a workable plan. Otherwise . . ."

"Sir?"

"I'll take—as they say—appropriate action."

Arthur sipped from his cup as Brand continued, "Anything else I should know? Any questions I should have asked?" His head throbbed abominably. "How did you learn Peter was traveling? Is Asian Investments an Agency front?"

"I can't answer that, sir."

"Why not?"

With a bleak expression Arthur said, "Need-to-know doctrine."

"Forgive me," said Brand dryly, "if that old cliché fails to impress me. Under the circumstances I need to know everything about this wretched operation—how Peter was spotted, his briefing."

"I understand your concern, sir."

"Not unless you've got a son who vanished on the Mainland. An only son," he added for emphasis. "All right, the situation is clear. And I'm prepared to do anything and everything I have to to get Peter out of China. Tell Ray Applegate. He knows what I'm capable of."

"Yes, sir."

"Today." Brand rose from his chair. "If I hadn't recalled the contact number and phoned I'd still be in the dark. No one in your shop would have bothered to tell me Peter's in trouble. Right?"

"I guess not, sir—not for a while."

"Because the Agency mustn't be embarrassed. But I don't mind embarrassing the Agency when my son's life is at stake. Remember that."

Arthur nodded and got up, clearly relieved to be going. "I'm sorry about what happened, Mr. Brand. At the time it didn't seem like much of a mission for your son, and no one thought there was any risk."

"Obviously, there was. And assuming Peter did exactly as he was told, what's the logical conclusion?"

Arthur swallowed again. "That the drop was watched. Or he was betrayed."

Alone, Brand ate cereal and phoned Gray at GlobEco to say he'd be there before noon. Then he got out Peter's notebook and called the other five numbers in turn.

One was a dry cleaner, one a taxi, two were Chinese restaurants, and the fifth a store that sold secondhand furniture. Peter had enough tradecraft to include the contact number among them, he reflected, and enough patriotism to service a dead-drop in enemy territory. Unthinking, unquestioning patriotism, he thought bitterly, of which the Agency had taken advantage. Now Peter had disappeared and the Agency had no plans to retrieve him. Except for me, he told himself, no one gives a damn what happens to my son. So if any action is to be taken it's up to me.

Silently he cursed the Agency for reviving the Legal Traveler Program, using the uninitiated for chores with a hazardous potential, and decided that Darman Gerold was at least philosophically responsible. MI6 had sent businessman Greville Wynne to service GRU Colonel Oleg Penkovsky in Moscow. The Colonel was under surveillance, so Wynne was bagged, sentenced, and imprisoned. Greville Wynne was no trained agent but a Legal Traveler, who suffered for his patriotism and innocence. Since then, at least among the Brits, Legal Travelers were an ultimate recourse, the hard lesson having been learned.

Too bad, Brand thought, the Agency hadn't learned it, too. Then my son wouldn't be wherever he is. A prisoner.

He felt no optimism that Arthur and his colleagues would or could devise an extraction plan for Peter. If they had so few assets that they had to send a virgin to service a drop in nearby Canton, what plausible assets could be organized to regain him?

It was a sobering, desolate thought. He'd try Irv Chenow, maybe Win Hilyard, too, but expectations of action from State were slim. How many MIAs still rotted in Vietnam and Cambodia? How effective had

State been in retrieving them, dead or alive? The diplomatic card was lighter than rice paper.

He imagined Peter jailed in some foul-smelling prison while his captors decided whether to stage a large-scale propaganda trial now, or at some future time when it would better serve their interests. Meanwhile, Peter would remain imprisoned and subject to their cruelties and whims. The realization chilled him.

Then, thinking back to dinner with La-li—his unfinished dinner— Brand felt less anger at the girl; Peter hadn't been snatched because he'd taken paper to Chen Lu-chih in Hong Kong, but because he'd ventured to the Mainland for the CIA. That secret could not be revealed to his daughter-in-law-to-be. Need-to-know doctrine.

After noting the time, Brand locked his apartment and drove to his office, where Tommy Gray was absorbed in the midday take from NRO. When the transmission concluded Brand showed him how to detect and analyze late progress in silo-hardening, and by using the computer's profile, estimate completion dates.

Wiping his lenses, Gray said, "This is really interesting stuff, Mark; less formidable than I feared."

"Like anything new it takes time to get used to." Brand paused. "Trouble is, I haven't got a lot of time to indoctrinate you. But while I'm gone you'll have Nelly and Phil to help you."

"Traveling, eh? How long?"

"Can't say."

"Hong Kong?"

"To start with. Tommy, keep this to yourself, okay? It looks as though Peter was grabbed in Canton—doing a job for the Agency."

"Why that's—Mark, are you *sure?*"

He told Gray the little he'd learned from Arthur, and said, "That's what I've got to go on." He snapped a pencil and slammed the pieces into the wastebasket.

"Mark, I'm really sorry. If I'd known Peter was being sent I'd have told you."

Brand nodded. "I believe you would. And I'd have told my son to stay clear of the Agency." He watched elm branches sway in the spring breeze. "I have some contacts in Hong Kong, they may be able to help."

"Hope you don't feel you have to visit the Mainland—you'd be a prize catch for the Public Security Bureau."

"Yeah. My clearances don't even allow me in the New Territories."
But, screw those prohibitions, he thought. If the Agency can't get Peter
back it will have forfeited my travel limitations. "Anyway, let's get back
to work, Tommy, there's something else on that photo I want to tell you
about."

An hour later Brand took a call from Nina Kenton. "Workaholic! I
was afraid I'd find you there, but glad I found you at all. Unless you're
hopelessly occupied, I have two tickets to the Symphony—Mehta conducting. And I'll sweeten the offer with supper at a restaurant of your
choice. Do I hear a reaction?"

"Positive," Brand replied, grateful for the opportunity to distract
his thoughts for an entire evening. "How about the Georgetown Inn? I'll
phone for a table."

"Perfect. It's a long program, mostly Bartok, starting at seven-
thirty."

"I'll come by before seven."

"Oh—earlier if you can; we'll have a drink before leaving. And—
Mark—any word from Peter?"

"Afraid not." Never should have told her Peter was missing; her
question brought his son's image into his mind.

"See you then."

He worked with Gray until five, declined a drink at a Connecticut
Avenue bar that Tommy found congenial, and drove to his apartment.

AFTER THE CONCERT, with its champagne intermission, and the supper at
the Georgetown Inn listening to John Eaton's fine jazz piano, they drove
to Nina's building, where Brand accepted an invitation to stay over.

The Hine cognac was exceptional, the music of Albeniz soothing,
and Brand felt himself drifting in a sort of Elysian reverie. Until Nina
kissed him lingeringly and murmured, "I know you're preoccupied over
Peter, dear, and I quite understand. Is there anything I can do to help?
Anything at all?"

"There is." He kissed her deeply, unshouldered her white silk
blouse, and touched her nipples with his tongue.

Later, after making love, when Brand was on the verge of sleep, she
said, "You aren't planning to do anything—impulsive, I hope."

"Impulsive? Like what?"

"Try finding Peter in that human anthill."

"I'm considering looking around Hong Kong," he said sleepily.

"Haven't been there in ages, and I love it. So if you do go, I'll go, too."

He was about to say no, decided not to make an issue of it. "You're good company, Nina. Would you be willing to shop while I go looking?"

"Perfect. Then I'll be there when Peter arrives."

If it were only that easy, he mused, and fell asleep.

MOST OF SUNDAY he spent at the office with Tommy Gray, and on Monday—having heard nothing from "Arthur"—Brand phoned Irving Chenow's office, and was granted a five o'clock appointment.

Entering the Department of State lobby, Brand experienced his usual distaste for the organization he held responsible for many of the country's worst misadventures. It was perhaps unjust, he thought as he rode the elevator to the sixth floor, to accuse State of habitually sublimating the nation's interests when there were few in the building able to define what the national interest was. It was also an inbred place where inertia was taken for wisdom. And in his view State remained guilty of high crimes and misdemeanors.

In the large reception area Brand gave his name to the nearest of several secretaries and was invited to take a seat while she used the intercom. The furniture was covered in gray tufted fabric, the carpeting was deep, and workers spoke in low conversational tones. Even the air-conditioning was barely audible. The overall atmosphere made a calm, laid-back contrast to CIA offices he remembered, where there was a good deal of noise, movement, and bare GSA furnishings.

In these surroundings, Brand told himself, a high-level public servant like Chenow would be at least marginally comfortable and able to contemplate grave issues without disruption. Before his presidential appointment, Irving Chenow had been an enormously successful Chicago corporate attorney, whose law offices, Brand imagined, were paneled in black walnut and other rare woods, hung with museum-quality paintings, and decorated biennially by an expensive London firm. So, State's near-best (top decor was afforded the Secretary) was by comparison bare bones.

After twelve minutes the Assistant Secretary's door opened and two men came out, both carrying thick folders and conversing in hushed tones. Identical dark suits reminded Brand of two penguins, as with brief nods at the receptionist they left the premises.

Presently Irving Chenow appeared and beckoned Brand into his office. They shook hands perfunctorily, after which Chenow loosened collar and tie, undid the top two buttons of his vest, and fingered his gold Phi Beta Kappa key. He stretched back in his large leather-upholstered chair and said, "Haven't seen you in a while, Mark. How you been keeping?"

"Okay, Irving. Yourself?"

"Eat too much, drink too much, not enough exercise," he grunted. "So, what else is new?"

He was a short man, with the inbred pugnacity of those ill-favored in height, and his hair was parted over the right ear and combed across a nearly bald skull. Thick, sloping nose; plump, unlined cheeks; and brooding, watchful eyes. Brand had long classified him as a tough, relentless opponent in any legal clash; he eased forward in his chair and said, "My son, Peter, went to Hong Kong on business for his bank and disappeared."

Chenow's thick eyebrows drew together. "Peter Brand is *your* son? I heard about—wait a minute—what do you mean disappeared?"

"No word, no contact, and his return is long overdue. That's bad enough, Irv, but there's an unsettling aspect I dug out of the Agency."

"CIA? You can speak freely here, the room's constantly swept."

"Habit," Brand explained. "Yes, CIA," and told Chenow what he knew of Peter's clandestine mission.

For a while the Assistant Secretary said nothing, although his lips moved as though chewing something unappetizing. Finally, he said, "You've considered alternate explanations to arrest."

"Arrest explains everything; nothing else does."

"Death—sorry, Mark, the legal mind at work. Shouldn't have said that. Apologies. Last thing I want is adding to your distress." He scratched the side of his neck and sat forward, thumbs and fingertips together. Brand decided it was a posture carried over from boardrooms. "Two things leap out at me. First, recruiting your son was ill-advised by the CIA, and they'll hear from me about it. Secondly, and with hundred percent hindsight, your son shouldn't have cooperated. But he knew you'd been with the CIA and probably wanted to show Dad he could do the same sort of thing. On top of patriotic motivation. But none of that is pertinent to what you're up against. I can alert our Canton consulate, have someone contact city and provincial authorities. I doubt we'll learn anything from that approach but it will warn the Chinese we're concerned about Peter Brand. That might help down the line."

"It might," Brand agreed.

"Right here in this building there is a major problem," Chenow continued, "and it surfaced in connection with the Tiananmen Square massacres. Briefly, my office advocated placing extremely strong sanctions on China for gross violation of basic human rights. However, the Secretary"—he sighed—"being responsive to the White House, took a more relaxed view. So Beijing gave us the finger and got away with it. Meaning there is no disposition at State or in the Administration to confront or penalize China for anything it does."

Brand considered. "Will the Secretary authorize a note to Beijing?"

Chenow frowned. "Probably not. But I can call in the Chinese Ambassador and raise hell—off the record, of course."

"Better than a note."

"Is there anything else that might be useful?"

"If you'll instruct the consulate and brace the Chinese Ambassador I'll be very grateful."

The Assistant Secretary rose, signaling an end to the meeting. "I don't like to see our citizens get pushed around overseas. Sometimes I can do something about it, most times not. Maybe this time I'll get lucky."

Brand nodded. He was turning away when Chenow said, "Mark, are you contented with the work you're doing—that ecological survey stuff? Satisfy you?"

"Pretty much—why?"

"Because I need people here who know something about China. Would you consider taking over China Desk?"

Startled, Brand stared at the Assistant Secretary. "Win Hilyard has the Desk."

"Win's leaving—got himself a plush job at Rand. I endorsed the move because Win—well, he needs more than a government salary. What I know of you that's not a primary concern."

"I—I'm flattered," Brand told him, "but I—well, I'm not an enthusiastic administrator by any means. And working in another bureaucracy, after the Agency"—he shook his head—"that would suffocate me."

"Well, look," Chenow said almost plaintively, "I'm doing something for you, risking the Secretary's displeasure—least you can do is give the offer more than a moment's consideration."

"You're serious, aren't you? What makes you think I'm the man for the job—that I wouldn't disappoint you?"

The Assistant Secretary smiled. "Partly coincidence. My father came here from East Poland in the early thirties, learned pharmacy, and kept a drugstore. World War Two erupted and Dad volunteered, went to China with Chennault's Fourteenth Air Force. Not as an airman—he lacked college education and wore thick glasses—but as a medic, a hospital corpsman in Kunming. When I was old enough to understand about the war Dad told me tales of China days—among them, this missionary doctor who worked in Kunming for the OSS."

"My father!"

Chenow nodded. "Abe Chenowitz, my father, used to cop medicine from army stores and help your father treat Chinese. It was inspiring to watch, Dad said, and called your father the kindliest American he'd ever met. He remembered when the doctor had a son, and how his wife was lost over the Hump—a tragedy for everyone. I never made the connection until a few weeks ago when I was sorting through my father's wartime things. Found a snapshot of two men and Dad had printed their names—his and Dr. Simon Brand. So, we go way back, Mark, through our families. That's one reason I want you with me: a Chenowitz and a Brand working together again. Now, will you seriously consider what I've said?"

"After what you've told me, how could I not? But I can't plan ahead until Peter's safe again."

"Of course. I understand. And I can hold the job open through June when Hilyard leaves. If you're not available I'll have to settle for some troll from the caverns below—but I hope not."

"You've given me a lot to think about," Brand told him, "and I will. My father will be surprised and pleased that I know the medic's son."

"He's alive then? I didn't want to ask straight out."

"Alive, well, and practicing the healing arts in rural Pennsylvania."

"If he ever comes to Washington I want to lay on something special for him—you tell him that."

"Might encourage him to come. He regards Washington as a source of plague and corruption."

Chenow chuckled. "Not unreasonable. Mark, keep me posted on your plans, and I'll stay in touch."

Brand left the building, feeling he had accomplished much more than he'd had any reason to anticipate.

He drove to his apartment garage, eased into the numbered slot, and noticed a black Ford sedan in the visitor's area. He was locking the BMW when two men got out of the Ford and walked toward him. Their approach made him uneasy. Robbers? Brand made for the elevator door, stopped when one of them called his name.

Turning to face them, he said, "I'm Brand. Who're you?"

As they neared him one said, "FBI." They produced laminated credentials for Brand's inspection. "I'm Special Agent Hoffman," the gray-haired man said, "and this is Special Agent Gearing, Washington Field Office."

"Okay," Brand said, relieved. "What can I do for you? Don't recall I've robbed a bank lately."

Hoffman made an effort to smile. "No, I don't think you have. Anyway, we work the Counterespionage Detail."

"And I haven't given away national secrets. We can talk in my apartment."

"Let's get into our Ford," Gearing said. "Your apartment may be bugged."

"Are you serious?"

"We believe you're an espionage target, Mr. Brand, and bugging a target apartment is routine."

"I don't understand what you're talking about. Who would want to bug my apartment?"

"The KGB."

"Unlikely," Brand grunted, but followed the agents to their car and got into the backseat. "What's this all about?"

"In a nutshell," Hoffman said, "you're being cultivated by an agent of the KGB."

"Who, for God's sake?"

"A lady you've been dating—Nina Kenton."

"Impossible!" These guys were way off base.

"Fact, Mr. Brand. She's in frequent contact with a controller we've identified as Oleg Tarnovski, a known officer of the KGB."

Eight

Brand said, "I can't disbelieve you, but Nina couldn't be involved in anything like that."

Gearing handed Brand a deck of photos, black-and-white enlargements. Each showed Nina in a restaurant setting, her companion always the same man. He handed back the photos. "What else?"

Gearing gave him a Bureau file photo. Nina's companion. It was labeled Oleg V. Tarnovski. "From the RCMP," Gearing said, "taken before subject was booted out of Ottawa. PNG'd. Excellent English. Specializes in recruiting the elite. Ever see him?"

"No." Brand returned the photo. "I can't imagine Nina being involved. Why would she? She wouldn't work for money—she's wealthy."

"Was—before being divorced. Her husband charged flagrant adultery. She settled for a hundred thousand and a sealed court record. Between gambling and lavish living she used up most of the payoff in a year. The KGB approached her, targeted you, and set her up in that condo you visit."

Hoffman said, "She contrived to meet you at a dinner party. We've checked with the hostess and learned that Nina wanted you included. Step one accomplished. After that . . ."

Brand shook his head. It was still incredible. "I've never discussed my work with her. And I can't recall she ever asked."

"You were with CIA, Mr. Brand, before you joined GlobEco, a

high-classification think tank with covert government connections. I can't ask the precise nature of your work—"

"Couldn't tell you anyway."

"Understood. But whatever you do must be of considerable interest to the KGB. They're spending a fortune maintaining the lady's lifestyle, and they're not known for extravagance."

Brand said, "I can tell you my work generally concerns China, but why would that interest the KGB? If you told me the Public Security Bureau was interested in me, that would make more sense."

"Surely you know the old Soviet Union had a traditional interest in China. They backed the postwar revolution before becoming ideological antagonists. Relations on the surface are cordial once again, but the two countries don't trust each other. Since glasnost the country is relatively open to foreign travelers, including Chinese. But that's not the same in China. The KGB knows we monitor China with high-tech satellites, something they can't yet do. So their shortcut to acquiring strategic intelligence on China is to get it from a specialized source—GlobEco. Specifically you."

Yes, Brand thought reluctantly, my target and missile-site knowledge *would* interest the KGB. He shook his head. "So it's a bullshit cover story that the KGB went out of business when Yeltsin came in?"

"Not entirely. But it was—is—a vast organization with sections and cells that can operate independently of the KGB Chairman. The KGB was always atrociously corrupt, and elements of it stashed away funds from Gulag gold mines, from extortion, black marketing, and just plain theft. So they've got operating money, plenty of it."

"And Tarnovski's operating independently?"

"Let's say he's a rogue operator working for hard-line seniors who haven't submitted to the new order." He cleared his throat. "The CIS isn't one big happy family, and may never be."

Brand nodded thoughtfully. "So if Tarnovski's Directorate could bring off an intelligence coup involving China it would gain a lot of prestige and influence."

"The catbird seat," Gearing agreed. "Perhaps able to change foreign and military policy."

Hoffman said, "Think what the KGB got from the Walkers, the spies inside our Navy. Codes, fleet dispositions, war plans . . . the whole nine yards. For years they were draining our blood with impunity.

Achievements like that made them bold again. They've been spotting and recruiting vulnerable Americans all over the country, and abroad. Aldrich Ames is a standout example. Plus disaffected intellectuals and scientists, the socially elite—like Madame Kenton—who can do the inside work for them. And it's highly cost-effective."

"Okay," said Brand, "I get the point, and there's something you probably ought to know: I'm going to Hong Kong and when I mentioned it to Nina she more or less insisted on going along."

"Mind telling us the purpose of your trip?"

In other circumstances he might have declined, but having told Nina he had no valid reason for withholding the truth from the Bureau. So he summarized the circumstances of Peter's disappearance, and his resolve to follow his son's trail. Hoffman and Gearing glanced at each other from time to time but said nothing until Brand stopped speaking. Then Hoffman said, "That explains portions of a conversation we picked up between Madame Kenton and Tarnovski last Saturday. Seems he doesn't want you on the Mainland. Tarnovski pays Kenton a bonus if she keeps you in Hong Kong."

"Can you clarify?"

Gearing shrugged. "Obvious. Potentially you're a prime source for the KGB. After what they've put into developing you they don't want their investment snatched and squeezed by the Chinese. They don't want it so bad Tarnovski told Kenton if she couldn't prevent it you'd have to be destroyed."

His throat constricted, his face felt clammy-cold. "Shall I break off with her? How shall I play it?"

"Don't break off, and try not to let her feel you're witting to her background, what she's up to. Normally I'd see you as a good channel for deception material but that would require time and more technical backup than we can organize just now."

"Also," Hoffman added, "Kenton doesn't have a technical background, so a lot of effort could be wasted. Just continue seeing her as you've been doing, keep it natural, and when you decide to, fade away. Okay?"

"I suppose," said Brand, "you've considered playing her back against her controller."

The agents exchanged glances. "We have," Hoffman admitted.

"You've handled agents, how do you evaluate her as a potential double?"

"Well," Brand said slowly, "I've never doubled an American, but with me she's been completely plausible, very effective in concealing her goals. If you've got a wealth of doubles you might pass on her. If not, you could develop her and see what you've got." He paused, thinking of something to add. "In one respect she qualifies—she can follow instructions."

"Certainly a basic qualification," Hoffman agreed. "Well, we'll think it over, come to a decision after she returns from Hong Kong. Whichever way it goes I doubt you'll be informed."

"I'd rather not know."

"Good," said Hoffman. "This clears the air a good deal. If anything unusual comes up, give us a call." He handed Brand a card with his name and phone number, nothing more. "Oh—don't mention this chat to GlobEco Security or anyone at CIA. Okay?"

"Hadn't planned to. Anything else?"

"There's this," Gearing said after a pause. "If Tarnovski thought you'd tumbled to the setup I suspect he'd silence the lady to preserve his personal security. So—"

"Yeah," Hoffman interrupted, "he might just do that. It's the KGB way of avoiding embarrassment, y'know. So if you were to tell her you're on to the game, she might blurt it out to Tarnovski, never realizing she was subjecting herself to disposal."

"I understand," Brand told them. "I don't want her hurt or killed so I'll act normally and let things wind down."

"Good," Hoffman responded, "because we may have future use for Tarnovski—but not if he murdered her."

Brand said, "I'll let you know if anything develops. That all?"

Hoffman nodded. "We hope your son shows up."

"Thanks." Brand left the car and continued on to the elevator. He punched sequential call buttons, and after entering his apartment stood by the telephone, staring at it, wondering if it was, in fact, bugged by the KGB. His impulse was to unscrew the speaker plate and check for a button mike, but decided to leave things as they were.

He poured a drink and thought it more likely that Nina's place was bugged, her phone tapped by her employers. Perhaps some hidden camera had recorded even their bedroom scenes, those intimate couplings that formed the beast with two backs. And why not? Nina was serving as a "sparrow"; the KGB would be remiss not exploiting her all the way.

As he sipped scotch, Brand remembered his resistance to the agents' revelations, his grudging acceptance of their truth. Now, even though he had done nothing wrong, Nina's treachery made him feel unclean. Like a fool he had been seduced, never questioning her motives, and he ascribed his unwariness to long separation from active operations. The lesson just learned was keep your guard up, accept nothing at face value. For years he'd lived by that protective format and it was necessary to follow it again.

Especially, he told himself, when I reach the Mainland.

His machine's message light was dark, Arthur hadn't called. Meaning the Agency was doing nothing, would do nothing to retrieve the missing Legal Traveler, his son.

Ultimately, he thought, Darman Gerold is accountable for Peter's fate. Can't let him wash his delicate hands of all responsibility so I'll put it to him plainly: If he doesn't feel responsible to Peter he's damn well accountable to me.

He reviewed Irv Chenow's unexpected offer to take over State's China Affairs Desk. If he did it would infuriate Darman Gerold. But, attractive as that reaction was, Brand realized it was a petty and insufficient reason to work for Irving Chenow. Despite their fathers' old connection. That revelation had been surprising, in a surprise-filled afternoon topped off by all that the Bureau agents had to say.

Toward Nina he felt disgust, bitterness, and loathing, emotions difficult to conceal over time. The agents had left termination to his discretion so he would drop out sooner than later. He had no interest in playing any role in a Bureau CE operation. The embarrassment of Nina's duplicity and his ingenuousness was not something he wanted to prolong.

MIDMORNING AT THE OFFICE Brand took a call from Darman Gerold, who said archly, "You've been talking out of school, Mark, when you could have brought your complaints to me. Indeed, should have."

"Gosh, Darman, I must of forgot. Do I get a whippin'?"

"What you get," said Gerold irritably, "is lunch at the club. Twelve o'clock. Do be there."

Smiling, Brand replaced the receiver. He'd planned to call Gerold, arrange a meeting, but thanks to Irv Chenow, Gerold had moved first. To Tommy Gray he said, "That was the Maharajah himself."

"Lucky you."

"Indeed—no, that's one of his much-used words. So I'll say No Comment."

"Better. Ah—planning to tell him you'll be away?"

"Undecided. Need-to-know doctrine, y'know."

"Oh, yes, it can be useful. And Gerold's a man of impenetrable ignorance."

Brand nodded. "He may pick at you while I'm away but don't let it get to you. Make memos for the record and I'll brace him when I get back." Briefly he considered telling Tommy of Irv Chenow's offer, but that was between Chenow and himself and discretion should be observed.

He met Gerold in the club's main dining room, at a corner table removed from power-lunching males and ladies who were stoking up for an arduous afternoon of bridge.

Without greeting Brand, Gerold lifted his martini glass and sipped. "Scotch for you okay?"

"So long as it's Black Label." He couldn't avoid staring at the man who was said to have been fucking his mother since puberty.

Gerold took a deep breath. "Amigo, I don't enjoy being hauled on the carpet by an Assistant Secretary and chewed out over something I knew nothing about."

Brand accepted his drink from the waiter, who left menus for them and went away. "You didn't know my son had been co-opted as a Legal Traveler?"

"No, I did not. Mark, surely you realize I'm not involved in every recruitment the staff makes."

"This recruitment was one that should never have been made," Brand said evenly. "The Legal Traveler program was abandoned years ago."

"I've reprimanded the people responsible."

"Doesn't bring Peter back, does it? And since Hong Kong Base doesn't have assets who can service a drop in Canton—the simplest operation imaginable—the Base Chief needs an ass-chewing for incompetence."

"He'll get it."

"Who's the current Chief?"

"Briggs Dockerty."

"Taipei?"

"Phil Lichter."

"Too light for the front line, Darman."

"That's your opinion. Let's order, Mark, I have an ops meeting to chair."

Midway through the meal Brand said, "I'll probably go to Hong Kong, nose around, see if I can pick up Peter's trail."

"I have no problem with that. Just remember clearance restrictions—no visiting the Mainland."

"Not even the New Territories. I know." He finished his minute steak and sipped iced tea. "Tommy's got a firm grasp of *Galaxy*. He'll do well while I'm away. Good selection."

"Well, thanks, Mark. Compliments on my judgment are rare indeed."

"This one's deserved. And there's something else I need to mention."

"What's that?" He gazed at Brand uneasily.

"Asian Investments, where Peter works, is a proprietary institution. I should have been informed."

"Why?" he asked defensively. "Your son was employed routinely, without Agency intervention. Anyway, he wasn't witting."

"By now," Brand said, "he probably is. Considering the unpleasant consequences."

"That's an assumption of yours. No supporting evidence."

"Peter's absence is evidence enough, Darman. He's missing because, unwisely, he took on an Agency chore."

Gerold sipped iced tea. "There's at least a possibility your son was picked up because he drew attention to himself in the wrong quarters."

"Suppose he did—Peter wasn't trained to detect surveillance, had no training at all. So the Agency can't avoid causal blame, nor can you. Now we've got the situation defined, what are you going to do to get Peter back?"

"We're working on it."

"Specifically?"

"Well, I'm not prepared to give you line and verse. These things take time."

"They take time when nobody gives a damn."

"What do you expect me to do? Any suggestions from your vast reservoir of operational experience?"

"C'mon, Darman, don't dodge it. You control an organization that's chartered to operate abroad, get things done. What do you do at your ops meetings—review the *Times*'s best-seller list?"

"Now, Mark, I know you're under stress and I won't let you provoke me. But you have to realize that when the DCI was old Admiral Purvis—with whom I agreed on many things and supported against a lot of senior people—he pared down our case officers, and assets withered. He was a technocrat and—"

"—a drinking pal of the President's."

"Right. Purvis didn't believe in classical acquisition ops, you know that, or shoot-'em-up reprisal teams. HumInt was a dirty word, and we're still suffering the consequences."

Brand grunted. "What the Admiral believed in were long lunches at the Army & Navy Club and as much first-class foreign travel as he could justify. You read his memoirs?"

Gerold shifted nervously. "I scanned them—like everybody did."

"He was dumb enough to show himself as a double-dip gravy-trainer." He eyed Gerold. "So it comes down to no ideas and no assets—that about it?"

Gerold looked away. "If you come up with a rescue plan, we'll give it every consideration."

"Yeah. So I'm suggesting you send an Eyes Only to Briggs and Phil summarizing Peter's situation. Tell them to cooperate if I require it. Otherwise they stay clear of me."

Gerold pushed aside his plate and reached for the finger bowl.

"Do it today, okay? And phone me to confirm."

"I will." He glanced at his watch. Brand motioned over the waiter who presented the check to Gerold. After signing, Gerold stood up. "Mark, we've had a lot of disagreements, but I'm truly sorry about your son. Anything else you think I might do, just let me know."

"Who do I call for alias documentation?"

"Me. I'll take care of it." He seemed grateful to have something constructive to do. "Thought of a name?"

"Something to go with a Canadian passport. Let Technical Services choose a random identity."

"I'll get on it today." He hurried off and Brand sipped the last of his iced tea, thinking that ordinarily Gerold would have refused alias documentation outright—which was why he'd left it till last. After humiliating him.

Back at his office Brand responded to a message from Nina Kenton. She'd accepted a spur-of-the-moment dinner invitation on condition Brand could escort her. Could he? Would he? Brand said he'd be delighted and would come by around seven. Now that he knew her clandestine motivation Brand found Nina more interesting than before. He'd never been involved with an American agent of the KGB and he looked forward to evaluating her deceptions with a critical eye. While giving her a piece of disinformation to pass along.

She didn't ask the question until late that night, after they'd made love and were lying side by side in her majestic bed. "When are you leaving for Hong Kong, dear? With a bit of notice I can shop for the right things."

"No need to," he said, quasi-sleepily. "Decided not to go."

"But why? You've heard from Peter?"

"Uh-uh. It's futile to search. And he'll come back when he's ready."

"Oh, Mark, are you *sure?* I'd so looked forward to Hong Kong with you. I could go alone, but it wouldn't be the same without you."

"No," he muttered, "I guess it wouldn't."

BEIJING

YESTERDAY THE PRISONER had been hauled out for renewed interrogation. He was confident it was yesterday because he was aware of guard shifts, eight hours each. As guards arrived and departed he could hear their conversation, the clanking of exchanged keys, and from that he kept track of time.

The interrogation had been more of an interview. Was he ready to confess, implicate others in the antidemocratic conspiracy? Inducements were a bowl of warm rice, hot tea, and a cigarette. While appearing to consider, the prisoner had consumed the rice, downed the tea, and smoked the cigarette. Then said he had nothing to confess. And that was true. The evidence against him was more than sufficient to convict without confession.

Worse, he mused, the fault was his own. He had minimized the risk of visiting the Blue Dragon souvenir shop on Huanshi Donglu, giving the recognition phrase, and waiting for the proprietor to hand over the 35mm cassette. The delay should have alerted him to imminent danger, but he had passed time scanning shelves of cheap souvenirs unaware. And when he had finally accepted the film roll and walked out, four plainclothes agents arrested him.

Even then he had failed to recognize the seriousness of his situation, thinking the offense too minor to warrant more than a fine and perhaps a week in jail before expulsion.

Now, weeks later, the prisoner understood that he was not going to be expelled from China. They had caught an American agent in an act of espionage and were going to hold and exploit him for their own purposes.

During that first week in Canton jail he had expected a consular visit, but no one came. Or if a consul tried to see him, had been turned away. In China one could become a nonperson very quickly. Overnight tides smoothed footprints in the sand.

His cell lock was large and metal-sheathed, the iron key close to five inches long for lock penetration and turning leverage, the key blade intricately cut to prevent duplication. Taking those factors into consideration, the prisoner had realized only the guard's key could unlock his cell. He had nothing of value to bribe a guard, no knife or gun for coercion. And he had abandoned the idea of inducing choleralike diarrhea to force his transfer to a clinic; weak and dehydrated, he would stand no chance of escape. He had to be reasonably strong to succeed, and yesterday's full bowl of rice had strengthened his body.

Inside his mattress tick the cords still lay concealed. Were he moved to another cell or prison they would be lost forever, and he suspected that sooner or later he would be transferred to a remote *laogai*, a forced labor camp to serve his sentence.

Unless, of course, the Agency could somehow intervene.

The Agency having persuaded him to go to the Mainland, he saw himself as the CIA's responsibility. His father, he knew, had worked long and faithfully for the CIA, as his grandfather had for OSS. Three generations of service could not be ignored. Even now, he told himself, an operation was being mounted to gain his freedom. Should he wait for it, or try to escape alone? Waiting would be easier if his trial and sentence had been public, his prison known. But because the prisoner did not know his place of imprisonment, how, he wondered, could he be located by the CIA?

In adolescence he had come to believe the Agency all-knowing, all-powerful—not that his father had so described it—but because it was something he wanted to believe.

Then, as the prison weeks passed, the prisoner reasoned that because the Agency had asked *him* to perform a minor service on the Mainland, logic told him it had no one else to send. Making the Agency no longer omnipotent, but powerless to effect his freedom.

His father, however, had contacts and influence. By now his father must have inferred his fate, mobilized resources to change it, set him free. Family friends in Hong Kong and Taiwan would help, he was sure, and his father would not be slow to use them.

But even his father would have to know where he was in order to free him, and the Chinese were masters of concealment. So he had to decide whether to wait for his father to act, or try escaping on his own. Penalties for failure would be severe, the prisoner knew, but death was not one of them; he was too valuable a pawn to destroy. If caught, he would be beaten and starved, reprisals he thought he could survive, so the risk was worth taking.

Only it would have to be soon.

Nine

IN HIS BED, BRAND was watching late TV news when the phone rang. His father said, "Wake you? If so, apologies, but I seem to be busier than ever. Whether these people are getting scalded with maple sap or cutting limbs with axes and chain saws, there's a lot of mountain activity this spring. Not to mention babies."

"Good to hear from you, Dad. Anything special?"

"Well, I hoped you'd have word from Peter." He paused. "Anything?"

"Afraid not. So I'm going to Hong Kong."

"Thought you would. You'll check with our friends, won't you?"

"Of course, the old Taiwan gang."

"Good. If you need money—"

"Thanks, I can manage." If necessary he'd draw on Peter's fund. Sela would be outraged were any of it to finance an anti-Communist purpose. But Sela was no longer of this world.

"Hardly need tell you I'll be worried."

"I'm worried about Peter, Dad. One worrier in the family is enough. I just want you to take care of yourself up there."

Dr. Brand grunted. "Want me in a Florida retirement cell, don't you?"

"You know better than that. But I know how you are and I want you to have some consideration for yourself."

"These people need me, Mark. Before I came they lacked a doctor for twenty years."

"And survived. Well, I have a claim on your life and so does your grandson. Not to mention your great-grandchild-to-be."

His father sighed. "Putting it that way persuades me. How is La-li, by the way?"

"I'm going to see her tomorrow."

"Tell her to call me if she needs anything while you're away."

"I will." There was something . . . "Dad, do you remember a Kunming Army medic named Abe Chenowitz?"

"Abe? Of course I do. How did you uncover his name?"

Brand repeated what Irving Chenow had told him, and said, "Because of that relationship Irv offered me the China Desk."

"He did? Then he's got a professional regard for you that has nothing to do with your father. Mark—did you accept?"

"I'm sure I won't—but I said I'd think it over. Everything's on hold until Peter's home again. Irv understands."

"So do I, and you gave the right answer. You're China-born so you can't be President, but it would give me a lot of satisfaction to see you Director of China Affairs."

"I'll bear it in mind. So when Peter's here I expect you to come down and celebrate with us."

"Gladly. And tell Irving I look forward to meeting Abe's son—a very fine man, his father. Did a lot of good for a lot of people at the time." His voice sobered. "What did it really accomplish in the long run? Communists killed almost everyone who'd had contact with Americans."

"You couldn't anticipate that."

"Never even thought about it, to tell the truth. We were too busy fighting Japanese to ponder postwar China. American trait, Mark. Tactically minded, no long view of the future."

"I agree, and it's disheartening."

"Well, you've got enough to depress you without replaying America's international mistakes. Now, get Peter back and take care of yourself."

AFTER WORK THE FOLLOWING DAY Brand called on La-li and found a visitor with her. Feng Wah, the scar-faced extortionist.

"Hello, Jethro," Brand greeted him, and saw the Chinese cringe in his chair. "We have anything to discuss?"

"No—no, Mr. Brand."

"No further word from Macao, eh? Sources dried up."

Feng Wah got up and spoke to La-li. "I think I better go."

"Excellent idea," said Brand. "You're not welcome here. Is he, La-li?"

"N-no," she faltered. "Please do not come again."

With a venomous look the Chinese student made for the door and left. Turning to La-li Brand said, "What did he want?"

"Money—always he wants money."

"I can't forbid you helping him, but I strongly suggest you don't."

"After what he did to you—no, never."

"Good." He gave her a card with his father's name and phone number. "Peter's grandfather," he told her. "Any problems while I'm away, you call him."

"I will. Then you're going to Hong Kong."

"In a few days."

"For how long?"

"No way to tell. A week, a month . . ." He shrugged. "Depends."

She dabbed at her eyes. "I miss him so."

"We both do. La-li, you're not to tell anyone where I've gone. That's important."

"I understand." She paused. "Will—do you think of going to the Mainland?"

"If necessary. But not until I know much more than I do."

"But you think Peter is alive?"

"I'm sure of it." He took her hands between his. "Trust me to do everything possible to find him and bring him back. And while I'm doing that, try to get on with your life, your job. Too much brooding will affect the baby."

Her eyebrows lifted. "Really? The doctor didn't tell me that."

"What did he say?"

"That I'm in good health, and so is the baby."

"That's the first thing I'll tell Peter."

For a while she seemed immersed in thought. Finally she said, "I haven't thanked you for the table settings you sent. They're lovely. Noritake—the best."

"Glad you like the pattern." He looked around. "Anything else I can do?"

"No—you've done so much, sir. More than I had any reason to expect."

"This is just a beginning for our family," he said, and kissed her forehead, left as tears began welling in her eyes.

FROM A PAY PHONE he called the FBI office and told Special Agent Gearing he was planning the Hong Kong trip.

"What about the lady?"

"She doesn't know. I said I had meetings at the Hudson Institute, be gone for several days."

"How did she react?"

"Disappointed."

"Naturally. No bonus. Say, if you need HK support, look up the consulate's Legal Attaché. Mention me or Hoffman and he'll do what he can."

"Thanks, but I doubt I'll be calling on him." To keep his toe in foreign doors, J. Edgar Hoover had pressured State to accept FBI offices in diplomatic installations abroad, citing stolen cars and fugitives from justice. And although Hoover was long gone, the Legal Attachés remained, barely tolerated by State and CIA, which tried to limit their contacts to local law enforcement agencies.

"Call when you get back," Gearing requested, and Brand said he would.

His message machine registered a call from Irv Chenow. Brand thought Irv might still be at his office and called there. After a short wait Chenow said, "Wanted to tell you I cabled the consulate about Peter. And I called in the Chinese Ambassador. As expected he was pretty taciturn, disclaimed any knowledge of Peter Brand, said no U.S. citizens were being held by his government. I pressed the matter, he got surly and I got hotter. He finally agreed to send an inquiry to Beijing, so that's where we stand."

"Irv, I'm very grateful; can't thank you enough."

"Hmmm. Just give utmost consideration to my offer, will you?"

"Said I would. And I'm visiting Hong Kong in a few days."

"Any leads?"

"No, but I haven't begun looking."

"Bon voyage, then, and may the saints attend."

After pouring a drink Brand found his thoughts returning to the unexpected presence of Feng Wah in Peter's apartment. If he was pan-handling, as La-li said, that was in keeping with what Brand knew of him. Still, it troubled him. Was he snooping for information to use for personal benefit? Or had he volunteered his services to the Chinese embassy? To do what? Report on those closest to Peter Brand? The embassy might not pay for such marginal service, but it might offer repatriation with immunity from punishment, and Feng Wah's character seemed insufficiently sterling to resist. He was, after all, a Communist, nurtured in Communist society, accorded rare preferment as a student allowed to study abroad. Having found himself in difficult circum-stances, Feng Wah sought to improve them.

Well, nothing to do about him, Brand mused, and hoped La-li had not revealed his planned Hong Kong travel.

In the morning Darman Gerold called to say that the requested material was ready. How did he want it delivered?

"By safehand," Brand replied. "Double-wrapped package. When can I expect it?"

"Within the hour, Mark."

When Brand said nothing, Gerold said, "No word of appreciation?"

Brand grunted. "We'll tote the balance sheet when I get back. For now I'm reminded of the man who cut a fellow with a knife, offered him a Band-Aid, and expected gratitude."

Gerold sighed, "Point taken. Watch your ass out there."

"Always have."

After the package was delivered Brand waited until Gray went to lunch before opening it. The Canadian passport seemed authentic, with a variety of visas and stamps showing travel to Malaysia, Thailand, and Japan, among other places. The issue name was Thomas Vincent Lang, born in Toronto. A dozen business cards were printed with his name and that of a Toronto firm, CanToyCo, importers of novelties and toys. A plastic envelope contained pocket litter that included letters from Lang's wife, a sleeping pill prescription, credit cards, and half a dozen low-denomination traveler's cheques. Brand signed them as Lang, locked the package in his safe, and went to his Georgetown bank. He tapped his money market account for ten thousand in cash, and had lunch at Chez Grandmère on M Street near his club. Before returning to his office, Brand stopped at a travel agency, where he bought a round-trip ticket to Hong Kong on Japan Air Lines, paying with his true-name credit card. It was the polar route departing from Dulles the following evening, and stopping at Tokyo.

Brand enjoyed JAL's first-class amenities, and felt the flight provided an easy transition from America to the Orient.

Next day he took care of pending matters with Tommy Gray, ignored two calls from Nina, and with one suitcase and a carry-on—both stripped of personal identification—taxied to Dulles and boarded the JAL 747 at dusk.

After accepting a scotch from the kimonoed attendant and pulling on soft flight slippers, Brand eased back his seat and watched the lights of Washington recede.

Ahead lay—what? he wondered. Hong Kong for information and possible assistance. Step one. Mentally he was prepared to brave the Mainland and its hazards, all of which were inconsequential compared to the chance of bringing Peter back.

My own life, he reflected, has been pretty much lived and so I'm not afraid to lose it. But Peter's life still lies ahead of him . . .

He drank deeply, and as the plane broke through clouds he saw the pale, ghostly light of the moon. He closed his eyes and silently asked, Where, merciful God, is my only son?

PART
TWO

Ten

HONG KONG

MARK BRAND WOKE in his room at the Manchu, opened the blinds, and gazed out over the Central District's high-rise buildings to Victoria Harbor where a Star Ferry was crossing to Kowloon.

He had slept during most of the trans-polar flight, waking at the Tokyo stopover for another meal and more drinks. His tongue was furry, his mouth tasted like the bottom of a trash bin and he recognized signs of dehydration. Before showering he drank most of a chilled bottle of Polaris to restore fluid balance and surrendered to the shower's rehabilitating steam. Shaved and dressed, he noticed a collection of cards, leaflets, and brochures thrust under his door. They advertised tailors, shoemakers, jewelers, tour guides, restaurants, camera shops, dance halls, and massage parlors. Brand dropped them in the wastebasket, hoping no tailors would appear with swatches and promises of twenty-four-hour completion. Tailors were the hardest to get rid of.

From the taxi rank in front of the hotel he took a taxi over Chater and Des Voeux roads to Man Yee Lane and went into a medium-size restaurant named Johnny's Kitchen.

The hostess wore a lavishly embroidered pink cheongsam and carried an armful of menus. "One, sir?" she asked.

"One. And tell Johnny Shek I want to see him."

"You're a friend of Johnny's?"

"Old friend. The name is Brand." He followed her to a wall table and declined a menu. "Stein of Tuborg, please, as cold as possible."

She nodded and went away. Presently a waiter delivered a large dripping stein, and Brand drank gratefully as he looked around. His body clock was set for breakfast but in Hong Kong it was lunchtime and the restaurant was doing a brisk business. He needed no menu, having

decided in the taxi to feast on the large beer-steamed prawns for which
the restaurant was famous. Maybe some dim sums to begin with, and
jiaozi for dessert. He was telling the waiter what he wanted when Johnny
Shek arrived. Before greeting Brand the owner told the waiter there
would be no luncheon check for the table, and thrust out his plump,
moist hand. "Mark! Damn good to see you. Been here long?"

"Just arrived. Naturally I came here first."

"As you damn well should." He eased his bulk onto the facing
chair and grinned at Brand. "You look the same, pal, no visible change.
Me"—he patted his paunch—"twelve kilos I don't need. So, how's
everything?"

"Ding hao, Buhao." He made the good-bad gesture with one hand.
"Drink?"

"Why not?" He gestured at a waiter and ordered a wine spritzer.
"How long's it been, Mark?"

"Last year, remember?"

"Yeah. Time goes so damn fast."

"How's your mother?"

"Same-same. Good. In Macao, of course."

Brand nodded. Eighteen years ago he had helped bring Johnny's
mother from the Mainland to Taiwan, then on to Macao, where her
husband, Johnny's father, waited. She had gone to Shansi Province for
her father's funeral rites (a bookseller, he had been slaughtered by Red
Guards) and denied an exit visa. Johnny, then a Nat agent-in-training,
had beseeched his instructor to help him, and that instructor had been
Brand. Because Johnny was half Portuguese, half Chinese, he had not
been dispatched to the Mainland (to be captured and killed by ChiCom
security forces) but to Burma and Thailand, where half-caste features
attracted less attention. Now, Johnny wore a drooping black mustache,
his hair was thinning, and Brand estimated his weight at two hundred
pounds on a five-foot-seven frame. "How's your dad?" he asked.

"Aside from diabetes, he's okay. Still runs the exchange house,
owns an interest in the Red Lotus Casino."

"A shrewd operator," Brand said reminiscently. "What are his
plans for the takeover?"

Johnny took his spritzer from the waiter, sipped, and shrugged.
"He's an optimist, figures the ChiComs won't interfere in Macao."

Brand surveyed the dining room. "And you?"

"I'm planning to liquidate before panic selling starts." He drank again and gazed at Brand. "What's your advice?"

"Do it," Brand said flatly as an assortment of dim sums arrived. For a while they shared the Chinese hors d'oeuvres, Brand ordered another Tuborg, and they munched and drank contentedly.

Before Brand's prawns were served Johnny asked, "So, what brings you back to Hong Kong? Last views of a once-heavenly place?"

He shook his head. "How are you fixed for Mainland contacts?"

"Not good. Looking for agent material?"

"I'm looking for ways to locate my son and bring him out."

"Mark—you mean—like my mother?"

"That's right, Johnny," Brand said soberly, "like your mother," and told him how Peter had disappeared, and why. When he finished he drank from the stein and set it down.

Johnny Shek shook his head sorrowfully. "God damn," he said quietly, "what a lousy break. And the Agency put him up to it, that's the worst part."

"The worst part is they have no rescue assets, nothing. I'm in this alone."

"There's me," Johnny told him, "and anything I can do."

"Thanks." He lifted a shelled prawn by the tail, dipped it into sweet-and-sour sauce, and bit into the crayfish-size shrimp. Johnny said, "Money? I'm good for whatever you need, you know that."

Brand nodded. "If I can bribe—and it's more than what I've got— I'll turn to you. Right now I need information." He ate more of the prawn, savoring its fresh iodine flavor. Johnny bought baskets of them every morning from fishermen whose sampans crowded Aberdeen harbor on the far side of the island. "To start with I want to find Eddie Wong, Sammy Lu, and Tommy Ning."

"Those bandits?" Johnny exclaimed, then sat back. "Sorry, I forgot you were blood brothers. Fang-tse family."

"Tell me about them."

He leaned forward. "You want me to tell you they're okay citizens making an honest living in the Crown Colony? Bullshit! They started running protection rackets in Wanchai, pressuring whores and houses, bars, noodle joints, got into waterfront theft, stirred up labor trouble for compradors, got rich." He sucked noisily at his spritzer, set the empty glass aside. "Bought land, put up housing, reached over into the New

Territories and collected from those poor Hakka rice farmers." He shook his head. "Mark, I hate to see you with them."

Brand shrugged. "If I have to I'll dine with the devil." He looked at his plate. Four white-pink prawns remained but his appetite was gone. He shoved the plate toward Johnny, dabbed his mouth with a napkin. "Can you put me in contact?"

Johnny nodded. "Where you staying?"

"Manchu, eleven-fifteen. True name."

"I'll get word."

"What's their pecking order?"

"Eddie Wong's the brains—if it takes brains to be a criminal."

"They in dope?"

"Don't think so. That's one thing the Crown Commissioner won't stand for. Anyway, since Vietnam quieted down the Navy don't come here like it did and demand's way down. Not that shit don't flow in and out of here but Japs and Europeans looking to buy take the ferry to Macao. Not much enforcement there." He grunted. "Not much of anything but money." Selecting a prawn he bit into it, swallowed, and asked, "Married?"

"No. I raised Peter alone . . . he's all I've got." Feeling his throat constrict, Brand drank the rest of the beer and handed Johnny a Lang business card. "Thanks for listening and thanks for lunch."

"Least I can do. You'll stay in touch?"

"Count on it." He left the restaurant and went out on Man Yee Lane, wanting fresh air and a walk to clear his head. At the big Teac hi-fi center he turned and made his way along Connaught Road past the main bus terminal and the General Post Office, reaching the waterfront between ferry piers.

The afternoon was bright and clear, harbor water glistening in the wakes of sampans, walla-boats, and stub-nosed ferries. A China Air Lines plane dipped gracefully over Kowloon Peak in the distance, starting its final approach to the narrow finger of land that was Kai Tak airport. The runways, nearly two miles long, had been extended with rock cropped from the island and the labor of a thousand half-naked coolies. A construction project, Brand reflected, comparable to building the Sakkara pyramid.

Because he had been raised Chinese Brand felt pride in the industriousness of the Chinese race, their capacity to endure privation, their ability to create beauty from paper, stone, and wood, their meticulous craftsmanship, and he thought that their millions on the Mainland deserved far better than the cruel, despotic system that had been imposed on them, and which he had fought—futilely—so many years.

Johnny's mother had been one small success, one the Agency never knew about. Brand had dispatched two Taiwan-based agents to the Mainland to locate a female resembling Johnny's mother. In three weeks they found a visually suitable candidate, a Lanchow Party deputy, and transferred her passport, clothing, and Party ID to Johnny's mother. The agents escorted her to Canton and put her aboard the train to Kowloon and freedom.

Weeks later, when the agents returned, Brand learned that the Party deputy had resisted despoliation and suffered a broken neck. River eels, Brand was assured, rapidly devoured the corpse. Johnny, however, never knew. Nor the Agency.

In those days, he mused, you could accomplish things that were later proscribed, do them with a nod and a handshake, and go on to other matters. No guilt, no fear of betrayal. Trust was the binder between case officer and agent, and in those times it was inviolable.

Today was far different. Between congressional snoopers and talkative employees secrecy had become a bygone word. And it was to preserve secrecy that GlobEco had been established; the only latent threats to its integrity resided in self-seeking incompetents like Darman Gerold and dreary malcontents unsuited to the disciplined requirements of the secret world.

Gulls cawed, circled, and plunged off the stern of a fishing sampan whose crew were gutting fish and discarding the offal, much of it snatched by gulls before it hit the water. There were scores of islands off Hong Kong, some mere rocky outcrops where gulls nested and deposited abundant guano that was harvested by Chinese whose life work it was. Sailing past Kau Yi Chau on a pleasant afternoon years ago, Brand had seen harvesters fending off screeching gulls while they dug and filled their baskets. Sela had found the scene revolting, and after her abandonment, when Brand forced himself to inventory their mutual grievances, he realized that her professed concern for the poor of the world was superficial. Her privileged, insulated rearing had kept her from contact with the working class and imbued her, he thought, with a false sense of values. How then, he often wondered, had she discarded all values and become a revolutionary? What was the irresistible lure? And in what ways had he failed her?

An urchin with a shoe box intruded on his thoughts. Brand let the boy—no more than six or seven—shine his shoes, rewarding him with ten HK dollars, as much as a dock laborer might earn in a day. The boy's thanks were profuse, and as he trudged away Brand knew that the money would fill the family's rice bowls for several days.

He continued along the waterfront, past Royal Naval Headquarters, reflecting on how the sights, smells, and bustle of Hong Kong always energized him. It was exciting to fly into Kai Tak at dusk, seeing the lighted Peak, the crowded streets below, wondering if some new and unforeseen adventure was going to unfold. And he thought, too, that the Crown Colony's few square miles seemed to contain the distillate of the entire Mainland; everything was there, available at one's fingertips.

At the Star Ferry piers he turned inland and walked the underpass until it emerged at Statue Square beside the Manchu. After checking the desk for messages—none—he took the elevator to his room. More advertisements had been thrust under his door; he collected them for the wastebasket, wondering why a three-star hotel allowed the annoying practice by bellboys, room maids, and hall porters who received a few HK dollars weekly for their complicity.

He poured a drink of duty-free scotch and sat down to think about his son. Assuming Peter had been captured in an illegal act, his captors would realize they had a prisoner potentially too valuable to execute. And it would take the authorities time to decide how best to exploit him and maximize their gain.

Having studied the ChiCom bureaucracy, Brand knew that several decision-making levels would be involved. From the provincial Public Security Bureau—the secret police—and Party authorities up to Party and PSB headquarters in Beijing. Some sort of judicial ruling would be made, probably in secret, to maintain a legal facade. After which, Peter would be held to await eventual disposition of his case.

It was not, he mused, a case of arresting an innocent tourist, for what Peter had done—servicing a clandestine drop—was clearly illegal in any country. His case paralleled that of Fecteau and Downey, whose black flight had crashed, and who spent long years in prison despite all efforts to free them.

As a spy Peter would be confined in a high security prison, isolated from other prisoners to prevent communication with the outside world. And it was likely the prison was located in or near Beijing to keep Peter immediately available when the ultimate decision was made. He would be fed a marginal diet but not allowed courtyard exercise lest the foreigner be seen by other prisoners. So, he told himself, his son was not in danger of execution or death from starvation; thus, no clear urgency in arranging his exfiltration.

Thinking operationally, Brand saw three phases ahead: locate Peter, organize his escape, and flee the Mainland. None of them, he conceded, could he accomplish without help.

The only alternative, he theorized, would be to kidnap a high Party official and exchange him for Peter. But that possibility was so remote as to be impracticable.

He finished his drink, and still feeling the effects of jet lag, lay on his bed and drowsed, finally falling asleep.

Repeated knocking at his door roused him. Brand sat up groggily. Outside it was dark but for the radiance of lighted buildings. "Who is it?" he called.

"Wong Luk-hoi," came the reply. "Open up, brother."

Eleven

THEY EXCHANGED RITUAL HANDSHAKES and body contact, sat down, and stared at each other. Luk-hoi "Eddie" Wong had not been a handsome young man and was less so now. His features had coarsened and a keloid scar half circled his neck, long black hair gathered in a ponytail, gleaming rings on his fingers, and a wispy mustache and goatee. He wore a beige linen suit, lavender shirt, and white cowboy boots with pointed toes. When they pressed together, Brand had felt a gun in its shoulder holster.

His old friend, he thought, was turned out like a Colombian drug baron.

"Long time," Eddie said, "since Taiwan. Who told you I was here?"

"My father."

"Ah . . . then he's—"

"Alive and well. He said Sammy and Tommy were here."

Eddie nodded. "They're available, and want to see you." His forehead wrinkled. "You used that kid, Shek, to make contact. Not one of my favorite characters."

"Quickest channel I could think of."

He shrugged again. "Yeah. I guess you know I'm not entirely legit."

Brand smiled. "Entirely? Would zero be more accurate?"

Eddie glowered. "That matter?"

"If it did I wouldn't have sent the message."

Eddie's features relaxed. "So you need help and you're not particular how it's packaged."

"Not where my son's concerned."

He grimaced. "What's wrong, Mark? Give me the picture."

Brand poured two drinks, sat facing Eddie Wong, and began to talk.

EDDIE PUT ASIDE the stub of a long panatela Brand recognized as Cuban. Hong Kong was the warehouse of the world. Eddie got out another Upmann, rotated it briefly, and put it away. "That's it?" he said finally.

Brand nodded. His throat was tired and he felt emotionally depleted from recounting Peter's story.

"So the kid went Canton-side to play spy," Eddie said musingly. "Natural, I suppose, seeing as Dad and Granddad were both in it."

"My father was never in espionage directly," Brand corrected, "he was the OSS detachment's doctor." He paused. "Not that it makes any difference."

"But you were," said Eddie and his smile became calculating. "Maybe still are."

"No."

"Because if you're involved in some CIA game, count me out."

"Why, Eddie?"

"Oh, a few years ago I had some business down in the Golden Triangle. CIA got wind of it and tried to cut off my balls." He fingered his goatee reflectively. "Actually, they succeeded."

Tacit admission, Brand thought, that Eddie was involved in narcotics. But bad as that was Brand was not in law enforcement. Besides, Eddie used the past tense, so perhaps he was now only a whoremaster and extortionist. Well, the ChiComs holding Peter were torturers and mass murderers; compared to them Eddie and his associates were pure as the Pope. He said, "The Chinese part of me doesn't show in my face, so I can't travel the Mainland unnoticed."

"True."

"So to locate Peter I need penetration of their prison system."

"Maybe he's not on inventory."

"That's possible," Brand agreed, "and if he's not listed that suggests the kind of prison he's in."

"Political."

Brand nodded.

Eddie grunted. "I'm not political myself, never was. I'm a businessman, do business where I can, with whoever's got goods or money. Compared to some of Chiang's buddies on Taiwan, ol' Mao looked pretty good to a lot of people."

"He had his day," Brand remarked, "and did more damage to China than anyone thought humanly possible."

"Well, he got rid of flies."

"And kicked our ass in Korea and Vietnam. But to get back to why I'm here, have you got assets—I mean people—who can do a reconnaissance job for me?"

"Probably. And if I don't, Sammy and Tommy will. They do more Mainland business than me."

"So there's business to be done on the Mainland."

"Plenty. Ever hear of a Chinese not interested in money?"

"A dead one."

"Right. It's a big country, Mark, hundreds of thousands of old graves yet to be robbed."

"Meaning a lot have been robbed."

"And the ornaments and jewelry and ceramics sent out. Payoffs, of course—way of the world—but everyone ends up happy. Especially those dedicated servants of the People's Republic—customs inspectors, police, warehouse agents—always got a hand out to look the other way."

"Airline pilots?"

"I never heard. Sampans, trains, and buses are cheaper transportation. Pilots usually deal in small packages—White Flowers." The generic term for heroin and cocaine. "So," he continued, "there are people over there to do business with—the problem is to spot the right ones."

Brand nodded. "The second problem is getting Peter out of prison; the third is getting him off the Mainland."

"With you."

"I'd prefer it." They both smiled.

"Yeah," said Eddie, "you're getting a little old to do hard time. Hell, so am I—so I'm careful not to get sent away. It's been tried, of course, but Crown barristers can do wonders when properly motivated." He flashed a smile of satisfaction.

"And you keep them well motivated."

"I do what has to be done," he said smugly, and to Brand it sounded like a Mafia cliché.

Eddie got up and brought back the scotch bottle, poured each a drink. "Before getting off old times," he said, "remember a big kid, older than us named Cheong Wing-dah?"

"Vaguely."

"His dad came from Shanghai with the Gimo, sort of oversaw what remained of the Nats' treasury. Cheong schooled with the French sisters—remember him now?"

Brand shrugged. "Why?"

"After his dad died Cheong drifted down here with plenty of capital. Got into money-changing, curio shops, like that. Then he opened art galleries on the island and Kowloon. He's a major buyer of Mainland grave stuff, made many fortunes."

Brand said, "An American needs a certificate of provenance to get that sort of thing through U.S. Customs. Doesn't that limit the buyer market?"

"Uh-uh. Cheong can have a crate of antiques flown to Bangkok, say, where it's repackaged and sent on to the States." He shrugged. "Routine."

Brand smiled. "Interesting, but why tell me all this?"

"Thought you might know Cheong; his contacts could be useful."

"Let's see what Sammy and Tommy come up with, okay? I don't want to deal with strangers where my son's life is concerned. And Peter can't be packaged and shipped to the States like a statuette."

Eddie sipped thoughtfully. "If your blood brothers can't help, no one can."

"What I figured," Brand said, "so let's bring in the brothers."

Eddie looked at his platinum Rolex. "We usually get together for dinner around ten. You know Shing Hong's?"

"I can find it."

"I'll send a car."

They got up and gave each other fraternal hugs. Eddie went to the door, and when it was half-open he closed it and turned around. "There was something floating around in my mind when I was talking about Cheong—now I've got it." He paused as though searching memory. "Remember old Chen who set up the Nats' antiquities museum?"

"What about him?" Brand felt a frisson of—expectation? "I heard he was dead—is he here?"

"No, but his daughter is—Chen Ling-mei."

Wordless, Brand stiffened.

"Cheong brought her here years ago. She runs the biggest art gallery in town. You've got to remember Maria—Mary—Chen."

In a voice Brand hardly recognized he said, "I remember her—very well."

Then Eddie was gone.

Dazedly Brand sat down. After all those years someone had voiced her name. Ling-mei, the love of his younger years. Here in Hong Kong.

He could hardly believe it.

He gulped down a drink to steady himself, then closed his eyes as memories engulfed him.

HE HAD BEEN VISITING Museum Director Chen to discuss aboriginal artifacts when a girl came into the office. She was delicately built, with almond eyes and skin the color of aged porcelain. After bowing gracefully to Brand she was introduced as Chen's daughter, Ling-mei. "But at school," she said, "they call me Mary or Maria. I apologize for interrupting—I'll come back later." And before Brand could object she glided away. Leaving him convinced she was the most beautiful young Chinese woman he had ever seen.

"A very good student," her father said. "A dutiful daughter and my pride and joy. The son I never had."

A week later Brand was walking along Plum Blossom Way when he noticed Chen's daughter alone at a teahouse table. Her features were perfectly composed until she saw Brand, then her gaze lowered as he came toward her. "May I join you?" he asked.

"I would like that, sir, but it would not do to be seen with a foreigner," she said apologetically. "My father would understand, but others . . ."

"Of course. I wouldn't want to embarrass you—or your father."

He was about to leave when she said, "Nearby there is a less public place where we could have tea—if you care to."

"Very much. I'll follow."

So they sat in the cool, shaded room where Brand found it both easy and pleasant to talk with this incredibly attractive girl, and hear her melodic voice as she spoke of her birth in Chengtu a year before the Communist takeover, of flight to Taiwan she was too young to remember, and the death of her mother when she was still a child.

In turn, Brand told her that his wife had left Taiwan for America, and died there, leaving their small son in his care; that he worked at the big Navy communications compound and led a quiet life devoted to his child.

"So, you are often lonely," she suggested.

"Yes, Ling-mei, and that is why I wanted to share an hour with you."

Again her gaze lowered. "It is unusual to meet a foreigner who speaks such perfect Chinese, and I enjoy speaking with you. Also, my father said you are a learned man, having studied our island aborigines."

"That was kind of him," Brand responded, "but that was in the past. Now I work for my government."

"Is it interesting to you?"

"At times."

"Oh? It is said that in your compound you can listen to Mainland officials talking—is that so?"

"It's an exaggeration."

She leaned slightly toward him. "Will you give me your frank opinion—do you think we will ever return to the Mainland?"

"Do you want to—very much?"

"I'm not sure—I don't remember what it was like."

"Then it won't upset you if I say that I don't believe the Nationalists will ever return—except as tourists.

"The Communist Army is very large, much larger than the few soldiers who came with Chiang from the Mainland. And the Communists are very determined to stay in power." He paused. "They proclaim Taiwan part of China and say it will be reunited one day."

While she considered his words he studied her face with its finely slanted cheekbones, slightly concave cheeks, and perfectly symmetrical lips. The depth of her eyes was remarkable, and Brand felt uncomfortably filled with desire. Yet that was an unworthy emotion and he suppressed it.

She said, "I will not tell my father what you said, because he, like all of the old Kuomintang, plan, live, and plot to regain what was so foolishly lost."

"Foolishly?"

"Chiang's armies cared nothing for the common people."

"They were fighting the Japanese, Ling-mei. The Communists waited out the war in Yenan, then attacked the exhausted armies of Chiang."

She nodded. "I understand your point. But it was a great tragedy for everyone."

"For everyone," he agreed, saw her glance at her watch and rise.

"I must go, sir."

Throat tight, Brand asked, "Were I to invite your father to dine, would you come with him?"

"I'm not sure. But I would like to see your home—your child."

"Then—?"

"Invite him—us—and hear what he replies." Then she was moving gracefully away and his gaze followed until she was gone.

DIRECTOR CHEN DID BRING his daughter to dine with Brand who felt himself tongue-tied and incapable of fully responding to Chen's comments and questions, so deeply was he affected by Ling-mei's presence at the table. She deferred to her father, never taking a conversational initiative and limiting her speech to Brand's occasional questions. And when Chen invited Brand to tour the museum guided by his daughter Brand quickly agreed.

The tour of Chinese antiquities was enhanced by Ling-mei's extensive knowledge of their dynastic origins and provenance. To Brand her presence was electrifying and he did all he could to establish deeper rapport.

Over the next weeks she met him occasionally at the teahouse, and when Brand learned that her father was traveling to Hong Kong he gathered courage and asked her to dine with him—alone.

Hesitantly, she said she would consider the invitation even though it was not proper for a maiden to be alone with a man. "Still," she said thoughtfully, "you are not a stranger but a foreign friend of my father's. So it is possible."

"Will you let me know?"

"Soon," she promised, and a few nights later came by rickshaw to his door. She wore a dark hooded cloak, and under it a red cheongsam of clinging silk. She carried a silk purse and clutched it as she looked nervously around. Brand felt as unsettled and awkward as though it were his first date. Making small talk was an effort, so after a small glass of rice wine Brand escorted Ling-mei to the dining table that number one maid had set with exquisitely arranged flowers, candles, and gleaming china. They were served a thin, spicy broth, then Keelung shrimp in a sauce of wine, ginger, and water chestnuts. Ling-mei took small delicate bites, moving her ivory chopsticks like magic wands.

Although he had no appetite Brand made a show of eating hoping to disguise the desire that suffused his body, and after serving them the servants retired.

In the living room Brand poured two small glasses of cognac and offered one to Ling-mei. Hesitantly she took it, sniffed, and asked, "What is it?"

"A Western custom."

After tasting she said, "It seems very strong."

"Then put it aside." He set a Debussy LP record on his player and took her in his arms.

"I don't know how to dance," she murmured, moving uncertainly against him.

"Doesn't matter," he said hoarsely, and touched her nose with his in a Chinese kiss. Her body trembled and he pressed his lips to hers. He was afraid she would draw away, but her eyes closed and presently her mouth opened to his tongue. Aroused, Brand lifted and carried her yielding body to the bedroom lighted by a single perfumed candle.

For a few moments she lay on the bed, Brand gazing down at her in awe. Then she rose and left the room. Brand felt it was the end of everything. But she came back, holding her purse, and placed it under the pillow. Then she turned and reached back for the zipper. Brand's fingers found and opened it, the silk whispering away as it fell and pooled at her feet. Breath caught in his throat, his heart pounded, for she was completely naked. Then, he too was naked, holding her tightly in his arms, caressing her body, invading its mysteries, pressing her small, budlike breasts until she reached under the pillow for her purse. From it she extracted an ivory object shaped like a small parsnip, parted her thighs, and said, "I have never been with a man before."

"I know." He saw her insert the smaller end, then force it into her vagina. Her face tightened with the pain of rupture, and after a few moments she withdrew the bloody instrument.

"Now," she whispered, and Brand entered where the ivory phallus had been. For a time she received his thrusts passively, then moved with him, rolling her hips and panting until passion rose to climax. In an agony of self-restraint Brand withdrew and ejaculated above the dark, silken beard, then clasped her tightly, murmuring, "I love you, Ling-mei, I love you."

"I was sure of that, or I would not have come."

They made love twice more before he called a rickshaw to take her to her home by the museum, and after it creaked off into darkness, Brand returned to bed and lay there, scenting her perfume, realizing that she had been prepared for the seduction by bringing the deflowering instrument and studying illustrations in the Bride's Book, both legacies of her mother, handed down from one female generation to another.

It troubled Brand that he had blurted out "I love you" not once but many times, and he justified it by believing he had meant it in those climactic moments. Not forever, of course, he reasoned, just then. When her fine-boned body was gathered in his arms and their hearts were pulsing together. Unfortunately, he reflected, Ling-mei, as a young, very recent virgin, could easily believe her lover was making an eternal vow. Particularly a young, unsophisticated Oriental girl.

In college he had learned by his junior year to avoid declarations of love, particularly anything that could be interpreted as a hint of marital intentions, which Bryn Mawr, Penn, and Temple girls were eager to extract and believe. Fucking friendships were one thing, serious relationships another, and so he had gone from one accommodating female to another. Until he met Selina Wayburn.

But that had proved the most monumental and lasting mistake of his life, and he avoided recalling it until their son was the only reminder.

Over the months until Brand left Taiwan, Ling-mei contrived to meet Brand in teahouse special rooms, at first bringing the Bride's Book to sample the illustrated positions, each untried one bringing new erotic delight.

Her father seemed unaware of his daughter's furtive absences and Brand avoided seeing old Chen lest he be questioned.

On the day Brand flew away with Peter, the museum director and his daughter joined the small group of Agency personnel to see them off. He saw tears streaking Ling-mei's cheeks and turned away, heartsick that he was leaving her. But his work had become unrewarding and he had assured Ling-mei that he would soon return.

So many years ago, he thought in the darkness of his room. The *Madame Butterfly* story reprised on Taiwan to the strains of Debussy, and it shamed him that he had not kept his vow.

Still, he knew that his failure to remarry had not been out of lasting reverence for his wife, but perhaps, subconsciously, because he was still bound emotionally to Chen Ling-mei.

Now it was said she was in Hong Kong. Would he dare to see her? Was it wise? What was her relationship to Cheong Wing-dah? Wife? Concubine? If he appeared at her gallery would she spurn him as she had every right to do? Uncertainties tortured him. Damn Eddie for mentioning her name. His first duty was to Peter; he could not let memories of the past overwhelm and deviate him from what he had come to accomplish. So, let the memories fade, the ashes grow cold again. Her life was her own, while his was dedicated to his son.

To detour his thoughts Brand showered and shaved, changed clothing and stood by the window watching the night lights of Hong Kong and the harbor. Beyond lay the New Territories and across the narrow Shamchun River, the southernmost district of Kwantung Province; then the vast earth mass of Mainland China, where his son was somewhere hidden.

When the phone rang it was the desk announcing that a car waited at the entrance.

Brand walked through the lobby to a gleaming black Bentley limousine, whose chauffeur bowed, opened the door, and drove Brand into the night.

Twelve

SHING HONG RESTAURANT was set partway up the Peak above the Governor's residence and the Zoological Gardens, for an unobstructed view of Victoria Harbor. Brand followed the chauffeur through the crowded, brightly lit dining room and up a winding staircase to a loft-style second floor. Were the barnlike interior stripped of tables and chandeliers it would be large enough for a Judy-Mickey musical: kids busy sweeping straw from the floor; cantankerous Harry Davenport stomping around; Ben Blue swinging down from the loft to everyone's merriment, keying the opening number of a Busby Berkeley hoedown.

But this was Hong Kong, not farmland Kansas, and two serious-faced young men stood on either side of a carved teak door. As the chauffeur spoke to them Brand reflected that though American Mafiosi favored clam-linguini trattorias for conclaves, their Hong Kong counterparts chose *fanguan zai* emporiums of their own.

The door guards wore identical black suits, white shirts, and black ties. They were clean-shaven and their hair neatly trimmed. One bowed to Brand and opened the door to the private dining room beyond. A round rosewood table could seat a dozen men, but only three stood near the corner bar looking expectantly at Brand.

Sammy Lu, he saw, was as lean as ever, dressed in a white leisure suit, black hair slicked back from his forehead. Tommy Ning's squat muscular build was accented by a shaven bullet-shaped head and almost invisible neck. They came toward him, wordlessly exchanging handclasps and body hugs until Sammy exclaimed, "Jesus, man, it's good to see you!"

"Yeah," Tommy echoed, pounding Brand's shoulders, "but you been a bad brother never comin' back." His eyes narrowed. "You been missed, know that?"

"Now I do."

Brand accepted a mao-tai cup from Eddie, who said, "I went ahead and ordered—save time, okay?"

Brand nodded. "You guys know why I'm here?"

"Eddie said," Tommy replied. "We're sorry, Mark. Sounds like your boy is in deep shit."

Brand looked at them. Affluence and corruption had altered their faces, the way they stood and dressed. They'd picked up sidewalk slang from U.S. servicemen, mannerisms from gangster movies. But they were real-life gangsters, gunslingers capable of murder for profit or revenge. They were also Brand's blood brothers and he had turned to them because he needed gunslingers to free his son, not sallow-faced consular clerks.

Sammy touched his cup to Brand's. "You figure the Gong An Ju's got—what's his name—Peter?"

"Who else? So it's a long reach." No reason to minimize the difficulties; they'd know them better than he did. Firsthand.

The door opened and two white-jacketed waiters came in pushing steam carts. One quickly set the table for four, while the other uncovered serving bowls and dishes until the air was steamy with the pungent flavors of the East.

Seated, they waited until the waiters left, then Eddie said, "Tommy's got a Gong An Ju contact in Canton he can work on. If that's where Peter was grabbed the guy ought to know."

"Or find out fast." Tommy dipped a porcelain spoon into spidery egg-drop soup. "He can choose between money or his nose."

"Sounds like a good start," Brand told them. "How soon?"

"I'll send a guy tonight. He'll be gone a couple days, no more than three."

Sammy wiped liquid from his goatee. "What else to get started?"

"I haven't thought ahead," Brand admitted, "because I didn't know how to begin. But if we can get a location from this Gong creep . . ."

"Job one," Eddie pronounced. "The rest comes from that."

"So," said Tommy, "might as well get started." He shoved back his chair and went to a wall phone.

While he was gone Sammy studied Brand's face before saying, "In HK we got anything a man could need—money, entertainment, girls. Mark, stay here, lead the good life where you're welcome."

Sensing that a direct refusal would be offensive, Brand temporized. "Haven't thought about it—but I will. When Peter's free."

"Well," Sammy said, "so long's you consider it. Peter, too."

Tommy settled down in his chair and reached for chopsticks. "Guy's on his way to Star Ferry. By midnight he's at Lo Wu. Tomorrow he sees our police creep, okay?"

"Okay," Brand said, "confirming I was right to come here. What I do next depends on what we hear from Canton."

"What *we* do next," Eddie said reprovingly. "I figure it's all gonna be *real* interesting."

Then for a while they concentrated on bowls of steamed rice, shrimp, lobster, oysters, Peking duck's crispy skin and succulent flesh, soft and fried noodles . . . on and on, thought Brand, who had seldom seen a feast like this. Sipping mao-tai, he conceded that, legend to the contrary, crime paid, and well.

As they loosened ties and jackets, Brand glimpsed their holstered guns and felt more secure than he had in all his Washington years.

WASHINGTON

When Nina Kenton opened the door "John" entered and locked the door behind him. He was wearing a dinner jacket, a red bow tie against a wing collar, and a white ruffled shirt—a combination she detested. Nina was in an embroidered housecoat and matching ballet flats, comfortably appropriate for an evening of VCR movies. After a critical glance at her visitor she backed farther into the room and said, "Is it prudent to come here? You said you never would."

He ignored her while he went to the small bar and poured vodka into a glass. After downing it he said, "Except for special circumstances. It's not as if Brand is likely to appear."

"I told you he was out of town." She arranged herself on the sofa. "No danger of that."

"None at all," he agreed and sat at the far end of the sofa. "Where was it you said he was going?"

"The Hudson Institute—upstate New York, somewhere."

"It has a branch in Hong Kong?"

"Why—I—" She sat forward suddenly alert. "Why?"

"Because that's where he is."

"I don't believe it!"

"Believe it, dear Nina. He flew there on Japan Air Lines two nights ago."

"Damn! *Damn him!*" She stared at John. "Why would he lie to me?"

"I thought you could tell me."

She shrugged. "Haven't the faintest. Maybe he's got a slant-eyed broad out there."

"Maybe. But isn't it more likely he's following his son? We discussed the possibility—and its consequences."

She shot up from the sofa, clenched her fist, and chewed a knuckle. "That bastard! He said we'd go together—I was counting on it. Then sneaking away—that miserable *shit!*"

He rotated the empty glass in one hand. "Why would he do a thing like that, Nina—abandon you so unfeelingly?"

"I—I don't know."

He considered her reply. "Is it possible your charms became commonplace to him? Boring?"

Collecting her thoughts she snapped, "Unlikely. Very damn unlikely."

"Then, what am I to presume?"

"Presume whatever you want." Her eyes narrowed. "How do you know he took JAL?"

"Passenger manifests are almost public records. Anyone with a plausible reason can find out who flew when, and where."

"I didn't know that." She resumed her seat.

"Now you do." He got up and walked toward the bar.

"Do I get a drink?"

"Get it yourself," he said coldly and tilted the vodka bottle. "I'm not one of those Western 'gentlemen' who bow and scrape and treat women like empresses and queens."

"You're certainly not." Why had he used the word "Western"? "You're not a gentleman at all."

Her ingenuousness made him smile. "Never aspired to be." He brought back his drink, sipped thoughtfully. "Not my line at all." He was tempted to tell this American cunt exactly *what* he was and reveal their real relationship. But the less she knew, the less she could tell—if it ever came to that.

"So," she said, "he's in Hong Kong looking for his son. We expected that—no big deal."

"But he gave you no notice, disguised his departure."

He had, she conceded, never returned her calls to his office. "I doubt he's foolish enough to try finding Peter on the Mainland. One man?" She waved a hand dismissively, noticed teeth marks on the knuckle.

"He could have friends, Nina, Chinese friends. In the Orient friendship means a great deal more than it does in the West."

There was that geographical allusion again. Why was he using it? She said, "You want me to go there, bring him back?"

"I didn't say so but it's not a bad idea. The crucial point is he doesn't get to the Mainland."

"And to prevent that you'd destroy him."

He grunted. "Not me—you."

She recoiled. "What a horrible idea! Even if I agreed how would I do it?"

"In the Orient the use of poison has a long tradition." From his jacket pocket he brought out two vials. One held several small pills, the other a clear liquid. "If you decide to go."

Shuddering, she turned away. "Who *are* you, John? Is murder your line of work?"

"Occasionally." He placed both vials on the coffee table. Nina got up and strode rapidly to the bar. She splashed cognac into a glass, swallowed, and shivered from the impact. "I'm not sure I could bring myself to do murder."

He sighed. "I get tired of reminding you what you stand to lose through disobedience." He moved an arm sweepingly. "All this, Nina, everything you hold dear." How devoted to material possessions these decadent capitalists were. How predictable and pliable it made them.

"You're insulting," she snapped.

"The fur coat is insulting?"

She thought it over and felt trapped by her own words. "That wasn't for—murder."

He nodded. "The reward would be greater."

"It would have to be. Much greater." The very idea made her want to vomit, but she recalled a time not long ago when she could cheerfully have murdered Bernie. But then, of course, she lacked the means to do it. Unwillingly her gaze returned to the poison vials.

Recognizing tacit acquiescence, John drew two envelopes from inside his dinner jacket and placed them beside the vials. "Ticket," he said. "JAL to Hong Kong tomorrow evening—Brand's flight." He gestured at the companion envelope. "Expense money."

"How much?"

"Five thousand."

She opened the envelope and thumbed hundred-dollar bills. "Exclusive of my bonus, right?"

He nodded. "And now that is settled there is a service you can perform for me." He stood and pulled off his jacket. "A personal service."

She stared at him. "What do you mean?"

He unhooked the trouser waistband to draw off his trousers. "Guess," he said with a leer.

"Fuck you," she sneered.

"That's exactly what you'll do, Nina. Don't I pay you to fuck Mark Brand? That five thousand includes a fuck for me."

She grimaced condescendingly. "I don't think so, John. I'm not in the mood."

He dropped blue-patterned shorts—underwear that affronted her sense of taste—and touched his wrinkled penis. "Now," he ordered, and before she could retreat he caught her arm and twisted it. His other hand jerked down her frontal zipper and when she tried to cover her nakedness he struck her face so hard she staggered back and dropped on the sofa, mewling and whimpering. He got astride her, knees on either side of her chest, clamping her mouth. "If you hurt me," he snarled, "I'll kill you. Now, suck, you bitch!"

Gasping, she palated the swelling glans, choked as he began thrusting more deeply. "Pretend you're Linda Lovelace," he gloated. "Eat the whole thing."

Fighting for breath, Nina told herself she would do anything to survive, anything at all. His penis and hair had a rank smell but if she retched she would choke. Gradually she relaxed, hoping he would come and leave her.

But when his penis was fully hard he got up and roughly pulled her over until she was facedown on the sofa. She gulped deep breaths of air, wondering what he would do next. At least she wasn't going to suffocate.

His hands grabbed her hips and drew upward until she was on her knees. Okay, she thought, doggy style, and felt him search for entry until he was housed and the thrusting began. Unwillingly she was becoming aroused but she didn't expect climax, just wanted him to finish and leave.

Then he withdrew and said, "Spread your cheeks."

"No!"

He slapped her buttock painfully hard. She yelped and reached back to part her buns, felt his thumb probe her anus.

She screamed, "You're hurting me, don't hurt me."

This bastard was raping her like a Mongol. The thumb withdrew to be replaced by the thicker glans of his prick. "Ugh," she groaned, and hammered her fists against the sofa. "You're tearing me," she sobbed, "ripping me up," but he was all the way in and grunting with pleasure as he sawed and thrust fast and hard. The pain was more intense than it had ever been before. He didn't give a shit for her. Why wasn't he satisfied with her cunt? She could hear guttural sounds from his throat. He clenched her hips, uttered a loud growl, and exploded. For a time he was motionless but for the tremors of his engine; gradually it shrank within her. As he withdrew she looked around and saw him dripping the last few drops onto her flesh.

Contemptuously, she thought, he'd used her like an inflatable doll, and for that she hated him. Her rectum was afire, burning. Her teeth clenched, she wasn't going to give him the satisfaction of hearing her moan again as he pulled on his trousers.

Dressed, he turned to her. She was sitting on the sofa, arms crossed over her breasts, rocking back and forth. Her eyes glared stonily, her face was twisted with hatred. "Next time," he warned, "don't resist. Pretend I'm Brand."

When he was gone she tottered to her bathroom medicine cabinet and got out prescription pain pills. After swallowing three she glanced at the haggard face in the mirror. She looked like a bag woman—and that dark bruise on her left cheek . . . painful to the touch. How could she explain it to anyone? To Brand?

She drew a hot tub and sank into it. Presently the pills diminished pain and she began to feel better. What a bastard he was. A gentleman would have seduced her, stimulated her, and made it pleasurable for both. Instead, the barbarian had rammed his fencepost into her ass for his pleasure alone. She hated him for that, for his ignominious, humiliating treatment. For his control over her life. Loathed him and felt utterly helpless to break away.

If the day ever came when she could hurt John she would do so. Without hesitation. If she told Mark maybe Brand would kill him for her. Or perhaps she'd save some poison for John's vodka the next time he came sniffing around for a blow job and a bottom-fuck.

She had never been raped before though she knew that many women were. She was reminded how the Russians raped and murdered when they conquered Berlin, their unleashed animal savagery. John had ravaged her as though she were a German woman and he a Russian soldier, for there was more than pent-up lust in his actions; there was a hint of vengeance, too. Was he Russian? she wondered. What was he? *Who* was he?

Closing her eyes, she eased back while the water's warmth relaxed and soothed her tortured nerves. For a time she wept in self-pity. Other women, she reflected, were able to lead lives of ease and comfort, with servile husbands who did their bidding. Why, she wondered, hadn't she been one of them?

SHE LOVED THE EUPHORIA of a Percodan reverie, the way it unleashed memories that otherwise seldom occurred. Often, she thought herself at the family home in Santa Monica, the white stucco, Mediterranean-style house with its tall clerestory and rolling lawn. There were servants then, before the Crash cost Daddy everything, a French-Canadian nanny, and a Japanese gardener, who lived in the shed with tools, seedlings, and growing plants. She was eleven and had quarreled that day over Derek; her best friend, Lila, had been envious and catty, and they had quarreled. Not wanting to sulk in the house until Daddy and Mummy returned from whatever they'd been doing, she strolled down to the potting shed and looked in to glimpse wall orchids, potted plants, and trailing vines. The shed's warm, humid air let her pretend she was in a jungle.

Taki was sitting on the edge of his cot, legs apart, gripping and stroking his Thing. Its size startled her, for she had only seen boys' Things by peeking inside the club bathhouse from the transom window, and been unimpressed. Taki's eyes were closed, his expression dreamy, and he seemed lost in another world. What he was doing—rubbing his Thing so fast—fascinated her, though she sensed something grown-up and forbidden.

As she watched, his Thing began to spit cream, globs of it that arched to the floor. She thought of a cow giving milk and giggled. Taki's eyes opened and stared at her. The cream was dribbling over his clenched fingers. "Missy," he said and grinned, "you never see porren before?"

"Porren?" She felt stupid.

"Men stuff." He held up his dripping hand. "When too much, gotta go."

Half understanding, she nodded, not knowing what to say.

"Come in, crose door, I show you, okay?"

She closed the door and went toward him staring at his Thing. A tingling sensation flooded her loins. As though she had to make pee-pee.

Taki beckoned her closer and with his dry hand began stroking where Mummy said no one must ever touch. But it increased the warmth in her crotch and she let him lift her dress. Somehow her panties were around her ankles, and his finger was rubbing a certain spot until she gasped with pleasure. He pried her thighs apart, and while she was trembling and shivering to his touch he lowered his head and began tonguing where his fingers had been.

Nothing had ever been more exciting.

Finally, he turned her around and told her to bend over. Then she felt his nose and tongue probing her anus—she knew the word from doctor books—and wondered why he would want to do such a nasty thing. But she was still in the spell of excitement; her knees were jelly and she could hardly stand. She was aware that he was rubbing his Thing again and sounds like moans came from his throat. Was Taki hurting himself? She hoped not; she wanted the pleasure to go on. He drew her onto his lap, and she could feel the stickiness along his Thing as he moved it up and down—not entering her private parts, it was too big, but rubbing the bottom side against them. Then, too soon, it was all over, with Nina swearing never to tell a soul and promising to come back next day.

At school she ached to tell Lila, but she was loyal to Taki and joined him in the shed that afternoon, the second of many. She learned to take his Thing in her mouth and lick and suck it like a lollipop, while he tongued the little fleshy button just above her pee-pee hole. Sometimes he would oil a finger and slide it in her anus, a sensation she grew to like, even though it sometimes made her want to do number two. And she loved watching him harden his Thing, then rub it between her buns until it creamed. When Marie asked about spots on her panties, she said it was ice cream and the nanny never asked again. Taki told her that together they were doing everything that grown-ups did—even Mummy and Daddy—except fucking what he called her twat. That would be dangerous, he explained, because people would find out and she would be shamed. Shame was when you had an accident in your panties and everyone giggled. Or when you stole a pencil and teacher found out.

Taki was no taller than she was, and they could lie together facing, or her behind against his front, and she knew just where he was. His small size kept her unafraid, and his gentleness, the sharing of grown-up secrets, the wonderful feelings he could arouse, bonded her to him until Daddy had no money and let Taki go.

She missed him terribly and rode her bike around looking for him until the day they moved to Covington and left all her friends behind.

Later she learned that Taki could have been sent to jail for "child molesting" even though that would not have been right because she had only done what she wanted to do, with Taki teaching.

Through high school her special knowledge made her feel superior to girl classmates because she understood what boys wanted while they were uncertain how to deal with them. But Nina always knew.

It was the same at Cal Davis after Daddy was promoted in
JCPenney and could afford to send her. Her fondness for sex play was an
open campus secret and she was popular because of it. And though she
didn't graduate—having married a baseball player—she never felt she'd
missed anything at all.

Though the child by Bernie had been a boy, Nina had occasionally
considered how she would react if she learned that a prepubescent
daughter was being violated by a man. Outrage, of course, and the
impulse to kill the ravisher. She regarded her own initiation by Taki as
special, unique, in no way comparable to the trauma a (nonexistent)
daughter might experience at the hands of a lustful male. She recognized the paradox but disallowed it.

As she slowly woke from the dream, Nina realized that John's
sodomizing had brought it on, renewed memories of Taki—who must be
dead by now—and all they had done together in the close, musky
warmth of the old garden shed.

Languorously she dried her body, inserted a Preparation H suppos-
itory where it would do the most good, and plodded off to bed.

She needed a good night's sleep because she had a lot to accomplish before flying from Dulles to Hong Kong—and Mark Brand.

With John's five thousand bucks.

BEIJING

Opportunity came for the prisoner on a night when block guards held a
party. Their shouted remarks told him bottles of rice wine had been
given to one of them, who was sharing in communal fashion. After
listening to their drunken revelry for an hour the prisoner got out the
hidden bonds and tied them into a three-foot cord. He tested it with all
his strength and waited.

Couldn't wait too long, he told himself, because the shift would
change and sober guards arrive. Success depended on a guard with
impaired judgment.

The prisoner began to groan, heard the guards quiet down, and
groaned more loudly. He lay on the mattress, knees to chest, and uttered
a sharp cry of pain. One guard ordered another to find out what was
wrong. The prisoner heard grumbling, then uneven footsteps as a guard

approached his cell. Light played over him. "What is it?" the guard demanded.

"Stomach . . . bleeding . . . take me to doctor," he gasped. "Sick—dying." He groaned again.

The guard grunted disgustedly. "Get up, be a man. Let me see you."

Clenching his coiled rope, the prisoner staggered to the bars, leaned against them. The guard cursed, weaved unsteadily, and got out his keys. He fumbled for the longest one, fitted it into the lock—and stopped. "Maybe—" he began, and turned away.

Quickly the prisoner dropped the cord over his head and jerked back, pulling the guard against the bars. Feet kicked and the guard went limp. Slowly the prisoner lowered the unconscious body, reached out and around, and turned the key. A slight shove and the door opened. Heart pounding, the prisoner listened, but the unseen guards were laughing boisterously. It was safe to move.

The prisoner dragged the guard into his cell, removed the holstered pistol and belt, then stripped off his uniform. It was small for the prisoner but it would have to do. He covered the still-unconscious guard with his ragged clothing, tiptoed to the cell door, and looked around. Three guards were grouped around a table. There were two bottles on the table, empties on the floor.

Turning the other way, the now-uniformed prisoner made for the corridor's far end, unlocked the metal-sheathed door, and went out.

Night. He gulped clean cool air and locked the door behind him, then walked into the courtyard, keeping close to the high wall. He adjusted the cap low on his forehead, so the bill nearly touched his nose. Western eyes were a dead giveaway.

Ahead was an open doorway. He was almost there when he saw a guard seated in a sentry box. The man's head tilted back, a sonorous snore issued from his nose. The prisoner tiptoed past him and crossed a narrow street. Behind him courtyard lights came on, a siren wailed.

The prisoner ducked down the nearest alley to the rear overhang of a noodle shop. He couldn't stop there, even if it was empty, for it was the custom for people to sleep where they worked. Cauldrons had been set on a bench for cleaning. From one he clawed a few dried noodles, scraped grains of rice from another, and wolfed them down. He was weak from exertion but he had to get far from the prison before daylight disclosed him, cross the Yong Ding River, and reach Sanlitun, the diplomatic area. The American embassy was on Kwanghua lu, near the Friendship Store. But first he had to orient himself, find out where he was.

The moon, low in the sky, gave him east-west directions, but because he was unfamiliar with Beijing's skyline he could only guess which way was north. He searched the sky for Polaris, the Dipper, but the stars were too faint. Nearby, a dog barked, inside the shop someone was stirring.

He began walking toward the moon.

Thirteen

Hong Kong

Brand was finishing late breakfast in his room when the phone rang. He answered, hoping it would be Sammy or Eddie with positive news; instead, the caller identified himself as Briggs Dockerty from the consulate and asked if he could come up. "Sure," Brand told him, and hung up.

Dockerty was Hong Kong Base Chief and Brand remembered him from the halls of Langley as a tall, skinny man with a prominent nose and a thin, canine face. When last seen, Dockerty had been an FE Desk trainee just in from the Farm who had yet to prove himself. Apparently, Brand mused, as he drank the last of his coffee, Dockerty had found favor with Darman Gerold, for Hong Kong was a choice assignment.

When Brand opened the door he asked, "Any news of my son?"

"Sorry, sir, not a word—but we're hopeful." Dockerty sat in a cushioned rattan chair and crossed spindly legs. He was wearing a blue-striped seersucker suit, white starched collar, and blue polka-dot tie. Polished black shoes and black stockings. His hands opened and closed nervously.

Brand resumed his chair and gazed at the Base Chief.

"So, why are you here?"

"A headquarters cable directed me to offer assistance. And at morning staff meeting the Consul-General mentioned your son's disappearance." He cleared his throat. "State sent him a rocket."

"What did you know about Peter's mission?"

He cleared his throat again. "Well, I knew someone was going to service the Blue Dragon drop—a Legal Traveler—but he wasn't identified as your son Peter." When Brand said nothing, Dockerty added, "The Blue Dragon's a curio and novelty shop catering to foreigners."

"It's on the burn list now, I trust."

"It is—definitely." He glanced around as though fearful of being overheard.

"It had to be under surveillance," Brand said heavily. "They must have been expecting Peter."

"We don't know that."

"And probably won't until Peter's free to tell the story." He shook his head disgustedly. "You had no Base assets to send there?"

Dockerty smiled bleakly. "You know how it is here—anything we do is by sufferance of the Brits and they don't want to irritate the Chinese. Not with Colony turnover so close at hand."

"What was Peter supposed to pick up?"

"Rolls of undeveloped film."

"From where?"

"Beijing—I guess."

"You don't *know?*"

"Look, I don't process the take, I just pouch the stuff to headquarters." He looked away.

"So it could be good stuff or trash."

Dockerty nodded.

Brand grimaced. "If Peter's harmed because he picked up a roll of worthless information—" He stopped. "But we won't know, will we? Because the Gong An Ju have the film." His eyes narrowed. "And they probably bagged the source as soon as the film was developed. Any thoughts on that?"

"Worst scenario," Dockerty replied, "you're probably right. And my guess is the source was probably a student."

"Lacking high-level access."

"Without significant access," Dockerty agreed, "if we're talking about Central Committee penetration."

"That'll be the day." Brand laughed bitterly. He was on the point of telling the Base Chief about Peter's delivering money and leaflets to a Mainland contact, decided it would only cloud the issue, give Gerold a hook to avoid full responsibility. "Who's the Beijing Station Chief?"

Dockerty cleared his throat again. "He's deep, sir. I'm not able to name him."

"Can't or won't?"

"Not authorized." Brand felt like hitting him. After a deep breath Dockerty said, "The cable told me to remind you your clearance status forbids your going to the Mainland."

"I know that," Brand said roughly, "and I don't need a junior officer to remind me."

"Sorry, sir, just carrying out orders."

Brand eyed him. "Any other orders I should know about?"

Dockerty shifted in his chair. "I—I guess you know Darman Gerold pretty well."

"We've known each other a long time. Why?"

"Makes it easier to tell you about the side channel I got from him." Interested, Brand nodded. "About me?"

"Well," he said uncertainly, "it mentions you by name. You probably know he's had trouble with his kids running away, getting their names in the paper. Fitzhugh and Doreen."

"Fitz and Dory. Go on."

"Doreen ran up big hotel bills in Bangkok and disappeared. Mr. Gerold paid them and alerted Far East Stations to locate her."

"How's that involve me?"

"The cable said if she showed up in Hong Kong I was to notify you—you'd know what to do."

Brand shook his head. "Fantastic. He wants to keep his name out of State and Agency traffic by appointing me truant officer. Well, I doubt she'll come here. Honkers doesn't welcome penniless runaways."

"She might go to Macao or the Mainland."

"Then too bad for Dory," Brand said coldly. "At garden parties the kids ran around making nuisances of themselves but I haven't seen them for years. How old's the girl now?"

"Twenty-three. Five-eight, long blond hair, hundred and twelve pounds—that's from her passport application. The consulate has her photo if you want a copy."

"I suppose she's involved with drugs."

"Used to be, but—"

"In Bangkok she probably spent her money on drugs and stiffed her hotel. It's what kids like her usually do."

"I know," Dockerty said sadly. "Anyway, I thought I better describe the situation to you."

"Being under orders to do so," Brand said with a thin smile. "Briggs, I've got plenty to do without trying to resolve Gerold's domestic problems."

Dockerty leaned forward. "You have contacts here."

"A few old friends from Taiwan," Brand acknowledged.

Dockerty swallowed and his large Adam's apple bobbed. "Special Branch Liaison asked me why you were hanging out with known gangsters."

"Oh? And what did you tell Special Branch Liaison?"

"That I didn't know."

"That's sufficient answer," Brand told him, "and I don't want anyone tailing me, whether Base or Brits. As long as I'm not breaking Colony law what I do and who I see is my own business." He reflected a moment before saying, "I suppose the Brits pulled my name off the airline passenger list."

Dockerty shrugged. "If you were ever declared to MI6 they'd have you in their computers."

"If pressed you can say I'm not an active agent; that should soothe them and absolve you."

The Base Chief nodded. "Oh, something I forgot to mention—she has green eyes. Doreen Gerold, I mean."

Brand grunted. "Like her mother, Darman's first wife. Any reason to think she'll come to Hong Kong?"

"She charged a round-the-world ticket that included HK and Tokyo."

"Well, I hope I don't have to check out the green eyes. I'm confident you can handle the problem without me." With a smile, he got up. "If there's nothing else . . ."

"That's it, sir." Dockerty rose, clearly relieved to be going. Brand showed him out and locked the door, reflecting on the strange coincidence that both he and Gerold were searching for a lost child, though lost for different reasons, and he felt a moment's sympathy for his old antagonist.

He would, of course, help return Gerold's missing daughter in the unlikely event she came to his attention. Not only as a normal human gesture, but because it would place Gerold under obligation to him. It was a degrading game, but one at which Gerold was a skilled and long-time player. So if Dory was in Hong Kong and Special Branch couldn't find her, chances were his old friends could. Especially if the girl was using drugs. Her Asian itinerary and what Brand knew of her past suggested that she was.

He spent the next hour in the hotel's health room, using treadmill, friction bike, and arm and leg weight machines. Then a cold plunge and massage under the skilled hands of a Chinese masseuse, a middle-aged, no-nonsense woman wearing a white cap and loose white frock.

After dressing in street clothes, Brand rode the tram to the Peak and checked for surveillants. In a clearing among mimosa trees Brand sipped jasmine tea and gazed out over Victoria Harbor, where sampans, junks, and walla-wallas plied their trade. Over the decades he had known Hong Kong, the city had grown enormously. Commerce fomented by the Vietnam War had brought about part of the growth (Asian boat people were carefully hidden from view) and where the China National Bank building had once been the island's tallest, it was now topped by a dozen other buildings including several of the world's finest luxury hotels. Under British domination Hong Kong had fattened off the growth economies of Thailand, Singapore, Taiwan, Japan, and Seoul, becoming a lush prize for Beijing after Turnover took place. How the Communists would manage this quintessential capitalist outpost was a question that worried every property owner—including Jimmy Shek.

The harbor's piers and anchorages were crowded with tankers and cargo vessels, and Brand's gaze lifted to Kowloon and the New Territories still hazy with morning mist.

Somewhere beyond the invisible bamboo curtain his only son was imprisoned and Brand reflected that it need never have happened. Pe-

ter's lack of information, his inability to divulge agent names, was sure
to anger his captors even if they believed him, so perhaps optimum hope
lay in a public show trial, then banishment from the Celestial Kingdom.

He paid for his tea, looking around for surveillants, then walked
toward the tram station, where he stopped at a telephone kiosk and
placed a call to Tommy Ning.

T OMMY'S OFFICE WAS in a medium-size godown on Hung Hing Road near
the cargo-handling basin. The main floor was filled with wood and
wicker crates and large bales of fabric. Forklifts moved here and there
as they loaded flatbed trucks. Brand wondered how many of the bales
contained grave-robbed artifacts. Brand watched from Tommy's enclosed, loft-level office while Tommy was on the telephone. Furnishings
were traditional Chinese supplemented by a modern computer console.
The room was air-conditioned against the harbor's high humidity and
soundproofing eliminated engine noise from the floor below. When
Tommy replaced the receiver he said, "That was my man calling from
the Star Ferry terminal, just came over from Canton."

Tensely, Brand leaned forward. "News?"

Tommy nodded. "Over a month ago plainclothes police and Gong
An Ju men arrested a foreigner." He paused. "The Blue Dragon shop
mean anything?"

"It's where the drop was." He felt excitement rise.

"That's where the foreigner was arrested. The place was being
watched. The owner was working for the police."

"Which Peter couldn't know. Where is he? Canton?"

Tommy shook his head. "The foreigner, probably your son, was
kept two days in Canton and then flown under guard to Beijing."

"Shit!" Brand sat back dejectedly. "What else, Tommy? Don't
make me drag it from you."

"Okay. The Canton cop doesn't know where the foreigner is being
held in Beijing, but thinks he has a chance of finding out. Unfortunately,
there's no way of telling how long it will take. See, it's too risky to phone
his Beijing contacts, so he has to go there, make payoffs, and get back to
Canton with whatever he can learn. One other thing, it's likely your son
has already had a secret trial and been sentenced."

"I've been afraid of that."

"But the Central Committee still might decide on a public trial if it suits them. Before that happens is the best chance of freeing Peter. Maybe he can be ransomed now, but later would mean loss of face. Anyway, he'd be stuck away in some reeducation commune where they'd make sure he could never be found."

"So it's a prison break, or nothing."

"Afraid so, Mark. And the sooner the better." He got up and went over to a lacquered coromandel cabinet, opened it, and took out a stone jug and two cups.

He filled both with mao-tai and handed one to Brand, who said, "For now everything depends on locating Peter. But until we have that information we've some time to plan ahead."

They touched cups and drank. Tommy said, "I was thinking the same thing. But it's one job to free him, another to get him out of China. That could be a lot tougher."

Brand sipped moodily. "How many men will it take?"

"Four experienced burglars might be able to do it. With bribe money, transportation, and weapons. Money's the easiest to lay on. They'll have to buy or steal a truck on the Mainland, same with weapons. Beijing's what—a hundred miles from the coast. Hijack a sampan and sail across to Inchon."

Brand considered. "That's about five hundred miles of open sea, Tommy, with aircraft and patrol boats looking for us every mile of the way. I'd rather hijack a plane."

He shook his head. "They expect hijackings, had so many of them they've got guards around every—wait a minute. *You're* not thinking of going?"

"Of course I am."

"That's crazy, Mark!"

"What kind of father wouldn't want to take part in rescuing his son? So, I'm going, count on it."

"I don't want to burn prayer scrolls and incense at your grave. Maybe Peter's grave, too."

"Unless we get him out he's already as good as buried. I have to be with him however it turns out."

Tommy sighed, shrugged fatalistically. Brand said, "I've got papers that'll get me to Beijing. I'll meet the team there and do the job."

"Mark, listen to me. How long since you were on the Mainland?"

"Forty years," he admitted.

"Security is tight everywhere, even in villages. Any men I pick can move freely but you'll attract instant attention."

"Why should I? Foreign tourists and businessmen are commonplace. Tourism is off since the Tiananmen massacre. Hell, they'll welcome me."

"So you can get to Beijing, but like I said it's a hell of a lot tougher to get out. And for that run from prison to the coast your son will need papers."

"I figure my brothers can provide them."

"Yeah, we've got our own press and forgers."

"Then that problem's solved." From his wallet he got out the photo of Peter he always carried, handed it to Tommy. "British passport?"

"Swedish might be better. Swedes trade their passports here for dope. British tourists hang on to theirs because replacement takes so long. Anyway, leave it to me." He studied the photo for a moment, then placed it in an envelope.

Tommy's mention of drugs and passports reminded Brand of Doreen Gerold, so he told Tommy about the girl and why he hoped to help restore her to her father. Tommy listened without comment until Brand began to describe Dory, then Tommy said, "Wait a minute, I'm not the guy you need."

"Who is?"

"Sammy." Tommy Ning picked up the telephone, dialed, and after a pause spoke rapidly. To Brand he said, "Sammy says you should come see him."

"Where is he?"

"At his studio. Kowloon side."

"A film studio?"

"Yeah, motion pictures. He makes them for Oriental exhibitors. Big money and it's legit."

"Like Run Run Shaw?" Brand visualized Bruce Lee-type martial arts movies and the kind of endless romantic films that were shown to Oriental audiences around the world, including Hawaii and San Francisco.

Tommy smiled slyly. "Mostly legit, Mark. Anyway, Sammy's expecting you. My driver will have you there in half an hour. Meanwhile,

I'll start putting together a rescue team. I'll make it three, in case of . . . injuries."

In the air-conditioned comfort of Tommy's stretch Mercedes Brand rode from the cross harbor tunnel's entrance by the Royal Hong Kong Yacht Club under the harbor to Kowloon peninsula. The driver took Hong Chong highway avoiding street crowds and marketplaces and turned west on Argyle Road, heading into the Mong Kok section with its narrow streets and busy market stalls. The limousine moved slowly onto Fuk Tsun Street, and after two more blocks stopped beside a large white-painted building whose walls were windowless. A black sign with gold letters proclaimed Mong Kok Films in English and Chinese. The driver got out and pressed a button beside the entrance door. In a few moments the door opened and the driver spoke with the doorkeeper, gesturing at Brand. He came back, opened Brand's door, and said he should go inside.

The doorkeeper, an elderly man, wore wispy white whiskers and the loose black garb of a Hakka peasant. Bowing, he greeted Brand respectfully and led him behind the flats of a sound stage where filming was under way, then to a corridor and up a flight of stairs and along another corridor, one side of which was glassed. Looking down, Brand could see four active sets with their kliegs, reflectors, cameras, and crews. The nearest had kung fu combat among five men; adjacent was a rural scene where an elderly farm couple was struggling with heavy burdens. The third stage represented an ornate throne room: emperor and empress surrounded by courtiers. Stage four's set was much simpler: a round, revolving bed on which two muscular men copulated vigorously with a naked Chinese girl. Then Brand was past the overlook and waiting while the doorkeeper knocked on a carved wood door.

A smartly dressed Chinese girl opened it, bowed to Brand, and said, "Please come in, sir. Mr. Lu is expecting you."

Unlike Tommy's godown office, Sammy's was patterned in black and white, stainless-steel furniture, and black onyx. Floor tiles alternated black and white, and window drapes were deep black.

"Well," said Sammy as the girl left them, "whaddya think, brother?"

"You've gone Hollywood—all the way."

"You like it, eh? Me, too. The guy I got it from had great taste." He rose from the depths of a padded black executive chair and gripped Brand fraternally. "Drink?"

"Why not?" As Sammy poured from a mao-tai jug Brand asked, "How'd you get into the movie business?"

"The guy who started the studio lost his nuts when the BCCI branch bank folded." Sammy shrugged. "I took the place off his hands. It was a good deal for both of us."

Brand grimaced. "Better for you."

"I've got the studio, haven't I? Now, what's this about some girl you're looking for?"

After identifying Doreen as the daughter of an old friend, Brand described her—including green eyes—and said she was a drug user. Frowning, Sammy said, "We use three, four Western chicks a month, Mark, mostly experienced ones, reliable, know what I mean?"

Brand nodded, he did.

"A girl needing hop to keep her spirits up can slow production, make a mess of it. Strict shooting schedule, see? Average flick takes a week, and I try to keep every stage busy. When lights are out no money's being made." He refilled his cup but Brand declined. "Since I took over the studio I got into something the poor bastard who organized it never thought of—the videocassette market. We duplicate from the edited master and deal direct with wholesalers and exhibitors. Overseas markets can't get enough." He smiled in satisfaction. "So we need new faces, new skin, to keep audiences buying and coming."

"I assume porno film production isn't exactly encouraged by the Crown Commissioner."

"Very little is—except banking. But, hell, where there's a demand someone's going to supply product. And unlike the Mafia that makes skin flicks for Westerners, I've got a good share of the Oriental market and it's expanding all the time."

"It's long been said the business of Hong Kong is business."

He nodded. "Understand, I don't find players and cast productions. I give budgets to line producers and they turn out their little gems."

Brand asked, "Where do the Western females come from?"

"A little advertising, and girls come over here to apply. Or some studio-connected guy will spot a good-looker in a bar or restaurant— they look for Swedes, Danes, German girls—blondes are what Orientals like seeing in action. Big boobs preferred since our Oriental women don't have naturally great breastworks."

"What I'd like you to do, Sammy, is circulate Dory's description among your employees, let me know if they spot anyone resembling her."

"Is she good-looking?"

"Her mother was, but I haven't seen Dory in, oh, at least ten years. If she's in Hong Kong she may not be too hard to find—she'll be low on money, maybe broke, and looking for drugs."

"And maybe in the morgue," Sammy grunted. "That could be a hundred Western chicks any day in Hong Kong—or night. But, sure, I'll pass out her description."

"Let's make it interesting for the lookers—offer a reward. Say ten thousand HK." About twelve hundred dollars. He got out his wallet.

"Ten thousand should do it—and put that away; your money's no good here. What're friends for?" He moved over to a table on which lay a thick three-ring binder. "Long's you're here, why not go through these photos? Maybe the girl's come through here."

The majority of the color glossies showed blond women naked from the hips up. Most were well endowed, but some of the girls looked no more than teenage. There was a scattering of full-length nudity, muff-shots and spreads typical of skin magazines. As Brand turned the viewing sheets Sammy said, "Any appeal to you I can probably get her to your room in a couple of hours."

"Thanks, I'll remember."

"No charge," Sammy added, and answered a ringing phone at his desk.

Of the hundred-odd females in the casting book, only six had blond hair; of them two wore dyke cuts and among the other four Brand could find no resemblance to Doreen Gerold. Closing the book he said, "Probably hopeless, but I promised to try."

"A promise is a promise," Sammy acknowledged. "We'll see what turns up."

"I'll send over a copy of Dory's passport photo in the next day or so." He went back to his chair, decided not to stay. "Is Cheong Wing-dah's gallery this side?"

"He's got two or three along Salisbury and Chatham roads, hotel district. But his showplace is Victoria side. Connaught Road near the

Chinese Club. If you want to go there, tell the driver." He eyed Brand. "Going to check on Mary Chen?"

"I've thought of it."

After thanking Sammy, Brand retraced his steps, slowing as he passed the overlook windows. One semidark set was being struck. On another the director was rehearsing the actor-emperor, and four different, naked actors were coupling on the revolving bed. Outside, the sunlight made him squint, then he was in the big, cool Mercedes and telling the driver to take him to Connaught Road.

As the limousine dipped down into the tunnel Brand asked himself if seeing Ling-mei after so many years was sensible, and reasoned that it was not. She had much to rebuke him for and she would have long felt that he had used her, then casually abandoned her. What she would not have comprehended, he realized, was his own psychological problems when they first met. He had been abandoned by his wife, the mother of his child, and was trying to survive a spiritual void. Had Ling-mei been older, more worldly, she might have been able to rationalize their affair without feeling exploited, profaned. And he admitted to himself, as he had not for years, that seducing her had been an act of unpardonable selfishness. Not only had he violated her body, he had destroyed her trust.

Even so, prudent or not, he wanted to see her again, learn about her life since they waved good-bye that long distant morning at the airport. There was no way now to set things right or even try. All he could do was apologize, ask for a forgiveness she had every right to deny.

BEIJING

NO LONGER A PRISONER, Peter Brand traveled through dark alleys and plot gardens, strengthened with the realization of freedom and flushed with new hope. He knew he would have to shed the ill-fitting uniform if he was to avoid detection before reaching the embassy, and so as he moved furtively by narrow back streets he scanned dwellings for line-hung clothing. Just before dawn he found what he was looking for: a man's blue cotton blouse and drawstring pants. He got into them and discarded the uniform at the next trash bin. Then moved on.

His plan was to find a hiding place before daylight made travel too hazardous, hole up until nightfall, and continue on to the embassy compound. Inside its gates would be Marine guards; outside, Chinese security police, a final obstacle to freedom.

Hunger was increasingly a factor. Without even a single five-fen coin in his pocket he could buy no rice, soup, noodles, or meat; to survive he would have to steal. He was reluctant to resort to theft, the Chinese having so little to sustain themselves from day to day, but his need had never been greater. By now his entire sensory apparatus was so finely tuned that he was aware of small gradations in dark and light, of an alley current slightly warmer than the last, of a rat's scurrying, a distant whistle, the faint bleat of a riverboat's horn. His ankles and knees ached from the unaccustomed strain of walking, his feet felt raw against the coarse straw soles. Without knowing where he was he decided to try to reach the Yong Ding River, hide and rest under a dock or inverted skiff. River folk were incurious and companionable, he thought, and he might be able to find a fish to chew on; its liquids would give him needed strength.

He had to keep going, stay ahead of his pursuers, for what he had learned of them—painfully—was that they would never give up. Already his cell-block guards would have been denounced if not executed for his escape.

His toe stubbed and lifted an object that clanged against the nearby wall. Peter scooped it up quickly and found it an old kitchen knife, the tip of whose rusty blade was broken off. The haft was intact, though, and the blade edge sharp enough to cut rope or sever a throat. He thrust it under the waist drawstring next to his skin and moved on.

The moon was no longer visible, but all around him roosters were crowing to signal dawn. He had, he thought, maybe half an hour to find shelter before people took to the streets. Then, keeping to the wall, he saw a tree branch projecting just above his head. The branch had come over the wall, and as he paused he saw something hanging from it. Fruit! A mango! Although it was not fully ripe, Peter severed the stem and circled the thick skin with his blade as he walked on. Before pulling the halves apart he licked juice from the skin, then tore out chunks of meat as voraciously as a starved monkey.

The unripe fruit, he thought, might bring on diarrhea, but its benefits far outweighed loose bowels.

In his bloodstream the mango's sugar produced a sort of euphoria that bolstered hope and let his mind turn to La-li and his father. Without warning tears filled his eyes, streamed down his cheeks. He wiped them away with his sleeve and lengthened his stride, less afraid now of exhaustion.

His nostrils first detected the river by its unmistakable scent of mold and decay, then he heard the rattle of oars in oarlocks, a voice lifted in hoarse, chanting song. Aware of boatmen ahead, Peter slowed and took an alley toward the sound.

The *hutung* ended at a sloping riverbank, and in the stream he could see the yellow glow of stern-hung lanterns as fishing boats moved onto the tide.

On hands and knees he crawled forward, glancing left and right for cover, saw only wisps of river grass that ended as the bank slanted downward into gooey mud. Then lantern light played briefly across the end of a sagging, broken-down pier. At its bank end he glimpsed a patchwork of slats behind which he could lay up if no one looked closely. It was the only refuge he'd found and he had to reach it before being seen. And it had the advantage of proximity to boats, one of which he could steal after dark.

If he survived the day.

On elbows and knees he crawled like an infiltrator toward the pier ruin forty yards away. It was slow, painful going and he feared that in the growing number of boatmen one would spot him and raise an outcry. So he ignored the pain of rock bruises in knees and elbows and crawled doggedly on.

He was almost there when he heard a sound behind him, higher on the bank. A sibilant voice whispered, "What are you doing here?"

Slowing, he turned and looked up, saw a woman holding a shallow basket. Staring down at him.

His hand gripped the haft of his knife.

Fourteen

AFTER RELEASING THE LIMOUSINE Brand walked slowly past the display windows of Celestial Galleries on the chance that Mary might be visible on the floor. The gallery was unusual in two ways that caught Brand's notice: its street fronting was at least fifty feet wide—in a city where prime real estate is valued at thousands of dollars a foot; and the gallery's interior was deep, spacious, and uncluttered. He passed the windows and paused beside the Chinese Club entrance.

Should he go back and enter the gallery? If Mary was there would she recognize him? What would he say?

More importantly, what would *she* say?

His hands clenched and unclenched; his palms were damp. Finally, he decided on a second look. Hell, he'd gone this far . . . inevitably he had to come to terms with the past, and it might as well be now, for he realized that he might never have another chance.

After mounting two low entrance steps Brand gripped a gold dragon handle and pulled on the thick glass door. It swung easily, and as he entered he felt the coolness of the inner atmosphere.

The interior was two stories high and indirectly lighted. Glass display cases had individual lighting to enhance jade and smaller artifacts of porcelain and cloisonné. But the eye-catching exhibits were mounted on spaced stands: a life-size terra-cotta military mandarin of the Han Dynasty, a patinaed bronze ritual vessel with a water-bird motif, a large Tang Buddha in the lotus position, whose polished metal gave off a coppery-gold glow, and a terra-cotta horse saddled, armored, and caparisoned for battle.

There were two couples in the gallery—Westerners by dress and appearance—one couple admiring a slim jade vase, the other couple seemed awed by the soft glow of a translucent green porcelain vase. In another venue Brand would have assumed these objets d'art were forgeries or replicas, but knowing what he did of Cheong Wing-dah's sources, he believed them authentic museum pieces whose value he could not begin to calculate.

Standing at an unobtrusive distance from the couples was a tall Chinese girl in a simple red-green cheongsam and matching slippers. Her hands were folded before her in a way that bespoke inner calm, and when she glanced back at Brand he caught his breath, for she was one of the most beautiful young Oriental women he had ever seen. Her skin was the shade of fresh ivory, her nose small and straight—not splayed as so many were—and her symmetrical lips were as brilliantly red as her cheongsam. Her face was almond-shaped, cheeks slightly concave, wisps of dark hair artfully arranged across her forehead. Lifting one finger tacitly signaled Brand she would attend him when she could. As her face turned away he realized that her eyes were untypical and lacked the epithelial fold. She'd had the cosmetic operation so popular in the Orient, he surmised, a fad resulting from exposure to Western movies and beauty magazines. Even so, the girl's features reminded him of Ling-mei's. She moved toward the nearest couple who nodded and spoke in French. With a smile she led them to a table and prepared a bill of sale. While she was writing, the other couple passed by and nodded appreciation before leaving. Brand occupied himself at a glass cube within which lay three matching bronze daggers, blades half-drawn from their ancient, ornate sheaths.

His attention was drawn to a pair of large animals carved in jadeite, and as he studied their marvelous craftsmanship a voice behind him said, "They're mythical representations."

"Oh?" Turning, he faced the salesgirl. "Tell me about them."

"*Xie chi* is the standing one, the crouched figure is called *qi lin.*"

"I see. And how old are they? Any idea?"

"The archaeologists who uncovered them estimated at least a thousand years," she said in fluid syllables.

"And their provenance?"

"Bianjing. If you're interested I can show you on a map."

"That's all right, afraid I'm a looker not a buyer." He paused. "Actually, I was hoping to see Chen Ling-mei. Is she here?"

The girl hesitated. "Do you have a transaction pending with her?"

"No—I'm someone she knew in Taipei—many years ago."

One fingertip touched her lips. "And your name?"

"Mark Brand. Yours?"

"Juli."

After he repeated the name she said, "It's Anglicized from Chu-li," and smiled charmingly. "If you like I'll mention you to Madame Ling-mei. Where can you be reached, Mr. Brand?"

"The Manchu."

"And will you be in Hong Kong long?"

"Probably not."

"What a shame." She fingered a single-strand pearl necklace. "There are many demands on Madame's time. This gallery is only one of her interests."

"Surely an important one. I remember when she assisted her father at the Taipei museum. Splendid background for dealing in antiquities."

"Taipei," she murmured. "When she was very young."

"We were young," Brand replied, "and time passes relentlessly."

"Like an unending torrent," she agreed, glided to the table, and gave him an engraved business card. "Even if you buy nothing you are quite welcome to return. And time permitting I would be glad to tell you the history of some of our offerings."

"I'd like that," Brand told her. "Perhaps I'll stop by again." She did not offer her hand or see him to the door, but watched him leave and walk down Connaught Street. As he vanished from sight her expression changed. She turned and went rapidly to the gallery's far wall, pressed an electronic lock, and opened a staircase door.

As she entered the second-floor office she said, "You had a visitor."

Chen Ling-mei turned from the one-way aperture through which she had been viewing the gallery floor. "I saw him."

"His name is Brand. Said he knew you in Taipei and wanted to see you again. Do you remember him?"

Ling-mei went slowly to an upholstered Chinese chair and sat down. "I remember him," she said tightly.

"He seemed pleasant. Will you see him?"

Ling-mei looked down at her hands, then at Chu-li before replying. "Perhaps. But I must think it over. So many years . . ."

For a few moments Chu-li said nothing. Then briskly, "Back to business. That French couple bought the Jin vase, you'll be glad to know."

Ling-mei managed a smile. "You have become an excellent sales-woman—but I hardly need tell you that." She replaced a strand of hair behind an ear.

"The vase sold itself, Mother—as many things do. What will I display to replace it?"

Ling-mei waved a hand distractedly. "I'll think of something, find something suitable."

"What's not displayed can't be sold."

"Soon," her mother conceded. "Don't hurry me, child. And the order from that Osaka toy-maker?"

"Packed and shipped, Mother. Don't worry over details. That's what I'm supposed to do."

Ling-mei sighed. "And you do it very well, daughter. Despite university you remained responsible—and practical."

"Like yourself." She bent over and kissed her mother's forehead. "*Must* I attend Father's banquet tonight?"

"You must. It's more business than social. Mainland associates, important people—and men from Bangkok and Singapore."

Her mouth twisted in distaste. "With their whores? It's insulting, and I despise the custom."

Again her mother sighed. "You were in Europe too long, daughter. You must not forget the ways of the Orient."

Irritably, Chu-li spat, "The ways of the Orient signify submissive women, female slaves, and I won't be one of them." Abruptly she left the office and her mother shrugged resignedly. Then she looked through the aperture again and saw her daughter emerge below in the gallery in time to greet a plump, brown-skinned woman in a purple dress of watered silk and a large, ornate hat that could have been discarded by the Queen Mother. The wife of some Latin dictator or drug dealer, Ling-mei decided, returned to her desk and covered her face with her hands.

Brand, she thought as tears welled in her eyes. Mark, my love. Here after all these years. How did you find me? Why?

AT JOHNNY SHEK'S RESTAURANT Brand ordered braised prawns in sweet-and-sour sauce, lo mein noodles with sauteed vegetables, and a tankard of Heineken's. While he was enjoying late lunch Johnny slid onto the banquette and said, "Food okay?"

"Great."

"How are things going?"

"Slowly." He swallowed noodles and sipped beer. "You didn't tell me Sammy makes porno films."

"Didn't think it was important." From a waiter he took a tankard like Brand's. Before drinking he said, *"Ting hao."*

"It's not important—you're right—but I was surprised."

"You saw the Mong Kok studio?"

Brand nodded, bit into a large prawn that was cooked to perfection. After swallowing he said, "I've learned my son was arrested in Canton by the Gong An Ju and taken to Beijing."

Johnny set elbows on the table and leaned forward. "Tried and sentenced?"

"We're trying to find out."

"Listen, Mark, if you need money for bribes, anything . . ." He left the offer unfinished.

"Thanks, Johnny. I've got enough for now." How much would it finally take? he wondered, though no price was too great for Peter's freedom. Morosely, he gazed at his nearly empty plate. "Guess I'll be around longer than I thought."

"Things move slowly on the Mainland, you know."

"Yeah. I went to Cheong Wing-dah's gallery—very impressive place."

"Highest prices in Hong Kong—and a lot of the stuff is authentic." He eyed Brand. "See Mary?"

"She wasn't there," he said, remembering the stunningly beautiful salesgirl. Effortlessly she had exuded a magnetism that disturbed him, and he resolved not to think of her again. More than likely Chu-li was one of Cheong's concubines, but she was also a considerable asset to the gallery. Multilingual, sophisticated, and knowledgeable—an extraordinary young woman. For Peter, he thought, she would make a perfect mate, but his son was already committed to La-li and scheduled for fatherhood.

Briefly he considered telephoning La-li, but realized he had nothing to convey that would ease her concern. His father would supply her with money, medical and spiritual advice when she needed those things.

Johnny said, "If you won't take money, I can let you have a gun."

Brand shook his head. "If the cops found it on me I'd be jailed and deported, but—"

"Knife, then?" From his pocket he brought out a spring-loaded switchblade and pressed the release button. The black matte blade shot out of the handle. "Take it, Mark, you might need it." He restored the blade and passed the knife to Brand. The black rubberized handle was knurled and indented for holding. Brand thanked him and dropped the weapon in a pocket.

A waiter bent over beside Johnny and whispered something. Johnny nodded, rose, and said, "Before you leave Honkers, let me know, will you?"

"Sure. And thanks for everything."

"Wish I could do more."

Brand finished his meal and tried to pay for it, but the waiter refused his money. Brand gave a sizable tip and left the restaurant. From a pay phone he called the consulate and asked Briggs Dockerty to send copies of Doreen's passport photo to his room.

" 'Bout an hour," the Base Chief told him. "Uh—got a lead?"

"Possibly."

Hot and perspiring from walking back to the Manchu, Brand took a long shower, dried off, and stretched out on the bed to relax while reading the *Manchester Guardian.* Eyes heavy, he dozed until knocking on the door roused him. A messenger from the consulate verified his name and handed him a plain envelope. Brand opened it at the writing table and took out four photographs. Studying them under light he saw the face of a young woman with shoulder-length blond hair and pale skin. Dory resembled her mother more than her father, he reflected, and that was to her advantage; though if she was an addict her appearance had probably deteriorated.

From the desk drawer he got out a hotel envelope and addressed it to Sammy Lu, Mong Kok Films, Fuk Tsun Street, Kowloon. He placed three prints in the envelope, the fourth in his wallet, and called down to the concierge for a messenger.

After paying the boy Brand returned to the bed telling himself he had done what he could for Darman Gerold and his wayward daughter, read for a while, and slept until dark.

Before dressing, he emptied his jacket pockets, noticing the card Chu-li had given him. Cheong Chu-li was engraved in English and

Chinese, telling him that she was not Cheong's concubine but his daughter. By Mary? he wondered, and considered inviting the girl to dinner; in relaxed surroundings she might tell him more about Madame Ling-mei, as she called her. Or she might not. Evasiveness was an Oriental art. Anyway, it was late for a dinner invitation, and he had only her gallery phone number. Maybe some other time, he told himself, though by now Mary must know he was in Hong Kong and where. He had taken the initial step and it was up to her if she cared to see him. He couldn't force a meeting; that would risk embarrassment with her husband. Better to leave things as they were.

After dressing, Brand considered dining in Aberdeen on the far side of the island. The harbor was crowded with floating restaurants and the sampans that caught their fish. Getting there meant a half-hour taxi ride over the island's steep spine but you could select your meal from a tank and have it prepared to order. Alternatively he could eat Chinese in some nearby restaurant or go to the Manchu dining room. On principle, Brand avoided hotel cuisine so it was Aberdeen or the street.

He was reaching a decision when someone knocked on the door. Thinking it might be Sammy Lu, Brand opened the door and stood back.

His caller held a large basket of flowers in one hand, a champagne bucket in the other. Startled, he took the basket and saw a familiar face.

"Surprise!" Nina Kenton caroled, and stepped in.

BEIJING

SEEING PETER'S KNIFE, THE old woman shrank back. "Do not hurt me," she pleaded.

"Then be quiet." He beckoned her close. Mumbling, she knelt beside him. "Are you ill? What are you doing here, young man?"

"I'm sick, need food, a place to rest." He tried to keep his tone balanced between begging and commanding; he knew and feared what was in her power to do to him, this simple old peasant woman.

She peered closer, becoming an easy target for his knife. *"Aiyee!"* she cried in a muffled voice. "You are not Chinese yet you speak as one of us. How can this be?"

"Help me, grandmother, take me to safety and I will explain." Glancing around he saw the dancing lights the fishermen carried on poles to light their way. Soon they would need no lanterns; already the haze above the river was turning gray. "Quickly," he told her. "We must go quickly, or—"

Her mouth tightened, then she stuffed grasses in her pockets and inverted the shallow basket on his head. "When you rise, stoop over," she ordered. "Pretend you are blind—I will lead you."

Slowly Peter got to his knees, extended his arm, and let her take his hand. Hers was like coarse sandpaper. Then he was on his feet following on her left as they moved to the crest of the bank and away from the fishing piers. Her straw pannier made an adequate peasant hat, he thought, and anyone seeing them from a distance would think them what they were pretending to be.

She took a packed earth trail and began humming a nursery song Peter remembered from his amah. He hummed along, too, and that brought a backward glance of surprise. "You *are* Chinese!" she exclaimed and grinned happily.

The trail slanted away from the river and toward a copse of tall bamboo where it ended. "Follow me," she said, and moved among thick trunks until in a small clearing Peter could see a hut of mud and wattle. To one side of it chickens scratched behind a woven bamboo fence. A cardboard carton formed a rabbit hutch: inside it the old woman strewed her grasses.

"Come." She gestured him inside, lifted a dented kettle from atop a baked-clay oven, and made tea. Ignoring the heat Peter drank gratefully, collapsed into a chair made from thin crating, and smiled weakly.

After sipping tea the old woman asked, "Are you a criminal?"

"A fugitive."

"From the police?"

He nodded. "And the Gong An Ju."

Fear flickered across her features. Peter said, "Don't be afraid, grandmother, if they catch me I'll never tell."

"I am not afraid," she said harshly, "of *them.*"

Her manner, her accent, and unexpected defiance told Peter that his savior was no mere peasant. Later, before he left, they might exchange confidences, but for the moment he busied himself wolfing cold rice from a bowl she had brought him unasked. "Fill your belly," she told him, "a man needs strength to carry on." A slice of bean curd was next, and while he was eating it she went to the chicken yard and brought back three eggs. After breaking them she added bean sprouts and fried the omelet in peanut oil. It was the first real protein he had eaten in weeks, and unwillingly he felt tears stream down his cheeks. He washed it all down with more unsweetened tea and sat back.

The old woman pointed to a blanketed straw mattress in a corner raised on duckboards from the dampness of the earthen floor. "Sleep," she told him and began washing utensils in an old dented basin. "No one comes here. If anyone should, I will know and wake you."

Uncertainly he eyed her. Had she helped him out of fear of his knife? Or was she a selfless Samaritan who spoke the truth?

Outside it was too light to return to the pier end and hide, too light now to steal a boat and float downstream. He had no place to go, no alternative to her offer. Thanking her, he got up and shuffled to the mattress on painful feet. Before sleep, as he lay there, he felt her remove his straw sandals and begin cleansing his feet with a warm wet rag. Then exhaustion mixed with relief surged over him in a dark wave and he knew nothing.

Fifteen

HONG KONG

"SURPRISE IS RIGHT," BRAND SAID, stepping back and closing the door behind Nina. He was furious at her but decided to play it differently. So he kissed her and placed the champagne bucket on a table. "You look wonderful," he told her. "And tonight I was feeling lonely and sorry for myself. Suddenly you change everything."

"Darling, if you'll pop the champagne I'll forgive you for coming without me. That was a very naughty thing to do."

"No," he said as he toweled the magnum dry, "this can be a very dangerous city and I didn't want you exposed."

"But we'll be together, won't we?" Catlike, she rubbed against him.

"Not when I'm in the less savory sections of the city. Ahhh—" He twisted out the cork. "Glasses, quick, in the loo." She hurried off and returned with tumblers. "Not elegant," he said, pouring, "but practical." Their glasses clinked and they drank.

"Ohhh, that was good!" She licked foam from her lips. "More, please."

When her glass was full she asked, "Any news of Peter?"

"None," he lied. "I'm still looking. Now, how did you find me?"

"Very simple—the tourist office called around and here I am, in a splendid suite just down the hall. This is a *good* hotel."

"And I can't tell you how glad I am to see you." He didn't dare, and was grateful for what the FBI had told him. That knowledge would keep him a long step ahead of her designs, help neutralize this treacherous succubus. He placed his arm around her shoulders, nuzzled the side of her neck. "Being together is marvelous."

She shivered. "Yes . . . wonderful. Oh, Mark, I tried to get the connecting room but it's taken." She frowned petulantly, then brightened. "Why not move in with me?"

"Hmmm. Great invitation, but I've put out feelers and I get messages here—some from very disreputable people."

"Oh, well," she said resignedly, "all we have to say at sundown is 'your place or mine?' "

"Right." He looked around. "Not spacious, but—"

"Oh, first night I need to unpack, find filmy things." Her expression was coquettish. "You won't mind?"

"Hardly." He took her hand and drew her to the sofa. Did she have a special reason for wanting him there? Interesting question, and he'd stay alert for clues. After sipping again he smacked his lips. "Cordon Rouge—must have cost you a fortune."

"Duty-free shop at Dulles. Besides, I want only the best for you, darling—you mean so much to me."

Double entendre? "And how much is that?"

"Why don't you guess," she teased. "I'm here, aren't I, after following you halfway around the world? Doesn't that speak volumes?"

"It does," he agreed, "and I feel pretty humble."

"That *all* you feel?"

He brushed the back of his hand across her nipples. Nina shivered and closed her eyes. Good, he thought, let her think I'm cunt-struck; she'll be less watchful. Setting aside his glass, he drew down her shoulder straps and freed her breasts. After fondling them he kissed, then licked the nipples. Her body shuddered and her thighs parted. Harshly she said, "Don't do that, lover, unless you're going to follow through."

"But I am." He pivoted her body back on the sofa, drew up her legs, and pulled off her panties. Then he opened his fly.

He fucked her fiercely, bitter at the knowledge this was what she was being paid to do. A freebie from the KGB, he thought, so take advantage of it.

She climaxed in a frenzy of clawing hands and kicking legs, shrieks and murmurs, and he thought that if she were simulating orgasm she was a true artist.

She had him finish in her mouth—a gesture of love, she told him—and then he held her in his arms for a while, stroking her hair and kissing her nose and chin. "Mark," she murmured, "you're so tender . . . I *am* glad I came."

"I'm glad you came so we could come together," he joked, at which she got up and went unsteadily to the loo.

Clothing replaced, hair combed, she joined him for more champagne. Taking his arm she drew him to the window and gazed over Victoria Harbor. "What a truly marvelous city," she said, drawing in breath. "The lights, the moving boats . . . all so incredible."

"That's the Mainland over there," he said soberly.

"I know." She kissed his cheek. "You believe Peter is there . . . somewhere?"

"Don't know what to believe. I've checked out some reports but when they're run down they turn into fabrications. Funny about Orientals, they say what they think you want to hear—not what actually is."

"Why in the world do they do that?"

"It's a way of being polite."

"How strange . . . I should think it the other way 'round."

"Which is why East and West have so much difficulty understanding each other."

She nodded thoughtfully. "With nothing to go on, you're surely not planning to look for Peter"—she gestured—"over there."

"That would be extremely foolish. No, I'd need verifiable information before I tried anything like that. But I've talked with the consulate and they say they're doing everything possible to locate Peter, Special Branch, too. And," he added, "word is out among old Chinese friends. So, I'm reasonably confident I'll have a fix on him before long."

"Meanwhile," she said, gazing up at the sky, "we have time together. Time to be ourselves, away from the phoniness of Washington."

He forced a smile. "Thought you liked all that Washington pretense."

"What's a single woman to do unless she goes to balls, dinner parties, and diplomatic receptions? I only met you because I was out dining with friends, not moping in my apartment."

Repeating the standard lie. He was growing to despise her. "My lucky night."

"And mine." She pressed his hand. "We've been together ever since." Facing him, she said, "I wasn't sure it would last any time at all, Mark, but now I don't want to let you go." She kissed him. "Ever."

"My thought, too," he said in a tone of longing. "Now let's have dinner and make a night of it. Celebrate."

Nina smiled enthusiastically. "Some special place of yours, Old China Hand?"

"The hotel dining room; the food is beyond compare." And it would spare him her duplicitous talky-talk riding over the Peak to Aberdeen and back. Instead, he'd order Westernized Chinese food for her, a bottle of plum wine to share, then back to her suite for the night. "I should shave," he said, "and try a fresh shirt."

"And I need to make repairs, unpack, and hang things. Half an hour?"

"I'll be knocking."

After showing her out, he felt suppressed rage at her for having followed and found him. From now on she was going to be an albatross around his neck—unless he came up with some way to rid himself of the bitch.

Beijing

It was dusk when Peter woke; he had slept through the entire day. From his pallet he watched her at the earthen stove while she tended a boiling pot. He sat up, and sensing his motion, the old woman turned to him. "You slept well," she remarked. "How do you feel?"

"Better, a lot better." He got up shakily, feeling pain from sore, stiff joints. "I have no money," he told her, "nothing to reward your kindness."

"Reward?" She shrugged. "Do not speak of such a thing." She peered at the boiling pot. "The rice will soon be ready."

Reflexively, his mouth began to water as it had when he heard the cell-block rice cart coming. He moved toward her and said, "Why are you helping me, grandmother? You don't know why I'm wanted, what crimes—"

She held up one hand, gestured at a small radio. "The government says a Westerner escaped prison where he was sentenced for espionage and crimes against the State. Is that true?"

"Part of it." He bent over the pot and inhaled the fragrant steam. "So you know my name."

"It was not mentioned. But if you are an enemy of the regime, that is enough for me to know." She smiled slyly. "I loathe the government, too."

"The broadcast described me?"

"It did. Here, hold our bowls while I fill them."

Facing each other in squatting position, they ate silently until she said, "Did you kill a prison guard?"

"I don't think so, didn't wait to find out."

"Doesn't matter," she said, "the broadcasts are filled with lies."

His fingers cleansed the inside of his eating bowl for the final grains. After licking them, he said, "My name is Peter. May I know yours?"

"Ah-peng," she replied, "and to see me as I am you would not think I was once a teacher, with a husband and a son."

He shook his head. "Almost from the first I realized you were not a night-soil peasant, but an educated woman."

Her head inclined, acknowledging the compliment. "I come from a village near Yangzhou in Jiangsu Province. Japanese soldiers did not bother us until they came looking for American pilots who had bombed Tokyo. They killed many villagers and burned our dwellings. With bayonets they killed my father but spared my mother and brother. After that we fled to Nanjing, and I went to school there, then university after the war ended." Her lips tightened at the painful memories. "My husband was a medical student, and when he was a doctor and I a teacher we faithfully served Chairman Mao." She paused and looked away. "Then came the Cultural Revolution, when almost anyone who could read, write, and did not work with his hands became Enemies of the State. Red Guards made me and my husband wear dunce caps and paraded us through the streets like animals. Even his patients and my students jeered and flung offal at us, some even kicked and beat us. My arms were broken, but my husband was strangled before my eyes." She drew in a deep breath. "Our son was taken off to a *laogai* and never seen again."

"I'm so sorry," Peter said and put his arm around her shoulders.

She nodded and went on. "Who knows how many thousands or millions of loyal Party members like us were degraded and killed? The State has never said—but I saw common graves heaped with corpses and felt myself lucky not to be among them." She swallowed. "After the Gang of Four was expelled, victims like me were amnestied and given small pensions, not even enough to live on. So I forage for food—I was doing so when I found you—and sell chickens, eggs, and rabbits—or trade them for rice, tea, charcoal, and fish." She shrugged stoically. "That is how I survive."

Peter said, "If you denounced me to the police you would be well rewarded."

"Perhaps. But I take joy in cheating them of something, and so you are safe here with me." She added a little peanut oil to the large bowl in which floated a lighted wick whose flame brightened. Then she wetted the glowing charcoal to save it for the next meal and turned to Peter. "Today I would have bartered eggs for a fish but did not want to leave you while you slept. Tomorrow we will have fish to feed us." She gestured at a tub where bean sprouts were growing. "That, too. Was the rice sufficient to fill your belly?"

"Yes," Peter lied, thinking he could have eaten three more bowls to satisfy his hunger.

"Then you must tell me what has been happening in the outside world, for I know what little news the State allows us to get is usually far from the truth."

So, sitting side by side on the straw mattress, Peter told her how the Soviet Union had come apart and ended Communism in Europe; told her of the Vietnam War, the Gulf War, Bosnia, the economic strength of Asian nations including Taiwan, and the unresolved dispute with North Korea over its nuclear missiles.

She was, he saw, drowning in the flood of information, and took pains to explain the location of unfamiliar places like Kuwait and Bosnia. After a while she made tea, sipping it while Peter talked on.

She did not seem surprised when he told her that the only large nations still embracing Communism were China, North Korea, Vietnam, and Cuba. Ah-peng pursed her lips and stroked her chin. After a while she said, "It is fated to end. Regimes that oppress and deceive their people cannot endure forever."

"How will Communism end in China?"

"Only after the Old Ones die off, and that will not be soon. Younger Party officials are eager to sip from the same sweet cup of privilege." She shrugged. "Only a few years ago I would have been executed for raising rabbits and chickens, bartering and selling. Private commerce is still forbidden, but the State ignores much of it."

"Why?"

"Because the State does not have to feed people who manage to feed themselves. People say openly that we are using capitalism to save socialism."

Logical, Peter thought, and described the horrors of the Tiananmen Square massacre when students demonstrating for freedom were shot and crushed by tanks. Uncounted hundreds of the young. "How much did you hear of it?" he asked.

"That loyal troops had put down an antirevolutionary uprising and peace had been restored. Have there been other such demonstrations?"

"None I know of." He sipped tea and studied her wrinkled features. "In Washington, where I work and live," he told her, "I have a Chinese fiancée. She dreams of returning here, as do other young Chinese expatriates in America. Some survived Tiananmen and fled abroad.

Others were students who refused to return to Deng's China. Life is very hard for them in America and they make do as best they can. I admire them, but I do not think their future is in China."

"No," she agreed, "but it is good that they have hope."

"It's strange," he said thoughtfully, "that La-li wants to come to China from America, while I want only to return to America."

"Not strange, natural; every creature seeks to return where it was born. Now, Pe-ter, have you thought of a way to leave China?"

He considered her question before saying, "I thought of stealing a fisherman's boat and following the river to the sea. Do you think that is possible?"

"It would be very dangerous," she said after a while. "Boatmen and fishermen know each other's boats and yours would soon be recognized. Also, the owner would tell the police of the theft, and the boat would be sought the length of the river. So that is not a good possibility." She emptied the teapot into their cups and set it aside. "Anything else?"

He nodded. "If I could get to the American embassy compound I would be safe." Unless the American Ambassador refused asylum, he quickly thought.

"Could you find it alone?"

"Not without a map of the city. Do you have such a map?"

She shook her head. "They are only available to officials and the China Travel Service. And asking the location would raise questions. But I agree your embassy is better than a riverboat. I will think how best to get you there."

She rose and said, "Pull aside the mattress, all the way."

He did so, she knelt and dug into the earth with her fingers, pulling up a loop of cord. Standing, she drew on the cord until the earth lifted, and Peter saw a board covering a coffinlike recess below. "A place to hide," she told him, "if a searching party comes. Go to it at once, and I will cover you."

"And if you're not here?"

Without replying, she knelt and reached down into the dark recess, brought up a cloth-wrapped bundle. Slowly unwrapping it on the table, she said, "After Red Guards killed my husband, one of them dragged me into the woods to rape me. I surprised and pleased him by letting him have his way, and when he was asleep—it was night by then—I crushed his throat under my foot and he died." From the wrappings she drew out a small blue-steel revolver. "I took this and have kept it ever since, to protect myself. Now I think you may have more need of it than I."

She handed over the revolver, and Peter held it near the candlelight. Oiled, it was in good condition. Peter opened the cylinder and five .32-caliber cartridges dropped into his hand. The lead bullets were coated with mold, but the primers were not corroded. The weapon was usable, should he ever need it.

"Now," she said, lowering the hatch cover and smoothing dirt over it, "we must think of a way to get you to your embassy."

Sixteen

Hong Kong

Tommy Ning said, "I think I've got some answers for you, brother."

Brand tensed. "You've located Peter?"

Tommy gave the thumbs-up, thumbs-down sign. "Maybe."

They were in Brand's room at the Manchu, facing across the writing table. "Go on, for God's sake," Brand urged. "What do you know?"

"Patience, brother. First, there's been radio broadcasts describing a wanted fugitive, a Westerner jailed for espionage against the State. Anyone spotting him is urged to denounce him immediately to the authorities."

"Was the fugitive named?"

Tommy shook his head. "That would acknowledge they've had a particular Westerner in prison, and they're not ready for that. Most likely they've been holding him for a show trial."

"Makes sense."

"Whoever the guy was—is—was held at Lingyuan Special Prison on the outskirts of Beijing. That's for political prisoners, dissidents, anyone bad-mouthing the regime, and probably your son Peter."

"But if he's escaped . . ." Brand's hands clenched into tight fists, and he shook his head. "How to find him before the cadres do?"

"Yeah. The broadcasts say the fugitive killed a guard escaping."

"Gets worse and worse," Brand said morosely. "If that's true he could be executed."

"They probably won't. Mark, I hate to say it, but we'd have a better chance of getting to Peter if he hadn't escaped. Now, he could be anywhere." He paused, gazing at Brand's strained face. "Does he know Beijing?"

Brand shook his head, then said, "I feel proud that he managed to escape even though it complicates things enormously."

"Then he has no Beijing contacts."

"None, but—he's smart enough to try reaching our embassy."

"Yeah, but that's where they'll be looking for him. Extra guards outside . . ."

"So he'll travel at night, have to." The idea made him feel a little better. "I guess I better get to Beijing, Tommy, get a feel for the situation, alert the embassy."

"Alone?"

"Can't get far with a commando team—but if I need help I'll phone you." He sighed deeply. "At least I know he's alive and free, though for how long . . ." He looked down at his whitened knuckles. "Anything else?"

"Wish there was. Oh—the Westerner was tried in secret and given a long sentence."

"No wonder he escaped. A long sentence is a powerful motive."

Tommy nodded and glanced around. "Anything to drink here?"

"Scotch okay?"

"Terrific."

Brand got up and poured Walker Black into glasses, added ice cubes. Their glasses clinked and Tommy sipped appreciatively. "It's a thirty-six-hour train ride to Beijing with very few comforts, so I doubt you're considering the train."

"I'll fly from here or Canton." He drank deeply, feeling the liquor ease his taut nerves.

"No trouble at the border?"

"I'm papered as a Canadian businessman, toy wholesaler. Should pass okay."

"Yeah, if they think you want to buy Chinese you'll get preferential treatment."

Brand squinted at the window. "I may need two or three helpers, Tommy. Any chance of that?"

"In Beijing?" He frowned. "Have to send them from here. They'll take the train, of course, not to attract attention. You want knee-breakers? Shooters?"

"Whatever it takes. Assuming Peter's still in the Beijing area, they can spread out and listen, report to me."

"Where?"

"The Beijing Hotel."

"Ah, that's the big one, a skyscraper, maybe five hundred rooms."

"If there's a thousand guests, the PSB can't watch us all."

"Good thinking." He sipped again, set down his glass. "Getting a visa could take a week."

"I know. Where's the China Travel Service?"

"Chater Road—easy walk from here."

"Ummm. Let's say I leave in a week. Can you recruit a band of desperadoes by then?"

"Two–three days should do it."

"Good. I want to meet them, let them see what I look like so they'll make no mistakes at the hotel."

The door buzzer sounded and Brand stiffened. To Tommy he said, "I'm not expecting anyone—sit easy." He got up and went to the door. "Who's there?"

"Nina, of course—who else?"

Brand turned and winked at Tommy before undoing the snub chain.

Nina came in with a box and two shopping bags. Seeing Tommy, she halted and said, "Oh, am I interrupting something?"

"Not really," Brand replied. "Two old friends having a drink together."

Tommy drained his glass and got up. "Just leaving anyway."

Brand said, "Nina, my old friend Tommy Ning. Tommy, Mrs. Kenton—Nina Kenton."

"Pleased to make your acquaintance, ma'am," Tommy responded and bowed slightly. To Brand he said, "We'll do this again, Mark, chat up old times."

"Thanks for coming."

Nina stepped aside as Tommy left and closed the door. "Well," she said archly, "one of your island brothers?"

Brand nodded. "Let's see what you've been buying."

She spread her purchases on the sofa: silk scarves, kid gloves, a cashmere shawl, and stepped back. "Aren't they beautiful?"

"Gorgeous," Brand agreed, "all of them. Drive a hard bargain?"

"I tried," she said with a laugh, "but whatever I paid it was much less than in Washington." Her arms circled his neck. "Sorry I broke up your meeting. Forgive me?"

"Of course." He felt her tongue dip into his ear, then her teeth nipped the lobe. The door buzzer sounded, and he left her. At the door he called, "Who is it?"

"Message, sir," the voice piped. Brand opened the door and saw a small, uniformed bellhop holding out a silver tray. On it there lay a parchment-colored envelope, addressed only with his name. He tipped the boy and closed the door, wondering who could have sent the envelope. Nina was at the bar pouring a drink. She looked around as Brand opened the envelope.

The folded sheet was engraved with a commercial address below the heading:

CELESTIAL GALLERIES

ORIENTAL ART

AUTHENTIC ARTIFACTS

Nina asked, "Something important?"

Throat dry, Brand said, "Could be," and read the delicate Chinese calligraphy. Chen Ling-mei would receive him if he cared to come to the gallery. Her chop impression was in red ink. Nothing more.

He refolded the note and put it in the envelope. "Concerns Peter," he lied. "Someone from the Mainland may have seen him there." If he didn't leave now, she'd have her skirt up and panties down, and they'd be coupling for the next hour. "Sorry, I have to go."

"Can't it wait?" she said petulantly. "For the last hour I've been thinking of what's between your legs."

"It'll be there when I come back. So, make yourself comfortable, and if I'm delayed I'll call."

"Well," she sighed, "all right. Can't say you didn't warn me." She went to him and planted a liquor-wet kiss on his lips. "But I do hope you'll get good news."

"So do I," he said, and left.

Not wanting to lose time walking, he took a taxi from the hotel and reached the gallery in five minutes. When he went in, Chu-li, the striking-looking salesgirl, approached him and said, "Madame Ling-mei expects you. This way, please."

He followed her the length of the gallery to a narrow staircase that led to an upper floor. The girl knocked and opened the paneled door. Brand entered a luxuriously furnished office and the woman behind the desk rose. "I'm glad you came, Mark," she said softly, and glided toward him.

BEIJING

PETER BRAND SLEPT through the night, disturbed by visions of his prison cell. Several times he woke perspiring, heart pounding, until reassured by the reality of his surroundings.

After a shared breakfast of egg-and-bean sprout omelet, Ah-peng gathered four eggs in a cloth and set out for the riverbank. In her absence Peter considered his situation. For a while he was safe with Ah-peng, but he knew his presence endangered her, and he hated taking food from her mouth. As long as he stayed there he was in limbo, when forward movement was required. Last night they had talked of ways to get him to the embassy, but each had its drawbacks. Steal a bicycle, both riding it to the diplomatic zone. Walk the distance, Ah-peng leading him as though he were blind. Entrust her with a note to be slipped to a Marine guard . . . he stroked the side of his face, feeling the incipient beard. He had neither razor nor lather, and could not hope to pass as Chinese wearing abundant facial hair. And there was the pallor of his skin—how could that be overcome? With sunglasses his Western eyes would pass unnoticed, an additional factor arguing for blindness as a disguise. Last night he had thanked Ah-peng for her offer of the revolver, but told her it would be more of a hazard for him than a help. If he were cornered and forced to kill, a knife would kill silently, affording him a better chance of getting away.

And as he looked around the bare interior he contrasted his surroundings with the spacious, well-equipped house he shared with La-li, and thought how little one really needed to live: really it came down to food and shelter. Ah-peng had survived degradation and the loss of her loved ones, yet she had not allowed herself to sink into destructive depression, but employed her intelligence to live independently in a cruel and oppressive land. He felt profound admiration for her, and realized that he was inspired by her resourcefulness and perseverance. Never give up. Never, never give up. Churchill's words? They could equally be those of Ah-peng.

When she returned, true to her promise, she brought a plump fresh-caught fish. It could be a species of carp, he thought, but knew it was neither trout nor salmon.

She produced a knife, gutted the fish, and set entrails and head aside. "We will steam this three-egg beauty," she announced, "and from the rest I will make a nourishing broth." She set water to boil, and suspended the fish in an openwork bamboo basket just above water level. That done, she turned to Peter. "Perhaps you do not like fish?"

"I love it, grandmother. And in prison I learned to eat anything and everything."

She smiled. "Good. Now, while our fish cooks, tell me if you have decided on a means to reach your embassy."

"I think of little else," he acknowledged, "but before I set out there is the problem of my foreign eyes, my beard, and the color of my skin." He paused. "And the embassy's location."

She nodded. "You will need a shave and sunglasses. I think I can color your skin to make it less noticeable." She turned his face away and examined it closely. "As to your embassy, I should be able to find it."

"How?"

With a smile, she said, "I will go to the Central Railroad Station and inquire. No one will be suspicious of an old woman, and if I am asked why I inquire I will say that I am a washerwoman and want to do washing at the embassy." She paused. "Of course, I will at first ask only the location of the diplomatic zone. Once there, the rest will be easy."

"Still," he said thoughtfully, "it is a risk I would prefer you not run."

She shrugged. "Is there another way? Can you think of one?"

"No," he conceded with a grimace.

"Very well. After we eat, and the broth is made, I will shave you." She picked up the kitchen knife and began stroking it expertly on a pumice stone. Watching, Peter thought, She'll nick and scar me, but worse things could happen. Abruptly she left, returning in a quarter hour with a collection of walnuts and unfamiliar herbals. After opening the nut shells she left the meats inside, and placed her gatherings in a small pan to which she added a few cups of water. Having tested the knife edge with her thumb, she dabbed peanut oil on his beard and began slowly to shave his face. The blade drew more than a sharp razor would have, but, Peter thought, you can't expect perfection from a field expedient.

Shaving done, she cleansed his face with a warm, wet cloth and stroked it with her fingertips. "My husband liked me to shave him, but in those days I had a good sharp razor and plenty of soapsuds. This will have to do." Going to the stove, she added charcoal and set aside the steaming kettle. In its place she set the pan of nuts and herbals and dropped in a handful of tea leaves. While the mixture steeped Ah-peng sat down and stared at Peter. Finally she said, "Take off your clothes."

Obediently he complied, leaving only the prison loincloth for modesty. "You're washing them?"

She shook her head. "I will trade them for a used Mao jacket and trousers, taking along a rabbit to seal the bargain." Her eyes half closed as she estimated his height. "Somewhat more than two meters, Pe-ter. Your height suggests Northern Chinese, so do you speak the dialects of Shanxi or Hebei?"

"Just a mix of Mandarin and Fukienese."

"If asked you can say you were born in North China, worked in Canton, explaining your dialect."

"But I hope nobody asks."

"If lucky." She opened her collar and brought out a string. From it was suspended a cross formed by two nails, held at the crux by fine wire or hair. "Should I not get needed information at the Central Railway Station I can go to Nan Tang, the Christian church. It is only a few blocks west of the station. There, a priest or pastor may be willing to help me." She restored the crude cross and buttoned her collar. "When we think of things," she remarked, "we often become aware of other things we had not considered before." Going to the stove she peered at the steeping mixture and nodded in satisfaction. "As soon as this cools it will be ready for use."

Silently he watched, admiring her ability to make much from little. Seating herself, Ah-peng said, "You will also need a hat with a large down-curving brim such as paddy workers wear for protection from the sun." She eyed him thoughtfully. "And sandals."

Peter said, "I shouldn't be surprised that you are Christian; my grandparents were missionaries in Yunnan-fu before my father was born."

"What happened to them?"

"When the Communist army invaded western China, Chiang's warlords defected or fled to Burma. My grandfather was able to reach Taiwan, with my father. His mother had been killed in a plane crash somewhere in the Himalayas—she had been bringing medical supplies from Calcutta. So it was that my grandfather raised my father, and my father raised me."

"Your mother?"

"Abandoned us on Taiwan and later died." He knew the true story of her death but did not want to explain it to Ah-peng.

"Your father did not remarry?"

"No—and I don't know why."

"But you have no wife either."

"A fiancée," he reminded her. "A dissident student who stayed in my country after the Tiananmen massacres, afraid to return. Her name is La-li." Voicing her name pained him because he knew she must be perplexed and suffering in his absence. Well, he was doing what he could to rejoin her—with Ah-peng's indispensable help.

"And you will marry La-li?" she inquired politely.

"As soon as I can."

Again, Ah-peng inspected the steeping mixture, nodded, and set the pan aside, replacing the fish-steaming kettle. She turned over the fish to steam on the other side, then reached into a terra-cotta jar and brought out a handful of bills. "When I stole the Red Guard's weapon," she said, "I also took his money. So far I have not needed to spend much of it, but we will take it along as we make our way to Beijing."

When the fish was done, Ah-peng divided it with her knife and they ate on pottery dishes, using chopsticks with the flaky flesh. Peter ate voraciously, it was the first protein he had consumed in many days, and when his half was eaten he sat back, patted his stomach, and belched in approval. "Delicious," he told her. "Again I am most grateful to you."

"That you enjoy our humble meals is thanks enough, Pe-ter." With that she left the table and dropped the fish head and entrails into the bubbling kettle. Then added a few onions and a handful of herbals. After that she tested the nut-and-herbal mixture and dipped a rag into it, applying the staining mix to his face, forehead, neck, hands, and arms. "The color should last several days," she told him. "By which time you will either be free or a prisoner. In either case it will not matter."

What he could see of his body—arms and hands—was darker than before, in keeping with his North China birth legend, and he thought he might get away with it.

Ah-peng said, "While I am away, tend the fish kettle, and when only half the water remains, remove it from the fire. Wet the charcoal as I have done, and I will be back by evening. Until then, rest and gain strength, for we will leave here tomorrow."

Seventeen

Hong Kong

Brand said, "I'm glad and grateful you chose to see me, Mary."

She extended her hands to take both of his. "We have much to say, Mark, after more than twenty years." She paused while her clear dark eyes searched his. "Can it really be so long?"

"Unfortunately so." His mouth was desert-dry and his limbs felt paralyzed. Her face was a bit fuller, but her skin still flawless, and he saw her as delicately beautiful as when they parted that day so long ago.

"Let's have tea, and talk." She gestured at a low table and turned to Chu-li. "Tea for two, please, if you don't mind."

"Not at all, madame." The girl left, closing the door behind her.

When Mary was seated across the table from him she said, "So, old friends meet in Hong Kong. How different from Taipei, is it not?"

He nodded, unsure that he could speak coherently. "Still," she said with a harmonic of nostalgia, "I find myself missing the island occasionally. The scent of camphor, the dusty streets, the view from the mountains . . ." Her voice trailed off. "Do you?"

"I've gone back a few times," he told her, "but always on business. It was there my wife abandoned Peter and me, and those memories are bitter. The good memories, the ones I cherish, are of you."

Ignoring the opening, she said, "But you did return."

He nodded. "Went to the museum and asked for Director Chen. His successor said he had died and knew not where you had gone."

"I see. So in a way you kept your promise to return."

"But not as I intended."

She shrugged. "No matter. Soon after you left I married my present husband—I believe you knew him on Taiwan—Cheong Wing-dah."

"A big kid, large for his age? Son of a Nat official?"

"Yes. Brought his father's money here and established a number of businesses." Her hand gestured toward the showroom below. "This is one of them."

"I've never seen a more tasteful gallery. You—own it?"

"In almost every respect. But by custom and Colony law I cannot own property—that right is reserved to males." Her lips closed in an almost-frown. "My husband has other galleries Kowloon-side but this is the showplace," she said with a trace of pride.

"And Wing-dah? He has other interests?"

"Mainly he arranges shipment here of Mainland artifacts. After I authenticate them they are placed in one of the galleries, or exported to, oh, Thailand, Jidda, Singapore, Japan—and the U.S. The business is quite lucrative."

"I can imagine. And you're fortunate to have an assistant so knowledgeable—and personable."

"I am indeed. Multilingual, too. Early education at St. Andrews here in Hong Kong, college preparatory in Lucerne, a degree in Oriental Art and Studies from Cambridge."

Behind him, the door opened and Chu-li entered carrying a formal tea setting on a silver tray. She set it between them, Mary thanked her and said, "Chu-li, Mr. Mark Brand is a very old friend from Taiwan, where he knew my father. Mark, my daughter, Cheong Chu-li."

Her head inclined and her palms joined below her breasts in traditional fashion. Brand rose. "I'm delighted to know you, Chu-li, and enchanted. You so resemble your mother when she was young that I should have guessed." To Mary he said, "A day of felicitous happenings. Thank you again for allowing me to come."

Chu-li's hands lowered. "Do you know my father?"

"Your mother thinks we met on Taiwan."

Mary said, "Child, it is not necessary to mention this encounter to your father."

Again her head inclined obediently. "I understand. And now, if you will excuse me, there are customers in the gallery."

She left with scarcely a sound, and Brand said, "I've never seen a more captivating young Oriental woman."

"Never, Mark?"

He felt his cheeks flush. "Present company excepted."

"I'm pleased you find her attractive. Mark, did you remarry?"

"No, I raised Peter alone." His face sobered. "A fine young man with a Chinese fiancée. Works for an international bank in Washington." He paused. "When he's there."

"Is Peter as handsome as you?"

"He's both handsome and intelligent. Organized his life well." He didn't want to talk about Peter now. He wanted to pour out his heart to his long-lost love, tell her how wrong he'd been to leave her, how he'd regretted it a thousand times and more. Swallowing, he began. "Mary, there are things I must tell you. For twenty years I've been haunted by—"

"Please, another time." She poured their tea and sipped. Brand did likewise, scenting the aroma of jasmine, the delicate, night-blooming flower of memory. Although chilled by her dismissal, he managed to say, "Delicious."

"This Chinese fiancée of your son's—where did they meet?"

"Washington. I'm not sure of the circumstances, but they've lived together for maybe a year. La-li came from the Mainland as a student, refused to return after Tiananmen. Her friends are mostly student dissidents like herself." He shook his head. "I feel so sorry for them."

"I, too, knowing what it is like to be a—refugee—and unwelcome." She set down her porcelain cup. "Why are you in Hong Kong? Business?"

"I wish it were that, Mary. Peter came here on bank business several weeks ago. La-li's friends persuaded him to deliver money and leaflets to a Hong Kong contact—and he did that. But unknown to me and his fiancée he accepted a side job for the CIA."

Her face stiffened. "What sort of job?"

"Simple enough on the face of it. Collect film cassettes from a Canton shop and bring them back to the consulate." His throat was tight. "From what I've been able to learn the shop was being watched. When Peter took the films he was arrested by Gong An Ju agents, taken to Beijing, tried in secret, and imprisoned." He looked down at his hands, noticing a tremor.

"Oh, Mark," she exclaimed, "I'm so very sorry. Then he's a prisoner . . . do you know where?"

Slowly he shook his head. "Mainland broadcasts report a Westerner escaped and is sought everywhere." He breathed deeply. "If he's captured they'll treat him harshly. I have to find Peter before the Chinese do."

One finger touched the corner of her mouth. "Have you a plan?"

"Go to Beijing, find out what I can. Seems hopeless, does it not, but I don't know what else to do. I can't just sit around doing nothing."

Impulsively, she touched his hand. "But, alone in Beijing, what can you do?"

"Some Taiwan friends are sending searchers to do what I can't."

"Taiwan friends? Your Fang-tse brothers?"

He nodded. "I know they live outside the law, but there is a bond of loyalty."

"Notorious criminals," she said disparagingly. "Extortionists, smugglers . . . even worse."

Defensively he said, "I understand that not all your husband's activities are entirely legal."

Stiffly, she said, "Nevertheless, he has Mainland connections who might be able to help. *Guanxi.* Shall I ask him?"

"All help is more than welcome." He considered before asking, "Does he know about me?"

"In Taipei he knew of you, and before we married I explained that you were an academic friend of my father's, that we took tea occasionally . . . nothing more."

"Then—?"

She leaned forward, speaking in a low voice. "On our wedding night I feigned chastity—the Bride's Book explained it all—so he never suspected I was already pregnant."

"Pregnant?"

"Shhh! Yes," she said almost inaudibly, "and I've sensed a certain feeling you have for my daughter, Chu-li. That's natural, Mark, because she is not Wing-dah's daughter, but yours."

Her words overwhelmed him. He stared at her before stammering, "Mine? Does—does Chu-li know?"

"No, and she may never know. You see, when my father learned I was with child he quickly arranged marriage with Wing-dah, who had once asked for my hand. Now my father is dead, and only you and I know the truth." She sat back and gazed at him. "So I will willingly ask my husband's help in finding my daughter's half brother. Your son."

He swallowed with difficulty. "I—I don't know what to say, but I'm thrilled to have a daughter I never knew."

"A daughter who must never know her father." She sighed. "Were Wing-dah ever to learn the truth, he would kill you to erase the stain on his honor. Now, go, Mark. I will see my husband and ask his assistance for you and your son." Standing, she said, "I invited you here so I could tell you of Chu-li, perhaps taunt you with the truth, but that is behind us now. If Wing-dah wants to see you, remember that he always envied you as a Westerner and a member of the Fang-tse that did not accept him."

"I understand."

Half turning, he glanced down into the gallery where Chu-li was talking with two customers. *His daughter!* The realization stunned him, and he barely heard Mary say, *"Zai Jian."* Good-bye.

"Zai Jian," he repeated hoarsely, and breathed, *"Qin Ai-De,"* darling, as he left.

AFTER THE DOOR CLOSED, Mary Chen went to the window and silently watched her daughter concluding a sale. All those years, she thought, I believed he would come one day. I planned to spit in his face for his betrayal, then show him living proof of the love I bore him, the daughter he can never claim.

But finding him contrite for the wrong he did me, and grieving over the loss of his son, I could not add to his misery. Chu-li now forms an enduring bond between us, and perhaps in some predestined way her father will help us as I will try to help his son.

BEIJING

WHILE AH-PENG WAS GONE, Peter rested on the mattress and let unbidden memories flood his mind. He thought of La-li, who must be distraught by now, and of his father, wondering what he might do to find and set him free. He found himself not caring what was thought and said at the bank—he could always get another job—but he faulted himself for not telling his father all he planned to do. Still, I knew then as now that he would have advised against the Canton journey, urged me not to go. I realize that going was an act of independence, proof that I could carry out missions within my father's secret world as he had for so long. And all it proved was my naiveté and immaturity, for which I continue to pay. Worse, I've involved an honorable and charitable old woman in dangerous things, something I had no right to do. Somehow I must make amends.

Toward evening he got up, fanned the charcoal into life, and warmed the fish stew kettle. Flavored with herbs and small onions the broth was delicious, and though he could have eaten it all he reserved half for his hostess and guardian. After nightfall he began to worry, thinking her inquiries might have drawn official attention. Still, her cover story was disprovable, and he hoped her intelligence would see her through.

He thought of grandfather Simon Brand, the stalwart, reclusive physician who continued caring for the needy as he had ministered to so many Chinese and Taiwanese. Peter admired his grandfather boundlessly, and thought that his forbears' genes were good ones that would enable him to endure, survive, and succeed.

Where was Ah-peng?

Sounds floated up from the river, the chanting of fishermen poling off to cast their nets. Unexpectedly, he was getting firsthand exposure to how ordinary Chinese worked and lived. Despite the misery of cruel oppression, their spirit was indomitable, and he wondered how many, like Ah-peng, would risk their lives to aid a ragged foreigner who was a fugitive. Grandfather had told him how the Japanese had slaughtered Chinese thought to have hidden Doolittle's Tokyo raiders, and razed whole villages in reprisal and warning to others. Today's killers were not Japanese but Chinese officials, who were if anything more ferociously vindictive than the *Riben* had been.

After dark he ventured outside to relieve himself beyond the rabbit hutch and returned quietly and cautiously. He was about to light the lamp wick when he heard approaching footsteps and froze.

His fear dissolved when Ah-peng's voice lifted in nasal song, and presently she was inside. "Pe-ter, Pe-ter," she said softly, "do you sleep? Wake now, for I have much to tell you."

He lit the wick and as it flared he saw her lower a large bundle from her back. Then she fanned the charcoal into life and said, "Now I must eat for I have not eaten today."

"There's plenty left," he told her as she stirred the stew. *"Chi baole."* I've had enough.

"Then eat again," she counseled, "eat until you can hold no more, for tomorrow your journey begins."

Hong Kong

Leaving the gallery, Brand glanced covertly at Chu-li and saw that she was looking at him, a questioning expression on her face. His impulse was to rush to her, crush her in his arms, and tell her he, not Wing-dah, was her father. He wanted to pour out his heart to her, beg forgiveness for having abandoned her, unknowingly, before she was born. But purging his conscience would ruin two lives: hers and her mother's. So he would preserve the secret and suffer in silence.

On the street, Brand let himself be carried along by the bustling crowd, too overwhelmed by emotion to strike out on his own. But when his mind cleared he turned toward Chater Road and walked as far as a street sign whose characters formed *Luxingshe*. Below, English lettering spelled out China Travel Service.

Before turning in he hesitated, mentally inventorying his cover documentation: Canadian passport in the name of Thomas Vincent Lang, CanToyCo business cards with a Toronto address, phone and fax numbers, credit cards and Traveler's Cheques, letters from Lang's notional wife, and a prescription for sleeping pills. All there. He opened the door and went in.

The office was spare, functional, and unattractive. The placement of desks and the long counter reminded Brand of a bank that was not doing well. Sections of the counter were partitioned according to function, so Brand lined up behind two men waiting at the section labeled Alien Travel Permits in both languages. He must remember, he told himself, neither to speak Chinese nor indicate that he understood it, for that would bring immediate and unwelcome attention from the *wai shike*, the foreign affairs branch of the Gong An Ju. Foreigners who spoke Chinese were routinely considered possible spies, and their travel curtailed.

He waited patiently, knowing that Chinese bureaucrats would not be rushed, and resented urgings to hurry. They would react by slowing whatever they were working on until the complainer produced *zha qu*, a bribe. Then matters would accelerate.

His thoughts returned to Mary, and he was thankful that she had refrained from reviling him as he'd half expected. Instead, her revenge had taken the form of presenting him with a lovely daughter he could never acknowledge. Bitter fruit, he reflected, but I deserved it.

After twenty minutes Brand was at the counter. Behind it a young Chinese woman with short black hair and thick lenses said in English, "You wish to travel to the People's Republic of China?"

"I do." He laid passport and a business card on the counter. After inspecting both, she asked, "For what reason?"

"Business. I'm looking for a source of toys to import."

With that she brought out a long bilingual form and began filling it with basic information. Then she asked, "Destination?"

"Beijing."

She shrugged. "There is a foreign trade center in Canton, so you need not travel so far."

He smiled engagingly. "But there is much more to see in Beijing, and the trade center there is perhaps more comprehensive. Besides, I would like to visit toy factories, check their quality control."

"If you limit travel to Canton I can issue a permit now, good for three days. But if you have to go to Beijing, approval will take longer."

"I think the wait will be worthwhile. How long is it likely to be?"

Her hands spread. "That is decided in Beijing. Sometimes a few days, perhaps as long as a week. For Beijing the travel permit costs more."

"I understand."

She went to a nearby copy machine and duplicated his passport pages. She stapled the business card to the sheet and asked him to sign at the bottom. Then she compared his passport signature with the new one, and said, "The permit fee to Beijing is forty U.S. dollars."

He got out Traveler's Cheques and countersigned two of twenty dollars each. Again she compared signatures and said, "Go to the second desk for travel and hotel arrangements."

"Thank you."

Again, he found himself third in line, took a chair, and waited. So far, so good. Ten minutes more and he was seated at the travel desk, behind which a young man was counting currency. That done, the man asked, "What is your travel destination?"

"Beijing." He handed over business card and passport.

"And the purpose?"

"Business. I want to find a reliable source for toys that I can import."

"Your current source is not reliable?"

Brand shrugged. "Malaysia. Quality control leaves much to be desired, and shipment schedules have not been met."

The clerk nodded understandingly. "You will surely find full satisfaction with our manufacturers." He paused. "When do you plan to depart?"

"As soon as my travel permit is granted."

He nodded. "Probably within a few days, Mr. Lang. Do you intend to fly?"

"Preferably by Japan Air Lines."

"Not our national airline?"

"I'm fond of Japanese food."

He frowned. "Have you selected a hotel?"

"The Beijing. A suite."

"It will be—expensive," the clerk cautioned.

"No matter. Beijing will be a once-in-a-lifetime experience for me," he said, hoping that would be so.

On a form the clerk filled in Brand's information, and said, "It will not be possible to make air and hotel reservations until the permit is received. Where are you staying in Hong Kong?"

"Kowloon-side, with friends."

"Telephone?"

"They lack one, so I will call here from time to time." He wondered if that sounded suspicious, so he added, "Service was cut off for nonpayment of tolls."

"Well, then, Mr. Lang, there is nothing more for the moment. You will pay here for the airline ticket and also place a deposit on your hotel room."

"Suite," he corrected.

The clerk nodded. "You can exchange money in Hong Kong, or on the Mainland, but only at authorized exchange centers. Penalties for black marketing are very severe."

"As they should be," Brand remarked, and got up, reclaiming his passport while the clerk stapled his business card to the completed form.

Leaving the office, Brand filled his lungs with air redolent of exhaust fumes, and decided to walk back to his hotel. It might be prudent to move to another hotel under the Lang name, where the CTS could contact him directly. But that would cause problems with Nina, and give Mary more information than she or her husband needed.

His brothers would understand, but for the present he did not want them to know his travel alias.

Back in his room there was a message from Nina asking about dinner arrangements as she wanted to dress appropriately.

Having seen Mary and his daughter, Brand found Nina less attractive and more irritating than ever. He disliked her passionately, but how to rid himself of her without an ugly scene? Well, he would accept her recriminations as the price of ending a relationship that had been false and treacherous from the start.

The telephone rang and he hesitated before picking up the receiver, thinking it was probably Nina with more importunings. Instead, it was Mary, who said, "My husband is interested in your problem and would like to hear more particulars."

"Of course. When and where?"

"Tomorrow if convenient. Eleven o'clock?"

"At the gallery?"

"No—he prefers you come to his apartment. This one overlooks Repulse Bay, and he will send a car for you."

"Thank you so much," he said, sensing anew the glow her voice used to inspire. "And thank Wing-dah, too. I look forward to seeing him again."

"Bearing in mind what I told you. And I believe he will be more cooperative if you appear humble."

"I understand. Humble it is. And thank you again." The line hummed and he replaced the receiver. Stroking Fatso Cheong was not going to be easy, but for Peter he was willing to grovel for assistance.

After pouring a drink, Brand took off his jacket and loosened his tie. Mary had come through, as expected, but the Nina problem remained. The most obvious solution was to leave without telling her; just taxi to Kai Tak and board the JAL flight to Beijing. Her Russian controller wouldn't like it, but that was Nina's problem to resolve. A clean break in Hong Kong would spare him ever seeing her when he returned to Washington, and he hated himself for ever, even slightly, considering marriage.

Again the telephone rang, and this time it *was* Nina. Controlling his voice, Brand said, "Just got in and was about to call you."

"Shall I come over?"

"Look," he said tiredly, "I'm hot and dusty and need the services of a masseur. After that—"

"Wouldn't I do, dear?"

"After that," he said doggedly, "I'm going to stretch out for a while."

"Sure you don't want me to come over and, ah, relax you?"

"I'll be in better form tonight—after dinner and wine at the Mandarin, okay?"

"Well, if you must," she said reluctantly, "so I'll dress for the occasion."

"Surprise me," he said, then, "Uh-oh, there's the masseur. I'll see you later," and broke the connection. Bitch, he thought, I don't even want to fuck you anymore.

He refilled his glass and focused his thoughts on tomorrow's meeting with Wing-dah. If he could smuggle artifacts from the Mainland, maybe he could get Peter out as well. But all that depended on finding his son.

The telephone rang and he answered, hoping it was Tommy Ning with more information from his contacts. Instead, he heard the voice of Sammy Lu. "Brother, I've got something for you."

"Great, what is it?"

"That white girl you were looking for."

Doreen Gerold. "You sure?"

"Looks like the photo and calls herself Dory."

"Life's full of surprises. How'd you find her?"

"One of my regular girls got talking with her in a bar—she said she was looking for work, so Silvia brought her to see me."

"The studio?"

"Yeah. If you don't want her, she can work for me. Good boobs but skinny. I can use her as a bit player until she puts on some weight. Whatta ya say?"

"Is she hooked?"

"Yeah, but I gave her a fix to quiet her down."

"Jesus, Sammy—"

"Hey, only way to handle junkies. Well?"

Brand glanced around the room, found no inspiration in the furnishings, and said, "Guess you'd better send her, Sammy."

"Okay. Ah—she'll be good for a while, but I'll send a fix along to quiet her down."

"Thanks, Sammy, good work, and I owe you."

"Bullshit. Brothers don't owe brothers." The line went dead.

Darman doesn't know it, he thought, but he's going to owe me big time. Then he phoned the Consulate General and asked for Briggs

Dockerty, the only Base officer who knew Gerold was looking for his daughter. "Sorry, sir, Mr. Dockerty is out of the city."

"When will he return?"

"Tomorrow morning. Care to leave a message?"

Brand left his name with a request to be called. Urgently.

Shit! He'd wanted Briggs to take custody of the girl, but that would have to wait for Dockerty's return. Until then he was in loco parentis. Unwillingly. Darman would probably fly out to repossess his daughter, take her back to Washington, and put her in rehab.

If only, he thought, Peter could be found so easily.

A TALL CHINESE DELIVERED Dory in less than an hour, and handed Brand a wrapped box. "You know what it is?"

"Sammy told me."

"Anything else?"

"No, and thank you."

"Mr. Lu says he was glad to help." He went out and closed the door. Brand turned to Gerold's daughter, sitting on the nearest twin bed. Her shoulder-length hair was stringy and her arms thin. Her eyes were deep-sunken, and her face was strained from the ravages of addiction. Still, he could see the resemblance to her mother in the girl's wasted beauty, and found himself wishing Darman could see her now.

He pulled over a chair and sat facing her. "How are you feeling?" he asked.

"Me? Oh, great, just great. Hey, never felt better." Her tongue licked thin lips. "You a producer? Director?"

He shook his head. "I knew you years ago, knew your mother, Suzie—Susan. From Portland."

"So?"

"Your father is Darman Gerold. You have a brother, too."

Her lips twisted. "Proves nothing."

"Have it your way."

She began pulling off her blouse. "Why talk? This is a tryout, right? You wanna fuck, let's get it on." Breasts swaying pendulously, she bent over to pull down her jeans, straightened up, naked.

He could count her ribs, see the concave abdomen above the pubic swatch. "Take a shower," he told her, "and we'll see what's next."

Taking her hand, he led her into the bathroom, turned on the stall shower, and said, "Use plenty of soap, fingernails, too." He closed the stall door and went back to open the box Sammy's man had left. It contained a hypodermic syringe partly filled with clear fluid. The stuff that dreams are made of, he thought, and placed the box in the night-table drawer. Then he called room service and ordered a steak sandwich with mashed potatoes and salad. Dory looked as though she hadn't eaten in days. He'd withhold the fix until she did.

In the bathroom he opened the stall door and saw her lazily soaping her body. After handing her a bottle of shampoo he left the bathroom and took off his shirt, intending to have it laundered overnight.

The door buzzer sounded, and he went to it, thinking the hotel's room service was exceptionally fast. Instead, there was Nina with a sly smile. "Massage over?" she asked coyly and stepped in.

"I was getting ready to shower," he lied. "Courtesy to the masseur."

"Then I'll wait," she said, "until you're spanking clean. May I have a drink?" She went to the bar and began pouring scotch in a glass. Just then the shower sound ended and Nina turned with a quizzical expression. Before he could stop her Nina strode into the bathroom just as Dory left the stall. For a few moments Nina stared at her, yelped, and strode back to Brand. "Since when does the masseuse shower, too?" she raged. "Oh, you bastard, you dirty bastard!" she screamed. "I'm not enough for you so you have to fuck whores?"

He caught her wrists. "Nina, it's not what you think. She's the daughter of a friend, and—"

"Pardon me if I don't believe you," she sneered as Dory, oblivious to the commotion, began toweling her hair. "Well, forget dinner, and tomorrow, when you've come to your senses, we'll talk. *If* I'm still here."

With a furious glance at Dory, Nina stormed out of the room.

Still toweling her hair, Dory came in and said, "Who's the big-mouth bitch? Your lady friend?"

"Was"—Brand smiled—"and you may have done me a big favor."

She sawed the towel between her legs to dry her crotch and said, "Dry enough?"

"Let's see your hands."

She held them out and he saw the nails had been gnawed to the quick. "Not much there," he said, "but clean. Get another towel and listen to me."

When she stared at him, he said, "Now, Dory, do it."

Through the open doorway he could see her finish drying her skinny body, and when she emerged again, she sat docilely on the bed. "Maybe," she suggested, "the bitch wants a three-way scene."

"Not tonight, Dory, so listen to me. I've been an associate of your father's for a lot of years. He knew I was coming to Hong Kong, and on the chance you'd show up he asked me to look for you."

"Well, I showed up. What now?"

"There's food on the way, and you're to eat it."

"I don't eat much these days," she said dully. "No appetite."

"Develop one. You won't get another fix until you've eaten."

"Promise?"

He nodded.

"Say it."

"I promise."

That pleased her, so she lay back on the bed and parted her thighs. "Anytime," she crooned, "any way, honey-man."

"Get real, Dory. I'm not going to fuck you. You'd tell your father just to make him mad. Right?"

"But he has no right to get mad over anything I do." Her nose wrinkled coquettishly. "Know why?"

"Maybe." Was it possible she knew that—

"He used to fuck his mother, that's why. I suppose you knew *that?*"

"I heard it said."

"And it's why Mother divorced him."

"Heard that, too, but it doesn't change anything. You'll stay with me until I can turn you over to one of Darman's people at the consulate. One bed for you, one for me, get it?"

She sat up and shrugged. "Okay, if that's how you want it." The fingers of one hand scratched track marks on her other arm. "But he'll take me back to our so-called home and stick me in a detox hole and forget about me again." She shivered. "He's done it before. I know the drill."

"Just don't give me any trouble, understand?"

She barely nodded. The buzzer sounded, and the food waiter was there. "Cover yourself," Brand told Dory, and when she was draped with towels, the waiter set his tray on the table. Paying him, Brand added a healthy tip and told him to send up a woman from the clothing boutique.

"Right away," the waiter said, and left.

Dory stared at the food and groaned, "You expect me to eat all *that?*"

"All of it." He pulled a chair to the table. "Start now."

She was partway through the salad when the hotel shopwoman arrived. In Chinese Brand told her the girl's clothing had been stolen and she needed underwear and a dress for street wear. Also shoes.

The woman knelt to outline Dory's foot on a sheet of paper and said she would bring up a selection of clothing in the girl's size. When the door closed behind her Dory said, "Say, you do things right. Maybe I'll stay with you."

"You will—until tomorrow." He gathered up her shabby clothing and stuffed it in the wastebasket.

After biting into the steak sandwich, she chewed slowly, distaste on her face, and said, "Don't even know your name."

"Mark. Call me Mark."

"And you're from the pickle factory?"

"Was."

"Got a wife?"

"No."

"Children?"

"Son. Don't talk, Dory, eat."

"I don't like this shit."

"Eat anyway."

"Because it's good for me?"

"Right." He poured a drink at the bar, filling Nina's abandoned glass, added ice, and watched Dory chew and swallow, one small bite at a time. Damn Dockerty, hell of a time to be away when I need him.

She got down the mashed potatoes without complaint, left toast ends, and finished the salad. Then burped loudly. "Do I get my fix?"

"When you need it—not until."

He looked out of the window at dusk enfolding the harbor. Lights twinkled on the Kowloon side, the ferry's string lights glowed like golden pearls.

The shopwoman delivered six dresses on a rack, with a box of underthings and three pairs of shoes. Brand let Dory choose what she wanted, and paid the woman, who took the rest away. Dory pulled on panty hose and nothing else. "I'm not big on clothing," she said reflectively.

"I guessed as much."

"So Dad will be surprised to see me in new duds. Pleased, too, the old motherfucker," she added bitterly. "I never liked Grandma, but Pop sure did."

"So it goes," Brand said, "in the best of families."

"And ours was one of the best," she muttered, and came to him. She brushed her nipples across his nose and whispered, "Maybe you're in the mood now."

"Sorry," he said, "now stop that," and pushed her away.

"I could yell rape," she threatened.

"And I'd kick the shit out of you, so calm down."

Swallowing, she stepped back. "You *mean* that, don't you?" Her tone registered disbelief. "Most men can't wait to stick it in."

Brand breathed deeply, patience wearing thin, "Dory, listen to me. I'm not going to make it with you, but if you keep it up I'll send you back to Mong Kok where Mr. Lu's studs will give you enough action for the rest of your life." He made a sinister smile. "See the donkey?"

"No!" She shrank back.

"It's there for a reason, so behave yourself."

"All right. I thought I was here to fuck you, but I guess not."

"You've finally got it," he sighed.

She turned on the TV to an English language station and lay on the bed watching. Brand realized the expected fix was not going to last overnight, so he phoned Sammy and said, "I can't move the package until tomorrow, so you'd better send another box, okay?"

"I'll make it two, brother. The kid's deep hooked."

"Whatever you say."

"In an hour."

After a while her body began twitching on the bed. She sat up and started scratching her track marks, then clawing them. He gave her ice water, and she drained the glass but said, *"That's* not what I need. You *know* what I need."

"Okay," he said reluctantly, and gave her the hypodermic syringe. She looked up at him helplessly. "Rubber?"

"No."

"Then squeeze my arm."

With both hands he choked the blood supply until a vein bulged visibly. She stuck a needle in it and fed the liquid heroin slowly into her vein. "Oh, Jesus," she gasped, and Brand thought, If Darman could see us now . . .

After the injection Dory lay back fully relaxed. Her eyes were closed and her breathing shallow. She was still out when Sammy's delivery arrived, and Brand stashed the hypos in his luggage.

Needing a change of scene, he dressed and went down to the hotel dining room for Leng Pan hors d'oeuvres; *chaiba ya tang,* duck soup; *cuipi zhaji,* crisp-skin chicken; and dessert of *bingdong hetao lu,* chilled walnut cream. After dining, he strolled around the block to settle his stomach and returned to his room. Still sleeping, Dory lay on her face in a childlike sprawl. So young, he thought. Far too young to be so utterly corrupt.

Undressing, Brand studied her and wished he could be optimistic for her future, but he believed her too far down the road of self-destruction to reverse it. Too bad, because her face and figure were basically attractive, she was educated, and could make some man a good wife, addiction aside. The waste was tragic.

Drained by stress, Brand turned out the room lights, got into the other bed, and fell asleep to the rhythm of Dory's subdued snoring.

During the night he felt he was having a wet dream, half woke and found a body crouched beside him. Dory was puffing on his shaft, gluttonous sounds coming from her throat. He knew he ought to push her away, but his excitement was too intense, and after climax, he saw her lift her head as moonlight showed her triumphant grin. "Fooled you," she breathed, "didn't I?"

"You fooled me, Dory, but you shouldn't have done it. Wasn't supposed to be this way."

The back of her hand wiped her lips. "Don't be angry, Mark. Do I get my fix now?"

Resignedly, he helped her with the injection, got her into bed, and covered her naked body. Then he half filled a glass with scotch and sipped it feeling angry, guilty, used, and remorseful for complicity. Damn her, he thought, I didn't want it to happen. If Dockerty doesn't show in the morning I'll send her back to Sammy until he does.

After the nightcap, Brand returned to his bed thinking that tonight had been Dory but tomorrow would be Wing-dah.

Beijing

In her bundle Ah-peng had brought used, loose-fitting peasant clothing, a woven reed hat with down-curving brim, sunglasses, sandals, and a knife. She had made a rough map of the city, and explained the route to the *Meiguo dashiguan* in case they were separated.

Peter protested that she had endangered herself once, and he would not hear of her going with him. Ah-peng dismissed his words saying, "You are young and therefore not wise. I am old and wise, and needed if you are to succeed. Pe-ter, I speak the truth."

Resignedly, he said, "Very well, grandmother, we will go together, but we have not decided whether by day or by night. By day the streets are crowded so we will be less likely to be noticed by soldiers or police. By night, we lose that advantage, though guards around the embassy may be less watchful." He took her rough hand. "What do you say?"

"Coming and going I thought of those things," she told him, "and I believe we should plan to enter the city by daylight, but not approach the embassy until well after nightfall. I marked a tradesmen's hostel where we can wait and rest. From there it is only a few minutes walk to your embassy."

The realization that freedom was nearing his grasp made his heart beat faster. His throat was dry.

Ah-peng went to the open doorway and peered up at the sky. Coming back, she said, "There is time for another meal. I suppose you are hungry as always?"

He nodded that he was.

"Very well, then. I will see what is to be found among the fishermen, though the hour is late and the best fish gone. Meanwhile, you can make yourself useful. Add charcoal, stoke the fire, and boil water in the kettle." A smile crinkled her face. "I think even a man can do such simple things."

"I will try, grandmother," he humored her, and she went out to gather eggs for bartering.

When the kettle was boiling, Peter got into his travel clothing:

loose black trousers with a waist drawstring and a large blouse of the same material. He fashioned a string to keep the hat positioned on his head and pulled on the woven-straw sandals. The knife he tucked into his waistband where it was hidden by the blouse.

Ah-peng came back and opened a large leaf in which she had brought a gutted eel. She chopped off head and tail, and said, "No good fish, but some say *shan yu* is even better."

"It is," he agreed as she added onions and herbs to the kettle and dropped in the eel. She took the eel head out to the chickens and brought back four eggs that she put into the boiling water. "For our journey," she explained, and drew him into the light for examination. "Remember to keep the hat brim low before your eyes."

"Yes, grandmother," he said dutifully.

"In public I will lead you with a cord to show your blindness, or take your hand at other times." She shook her head. "Success will not come easily."

"I'm told that it seldom does."

"A person of wisdom told you that."

"My grandfather. The doctor who healed in Kunming during the war."

"Yes, you have spoken of him. He still lives?"

Peter nodded. "Still healing the poor."

"Like my husband," she said sadly. "All his life he did only good for others. And for that he was murdered."

"So tragic," he said quietly and took her hand. "I don't know how I can ever repay you for all you've done for me, but I'll try for the rest of my life."

Her hand squeezed his. "What I do, I do in memory of my husband and the son I will never see again. So for now, you are my son, and so you must not think of repayment."

"But I will."

She cooked the eel until the flaky white flesh peeled easily from its snakelike spine. The savory meat almost melted in Peter's mouth and stimulated his hunger for the rice she next prepared. Again he marveled at how much she could do with almost nothing, and knew her example was one he would not forget.

"It will take us two hours to the city outskirts," she told him, "so we will leave very soon." After rinsing their bowls and quenching the charcoal, Ah-peng went outside to feed her chickens and rabbits. Returning, she said, "I gave them enough for two days. More, and they would kill themselves eating." The idea of having too much to eat made her chuckle, and Peter smiled, too.

From a large rag she made a bundle to hold a flask of water, boiled eggs, and a mango. Her money she carried inside her waistband. "And the gun?" she asked.

He shook his head. "If trouble comes the knife will do as well."

So, after tying her food bundle across her back, Ah-peng inspected Peter a final time, adjusted the hat brim low on his forehead, and set the sunglasses on the bridge of his nose. Then she looped a cord around his waist and payed out a four-foot length before knotting a handhold. "Always keep your eyes turned upward, Pe-ter. Let me guide you over and around potholes and obstacles. Our rulers claim to have accomplished much in our Great Socialist society, but building and maintaining roads remains beyond them." She pulled on the line and started off, Peter following.

As she led him through the bamboo copse to the trail where she had found him, Peter wondered if he would ever see the place again.

From now on there was no turning back; there was only the way ahead.

HONG KONG

SHORTLY AFTER DAWN BRAND placed another call to the consulate and left a second message for Briggs Dockerty with the switchboard operator: Call Brand ASAP.

Dory was still unconscious from her last fix, so Brand showered and soaped energetically, hoping the kid didn't have herpes or some Asian venereal disease. Then he went down to the hotel dining room, ordered breakfast, and began scanning *The South China Morning Post*. One Washington item he read carefully suggested that the present CIA Director was planning to leave and the White House was drawing up a list of potential replacements. Brand frowned. Darman was going to get on that list if it was humanly possible; he'd pull out all stops, enlist the support of congressmen, senators, corporate CEOs, Harvard Law School classmates, and the chairman of the President's party. He could do it, too, Brand thought angrily; the son of a bitch has all the qualifications—except integrity. He dug savagely into a chunk of sausage and swallowed it, nearly choking until coffee cleared his throat.

He felt helpless to stop Gerold's almost-predictable nomination until he recalled Tommy Gray's threat to pass the story of Gerold *mère et fils* to the Foreign Affairs Committee. Tommy would do it anonymously—as things were done inside the Beltway—and even though unprovable, the tale would cause influential members to question Gerold's suitability for the directorship.

So there was hope.

Brand continued eating the mushroom omelet, and when his plate was nearly clean he noticed Nina Kenton enter the dining room. Seeing Brand, she nodded and walked toward him. As Brand rose she said, "Good morning, may I join you?"

He gestured at a chair and sat down. "Mark," she said, "dear Mark. I couldn't sleep last night, replaying that unwholesome scene I provoked. I invaded your privacy, drew unwarranted conclusions, and acted the total bitch." Brand stared at her incredulously. She leaned forward and said, "I'm truly contrite and humble. Honestly. I can't bear letting everything end on that awful note. Is it within you to be charitable and forgive me?"

Shit, he thought, but said, "Why the sudden change, Nina? You wouldn't listen to me before, why now?"

She breathed deeply. "During the night I came to realize that I was replaying a scene that still pains me—catching my husband with a woman. He had no excuse for that, but you said—if I remember—the girl was the daughter of an old friend." She swallowed. "Care to tell me more?"

Why not? he asked himself. She's going to cling like a limpet regardless of what I say. He signaled a waiter who brought a coffee cup and filled it for Nina. "Thank you," she said, added sugar, and sat back. Waiting.

"That was the truth, Nina. Her father is an old associate of mine. When he learned I was coming here he asked me to look for his runaway daughter, admitted she was an addict." He sipped from his cup. "I'm not going to name the father because he's prominent in Georgetown circles and you may know him. To say the family is dysfunctional puts it mildly. Anyway, I circulated the girl's photo through Chinese friends, and yesterday she was brought to me. Now I can appreciate your reaction to bald appearances, but the girl was filthy when she arrived. She was showering off accumulated grime when you walked in, and I'd ordered food for her."

"Oh, Mark"—her hand reached over to cover his—"I'm so very sorry for misjudging you. What are you going to do with her?"

"Turn her over to the consulate—a moment that can't come too soon." He glanced at his wristwatch. "When the consulate opens I'm calling an officer who knows her father. He'll handle things from then on."

Her eyes looked upward. "Then she's—?"

"Asleep. Addicts don't have much energy, they sleep a lot."

Nina nodded solemnly. "Poor thing. Mark, I understand completely and respect what you're doing." She paused. "Can I help at all?"

"No, and I'll be busy with details the rest of the day."

"I see. And—tonight?"

He shrugged. "Things need cooling down," he replied noncommittally.

"But have you forgiven me?"

"I'm considering it," he told her, "and I'm preoccupied with finding Peter."

"Of course. Yesterday you left me to see someone. Was there new information?"

"Some. So I have a lot to do. In Washington, remember, I tried to discourage you from coming along, knowing I was going to be plenty busy, but—"

"I came anyway—thinking to show you my devotion."

"You have," he said wearily, "and I appreciate it. But I'm going to be out and around, no time for—diversions."

"I understand, of course. But you're not going to visit the Mainland, are you?"

"Wouldn't be wise, would it?"

"Quite unwise, I'd say."

He got up. "I'll keep in touch," he said and left.

After watching him walk the length of the dining room, Nina recalled last night's aftermath when, in her room, she had fought to suppress reflexive anger, reasoning that John would never pardon her breaking with Brand. She was still hungover from all the liquor she'd drunk, but it had helped her resolve to don a humble face and beg Brand's forgiveness for her harridan behavior.

I crawled, damn him, she told herself, and he still wouldn't bend. Last night I was so furious I even thought of poisoning him, but that would cost me the apartment and John's payments, and I desperately need both.

At least, she mused, he's not going to China, so from John's point of view my trip will have been worthwhile.

A waiter asked if she wanted a menu, produced one, and wrote down her order. While Nina sipped a second cup of coffee, she thought that even if Brand never slept with her again she would still have to watch his movements like a hawk.

IN BRAND'S ROOM, DORY was stirring. The phone showed a red message light, so he dialed the switchboard and learned that Dockerty had called. When he got Dockerty on the phone, Briggs said, "Jesus, Mark, what's so fuckin' urgent? Sky falling in?"

"I can't handle sarcasm this early, Briggs, so put on your consular cap and get the hell over here. I've got Darman's child."

He hung up and woke Dory. "Get dressed," he told her. "This is moving day."

"Don't want me to stay?" she asked sleepily.

"Too complicated, honey. Our lifestyles don't mesh."

She sat up and the sheet fell away, exposing her large breasts. One hand began scratching the inner side of her arm. "I'm needin'," she whined. "How about a fix?"

"Get dressed and eat breakfast. After that . . ." He called room service and ordered omelet, ham, toast, and coffee.

"Eating's all you think about," she said as she padded to the bathroom. "Oughta be fat as a pig." The door slammed shut.

While she was showering, Brand laid out her new clothing, let the waiter in, and after Dory was dressed and slowly eating, Briggs Dockerty arrived. After a glance at her the Base Chief said, "Sent off a Flash to Darman, side channel. This is Doreen Gerold, huh?"

She looked up hostilely. "Who the fuck are you?"

"The man who's going to restore you to your anguished parent. How's that grab you?"

"Ungood," she slurred. "Very damn ungood. Mark, I need that fix."

"Patience," he said, and drew Dockerty aside. "It'll take Darman a day or so to get here so I suggest you stash her in some rehab place for attitude remediation."

"You're bowing out?"

"Damn right I am. This refractory child is too much for me."

"What'd she mean, 'fix'?"

"She's an addict, man, get that in your skull." He went to his luggage and brought back the last of Sammy's hypos.

Dockerty said, "Is that what I think it is?"

Brand nodded.

"How'd you find her?"

"Through those 'criminal associates' Special Branch complained of. Leave it at that, Briggs, and after she eats she goes."

"You'll go with us?"

"Like hell. Call one of your gofers to bring 'round a car. Ask the consulate for a rehab referral, short-time. This is your day to make big points with Darman." He watched Dory swallow the last of her ham, and said, "Mr. Dockerty here will handle the fix, Dory, so be nice to him." He heard Briggs on the telephone, talking to his office, issuing orders. To Dory, Brand said, "You're a lucky young lady, you've got a home to go to. Thousands don't."

"Some home," she sneered. "Gimme a fuckin' break, man."

"You'll get all the breaks you deserve," he told her, and gave Dockerty the boxed hypo. "Let her shoot up when she gets frantic, not before. You need time to get her to a clinic."

Dockerty stared at him. "You're making me an accomplice."

"You're not in law enforcement, Briggs, so relax. Do what's necessary and put it behind you."

Suddenly Dory left the table and hurried to the bathroom. They heard retching sounds, and after a while the toilet flushed. "Not used to food," Brand explained. "Stomach's shrunk. Where in hell's your man?"

After a while Dory emerged from the bathroom, her face pale and gaunt.

The buzzer sounded, Brand opened the door, and a well-dressed young man came in. To Dockerty, he said, "Everything's laid on, sir. Car waiting."

"Dory," Briggs said, "you'll go down between us—you don't look too good, might stumble and mar that pretty face."

"Fuck you," she grated, but went to the men. Turning to Brand, she said, "I guess you expect me to thank you."

"Uh-uh, out of character. Just speak well of me to Dad."

He watched them leave, then closed the door behind them. He felt sudden relief, the flaky waif was gone. Let Briggs and Darman wrestle with the problem, he'd had enough of it.

His gaze turned to the bar, and he thought a shot wouldn't hurt, early in the day as it was. So he poured scotch in a tumbler, added ice, and gulped gratefully. Then he folded yesterday's clothing receipts and stuck them in his bag. He'd get them to Darman as a reminder of good deeds done and it would needle the shit out of him.

Besides, he mused, having an addict daughter wasn't going to play well for a man who wanted to be Director of the CIA.

With that he blocked Darman's troubled family from his mind and thought about his meeting with Cheong Wing-dah. He wouldn't have sought Fatso's help, but Mary had suggested and arranged the meeting, so he was obliged to follow through. Maybe something will come of it, he reasoned; anything to help me find my son.

The telephone's ringing interrupted his thoughts. Thinking it might be Sammy Lu, Brand heard instead a voice that resembled Mary's.

"Mr. Brand?"

"Yes."

"Cheong Chu-li. I—I'm in the hotel lobby—"

"Go on."

"I—if you're free, I would like a few minutes of your time."

"Of course. Shall I come down?"

"No—no, it is better that I come up. Thank you."

He replaced the receiver and began straightening the beds, rinsed his glass, and presently the buzzer sounded. When he opened the door the girl quickly came in. She was wearing a light hooded cloak over a scarlet cheongsam, and her features seemed strained.

"I have only a minute, sir, but there is something I wanted to tell you." Her cheeks were flushed and there was a film of perspiration on her upper lip.

Brand asked, "A message from your mother?"

"No—no, not that—though she would approve."

She glanced around uncertainly until Brand said, "Please be seated."

"Thank you." She did so gracefully, drawing the cloak aside and pulling back the hood to reveal perfectly coiffed dark hair.

Emotion tightened Brand's throat; memories flooded his mind. His daughter was here—alone with him for the first time in their lives. "What is it?" he asked gently. "Is there something I can do? For you? For your mother?"

"Oh, no," she said quickly, and glanced at the closed bathroom door. "Are we alone?"

"Yes, just the two of us. There's nothing to fear. Please take your time." Curiosity quickened his pulse. What on earth had brought her to him?

Composing herself, Chu-li said, "At the gallery . . . remember, I asked if you knew my father?"

"I remember."

"Well, Madame—that is, my mother—arranged for you to see my father today—is that not so?"

"It is."

"And you were once a good friend of my mother's—on Taiwan?"

"I still am. Please, if there's anything I can do, just tell me."

She drew in a deep breath. "I fear that what I am about to say is disloyal to my father, but he has never been a good husband to my mother, and so my loyalty is to her. Do—do you understand any of this?"

"Not really, so—"

"Cheong Wing-dah used to beat my mother. As a child I often fell asleep when she was sobbing beside me. My father can be a beast when he drinks—and he often does—so we see him as seldom as possible."

"Go on."

"And he keeps other women—concubines, I suppose." Her cheeks turned pink and she gazed down at her folded hands. "That is the least of it, though." She looked up at him. "I am taking a very long time, am I not?"

"Take all the time you need, child. So—"

She seemed to steel herself before saying, "Last night we were at a dinner he gave for Hong Kong officials—some brought wives, others their concubines—an insult to his wife, my mother. Afterward, I was in the powder room and heard him outside talking to a man—I don't know who—and my father said he was meeting today with a Westerner he had once known on Taiwan. That Westerner, he said, was asking for help with a Mainland problem, and while he would pretend to lend assistance, he had disliked you all his life and was planning to do you harm." Tears formed in her eyes. She reached out and clutched his jacket. "Oh, sir, I'm so confused. But my mother's friend is my friend, and I fear you may be in danger."

Brand patted her hand. "Your mother knows of this?"

She shook her head, dabbed at her eyes with a small kerchief. "Madame—Mother—told me of your son—Peter, is it? And you are here to search for him. So"—she swallowed again—"I did not want to keep secret from you knowledge that might prevent your finding him."

Brand thought it over. "I'm very grateful, Chu-li, and you shouldn't be confused. I think your duty was to your mother and her old friend, though she need not know of your coming."

Rising, she managed a bleak smile. "Sir—" she began, but Brand interrupted.

"Please, Chu-li, don't be formal as with a stranger. I'm Mark. Can you say it?"

"Mark. It is what my mother calls you. And you knew my grandfather Chen, so you *are* a family friend." The thought brightened her face. Almost shyly she said, "The French sisters who first taught me gave me another name. They called me Solange. Do you like it?"

Brand nodded. "A name that combines sunshine and angels—I like it very much—and it suits you well."

"I'm glad you like it, Mark. Now I must return to the gallery before I am missed. If my father's men followed me, as they sometimes do, I must find an excuse for my absence."

Impulsively, he drew her to him, brushed his lips against her cheek. She did not react, but stood passively until he stepped back. "Thank you again for everything, Chu-li, I'm so grateful you came."

She drew the hood over her hair, gathered the cloak, and said, "For your sake—and my mother's—you must be careful of Wing-dah."

"I will."

"And—Mark—when we meet again, please make no mention of this."

"I promise," he said, and she was gone.

That Chu-li had run risks to warn him of Wing-dah's deception filled Brand with gratitude and pride. She had been disloyal to one parent to be loyal to her mother, and Brand saw it as an honorable thing. His daughter's words reinforced Mary's concern, and now he was better armed than before. To cancel the meeting might arouse Wing-dah's suspicions, especially if a watcher had seen her enter the hotel. So his role would be to dissimulate, feign a friendliness he had never felt for Fatso Cheong, and pretend to accept whatever help he might suggest.

While telling him nothing in return.

From his suitcase Brand got out the black switchblade given to him by Johnny Shek. He pressed the spring release and a five-inch blade shot out. He thumbed the double edges lightly and found them sharp as a knife needed to be. Pressing the release button, he housed the blade in its protective haft and slid the switchblade in a trouser pocket.

As the Agency mantra went: Far better to have a weapon and not need it than need one and be without.

Eighteen

WASHINGTON

SEATED AT HIS GLOBECO DESK, Tom Gray watched Gorgon satellite photos move in slow procession across his monitor screen. Today's NRO feed was more interesting than what he'd become accustomed to, so he downloaded images selectively and heard hard copies slide into the tray behind him. When the feed ended Tommy gathered the prints and placed them under the strong light of a large magnifying lens. With a marker he circled areas of special interest, numbered them, and made identifying notes on a separate pad. Then he reexamined each photo and turned off the light.

For a while he considered the inferences he'd drawn from the photos, then lifted a red-and-white-striped receiver from its cradle and punched four buttons sequentially. At the Langley end of the secure landline, a similarly striped telephone rang on the desk of Darman Gerold. Gray heard it ring five times before Gerold's voice said irritably, "Mark? What the hell is it? Can't talk now because—"

Calmly, Gray said, "Mark's in Hong Kong, Darman. Gray speaking."

"Forgot. Okay, Tom, I'm on my way out of the office. Can't it wait?"

"Your decision, but you ought to see what just came in. NRO feed from Gorgon. Darman, I think it's important."

"Okay, okay, make it fast, I got a plane to catch. Talk, Tom."

Gray sighed. "About two hundred miles west of Beijing there's a warhead assembly plant, nearest town, Yangyuan."

"Yangyuan. Go on."

"Every ten days Gorgon covers it. Ten days ago five freight cars were lined up on a plant siding. As of last night they were gone, moved since previous coverage."

"So? What's the significance?"

"Last night—our time—Gorgon picked up the same freight cars on a factory siding at Zhuolu, a hundred miles east-northeast of Yangyuan."

"Bottom line, for God's sake, I'll miss my plane."

"Zhuolu's one of their chemical warfare plants, Darman." As you damn well ought to know, he thought disgustedly.

"Oh. That's the bottom line?"

"Inferentially, Darman, the warheads are being charged with lethal chemicals. Gas."

"But you don't know that as an absolute?"

"No," Gray conceded, "but arguing in the alternative, why else would the warheads be there?"

"Isn't that something you're being paid to determine?"

"Yes and no. We have photo indications only. But I think it's serious. I'm going to transmit the photos to you. At least look them over before you go."

"All right, I'll scan them, and pass them to Ray Applegate."

"Can't, hasn't got Gorgon clearance." Ray was Tom's replacement as Chief, Far East Operations.

"Damn. Then you better show a set to Win Hilyard. He's cleared, isn't he?"

"Yeah, but he's leaving State. Your call, Darman."

"If Win's not around, try Irving Chenow, okay?"

"Okay. Be in Hong Kong long?"

"Long enough to bring back my daughter—your ears only."

"I understand. Transmitting now." He replaced the receiver and sent the photos via secure facsimile line. After that he set the originals in a folder and placed a call to the China Desk at State.

Waiting for Hilyard to respond, Gray thought how futile it was to have an asshole like Gerold in a position of decision-making authority, so it was probably for the better that Darman was leaving town. Hilyard was bright, if languid, and could be counted on to move the intelligence up the chain of command. But as an Assistant Secretary, Irving Chenow could take the findings to the National Security Council if he was equally disturbed by the convergence of warheads and a weapon of mass destruction.

Hilyard's secretary said, "Mr. Hilyard's been clearing out his desk, sir; came in for an hour this morning and won't be back today."

"I see." Win's replacement hadn't been named or cleared for Gorgon. "Could I trouble you to transfer me to Mr. Chenow's office?"

"Certainly, sir. One moment."

"Assistant Secretary Chenow's office," a female voice said.

"I'm Tom Gray, miss. Mr. Chenow doesn't know me, but please tell him I'm acting for Mark Brand." He cleared his throat. "I need to see Mr. Chenow on an urgent matter. As soon as possible."

"Mr. Chenow is in a meeting, sir, but I suggest you come now, and Mr. Chenow will see you as soon as he's free."

"Thank you." Gray slid the photo folder into a red-striped envelope and put the envelope into a leather briefcase. Then he called for a car and walked downstairs to meet it.

CHENOW SAID, "SO YOU'RE taking Mark's place while he's away."

"Yes, sir."

"Before we get to your concerns, do you know if Mark located his son?"

"Not to my knowledge. He's in Hong Kong, that's all I know."

"Hell of a thing," Chenow said angrily and tapped a bound report on his desk. "Beijing broadcasts say a Westerner escaped from Lingyuan Special Prison and hasn't been recaptured." He stroked his chin. "Could be Peter."

Gray sat forward. "Didn't know that. We don't get foreign broadcast summaries at my place. Yes, could be Mark's son."

"How to find him?" the Assistant Secretary said musingly. "Like looking for a needle in a thousand haystacks." He shook his head. "Okay, what have we got here?"

After spreading the photos across Chenow's desk, Gray explained the sequence and said, "Yangyuan manufactures warhead casings. Normally the nuclear material is added at Wuhan where it's made. Instead, we see these casings sent to Zhuolu, a chemical warfare plant."

Putting on half glasses, Chenow bent over the photos to study them more closely. Straightening, he removed the lenses and said, "So you infer the warheads will carry—what?"

"Binary compounds that stay inert until united by explosion or impact. Then they form lethal gas."

The Assistant Secretary swiveled in his chair to look out over downtown Washington. After a while he asked, "These warheads—for what size missiles?"

"Intermediate range."

"Umm. Got a target or targets in mind?"

"Possibly. What I've got, sir, is a semi-educated guess."

"I understand. With that proviso, what's your thought?"

Uneasily, Gray said, "Well, the Chinese army has been test-firing missiles from mobile launchers at the Leping military base—Jiangxi Province." He swallowed. "Warheads didn't carry explosives so we don't really know what or why they've been testing. But you know that the Central Committee has threatened to invade Taiwan if Taiwan declares itself independent of the Mainland. And you know how it rankles Beijing that Taiwan—which they consider a mere province—is a free island."

"With enormous economic growth." The Assistant Secretary nodded. "Yes, I know the threats, but so far we've always considered them aimed at home consumption." He shrugged. "Maybe not. And it wouldn't make sense to invade an island destroyed by missiles, would it?"

"Not to Western logic. But the Chinese—" He spread his hands. "You never know."

"Still," Chenow said, "to hypothesize a bit further: it would make sense to destroy the population with a weapon that leaves buildings and factories intact." He eyed Gray. "That makes sense?"

"It does."

He gestured at the photos on his desk. "Gas-loaded warheads. What kind of gas is made at Zhuolu?"

"It's not gas until the compounds are combined, but the plant takes in all kinds of chemicals. There's nerve gas, of course, but it occurs to me the Chinese may have been inspired by what that Japanese cult did to the Tokyo subway. The lunatics used sarin."

Chenow paled. "Sarin," he echoed. "Can they make it at Zhuolu?"

"They can make it anywhere, but it has to be warhead-loaded at a site like Zhuolu."

"Then the warheads are joined to missiles, and the missiles are loaded on mobile launchers." He swallowed. "Aimed at Taiwan."

Gray said nothing. Chenow scanned the photos again and looked up. "Bad news, Mr. Gray. Who else have you told?"

"Darman Gerold—but he's left for Hong Kong."

"Win Hilyard?"

Gray shook his head. "He wasn't around, so I took it on myself to come here."

Chenow gathered the photos into a pile and inserted it into the classified envelope. "I'd better take these to the Secretary, ask him to schedule the matter for the NSC. I agree this is damn urgent, and I appreciate your taking action." He stood up. "You'll hear from me if an NSC briefing is called for. Meanwhile, this is between us. Don't inform anyone else."

Gray said, "That's understood." They shook hands across the desk, and Gray left the office, satisfied with what he'd done, though realizing he'd propounded what was no more than speculation based on inferences.

What was needed, of course, was an on-site agent who could identify what was being loaded into the warheads at Zhuolu, and tell where the assembled missiles were being delivered. Lacking such an agent, all he could do was increase Gorgon surveillance and keep Chenow informed.

Back at his desk, Gray transmitted a request to NRO, and slowly and thoughtfully composed a memorandum for the record detailing his conversations with Gerold and Chenow, and summarizing the qualified conclusions he had reached. He dated and initialed the printout, and stored it with the computer disk in his personal file.

This could be the start of something big, he told himself as he locked the safe, and I need to cover my ass.

AFTER GRAY LEFT HIS office the Assistant Secretary phoned the Secretary's office and was granted a brief appointment for later in the day.

Staring at the photo envelope, Chenow thought, He's not going to like this, not going to like it at all. The Secretary's a prime advocate of Administration policy to ignore Chinese lies, insults, and provocations in order to promote trade. Confrontation and sanctions would cost American jobs, according to the Secretary and his coterie of foreign policy wonks. So at all costs don't upset Beijing.

But we have a defense treaty with Taiwan. If the island were to be invaded, we'll have to honor that treaty—and that means sending American ground forces and getting involved in another Asian war against an army of overwhelming numbers. That could perhaps be avoided by a surgical air strike to eliminate the Zhuolu and Yangyuan factories, and the loaded freight cars. That action would save the Taiwanese from death by sarin or some other horrible gas, but it would certainly destroy trade relations with China.

Irresistibly, I'm reminded of Munich, umbrellas, and a far-off country named Czechoslovakia. Does history repeat itself? Unfortunately too often it does.

He left his desk and went over to the window. Looking down, he thought, This Secretary has never wanted to project American might where it could be useful. Let the U.N. do it has been his guiding philosophy. But to take this apparent problem to the Security Council would require proof positive, and that we don't have. If counteraction is to be taken we'd have to do it alone. Not that I'm ready to recommend air strikes on the basis of what Gray's shown me, but it's an option that should be considered. The proper place for that is with the NSC.

The government needs to be told what Gray and I know, so I'm going to ask the Secretary's permission to lay it before the NSC. He might warm to that approach because it would sideline him from the decision process, at least until the President requests his advice. The Secretary won't want to hear about Taiwan because it's an obstacle to bounteous exchanges with Beijing. All he wants is good tidings from Beijing, when all I can offer him are distressing suggestions of Beijing duplicity and murderous intent.

Through the intercom his secretary said, "Sir, there's been a cancellation in the Secretary's schedule and he can see you now."

Assistant Secretary Chenow picked up the photo envelope and squared his shoulders. I'm not expecting much, he told himself, but whatever the outcome, I gotta try.

Nineteen

HONG KONG

CHEONG WING-DAH'S WHITE STRETCH Mercedes picked up Brand at the Manchu and rode him smoothly over the island's spine to one of the many tall buildings perched high above Repulse Bay.

The driver steered into the garage entrance of a new apartment building and followed the corkscrew lane downward through levels of subterranean garage. Finally at the bottom, the driver stopped by an elevator door, got out, and opened Brand's door. He led Brand to the elevator door and opened it with a key. "Penthouse, sir," he said to Brand. "Mr. Cheong awaits you."

Stepping into the elevator, Brand noticed that it was stopped at sublevel five. He pushed the PH button, the door closed, and the elevator ascended rapidly. The penthouse was a stop above the twentieth floor, so, taking garage depth into consideration, the building was twenty-six stories overall.

When the elevator stopped, the doors opened and Brand stepped onto a crimson Chinese carpet. From one side of the foyer a neatly dressed man appeared and said, "Please follow me."

The long corridor was floored with patterned marble, and each wall displayed Chinese antiquities. One shelf held a dozen snuff bottles of crystal, amber, porcelain, and celadon. Framed under glass was a gold brocade coat, beside it a blue silk dragon robe. Opposite was a set of pink silk aprons, and above it a large mother-of-pearl inlaid tray. He glanced at a ceremonial dagger mounted beside its ornamented scabbard, and walked on.

On the floor stood a pair of Ming-style elephant seats, four hexagonal garden seats, and several tall aubergine jars surmounted with Fu lions forming cover handles. It was an awesome collection of Chinese artifacts, and Brand sensed that their value was close to incalculable.

Finally the corridor gave out into a spacious sunlit room, carpeted and furnished in modern Chinese style. To the right, ceiling-high glass separated the air-conditioned room from a broad open balcony, and at the room's far end two hallways led off into what Brand presumed were dining and living quarters.

Directly ahead was a modern version of a Manchu throne, slightly raised on a carpeted dais. On the throne sat an obese Oriental man wearing a coat ornamented in gold and silver brocade. His long black hair was swept back behind his ears, and his rotund face wore a mustache that outlined his mouth and joined with a short black beard. Eyeing Brand, he half rose, waved a hand in greeting, and settled himself back on his cushions. "Welcome, old friend," he said. "Too seldom am I privileged to welcome a noble brother of the Fang-tse clan."

Approaching, Brand bowed his head and tented his fingers against his chest. In humble tones, he replied, "You do me too much honor, old friend. And I am grateful that you were willing to receive me."

Wing-dah lifted one hand dismissively and Brand raised his head to look around. "This palace pays equal tribute to your elevated station, and to your respect for the ancient culture. I am overwhelmed with admiration."

Wing-dah smiled. "Thank you, Mark Brand. Your courtesy continues to mark you as a man of taste and discernment." He paused. "Tea? Something stronger?"

"Tea."

Wing-dah clapped and a servant appeared, bowing as Wing-dah instructed him. Then Wing-dah indicated a chair beside his and Brand seated himself. For a few moments there was silence, broken when Wing-dah asked, "Was it through chance you stopped by the Celestial Galleries and encountered my wife, Ling-mei?"

"Not entirely. As occasionally in the past, I lunched at Johnny Shek's restaurant. He joined me, and we spent a pleasant hour recounting old Taiwan memories. He mentioned that Museum Director Chen had died and his daughter married you. And he described a number of your successful enterprises, among which was the finest antiquities gallery in Hong Kong. So when opportunity arose, I went in and asked your daughter if it was possible to see Madame Cheong, identifying myself as a long-ago friend of her father's from Taiwan. Her mother was not there, she said, but a day or so later a note from your wife invited me for tea." He paused. "While we talked I revealed the quest that brought me to Hong Kong: searching for my son imprisoned on the Mainland."

Wing-dah nodded sympathetically. "So my wife told me. As I am not blessed with a son I am willing to do whatever I can to restore yours to you."

Tea arrived on two inlaid trays, the servant poured and went away. Before sipping, Brand said, "To your eternal health."

"And yours." After setting aside his tea, Wing-dah asked, "In what way do you feel I can be of possible service?"

Brand shrugged. "That would be for you to say. But my understanding that you import many things from the Mainland suggests it might be possible to—shall we say—import my son."

"Possible, yes," Wing-dah acknowledged, "after your son is found."

"That happy event," Brand said, "is yet to be realized, but it bolsters my spirits to think that an exit for him is not impossible." He paused. "Without inquiring impolitely, I would assume that the cooperation of certain Chinese officials would be required."

Wing-dah nodded. "In that respect nothing has changed from former times. *Zha qu* remains a powerful persuader."

"That being so," Brand responded, "permit me to say that where expense is incurred I will be only too happy to defray it."

Wing-dah shrugged. "If and when the time is appropriate we may consider the point. Meanwhile, please do not let it burden your thoughts." He sipped from his teacup and set it down. "Now, tell me how your son came to be arrested, and why."

"Gladly." As Brand began speaking, he noticed men standing in the shadows of the two hallways, and decided they had been posted to recognize him in the future. "My son Peter works for an investment banking firm in Washington and has a fiancée who is Chinese by birth. She is part of a circle of young dissident students who either fled the Mainland after Tiananmen or refused to return to China thereafter." He paused, noting the hallways now empty of watchers, and continued. "Unfortunately, Peter let himself be persuaded to perform a service for them in Canton while in Hong Kong on business for his firm. At the Blue Dragon curio shop he asked for and was given a roll or so of film that he planned to take back to Washington. At that point he was arrested by Gong An Ju officers and taken to Beijing."

Wing-dah's head moved regretfully. "Foolish of him to go there," he intoned, "but the importunings of a loved one are difficult to refuse."

"True. From the little I've been able to learn in Hong Kong, Peter was tried in secret, sentenced, and sent either to prison or to a distant Thought Reform Labor Camp."

Wing-dah stroked the point of his beard thoughtfully. "Do you know the specific charge against him?"

"Espionage, I suppose."

"The length of his sentence?"

"I have heard only that it is a long one."

"Then prison is more likely. A prison for political prisoners, you agree?"

Brand nodded.

"Your Beijing embassy has inquired of the authorities?"

"I believe so. And the consulate in Canton." He spread his hands, palms up. "Nothing. What concerns me most is the failure of the authorities to publicize my son's arrest and trial."

Wing-dah grunted. "Doubtless that is being withheld for some future political or economic advantage. You know how that system works."

"Only too well. And I should add that in recent days Beijing radio reported the prison escape of a Westerner." He sighed. "It could be Peter—but there must be a score of imprisoned Westerners. The escapee's name was not given."

Wing-dah frowned. "Complicating an already difficult situation. Tell me, old friend, do you plan to go to Beijing and—investigate?"

"A possibility," Brand told him, "but I have nothing to go on warranting such a trip."

"Personally," said Wing-dah, "I would recommend against it. But if you go, I may be able to clear the way for you somewhat."

"I'll remember that," Brand replied. "Now, it has occurred to me that if Peter were to escape and take refuge in, say, the embassy, the authorities would demand his return. I expect they would ring the embassy and examine everyone who leaves it. Consequently, he could not just walk out. But if he were to depart concealed in a van of diplomatic household effects, or a crate of valuable artifacts, he might pass undetected and reach Hong Kong by air."

Wing-dah said, "I was thinking along similar lines." He leaned forward and fat bulged upward under his chin. "Were your son able to escape to the embassy."

"Of course. And the embassy's attitude is crucial. My country appeases Beijing whenever possible. Once the authorities demand the embassy turn over an escaped prisoner convicted of espionage against the PRC, how long would the embassy protect him?"

Wing-dah sighed. "Not long, I fear. So I will make tentative arrangements to take effect in the happy event your son finds refuge in the embassy. Then he can be moved out with little delay."

"You have lightened my burdens immensely," Brand said, "and I will impose no further on your time." He stood up, ostensibly relieved, and Wing-dah said, "Once you have news of your son you have only to inform me. Then I will take such measures as are called for."

Brand's head bowed. "I am truly grateful," he said, "and I cannot leave without congratulating you on your daughter, Chu-li. So personable and well educated, she is a credit to her parents and does honor to her rearing."

Wing-dah smoothed the curve of his mustache. "As a father you will understand that no expense is too great where the welfare of a child is concerned."

"You excel in all things," Brand replied, and took two backward steps from the throne before turning around.

He heard Wing-dah utter the parting formula: "Do not hasten from this humble place which your presence has illuminated." Brand acknowledged the utterance with another bow of his head, and walked to the corridor through which he had come.

There he was joined by the previous escort who accompanied him down the elevator to the waiting Mercedes. Brand got in and was surprised when the escort got in beside him. "For your safety," the escort explained, and produced a nickled handgun from his shoulder holster. "Too often bandits rob cars on this road and kill the passengers."

"And the Colony police?"

"Too few to patrol our roads."

"Then I welcome your protection."

"Cheong Wing-dah insists on it."

Brand gazed out of the tinted window as portions of the bay flashed by through gaps in rocky outcrops. Fatso Cheong is still the smarmy kid I avoided in Taipei, he thought, despite the ostentatious opulence of his abode. He's circled and imprisoned in fat, and at his weight prefers not to move around.

It relieved Brand that Cheong's disability made sexual congress with Mary a near impossibility, though her expressed distaste for her husband suggested they had not coupled in years.

Besides, he remembered Chu-li's resentment over her presumed father's concubines, so if Fatso was not the eunuch he appeared to be, he had other means of sexual relief available.

As the Mercedes descended the steep spine, Brand reviewed what he and Cheong had said to each other. Brand had concealed the sponsor of Peter's Canton mission, the CIA, and indicated uncertainty over Peter's assumed escape. Through it all, Fatso had seemed polite and sympathetic; probably, Brand mused, to disarm me. But if Peter ever came into Fatso's power, I think he would kill him, there being no more horrific form of revenge. "Old friend" was on Fatso's tongue too readily, like all the blather about the noble brother of the Fang-tse clan.

What he'd learned from the interview was that Cheong Wing-dah was the last man in Hong Kong to whom he would entrust Peter's life, or his own.

After the limousine rounded a hairpin turn, the driver slowed and seemed headed toward a viewing overlook farther along. Peripherally, Brand saw his companion's hand edge toward the revolver in his lap.

Brand's right hand thrust into his pocket and gripped the switchblade handle. When the driver seemed committed to the overlook, Brand said, "Stopping here?"

"Only for a moment, it is a view worth seeing."

The driver was braking as he turned toward the overlook. Brand said, "Got a cigarette?" and the escort nodded. When the revolver hand dipped into his chest pocket, Brand said, "No, I've got things to do, we won't stop here." He pressed the handle's release button and the blade slid out with a muffled click.

Holding a pack of Marlboros, the escort said, "We really must stop," and hurriedly stuffed the cigarettes back into his pocket. The same hand dropped to cover the revolver, but by then the switchblade was out, and Brand dug the point into the man's wrist. The man yelped, jerked back his hand, and Brand grabbed the revolver.

As the man pressed the bleeding wound to his mouth, Brand pushed the gun muzzle against his ribs. "Whatever you had in mind," he snapped, "forget it."

The Mercedes slowed and turned into the overlook. The driver braked and looked around, eyes widening in disbelief. Brand swerved the pistol muzzle at the driver and said, "Eyes straight ahead," then told his escort to get out. When the man was standing, back to the precipice, he gasped, "Don't kill me."

"Why not?" Brand said through the open window. "You were going to kill me."

"No, no, it was only to frighten you."

"Why, son of a diseased sow, why?"

His face tightened at the insult, but he muttered, "To keep you from the gallery."

"What gallery?"

"Celestial Gallery, the place of Madame Cheong."

"Ah," said Brand, "so that's it." He let the man wrap his wrist with a handkerchief before saying, "I don't like threats. Tell that to the fat man if you want, or say nothing of what happened to you." He nudged the revolver into the back of the driver's neck. "You, too. And if I'm threatened again, followed, or interfered with in any way I'll shoot the street dog in the belly and watch him bleed to death. Understand that?"

"Yes," they said together. Brand ran up the window and told the driver to take him to the Manchu without delay. The Mercedes backed around and took to the road again. Brand looked back and saw his escort standing there, holding his wounded wrist. Brand smiled and put his knife away.

But, he thought farther down the road, Chu-li's fears were well founded. She thought she might have been followed to and from my hotel, and now I think she was. Hearing Mary plead for help to my son must have infuriated Fatso to the point of arranging this little episode. Perhaps the intent was only to frighten me, but the overlook is a high and isolated place where I could have been shoved over and fallen to my death. No bullet holes to prove murder, just another accidental death.

He shook his head, thinking there was nothing to be gained from telling Mary or their daughter; it was over with. If Mary asked the outcome of the meeting he would say only that a benevolent Wing-dah had offered assistance, and it had been accepted.

Before leaving the Mercedes at the hotel entrance, Brand advised the driver that silence was prudent, and went up to his room.

Responding to a message from Tommy Ling, Brand returned the call and learned that three men recruited to help him in Beijing could be seen at Brand's convenience. "Tonight," he told him, "after dark. Let me know when they're coming."

"Your room, right?"

"Right. By the way, I saw Cheong Wing-dah, and he's the same naughty boy we all disliked."

Tommy chuckled. "I want to hear about that, brother."

"You will," Brand said and hung up.

He put two ice cubes in a tumbler, filled it with scotch, and sipped as he watched freighters, sampans, ferries, and walla-wallas moving across the bay. Tomorrow, he thought, I'll check with the Travel Service for my permit. Hong Kong isn't the answer to finding Peter; it's only a beginning.

After dining alone Brand returned to his room for the arrival of Tommy Ning and his three recruits. They came promptly and Tommy introduced them as Wo, San, and Yang. The first two were slightly built men in their late twenties, while Yang was at least forty and the tallest of the three. Appraising them, Brand thought, If I'm not doing them an injustice, they all look like career criminals. He gave his Canadian business cards to Tommy and the recruits. Tommy said, "These ought to be done in Chinese, brother; I'll take care of it."

"Thanks. Have you briefed them?"

"No. I thought it best to leave it to you."

Addressing the search team, Brand said, "I need your help in and around Beijing. Have you ever been there?"

All three nodded.

"For some weeks my son Peter was a prisoner in Lingyuan Special Prison—at least that's what I believe. Somehow, he broke out and vanished. The government ordered a search for him and broadcast his description. But as far as I've heard he has not been recaptured."

The men exchanged glances, and Brand continued. "I want my son found and taken to the American embassy, where he'll be safe for a while. Then he'll need help leaving the embassy and getting to Hong Kong." He looked at them. "Any questions?"

They shook their heads. Brand said, "How you get to Beijing is your affair. I'll go there as soon as my travel permit is issued, and stay at the Beijing Hotel." He held up a business card. "Under this name. Now, I expect it will be several days before I can get to Beijing, but you three can leave before then. What I want you to do is spread out, listen, and ask questions. Since the whole area is looking for Peter your questions won't seem strange. So when you have any news at all, one of you is to come to me at the hotel." He considered. "One final thing, don't lose touch with each other. When Peter is found we will have to act rapidly, and I'll need all three of you."

Tommy asked, "Anything else, brother?"

"That's it, for now."

Tommy turned to his men. "This man is my clan brother. Whatever he tells you to do in Beijing, you will act on his order as though it came from me."

Brand shook hands with the men and said, "Until Beijing."

They nodded and filed out of the room. Tommy said, "Are you satisfied with them?"

"Of course."

"Then they'll slip across the border and take the train to Beijing. They'll work their Gong An Ju contacts as well as the streets. I have confidence they will come up with information."

Brand said, "I can't thank you enough, brother. I feel more hopeful now."

"So do I," said Tommy. They embraced fraternally, and Tommy was gone.

BRAND MIXED A DRINK and thought about Beijing. It was foolish to make plans now because everything depended on what the searchers came up with. But if Peter's recaptured, he mused, there's no option but to break him out—and that's when my three fine cutthroats can really show their worth.

The phone rang. Brand glanced at it, reluctant to answer lest it be Nina; it would be like her to call at night when, presumably, his defenses were down. Still, she hadn't bothered him since breakfast, so perhaps the caller was Tommy Ning with an afterthought.

Picking up the telephone, he said, "Yes?"

"Mark? Darman here. Got in a little while ago, and I need to talk with you."

"Feel like coming here?"

"Actually, I'm at my daughter's, ah, rest home and need to stay awhile." He paused. "Can you make breakfast tomorrow?"

"Sure."

"It's, ah, Tommy briefed me just as I was leaving for Dulles. He's come up with something that's possibly interesting." He paused again. "I think you should know about it."

"Breakfast here?"

"Good idea, I haven't checked into a hotel yet, and we should talk where we can't be, ah, overheard."

"Nine too early?"

"Sounds good—I'll have jet lag so the hour's not important."

Brand thought he heard a fatigued sigh and asked, "How's your daughter?"

"Oh, about as expected. We're flying back tomorrow." There was a long pause. "Briggs—I mean our mutual friend—told me you were responsible for bringing her in." Darman's phone discipline was always lousy, Brand thought, before Darman added, "So I have much to thank you for."

"Local contacts did it."

"Maybe so, but you had the contacts. Look, I've got some wrap-up here with the doctors and sisters, so I'll see you in the morning."

Brand replaced the receiver, wishing it were as easy to find Peter as it had been to recover Doreen. Self-centered Darman hadn't even asked about Peter. Typical, he thought as he poured a nightcap for himself and prepared for bed.

In the morning, Brand took Darman's arrival call at nine, went down and met him at the restaurant entrance. Gerold looked tired and there were circles under his eyes. They shook hands and were shown an isolated table. After ordering, they sipped coffee before Gerold said, "By no means is this the first time I've had to fetch Dory home. Six months ago from Rio. Before that, Marrakesh." He shook his head. "And each time I think she can be cured of her addiction."

"Natural to feel that way. And by you coming each time, Dory has to understand—even subliminally—that she's wanted and loved."

Gerold made a slight shrug. "What I dread is the phone call telling me she's OD'd—but I hope that never comes." He sipped orange juice and breathed deeply. "You've got a problem, too. Any word on your son, ah, Peter?"

"Nothing solid."

"So what are you going to do?"

"Put out word, keep my ears open."

Gerold nodded. "Don't know what you could accomplish in Beijing—even if your clearances didn't block Mainland travel."

Brand said, "I hardly need mention I'm still enraged that Peter was co-opted for a Mainland mission."

"No, I have it in mind. And the idiot who launched him has been censured. It'll be a long time before he sees promotion—if ever." He looked away, showing his best GQ profile. "Not that it's any satisfaction to you."

"None at all."

Gerold pursed his lips. "Briggs Dockerty didn't give me any details about finding Dory—where, what the circumstances were . . . could you fill me in?"

"Dory knows more about it than I do. Like I said, Darman, I passed her photo to some friends, and by great good luck she was brought to me. She'll probably remember in a day or so, though she may not want to talk about it."

"Yeah, she's never been forthcoming about those things." He let the waiter serve finnan haddie and eggs, place a silver toast-server nearby. He waited until Brand's plate was served before saying, "Guess you got her cleaned up, new clothing."

Brand nodded, and got out the store receipts, which he handed to Gerold. "Not a big deal," he said and cut into his omelet.

Gerold said, "I'm not great on exchange rates, Mark—how much in green?"

"Oh, fifty's plenty," he said casually, "but don't bother."

"*Au contraire.*" He fished a fifty from his billfold and gave it to Brand, who thanked him.

Then for a time they ate silently until Gerold finally said, "I ought to bring you up to speed on something Tommy Gray came across. He flashed me some Gorgon photos that suggest the Baddies are loading missile warheads with some kind of gas."

"Oh?"

"Course, he may be leaping to conclusions, but the coverage shows freight cars at the warhead factory, then at the gas plant."

"Go on."

"I was too rushed to get the photos analyzed in-house, so I told Tommy to get them over to State. Win Hilyard. For his input."

Win was the officer Irving Chenow wanted Brand to replace.

"I heard he was leaving for greener fields," Brand remarked.

"Alternatively, to Assistant Secretary Chenow. Now, Mark, no one's pushing alarm bells, but when you get back your input is going to be needed. Got to figure out what those sneaky bastards are up to."

Brand stirred his coffee. "Further coverage should give some indications. There could be a simple explanation—like a misrouted freight train, who knows?"

"Who knows indeed. And I doubt I need tell you the Administration's hell-bent on improving relations with China."

"No. We take every shit bucket they empty on us, grin, say it tastes like honey, ask for more." He shook his head disgustedly.

"China trade translates into U.S. jobs, and jobs mean elections. So if there's something menacing to be divined from Tommy's observations, the Administration won't want to hear about it."

"I'm sure of it," Brand responded. "When the Administration came into office it couldn't wait to threaten sanctions against China unless Beijing stopped violating what we call human rights. Then big-time corporations—campaign contributors—had their say, and the Administration began ignoring Chinese slave labor and all the rest." He paused. "So you're right about what impact new military nastiness might make on our betters. Probably none." He finished his omelet and the waiter added coffee to his cup. "Apropos of hardly anything, I recently read that our sainted Director may be leaving for an undisclosed . . . change. Any truth in it?"

Darman's pale cheeks flushed. "Still rumor stage, Mark."

"But you wouldn't mind a shot at the brass ring."

"Who's to say?" He moved fish bones to one side of his plate. "I have friends, associates outside the Agency, who might feel I was qualified, but I'm not a self-promoter. Give me that, Mark. I've never been a self-promoter."

"But should the halo descend on your head . . . ?"

"Why I'd remember friends and supporters—unlikely as that coronation is to happen." He gulped coffee and looked at his wristwatch. "Gotta pick up Dory, this is one flight I don't want to miss."

"Too bad you can't look in on your Stations while you're out this way. The boys always welcome visitations from on high."

"Pardon me if I disagree." He smiled the morning's first smile. "Like the first time I came through Taiwan and met you. Air pretty chilly that day."

"But no discourtesies."

"None at all." Shoving back his chair he got up. "So I'm grateful for all you did for Dory, Mark, and I owe you—big time." He started to leave, halted. "Any idea when you'll be back at GlobEco?"

"Couple weeks anyway. Meanwhile, looks like Tommy's handling things more than adequately."

"But lacking the Brand trademark of authenticity. That's a compliment, Mark—and I hope you'll have Peter with you very soon."

Brand's gaze followed Gerold from the dining room. He signed the check, deciding he ought not linger over coffee lest Nina appear.

As he rode the elevator to his floor, Brand recalled Darman bringing Taiwan into their conversation. Was it a chance mention, or was Darman giving me a subtle clue to something significant he failed to convey? Brand wondered. A connection between gas warheads and Taiwan? It would be like Darman to fly off, leaving me to figure out what it was all about. "Keep an eye on Korea," he'd enjoined not long ago, with no follow-up explanation. Since then, Paladar coverage had been negative, so I figured Darman was giving me busywork to occupy my time.

The elevator doors opened and Brand stepped out. Wherever Dory Gerold shows up next, he thought, I pray it won't be Hong Kong.

BEIJING

In addition to the bamboo staff she had cut for herself, Ah-peng fashioned a shorter probing rod for Peter, who poked the earth ahead of him from time to time. Eyes closed to help simulate blindness, Peter let his guide haul the tow rope around his waist for changes in direction. Occasionally she would snap, *"Peng yi peng,"* when he was to wait, then tug the rope to proceed.

When they were only a few miles from her hovel Peter's feet were sore and rasped from rough straw in his sandals. He likened the discomfort to walking on shoes filled with sandspurs and wondered how long he could keep the sandals on.

The country road was rutted from cart wheels and barrows. Donkeys strained to pull heavy loads on small carts piled high with vegetables, furniture, and other goods, and when they stopped, their owners lashed viciously to move them on. Peter reflected that considering Oriental disregard for human life, it was not surprising that abusing mere animals was commonplace. Still, he noticed that when peasants and bicyclists approached they often moved aside to avoid inconveniencing the old woman and the blind man she led. Paradoxical, he thought, as they neared a bent-over elderly man hobbling with a cane. He nodded to Ah-peng, and Peter heard him utter good wishes to them both. The customary courtesy of the countryside was unlikely to be duplicated within the great city.

Mostly they trudged in silence, stopping after two hours to share boiled eggs and mango under the shade of a roadside tree. Peter welcomed the relief to his aching feet, while wolfing his share of their food. Ah-peng passed him the water flask and said, "It is taking longer to reach Beijing because we cannot walk as fast as I did alone."

Peter drank gratefully and corked the flask. "How much longer?" he asked.

"I think it will be dark when we reach the hostel but we will be safer there than on these roads where robbers may set upon us."

Peter felt his knife, still secure under his waistband. "Let us continue, then," he said, "and not rest for another hour."

They picked up their staffs, rose, and took to the road again.

IT WAS DARK WHEN they entered the city on Guang-an Road and passed Lianhua Lake and the park that surrounded it. Now there was stone paving under their feet and Ah-peng quickened their pace. By now Peter was accustomed to the tugging rope—his umbilical cord, he thought—and to the tapping of her staff on cobbles and concrete. "Only a little farther," she told him, "less than an hour to go."

By now most workers were in their homes, but food shops were busy with customers, and as Peter passed them he sniffed the savory scents of ginger and frying fish, roast pork and delicate seasonings that made his mouth water and his hunger almost unbearable. Finally he said, "Can't we eat something now, grandmother?"

"Patience, young man. After we reach the hostel I will bring food, so think of other things."

Peter plodded on.

THE HOSTEL WAS a three-story brick building roofed with thatch and tile. The cheaper sleeping places were in the open courtyard, straw mattresses arranged under sloping eaves as partial shelter from rain. Ah-peng paid for two places in a communal room on the second floor, using more of her stolen yuan, and when she had guided Peter to his mattress she said, "Rest there until I come back with food."

After she left, Peter pulled off his torturing sandals and stretched out on uneven ticking that gave off the stench of old perspiration and body oils left by a thousand other travelers. To his weary body the thin mattress was as luxurious and restful as eiderdown. Sleep came almost at once.

Ah-peng was tugging his hand. Even as he woke he smelled the aroma of hot food and sat up. From a meal shop she had brought paper containers of rice, noodles, and fish fried in rice batter. She arranged the containers between them, knelt, and whispered, "Police below, so I will feed you." Deftly she fed him fish morsels from her chopsticks, noodles, and small balls of rice flavored with soya.

Peter heard the policemen clump up the wooden stairs. They walked slowly around the room eyeing each occupant in turn. They were wearing shabby khaki uniforms and scuffed boots, old Mauser pistols holstered around their belts supported by shoulder straps. Ah-peng began to croon tenderly, interspersing the tune with urgings to eat, nephew, eat to the full. When the policemen reached her they stopped and one bent over to say, "Can't he feed himself, grandmother?"

"He's blind, honorable official, and so I try to ease his burden as I am able."

The other said, "You're not from the city."

"No, honored sir, we come from Daxning in search of honest labor. I must feed myself as well as this son of my dead sister, and life in Daxning is not easy for an old woman such as myself." She dipped chopsticks into the noodles. "Would you care for a bite, sir?"

"Thank you, but we have eaten. Besides, it would be dishonorable to take food from your mouths." He straightened up. "May good fortune attend you and may you live many years in good health."

Ah-peng bowed her head slightly, and the policemen moved on. Peter heard their boots on the stairway, and breathed in relief. Ever since she'd warned him of their arrival his heart had been pounding, almost deafening his ears. Now he felt limp in the aftermath. "No more food, grandmother, it is time for you to eat."

"Are you sure?"

Patting his stomach, he belched to indicate full satisfaction, then stretched out on the mattress. Ah-peng ate then, cleaning out the emptied food containers with fingers and tongue. Then she dropped them in a covered container painted with the legend: *Killing flies is an obligation to the Revolution.* Also mice and rats, Peter thought, for he had seen rats as big as squirrels, hardy enough to take on feral cats.

He dozed off into a sleep of bone-deep fatigue, Ah-peng lying on her mattress beside him. Later, a gasp from Ah-peng wakened him, and when his eyes opened he saw two men kneeling beside her. One held a knife at her throat while the other shoved up her blouse to rifle her waistband. Cautiously, Peter gripped the handle of his knife, then tensed and lunged, slashing at both robbers. His knife bit deep into the leg of the plunderer and opened the bicep of the knife-holder. Peter slashed repeatedly until both robbers turned and fled noisily down the stairs. Ah-peng burst into tears and clung tightly to Peter's shoulders while he soothed her. "The money is safe," he assured her, "they hadn't time to find it."

Wakened sleepers came around them and asked what the disturbance was. Ah-peng told them, and added, "My nephew has enough sight to make out forms, thus was able to drive them off."

"Two? More?" one fellow asked.

When Peter shrugged, Ah-peng said, "Two—and one robber would have been more than enough." She dried her eyes, and the curious drifted back to their own places, muttering about crime and the evils of the city.

When all was quiet again, Peter cleaned his knife on the ticking and quietly suggested to Ah-peng that it was probably time to go. She nodded and began putting their few things in her bundle. They went stealthily down the staircase, past the snoring clerk, and emerged on a street dimly lit by moonlight.

After orienting herself, Ah-peng said, "This way, dear nephew," and tugged his cord to lead him.

Together they set out through darkened streets on what Peter Brand prayed would be his final steps to freedom. And as they filed along, he remembered irrelevantly that when he left Washington the NFL draft was under way, and he wondered how the 'Skins had fared in signing a few decent picks.

Twenty

To IRVING CHENOW, the Secretary of State's office resembled a Taos craft shop. Indian serapes on the walls draped beside horsehair belts decorated with silver and lapis lazuli; desk loaded with clay artifacts, and behind it a large oil of Sam Houston mounted on a pinto, his pose heroic. Decor calculated to remind visitors of the Secretary's southwestern origin, in contrast to the Eastern elite whom he early despised but had come to accept and finally embrace.

As a regional lawyer from a buffalo-chip law school, the Secretary had learned that accommodation and cooperation were far more profitable strategies than opposition to the reigning financial powers.

His appointment as Secretary was due exclusively to his presidential campaign fund-raising success among the oil, gas, and cattle barons who had been his clients. What courtroom skills he lacked were more than compensated by his proven abilities as a negotiator. LBJ had been the Secretary's role model and inspiration, and he seldom deviated from Lyndon's trademark call to reason together and amicably seek a solution to problems of the moment.

So, after scanning the Gorgon photos and hearing Chenow's explanation of their significance, the Secretary said, "Irv, tell you the truth, I don't see you've got a hell of a lot to go on. What I see here is pretty circumstantial."

"Circumstantial evidence brings in a lot of guilty verdicts," Chenow remarked, lawyer to lawyer. "Granted it's premature to predict an attack on Taiwan, but I'd be remiss in my responsibilities to you and the President if I neglected bringing this situation to your attention."

The Secretary peered at him over horn-rimmed half lenses. "You leave the President to me, Irv. I'm not taking him any half-baked theories, you understand? When you've got something probative—if it ever comes to that—it'll be time to inform the President."

Chenow nodded silently.

"Besides, I don't want him worryin' over Taiwan island when we got bigger bulls to brand. I mean, next week's Pacific Rim trade conference in Singapore. China's coming—the *real* China—and we want to negotiate a real breakthrough in our trade relations with Beijing."

"And Taiwan?"

"Not invited," the Secretary snapped. "China made it clear they wouldn't attend if Taiwan was there. So we persuaded the Taiwanese to stay home and keep their mouths shut tighter'n a bull's ass in fly-time." Seeing Chenow's pained expression at the earthy phrase, the Secretary smiled. Chenow's appointment had been imposed on him, and he hadn't liked that. And he didn't like the Chicago kike lawyer, never would. Had nothing in common with him or any of his breed.

Chenow said, "Sir, I appreciate your concerns. Still, I'd like to address the subject at the next meeting of the NSC Asia Working Group. Not to dwell on it unduly or advocate any particular course of action, but I think the members would appreciate a State alert on what might become a serious matter." He sat forward. "Give them lead time to evaluate response options to a defined threat. I feel that would not only be appropriate procedure, but would avoid State having to take a point position based on current findings alone."

The Secretary frowned, then his features relaxed. "You got some good ideas there, Irving, but until there's hard facts I don't want people talking and speculating. First thing you know it'll be all over the *Post* and the *Times,* and the Chinese will get madder'n hell. See my point?"

"I do, sir. And what we want to avoid is a situation like the one that escalated into the Cuban Missile Crisis."

The Secretary poked a finger at his chin. "Don't recall details."

Inwardly, Chenow smiled. "CIA had ground agent and U-2 photo intelligence that Khrushchev was installing nuke missiles in Cuba. Kennedy was campaigning at the time, and didn't welcome a foreign policy distraction. Accordingly, word didn't get out until the information was leaked to a senator, who gave it to the press. JFK, McNamara, and Rusk were boxed in, forced to take action."

"Well, they solved the crisis, didn't they?" he asked belligerently. "Quieted things down."

"With public embarrassment and egg all over their faces. So, drawing on that experience, it seems to me that a potential crisis with China could be avoided by a quiet, early warning to Beijing."

"When?"

"After we determine that a credible danger to Taiwan exists."

"We?"

"I mean the NSC," Chenow said hastily. "We should have more Gorgon coverage in the next few days. So if you're in Singapore and the situation seems to be heading toward a single conclusion, I'd like your prior authorization to present the findings to the NSC."

"No," the Secretary replied, shaking his head slowly. "What you do is cable me an Eyes Only briefing, and I'll decide whether to involve the NSC." He looked at the wall clock. "For all anyone knows the Chinese might point those missiles at North Korea, right?"

Chenow nodded reluctantly.

"Which might not be such a bad thing."

"Except for the fact that North Korea could retaliate with nuclear missiles, and"—he spread his hands—"the consequences are horrible to contemplate."

"Sure they are. So you keep watching spy photos, and if the situation worsens, you tell me first."

"Yes, Mr. Secretary," Chenow said stiffly.

"And nobody else." He brought the photos together and slid them into their envelope. Then he got up and came around his desk as Irving Chenow rose. He gave Chenow the envelope and laid an avuncular arm across his shoulders. "Don't fret, Irv," he counseled. "Nothing could come of this, nothing at all. So my motto is, don't buy trouble in advance. Tomorrow it could all blow away. Right?" He removed his arm and walked with Chenow to the door. "Always good to talk with you, Irv. We'll do it again after Singapore."

"I appreciate your time," Chenow responded, and left the Secretary's office. Walking down the corridor to his own office, Irving Chenow told himself not to be discouraged; the Secretary had acted predictably, if shortsightedly. From past experience he should have known better than to expect the Secretary's authorization to involve the NSC. But if the balloon ever went up the Secretary would be screaming and bellowing why he wasn't informed.

Okay, you shit-kicker cowboy, Chenow thought as he turned into his office, have it your way. But life exacts consequence for inaction as well as action, and you better pray fate's fickle finger doesn't point at your desk.

He sat down and after a few moments thought began dictating a memo for the record into his recorder. As meticulously as though he were preparing a legal brief, Chenow cited the date and time of dictation. Beginning with Tom Gray's request for an appointment, the Assistant Secretary detailed what had taken place after first viewing the Gorgon surveillance photos. He summarized his exchanges with Gray, then reconstructed his meeting with the Secretary almost verbatim. That done, he noted the time and stopped the recording.

Normally, he would have had his private secretary transcribe the tape but she lacked Gorgon clearance. What to do? He rewound the tape cassette and put it in his pocket. Before their marriage, his wife had been his legal secretary and he knew that she could still turn out fast, accurate pages on their home word processor. Long accustomed to keeping client secrets inviolate, Vivian would never question the memo, or mention Gorgon to him, or anyone.

Transcription problem solved, Chenow had his secretary place a call to Tom Gray. And while waiting for the GlobEco officer to respond, Chenow thought that although Gray seemed a perfectly responsible analyst, he would feel a lot more comfortable were he dealing with Mark Brand.

Still nosing around Hong Kong, he mused, and wondered when Mark would return to Washington, with or without his son. I need him at the China Desk, dammit; can't do it all alone.

Hearing Gray come on-line, Chenow said, "This isn't a secure phone, so I'd like you to come over at your early convenience."

"Umm. Of course. Tomorrow do?"

He scanned his appointment book. "It will. Meanwhile, to put things succinctly, Tom, we have a problem."

Beijing

Rats scurried across the street as Peter followed Ah-peng, still simulating blindness despite the dark of night. Every few blocks they passed a sort of sentry post, with a dozing or sleeping policeman inside. Maybe, Peter thought, they'll be sleeping outside the embassy and won't pay attention to our approach, but he knew that was probably too much to hope for.

He tugged the rope to stop Ah-peng, and in a low voice said, "The Marine guards may admit me to the embassy, but I'm not sure they'll let you in."

"You must not concern yourself with me, nephew," she countered. "Whatever happens, will happen. Your life is ahead of you. Mine"—she shrugged fatalistically—"it's not been an easy one. My few years of happiness I can hardly remember now, but I would take great joy if you were to reach your destination unharmed. So let us keep moving; your embassy is only a few blocks more."

As they resumed walking they heard the squawking of oncoming ambulance klaxons, the wail of police sirens, and the harsh barking of fire engine horns. Peter's first reaction was panic. Chilled, he thought, They're coming for me, then common sense prevailed and he realized that such a horde of emergency vehicles would not be dispatched to scoop up a single fugitive. No, had to be something else, something big scale . . .

A few windows lighted on either side of the street. People peered out through darkened windows. Two police motorcycles blatted past and turned left at the intersection. The volume of sirens and klaxons was cacophonous. Peter pressed his hands over his ears and Ah-peng shrank back against him. "What can it be?" she whispered in frightened tones. "Surely some catastrophe . . . an earthquake, perhaps. Nephew"—her eyes searched his face—"did you feel quaking underfoot?"

"No, grandmother," he replied, "so perhaps a fire, an explosion somewhere . . ." His voice trailed off as he sensed the sounds diminishing in volume, some dying away. "Come," Ah-peng urged, tugging on his cord, "let us find out what it is." Faster than usual she drew him on, and at the intersection they turned as the cyclists had.

"Lights," she said in an awed voice. "Many lights. Ah, now I see, trucks and ambulances reaching the hospital." She turned to him. "Yesterday when I passed nearby I noticed a sign pointing toward Shan-yuen People's Hospital. Yes, that is it, but what happened to the poor victims? What disaster . . . ?"

"I'm not curious," Peter said flatly. "Let us go on to the embassy—perhaps guards have been sent to assist at the hospital. We have come this far, now is no time for delay."

"Patience, patience. The embassy is four blocks away, and the hospital only two."

"In opposite directions. But," he said resignedly, "having followed your guidance since we met I cannot ignore it now." And through his dark lenses Peter saw the illuminated hospital, the ranks of vehicles offloading victims. "*Ai,*" Ah-peng shrilled, "*aiyee,* only see how many they bring. The dead they put aside to move the injured along." Excited by the spectacle, she pulled Peter closer, until they were beside the nearest ambulance. Approaching it from the hospital came a young woman in a white medical coat and gauze face mask. She walked tiredly, unsteadily, and at the ambulance she leaned back against it and began to weep. Ah-peng went to her and gently said, "Honored doctor, you have done all you could for the suffering, is that not so?" The girl pulled off the face mask and mopped her eyes and cheeks. "That is true—but I am not a doctor, only a nurse."

"Nevertheless, you comfort the sick and wounded and perform healing tasks for the Glorious Revolution, so what is the difference?"

The girl nodded. "Thank you for your good words, grandmother, but I wish I had not had to see so many dead and injured where the trains collided head-on."

"Collision? Where was that, comrade nurse?"

One hand waved vaguely. "This side of Changping."

"Where is that? The name is unfamiliar."

"Northwest, a dozen miles or so. Oh, grandmother, I hope we never see such a calamity again."

Peter placed a hand on the ambulance fender and felt vibration; the engine was running. Breathing deeply, the nurse said, "Few were killed by the crash itself. Most died from the gas."

"Gas?" Ah-peng inquired.

"Military canisters spilled from a freight train and broke open.

Villagers who hurried to the scene breathed the gas and died almost at once." She shook her head. "For them, nothing could be done."

Peter said, "You were at the scene but did not breathe gas?"

"By then it was gone." She shook her head and sighed. "I must return and do what I can. I think we will be working the rest of the night, perhaps through the day."

"May the example of Mao, our perfect leader, inspire your hands," Ah-peng intoned and turned to Peter as the nurse walked back toward the hospital. "Strange," she said, "the poor girl."

"Lucky girl," Peter remarked, and patted the fender. "This ambulance," he said, "can be my way to freedom. Take me behind it and close the doors. Then continue around to the driver side."

"Pe-ter," she said in an alarmed voice, "what is in your mind?"

"I will drive while you show me the way to the embassy. If the police guards are withdrawn I will go to the gate and talk to the Marine sentry. If police are still present—well, you must leave me. Hurry now, do as I say before others come."

She hesitated. "So this may be our last moment together. I pray to our God that you will succeed in safety." Then, drawing him behind her, she closed the rear doors and stopped by the cab. Peter untied the waist cord and said, "Get in beside me." And as he helped her mount, he felt imbued with enormous new strength and resolve.

Sunglasses off, he scanned the floor gearshift and shoved the stick in reverse to back slowly away. At the road he meshed the forward gears and steered from the hospital zone. "Straight ahead," she said tremulously, "and I will tell you where to turn."

He found a toggle switch to turn off the warning lights and gripped the steering wheel. On the dash was another switch to sound the klaxon horn. "Slowly," Ah-peng cautioned, and pulled off his straw hat. "Coolies do not drive, nephew."

Peter felt the thumping of his heart. The moment of ultimate danger was at hand, and he wondered if he would survive it. Mouth dry, he licked his lips, felt suddenly weak, and closed his eyes for a moment. Then steadied himself as Ah-peng said, "Left at the next crossroad and you will see the embassy beyond."

"Thank you for everything," he said and pressed her hand impulsively. "You have been the grandmother I never knew." Turning the wheel, he scanned the embassy compound, whose high wall was unbroken but for a wide grilled entrance gate behind which he could make out two sentry boxes and a white-capped Marine carrying his rifle at shoulder arms.

The way was clear but for five policemen standing at intervals in front of the embassy. He drove past them and continued around the block. After turning the corner, he braked and said, "Leave now, grandmother. I must finish this alone."

"But—"

"Now." He kissed her cheek and she climbed down to the street. Then he made a U-turn and headed back to the embassy. Setting his teeth, Peter pushed the gas pedal and the heavy vehicle accelerated. Switching on warning lights and klaxon, he steered straight at the gate.

Crash impact slammed him back against the seat as the gates buckled and came apart. The ambulance crashed through beyond the sentry boxes, and Peter braked. He got quickly down from the cab and walked back to the two sentries, who were pointing rifles at him. "Don't shoot," he said groggily, and raised his arms, "I'm an American."

Hong Kong

THE DOOR BUZZER WOKE BRAND, who left bed in pajamas and called, "Who is it?" fearing the caller was Nina Kenton. Instead, a voice piped, "Message, sir," and Brand opened the door. He took a small envelope from a lacquer tray, said "Wait," and got tip change from his night table. After the door closed, Brand opened the envelope, realizing it came from Mary, and read the enclosed message:

> Mark, we must talk. Please meet me on the Star Ferry pier at nine o'clock.

Nine, he thought, okay. His wristwatch showed a few minutes after eight. Plenty of time to dress and walk there, but what was the emergency? he wondered. Had Wing-dah visited his displeasure on her or Chu-li? Did Mary want to warn him of some new menace from her husband? Or in some indirect fashion perhaps she had acquired news of Peter.

From room service Brand ordered a Continental breakfast and after he had shaved and showered, found it waiting on the table. He dressed, between bites of croissant and gulps of coffee, and walked to the ferry pier, arriving shortly before nine. After buying a copy of the *Post*, Brand scanned it, looking around for surveillants, until a taxi stopped nearby and Mary got out. She was wearing pale linen slacks and an embroidered green Chinese jacket; she saw Brand almost at once. Walking slowly toward him, she said, "We'll talk on the ferry," and continued on to the ticket office.

While vehicles trundled aboard for the crossing to Kowloon, Brand went up the staircase to the upper deck and found her at the railing aft of the pilothouse, watching seamen cast off the heavy lines. The big ferry shuddered as it moved from pierside, and when it was clear Mary beckoned him closer. "Thank you for coming on little notice, Mark, but I felt I must see you before you leave for Beijing." She glanced around, cross-breeze feathering her dark hair. "I want to know how things went with Wing-dah."

"Not awfully well," he admitted. "I wasn't going to tell you, but I can't lie to you."

"What happened?" Her hand moved along the railing until it touched his.

"Ostensibly all was smiles and cooperation," he said with a grimace, then described the incident at the overlook.

Her face tightened in dismay, and she said, "I'm so relieved you heeded my warning—and Chu-li's."

"Kept me alert so nothing bad really happened." He paused. "Didn't know our daughter was going to tell you she'd seen me."

Mary smiled. "There have never been secrets between us—only the one: her true father, you."

"She's a remarkable young woman in every way. Perhaps a time will come when she can learn the truth."

Mary nodded. "I, too, hope for such a time. But for now I must continue the pretense. Were Wing-dah to learn the truth I know he would kill us both."

"Can't you leave him?"

She shrugged. "For the present, the benefits outweigh the disadvantages, and there is my—our—daughter's future to consider."

"She would be an asset to any gallery—here or in Europe or America." His hand closed over hers. "As would you."

"I've thought of that scores of times. But Wing-dah is so influential in the Colony that life would be very difficult for us." She smiled wanly. "This morning when I wrote the note I was reminded of the ways we used to contact each other—the secret meeting places." She sighed. "Were you reminded, too?"

"Of course I was."

"And since then—have you ever thought of me?"

"Often—with longing and pain. Mary, *Qin Ai De*, if only for the sake of our beautiful child I need your full forgiveness. Tell me I may hope for it one day."

The breeze freshened, and Brand glanced away to look out at sampans and walla-wallas threading through the busy harbor.

"I forgave you long ago," Mary replied softly, "for I never stopped loving you."

Too choked to speak, Brand lifted her hand to his lips while Mary stroked his head. After a while she said, "Between Wing-dah and me there has been nothing for years—except hatred. He knows he cannot rid himself of me, his wife, without losing Chu-li, whom he admires and cares for above all things." She shrugged. "A stalemate. But I have accommodated to it as has he. Mark, you have seen his gross obesity, it limits his movement and he cannot force himself on me, or beat me as he used to."

"Chu-li told me."

"Poor child. As soon as I could I sent her away from all the unpleasantness at home. But to do so I was made to promise Wing-dah never to divorce him. Not that he desired my presence, but to avoid losing face among his associates in the Colony."

The Kowloon pier was ahead, white-and-black gulls swarmed upward at the ferry's approach. Mary said, "You are resolved to go to Beijing, are you not?"

"I must."

"Were the Gong An Ju to learn that you worked against the PRC I fear you would be killed, or captured like your son. I pray that will not happen, but life is uncertain and there are events beyond our abilities to control. So I wanted at least to bid you godspeed on your mission and safe return."

The ferry shuddered as the propellers reversed to slow its approach to the pier, then it nosed in and bumped to a stop. "Will you go back with me now?" he asked.

"No, my excuse for crossing is to visit two of Wing-dah's Kowloon galleries, so we will part here. And when you return from Beijing, go past my gallery and let Chu-li see you. She will let me know that you came back safely."

"Dear Mary," he said emotionally, "you are as beautiful as the day I first saw you in the museum, and I know now that I want you with me always. So—"

Her fingers pressed his lips. "I want you, too, and we will meet again when you return."

She left him then, and joined other passengers going down the staircase. Brand watched until she was out of sight and then he sat on a bench, his mind in turmoil. The ticket taker brought him back to present reality, and he paid for the return crossing.

As the ferry moved out gulls fluttered overhead, and he thought that if Wing-dah refused to give Mary a divorce there was a final way to free her:

Kill him.

INSTEAD OF GOING BACK to his hotel, Brand stopped at the Travel Service office and asked if his travel permit had been issued. The agent said authorization had been granted, and his permit had been prepared. "How soon do you want to leave, Mr. Lang?"

"Today if possible."

"You want to fly by Japan Air Lines, do you not?"

Brand nodded.

"The next flight to Beijing leaves Kai Tak at two o'clock. If that flight is fully booked, would you go by China National Air?"

"I would. When does it leave?"

"At three-thirty. Flying time is just four hours. And"—he shuffled through papers on the desk—"you requested a suite at the Beijing Hotel."

"Yes."

The agent looked at his wristwatch. "Pay now for your air ticket and for two nights at the hotel. Canadian dollars?"

"American." Brand paid the total and received ticket, travel permit, and hotel vouchers. As he got up to leave, the clerk said, "Everything is in order. You are to be at the airport one hour before departure."

"I understand."

"That is all for now, Mr. Lang."

"Thank you," Brand said, and went out to the street.

From the Manchu lobby Brand called Nina's room and surmised from the five rings and her sleepy voice that he had wakened her.

"Morning," he said cheerfully, "sorry to intrude on pleasant dreams, but I'm leaving for the day, and thought you might have dinner with me."

"Wonderful!" she exclaimed. "What an exciting prospect. What time shall I be ready?"

"Six okay?"

"Perfect."

Brand smiled. By then he should be in Beijing, far from her wiles and deceptions. "Call you then." He hung up, went over to the desk, and told the cashier to ready his bill for midday departure.

In his room he began packing and answered the telephone, not caring if it was Nina. Instead, Tommy Ning said, "Our friends are on their way, brother, thought you'd like to know."

"Thanks for telling me."

"What about you?"

"After noon I'll be away."

"Away . . . ? I get it. Mark, anything I can do?"

"You've done more than enough. See you, brother." He replaced the receiver, and when he was packing the switchblade he had used only yesterday, he reflected that Wing-dah had only to inform the Gong An Ju in Beijing to rid himself of Mark Brand forever.

PART
THREE

Twenty-One

ASSISTANT SECRETARY OF STATE CHENOW looked up from the photo images Tom Gray had spread across his desk and said, "These are sequential to the photos you showed me yesterday, that right?"

"Yes, sir," Gray replied, "except for an eighteen-hour interval between the series."

"Long enough for the freight train to move from the Zhuolu gas plant to here"—he rapped a photo—"where it collided with the oncoming train."

"We've counted fifty-three bodies on the ground, near where the flatbed overturned and warheads spilled off. Our presumption is the victims were killed by gas."

"Why?"

"No evidence of maimed bodies typical of train wrecks. And if you'll notice close-up photo number four, it shows two smashed warheads. That impact breached the internal containers whose contents formed lethal gas."

Chenow nodded thoughtfully. "What else?"

"Most of the corpses are in garments worn in the countryside. Only two have railroad uniforms. So it appears that farmers and villagers went to the collision site, inhaled gas, and died there."

Chenow said wryly, "They certainly didn't die from simultaneous heart failure."

"Or Kool-Aid," Gray remarked. "The Gorgon satellite will make another pass over the Pingying area in about, oh, ten hours. It'll be interesting to see what's been done by way of cleanup by then."

Chenow nodded. "Sort of a small-scale Chernobyl disaster, eh? It's not the sort of thing the New China News Agency is likely to tell the world about." He leaned back in his chair and tented his fingers. "Since yesterday we've acquired facts to establish that warheads from Yangyuan were loaded with gas compounds at Zhuolu and moved by rail toward Beijing. The head-on collision occurred after the freight train cleared the city of Pingying—which is how far from Beijing?"

"Ten–twenty miles. I can get exact distance from NRO."

Chenow waved a hand. "A small city like Pingying wouldn't have enough emergency vehicles or personnel to handle a disaster on that scale, so vehicles would have had to be sent from Beijing to process victims, dead or alive."

"Good point. Land agents could check Beijing hospitals for unusual activity, and verify if victims were gassed to death." He paused. "Unfortunately, we lack on-ground agents for that kind of footwork."

"Can you send any?"

"Take days to instruct them," he said. "The Chinese know we've got satellite coverage of the area so they'll work double fast to clear the scene of damaged and undamaged warheads. Then they can report a train collision, quantify the victims, and say nothing more." He shook his head. "You could send a blind query to the embassy. Or CIA could ask Beijing Station for a report."

"That's preferable," Chenow remarked. "I'll take it up with Darman Gerold."

"Ah—he may be away, sir. Went to Hong Kong to bring back an errant daughter."

"Right—you told me that. Who's next in line?"

"Ray Applegate, my replacement, but he's not Gorgon-cleared."

"Damn," Chenow said, using one of the expletives he occasionally permitted himself. For a while he was silent, considering alternate courses of action. Finally he said, "We've always assumed the Chinese manufacture chemical warfare compounds and it hasn't been a large issue. Mating the compounds to a delivery system was a natural progression, and now we have proof positive. What we *don't* have is an indication—much less proof—of intended use. IRBMs can't reach Taiwan from North China so we need to determine where the warheads are sent by replacement train."

Gray said, "The results of the accident could persuade the army to keep the warheads out of Beijing and detour them around the city."

Chenow eyed him. "Is that feasible?"

"I don't know, sir, but I can find out." He thought for a moment. "Alternatively, the warheads could be shipped to a South China port and taken by truck or rail to the missile-launching site." He paused. "At present, of course, we don't *know* Chinese intentions. I'm even wondering if they intend threatening Taiwan."

"If they don't have a target in mind," Chenow objected, "why would they ready the warheads and move them?"

"Maybe to stockpile in a safe place for future deployment."

"That's credible," Chenow acknowledged. "In which case there is no immediate danger to Taiwan." He tapped the photos absently. "I was thinking of showing this series to the Secretary before he leaves for Singapore, but he'd want a bottom-line conclusion, and I can't give him one. Unfortunately, he's precluded me from taking up the situation with the NSC Asia Working Group." One thumb rubbed his chin. "Any ideas?"

"The next Gorgon pass may add to what we have."

"Yes," Chenow said, and returned the photos to Gray, "which means you'll have to monitor the images continuously. The geopolitical situation strongly suggests to me that a nasty Chinese move is in the making. Taiwan is their only proclaimed enemy, so I'll stay with the presumption that Taiwan will be the target. However, like every other bureaucrat in Washington I don't want to put myself out on a limb."

"I understand," Gray replied, "so I'll get back to work."

"Call anytime," Chenow told him, and after Gray left he dictated another memorandum for the record. They were due for cocktails at the Philippine Embassy, after which Vivian might have time to transcribe his dictation.

She was a wonder, he mused. With a son at Landon and a daughter at Holton-Arms, she helped with their homework, handled all PTA obligations, entertained in praiseworthy style, and was his helpmate in every way. He hoped Vivian had never regretted their marriage, because to him she was the indispensable wife, and he was the most fortunate of men.

BEIJING

Consul Jason Whitbread eyed Peter across the conference table and said, "So your name is Peter Brand."

"Peter Simon Brand," Peter acknowledged.

"Can you verify your identity?"

"My father, Mark Brand, can identify me, and you could have my passport photo faxed from Washington."

"We may do that." The Consul was a skinny, thin-faced man with reddish-blond hair and a wispy mustache. "You say your passport was taken when you were arrested in Canton."

"That's what happened."

Whitbread opened a thin file and produced a State Department circular telegram stamped NOFORN. "You pretty much fit the description, Mr. Brand, so for the time being I'll assume you are who you say you are. Nevertheless, I have to tell you that your, ah, unconventional arrival has shaken up the embassy pretty drastically. What are we to do with the smashed ambulance, the gates you destroyed?"

"Repair them," Peter said calmly, "and I'll pay whatever it costs."

"That's an interesting proposal," the Consul remarked, "and I'll make note of it. Actually, the Chinese towed the ambulance away just after dawn, and the Marine detachment jury-rigged the gates until ironwork can be done. Of more serious concern is your own statement that you escaped from a Chinese prison and hid until you stole this ambulance last night. If you arrived here as a fugitive, the Chinese will demand your return."

Peter shrugged. "I'm not sure they will."

"Oh? Why not?"

"Because my trial was in secret and I was secretly held. The Gong An Ju or the Foreign Affairs Bureau would have to acknowledge those things before asserting a credible claim to my person."

"Possibly," the Consul remarked, and bent over to read more of what Peter presumed was his file.

He had endured a long, stressful night, with only an hour's sleep in Marine quarters. There he had been allowed to shower and shave before being escorted to the Consul's office in borrowed off-duty clothes and moccasins. "When there's time," he said, "I'd like something to eat before the Station Chief debriefs me."

The Consul nodded. "I'll have a meal brought here. What would you like?"

"Anything that doesn't have rice. Plus coffee."

The Consul left the table for the outer office and came back. After resuming his chair, he said, "Why would the Station Chief—if any—see you?"

"Because I went to Canton to service a drop for CIA."

The Consul sat back and stared at him. "You were told to do that?"

"I was asked," Peter explained, "by a CIA officer from Langley, who learned that I was visiting Hong Kong on business for my firm."

"Who was the CIA officer?"

"Called himself Barney, but I doubt that was his true name. Incidentally, my father worked in CIA for a long time. Barney knew that."

"Did your father know what you'd been co-opted to do?"

Peter shook his head. "I wanted to show him I'd grown up and could do the sort of things he'd done for many years." He grimaced. "Not a wise decision."

"As things turned out." He examined file papers again. "Actually, Mr. Brand, we received two inquiries about you. One from State, the other from CIA."

"So I ought to talk with the Station Chief."

"And what would you tell him?"

"Things picked up along the way. Information about the— Never mind, I'll hold it for him."

Whitbread's lips formed a sly smile. "You're looking at him, but if you ever mention me as CIA I'll have your legs broken in painful places." He got up. "I'm going to do two things: inform State and headquarters that you're here, and bring back a tape recorder. The former will take a while, so feed yourself and get ready to talk." Looking down at Peter he said, "It's rare we get an agent back, so permit me to say, welcome home."

"Thank you, sir," Peter responded as the door opened and a tray of food arrived. "I'm glad and grateful to be here."

REPLETE WITH SCRAMBLED EGGS, bacon, biscuits, and honey, Peter answered Whitbread's questions for half an hour. They broke for fresh coffee and Peter said, "I'd like to telephone my fiancée in Washington."

"That can be arranged."

"And, of course, my father." He wrote down both phone numbers and gave them to the COS. "Bear in mind," Whitbread remarked, "that it's dead of night in Washington." He looked at his watch. "In two or three hours people will be up and around, able to celebrate the good news." He sipped from his cup. "But I have to tell you the Ambassador isn't at all happy over your arrival. One, you crashed a stolen vehicle into the compound, and two, you're an admitted fugitive from Chinese justice. Frankly, he doesn't know what to do with you."

The warning made Peter uneasy. "Surely he won't hand me back to the Gong An Ju."

"I'll do all I can to dissuade him," Whitbread said, "but the Secretary of State doesn't like the CIA cluttering up his embassies, and this Ambassador takes his cue from him. So I don't have much leverage. Your father have usable contacts around Washington?"

"I'm sure he does," Peter replied, "though I don't know who they are."

"Okay," Whitbread said, "back to work. How were you able to steal the ambulance?"

"It was parked, motor running, outside the Shan Yuen People's Hospital."

"That's a few blocks from here." He paused. "Now I think about it I heard a lot of sirens and horns last night, but got back to sleep and forgot about it until now. What was it all about?"

Peter summarized what he and Ah-peng had learned from the nurse about the train collision and many victims dead from gas.

"Gas? What kind of gas?"

"The nurse didn't know."

"She was there?"

"She was there. Emotionally frayed from the experience. Oh, she said the gas came from military canisters that smashed open when the freight train overturned."

"Canisters," the COS repeated, "whatever that means."

"She said most of the victims were farmers and villagers who'd come to the collision site just after the crash occurred—that's why they inhaled gas. By the time the nurse got there the gas had dissipated. But she was pretty scared."

"I can imagine, it would shake the hell out of me. But you didn't see the collision?"

"Was miles away with escape on my mind."

"Yeah. So you just hopped into the ambulance and drove here. Why did you think you'd have to crash through?"

"Well, I drove past the compound and saw five policemen stationed in front of the gate. If they hadn't been there I could have walked up to the sentry and asked to be let in. But it wasn't an option."

"Guess not."

Peter said, "Just after I escaped there were government radio broadcasts saying a Westerner had escaped from prison by killing a guard, and—"

"Did you? Did you kill a guard?" He frowned.

"I think I only knocked him out. But the authorities would lie about that to encourage people to look for me."

Whitbread nodded. "And there's no way to disprove it. I didn't hear those broadcasts, Peter. This is a small Station, and we can't monitor domestic radio. Was your name given?"

"No. Because the government had never admitted having me in prison. If I'd been recaptured they could kill me and no one would ever know."

Whitbread said, "I'm going to transmit a report on what you learned at the hospital—it could supplement information from other sources. Now, suppose you tell me more about Ah-peng, the sainted woman who cared for you through thick and thin."

Hong Kong

Nina Kenton waited until seven o'clock before calling Brand's room. For an hour she had sat by the telephone, dressed for dinner, expecting Brand to phone or come by. As the minutes passed she grew irritated, angry, and finally furious. *Where is he? Damn him!* She felt like shrieking, but grabbed the telephone and dialed Brand's room. After half a dozen rings she gave up and called the desk.

An Asian voice said, "May I help you?"

"Yes—I've been dialing Mr. Brand's room but there is no answer. I—I'm concerned something might have happened . . ."

"One moment, madame." There was silence until the clerk spoke again. "Sorry, madame, Mr. Brand released that room."

"Released?"

"Checked out."

Fear clutched her throat. "Did he take another room?"

"No, madame, he paid his bill and—departed."

"Oh, God," she breathed despairingly. "When—do you know when he left?"

"Let me see—it was just after noon today."

Noon! Why, that was after he asked her to dinner. Oh, the bastard, the dirty rotten son of a bitch. She fumbled replacing the receiver and sank back in her chair. Her first thought was that Mark had moved to another hotel, but if he'd done that it was because he wanted to avoid her. Tears welled in her eyes. She pounded chair arms with her fists. I thought things were smoothing over, and tonight I was going to be the uninhibited whore to seal our relationship.

Why? Never a problem between us until I erupted at the little bare-assed slut I caught in his room. For that, he's dumping me? Oh, Jesus, for *that?*

Tears rolled down her cheeks. Thoughts, words, whirled in her brain.

He's gone, accept it. And I know where. The miserable liar has gone to China, to Beijing to look for his wretched son. Oh, God, what can I do? How can I tell John? When will I tell him? How can I explain Mark's escape?

She dug fists into her cheeks to stem flowing tears.

When I had the chance I should have poisoned him, at breakfast. But he lied, saying he wasn't going to the Mainland. Oh, if I'd realized he was scheming even then . . .

Unsteadily she pushed out of the chair, went to the bar, and leaned on it. Her whole body was trembling, shaking from the sick realization she'd been outmaneuvered. She poured scotch in a tumbler and swallowed until she started to choke. Bleary-eyed, throat and nostrils filled with liquor fumes, she coughed and coughed until the spasm ended. Then she smashed the tumbler against the wall. Wish it were his head, she thought, and now I'll never see him anymore. Never again. John will cut me off, and I'll have no money, no place to go . . . Tears of self-pity soaked her cheeks. She dried them with a cocktail napkin and staggered from the bar. Pulling off her dress, she entered the bathroom and stared at the mirror. A makeup-stained witch-mask stared back.

With a shriek she toweled her face, wet the towel, and scrubbed at the horrid colors. Then she ran fingers through her hair and stepped back, feeling a warm liquor glow spread from her icy stomach.

I'll feel better soon, she told herself; one thing you can say about liquor, it's reliable. You can count on it—the way I thought I could count on Mark Brand. *"What went wrong?"* she wailed. *"What made him reject me?"* And burst into bitter tears again.

She dropped bra and panty hose and lurched naked to the bar, where she filled another tumbler and swallowed slowly. Smooth as honey, she thought in surprise, and drained it all.

Hiccuping, she made her way to the bed and lay back on the quilted covering. Don't give up, babe, you've got too much going for you to quit now, she told herself. You'll get over tonight, and tomorrow—well, let tomorrow come. Fuck Mark and fuck John, miserable bastards, were her thoughts before her clouded mind seemed to drift away.

Turning on one side, she drew her knees to her breasts and regressed into childhood.

"Oh, Taki," she crooned to the pillow, "dear old Taki. Come to me, I need you so. Comfort me, excite me the way you always do. Your little Nina needs you now."

Twenty-Two

BEIJING

As THOMAS V. LANG of Toronto, importer and distributor of toys, Mark Brand passed through Beijing airport Customs and Immigration with no more than routine scrutiny. After he made out the currency declaration form, his travel permit and Canadian passport were stamped without comment, and Brand chose an elderly BMW taxi to take him to the hotel.

Though expensive by Chinese standards, the suite was small by

Western norms. Sitting room large enough for a sofa, TV, two chairs, and a tea table. A single door opened into the bedroom that held a double bed and night table with reading lamp. The closet was empty but for the luggage rack, on which the porter had placed Brand's bag. No closet hangers, no soap bar or Kleenex, but a partial roll of tan toilet paper was recessed in the tiled wall. A shower head pointed downward toward an old-fashioned bathtub . . .

Bedroom wallpaper was bicolored from wall seepage, peeling here and there. On the tea table, no welcoming basket of fruit and flowers for the weary traveler, just a lone bottle of TianFu Cola; no ice or bucket to cool it . . . I might as well be in a hostel in Outer Mongolia, he told himself, and began to unpack.

From the suitcase he got out a sealed liter of Walker Black, opened it, and swallowed a shot. He needed bottled water from the room boy but decided not to test the purity of hotel ice. He hadn't repeated that mistake since cooling a drink with Djakarta hotel ice six years ago. That imprudence—or naiveté—had cost him ten days in bed with amoebic dysentery. Since then he used bottled water even to brush his teeth.

Anticipating spare amenities, Brand had packed coat hangers from the Manchu, and hung his clothes on them. That done, he rang for the room boy and asked for bottled water—in English.

While waiting for delivery he stretched out on the bed and congratulated himself on sloughing off Nina without complications. By now, he thought, she must be gnawing her knuckles in rage at his evasion. Still, she might linger in Hong Kong in hopes of his return, or stay on orders of her controller—what was his name?—Rostenkowski? No, a soundalike name. Tor—Tar . . . Tarnovski, that was it. First name Oleg. Oleg Tarnovski. Brand was pleased at recalling a name he had heard only once before.

Poor Nina, he thought with minimal sympathy, the Russian Intelligence Service was not famed for tolerating failure. But as a player in the game she had to accept consequences. Poor Nina.

And there was La-li to worry about. In principle he refused to accept the concept of failing to find and bring home his son. Sometime tomorrow Wo, San, and Yang, his three enrolled desperadoes, would reach Beijing and begin their search. Meanwhile, I ought to make myself known at the embassy so they'll realize Peter hasn't been forgotten.

Two bottles of Tiger Spring water arrived with the room boy. Peter paid for them but when he added a tip the boy refused, reminding Brand that tipping was illegal in the New China.

He uncapped a bottle, drank deeply, and mixed scotch and water. Sipping pleasurably, he went to the window, parted blinds, and looked out. Unlike Paris, Beijing was not a city of light; below lay broad spaces of darkness. But Tiananmen Square was outlined by lights. The immense Great Hall of the People was floodlit—parliament sat there—and in one of its ceremonial banquet halls Nixon had come close to giving away the store. Poor Dick, he mused, our late disgraced President. What you knew about China could be dropped in a thimble with room to spare.

As he had during the flight from Hong Kong, Brand reprised the stunning turn of events bringing him and Mary together again. Having been married to an urban revolutionary, and after keeping company of varied duration with at least a dozen women, he knew what had been missing from the equation of his life, and it was found in one word: Mary.

More than twenty years after her betrayal she was willing to join her life with his, and the realization of how enduring had been her love shamed him and rekindled the deep emotions he had felt when they were secret lovers long ago.

He wanted to claim Mary now, and with her the child and symbol of their love. But first the Wing-dah obstacle had to be displaced, and Peter found, the latter more difficult to accomplish than the other. So, he mused, despite the long years since Taipei I have more waiting to go through. Penance overdue, and more than deserved.

Somewhere in the city a police siren screamed high and stuttered into harsh staccato barks before the warning sequence repeated. The sounds tensed him, for his first reaction was that Peter had been caught; then he realized how unlikely that was. His nerves were on edge and he felt drained by the stress and emotions of the day. Forget all that. He was in Beijing, his goal, safely in place, and ready to take up the search for his son in the morning.

A Travel Service brochure had recommended dining at the Kang Le Happiness and Enjoyment Restaurant, or the Sichuan on Ron Xian Lane. But Brand had eaten well on the JAL flight and he was too tired to change and go out for another meal. Breakfast would come soon enough, he thought, and wondered how long it would be before he saw his son again.

Washington

During the week Darman Gerold used the Georgetown house on P Street to avoid the drive between Langley and the Upperville estate he shared with his second wife, Pauline. Hong Kong clinic doctors had sedated Doreen for the homeward flight, and Gerold still felt groggy from jet lag and the stress of watching his daughter on the plane.

He was having an abbreviated breakfast on the flagstone patio that overlooked the long, narrow, typically Georgetown garden. The time was seven forty-five, and clinic people were due at eight to take charge of Doreen. He sighed, recalling similar occasions when he had placed her in detox as the initial step in rehabilitation. Detox was effective, as far as it went, substituting methadone for heroin, a two-to-four-week dependency transition, with physical therapy, nutritious food, and psychological counseling. This time, he thought, she's not going to get out until I'm convinced she's clean and has at least a reasonable chance of leading an independent, drug-free life.

At this stage, he mused, I guess that's expecting a lot, but I'm not going to be swayed by pleas and hysterics. Addicts are liars and manipulators, I must remember that.

Jacques, the manservant, brought a portable phone to the table and said, "Call for you, sir."

Clinic people are delayed, damn them, he thought before asking, "Who is it?"

"A Mr. Chenow, sir."

Irving Chenow. "Okay, I'll take it." He pushed the receiver button and spoke. "Irving, what can I do for you?"

"First, Darman, I have to apologize for the early call, but I heard you got back last night, and I wanted to make contact before you're embroiled at the office."

"No problem. What's up?"

"Any chance you can fit me on the day's agenda?"

"Every chance." Irving was a personal friend of the President's and might put in a helping word when the time came. "What's convenient for you?"

"If you can come over around midday, we can lunch in my office and talk."

"Good idea, Irving. I'll be there."

"And I'm glad you were able to retrieve your daughter. Did you cross paths with Mark?"

"We had breakfast together so I could brief him on Tommy Gray's concerns."

"Glad you did." He paused. "Hasn't found his son yet, has he?"

"No, unfortunately. But Mark played a role in locating Doreen. Incidentally, I don't think he'll be back here for another two weeks or so—if then."

"Too bad, I feel we could use his input. Anyway, Darman, we'll talk later."

Gerold clicked off the telephone and set it on the table, thinking the day was going to be a hectic one; aside from Agency business he had a schedule of stroking calls to make. There were about twenty people who could help him toward the directorship, and reminding them of his availability was a crucial step. Following it with two or three Georgetown dinner parties and a larger do in Upperville. He could meet New York contacts at the Harvard Club to expand networking beyond the Beltway.

As he drank the last of his coffee, he saw Doreen sidle through the French doors and said, "Feel like breakfast?"

"God, no." She scratched the inside of an arm that showed red stripes from her fingernails. "All you and Mark think about is eating."

She was barefoot, he noticed, and wearing only bra and panties, material so flimsy her thatch and nipples showed through. "Doreen, I wish you would dress more appropriately when Jacques is around."

"Jacques?" She shrugged. "You trained me never to notice servants, so I don't." Leaning against the wall she smiled at him. Not a wholesome smile, he thought, but a calculating one with a hint of—malice? "You don't like Mark, do you, Dad?"

He hated the parental appellation, which was why, he knew, she used it. "Mark Brand? Not particularly, why?"

"You should be grateful to him—for finding me."

"I am." He got up from the table.

"I respect him, too. Mark took good care of me. A gentleman. Didn't want to fuck me."

"Doreen, *please* don't use that word in my presence."

Ignoring his plea, she said, "So I showed my appreciation by blowing him."

"*What?*"

"Head," she said calmly. "I gave him head, Dad, you know—oral sex."

"*The son of a bitch!*" he exploded, "I ought to—"

"Easy, Pop. Mark was sleeping when I took advantage of him—as it were. All my doing."

He stared at her. "Slut," he said coldly, "you little slut."

"Hey, Dad, I'm your daughter, remember? And if I'm a slut, what do we call Grandma Gerold?"

Mouth dry, he swallowed. Damn Amy for drunkenly revealing their affair. He stared fixedly at his daughter. She'd known for years. Some of her many psychologists and psychiatrists had told him it was one of the causes of her alienation and addiction. "Call her what you want," he responded, "but don't blame everything on me."

"Mother did. Why shouldn't I?"

"I'm not going to discuss it anymore." He stepped toward the doorway.

"You're in denial, Pop, that's what the shrinks call it. You'd feel better if you'd admit it—admit being a motherfucker."

His cheeks crimsoned. He loathed the word, it cursed and perverted the love they'd shared. Sin, the Bible said, but sin was foul, disgusting. Not like— Jacques interrupted his thoughts, saying, "They're here, sir."

"Good." Darman turned to his daughter. "Get on some clothes, time to go."

"Clothes? Who needs them? They'll give me white smocks at the clinic." She walked ahead of him through the house to the foyer where three people waited. A lady doctor—Hampill, something like that—and two white-jacketed male attendants.

"Morning, Doreen," the doctor said, smiling, "how are we today?"

"Lousy," Doreen replied. "Fuckin' lousy." She evaded her father's attempted kiss and said, "Take me as I am or not at all. Let's go."

Darman Gerold watched his daughter walk away. Why do I go through it, he asked himself, when every time it gets worse?

He watched her get into the clinic's stretch Lincoln, and sighed. As the limousine pulled away he thought that, at least, one phase was ended and another begun. Her rancor and contempt he had to tolerate, was forced to. For if she ever aired her charges in public he was finished. Marriage gone, career destroyed. The end.

Beside him Jacques said, "Will you be dining in, sir?"

"Probably not," Gerold replied, "so don't fix anything. First day back is always a bitch."

Driving across Key Bridge toward Langley, Gerold resolved not to think further of Doreen's nastiness, it was all part of the life she'd willfully destroyed. Cathedral School, Bennington . . . background and social position . . . by now she ought to be married to a young lawyer or doctor, taking the station in life he'd prepared her for. But, no, she was obsessed with what had happened long ago, before he'd married her mother, before Doreen was even born.

And as he drove automatically his mind slipped into a reverie that drew him back to boyhood. As though it were yesterday he remembered how it was those many nights when Amy slipped into his bed, his father unknowing, and cuddled and kissed and embraced him in knowing ways that brought incredible ecstasies to them both. *Always remember I made a man of you*, she'd murmured soon after that first experience, and he had never forgotten the dizzying excitement of her mouth and the sweetness of her breasts and loins. They had been everything to each other, their secret heightening pleasure almost unbearably. And on visiting weekends at St. George's she would come faithfully and share her room at the Viking until the weekend was over.

He remembered his first spring vacation when she had taken him to Havana and indulged them with lewd exhibitions, herself taking active part in some despite his jealousy. But later, in their Nacional room, she would make it up to him extravagantly, inhibitions drowned in the cognac and champagne she taught him to enjoy.

And there was the unforgettable Harvard summer when Amy had taken him to England, France, and Italy, where they passed as lady and gigolo and were never found out. There they could hold hands as they strolled and kiss over cocktails. Her lust was incredible and constant, and he had often wondered if his father had married her because of it. True, Amy made occasional allusions to his father's dedication to business, frequent travels, and diminished desire—the latter, Darman Gerold eventually realized, attributable to the prostate cancer that killed him. But she let him understand that he, not his father, was the one who shared her bed.

It made him inwardly proud to be her lover, to know that he, above all envious males, was loved by this incredibly gorgeous woman, with whom everything was possible, everything shared. They thought so much alike that speech was often needless; and she taught him tactics of self-interest, guile, and manipulation, knowledge that had proved priceless so many times throughout the course of his life.

Unbidden, he sensed the early pulse of an erection. It was a tribute to Amy that so long after her untimely death her memory could still arouse him. And why not? He owed her almost everything.

As he turned his pearl-gray Jaguar into the Agency access road, Gerold remembered how Doreen had appeared on the patio, practically naked but for a provocative smile. She was, he knew from school, police, and clinical reports, no stranger to sexual activity; she'd even boasted of an act with Mark Brand he found disgusting. He resented Mark's intimacy with his daughter and would hold it against him for reprisal at some future time.

Reflecting on Doreen's body language, Gerold recalled occasions at home, sailing, on the beach, and in their pool when she had displayed herself naked or near naked and unashamed. It made him wonder if Doreen had been sending a seductive message he'd been too dense and fatherly to comprehend. At first the thought was repugnant, but as it turned in his mind he found a certain logic.

His daughter knew he had slept with his mother; perhaps subliminally the little minx wanted to take his mother's place. If that was the case it could explain a great deal. First, he would ask Dr. Hempill whether, in her opinion, Doreen had a father fixation, say it was a troubling thought he wanted to lay to rest. Innocently, the psychiatrist would reply yes, or no. And depending on her answer he would take follow-up measures as seemed appropriate. Not excluding—

He braked at the entrance guard post, showed his badge to the guard, who smiled, saluted, and waved him in.

Steering toward his parking space in front of the headquarters main entrance, Darman Gerold visualized the faces of Amy and Doreen until they merged into one. There had always been a strong family likeness, he mused, and in good health Doreen could be a radiant beauty. Now, she was a dissolute shell of her former self, but after detox and rehab, she could become her true self once more. Even then, he reflected, her figure would lack the mature voluptuousness of his mother's, though that might develop in time.

And as he got out of his car, it came to him that he was seeing his daughter in a new and unexpected light. Aside from parental obligation to help her gain full health, he ought to show Doreen signs of true affection by word and deed. This time he was going to monitor her rehab progress very carefully and evaluate any behavioral changes that could open an entirely new relationship between them.

Beijing

While Peter Brand was having breakfast in the Marine mess, he saw COS Jason Whitbread come in and draw coffee from the stainless-steel urn, then bring his mug to a place across the table from Peter. "How you doing?" Whitbread asked.

"Better. Food and sleep make a big difference." He chewed on sausage the Marines called horse-cock, and swallowed. "What's happening in the outside world?"

Whitbread smiled and looked at his wristwatch. "As of now the Chinese haven't demanded your return, though a note from the *Wai-shike*—the Foreign Affairs branch—could come anytime." He sipped from his cup. "A couple of things occur to me: The authorities know a stolen ambulance crashed into our compound, but they don't really know the driver was you. They can surmise the truth, but they also have to consider some Chinese citizen, who couldn't wait for a visa, drove the ambulance."

Peter nodded and spread honey on a biscuit.

"Secondly," the Station Chief continued, "I'm inclining toward your thought that because the authorities never admitted having you, they can't easily do so now. Among other things it would mean loss of face and considerable bureaucratic confusion, including where blame is assigned, and so on. So I assume some infighting is going on right now."

"Sounds likely."

"I made those points to the Ambassador, and mollified him for the time being. Like most guys in the diplomatic racket, he doesn't want to hear about trouble, present, past, or future."

Peter smiled slightly. "Does the Ambassador know why I went to Canton?"

"No. It's not relevant at the moment, and if I have to admit you were acting in an agent capacity—a 'Legal Traveler' actually—I'd lose face, and so would the Agency. So for the present I don't think you have to worry about being handed back to the Chinese. The real question, though, is how we get you out of here, to an airport and home."

Peter drained his coffee mug and set it aside. "I telephoned my father's apartment. He didn't answer, so I left a message on his machine."

"But not your name, I hope. We assume the Chinese monitor all calls to and from the embassy."

"No, I didn't give my name. Then I phoned my fiancée, who was pretty relieved to hear my voice—but she said 'Peter' a couple of times. Is that bad?"

"Who knows."

"I was going to call my father's office, but La-li told me Dad was in Hong Kong." He grimaced. "Looking for me."

"Oh? Where in Hong Kong?"

"No idea. He may have friends there, but I don't know who they are. More than likely he went to a hotel. Last time we were there together I was pretty young, don't remember where we stayed."

Whitbread nodded thoughtfully. "Given his background, I'm sure your father can take care of himself, so we won't worry about him."

"Right."

"Oh, one thing the Ambassador doesn't want is any publicity about you and your escape. He's very firm about that. So long as the Chinese don't stir things up with a diplomatic note or street demonstrations, he's willing to keep you here. Of course, he wants you out of the embassy as soon as it can be arranged."

"Me, too."

"Yeah." He cleared his throat. "But I notice the police are still watching the embassy gate. Either they figure you're inside, or are waiting for you to try to leave.

"Whichever the case, getting you out of here isn't going to be easy. Any ideas?"

"Not yet. I used up a lot of ideas figuring how to get here. Seems to me it's your problem to solve."

"Probably," Whitbread conceded, "and for the time being I'm not going to consult headquarters for advice. They'd come up with a dozen cockamamie ideas with no connection to reality, maybe send some asshole here to supervise and second-guess me." He shook his head. "I've had all of that I can handle."

"I'm sure."

"Meanwhile, you're comfortable?"

Peter nodded. "I've got food, bed, and a telephone. I'm okay."

"Want anything, tell Gunny Samczak—Gunnery Sergeant—he heads the detail. If he can't supply it he'll let me know." Whitbread got up. "We're keeping your presence on a need-to-know basis to avoid speculation and leaks to the outside. Okay?"

"Okay."

"I'll get you some magazines and books. Like Clancy's stuff?"

"Sure do. Or anything by Elmore Leonard or Len Deighton."

"We both like the same guys. See you later." He left the mess hall and Peter got more coffee.

True, he reflected as he returned to the table, he hadn't given consideration to leaving the embassy without getting arrested, but it was an immediate problem that had to be resolved. Ah-peng would have ideas, he told himself, but she was no longer at his side to counsel him. Surely she was safely in her hut by now, resuming the daily routine his presence had interrupted, and he wanted to get money to her—food, money, anything—before he left Beijing.

MARK BRAND SLEPT LATE, had breakfast in the hotel's restaurant off the lobby, and decided he ought to strengthen his cover legend before going to the embassy.

A taxi took him to the Foreign Trade Office half a mile away, where he was courteously received by an English-speaking trade official who examined one of Brand's Canadian business cards and said, "If you will go to the third floor, you will find sample toys with the locations of manufacturers. Have you bought Chinese toys before, Mr. Lang?"

"No. I've been dealing with South Asian factories with which I'm not fully satisfied. That's why I've come here." He paused. "Are any of your toy factories located within easy reach of Beijing?"

"I'm sure some are, but I'm not familiar with toy manufacture. In any case, you would be able to place export orders upstairs and save yourself the bother of traveling to visit factories."

"I understand," Brand replied, "and thank you." He walked up a broad staircase to the third floor, wondering what the building had been prior to the Glorious October Revolution.

An area the size of a basketball court was given over to tables holding an extensive assortment of toys. As he approached the nearest display, a woman in black Mao-style blouse and trousers approached him and bowed. In Chinese she asked if she could help him. Brand shook his head and said, "English only, sorry."

To which she responded, in English, "Then we will speak your language, sir."

He gave her a business card, and after inspecting it she asked, "Where are you staying in Beijing?"

"Hotel Beijing."

"And will you be long in Beijing?"

"A few days," he told her, "and after business is concluded I plan on some sight-seeing—the Great Wall, Ming Tombs, the works."

"How satisfying to combine pleasure with business," she exclaimed, "and I hope that both will edify you before departure."

"Me, too. By the way, your English is excellent."

"Oh, thank you," she beamed. "Now you may inspect exhibits undisturbed, letting me know when I can be of assistance."

Slowly Brand walked along the display tables, pausing now and then to pick up a toy and examine it. At each toy grouping were bilingual cards providing name and address of the manufacturer, and Brand pocketed half a dozen before completing his tour of the display.

When the aide came to him, Brand said, "What about prices? I don't see any prices listed."

"That is true, Mr. Lang. Price depends on your arrangement with individual factories, mainly the order size."

"Still," he said, "an indication of price range would be helpful."

"An excellent suggestion, and I will make it known to my supervisors." Her hand thrust out. "Thank you for coming."

"My pleasure."

"Your hotel can provide translators and secretarial services, also facsimile transmitters for reaching some of the manufacturers without delay."

"Yeah, that'll speed things along. And thanks again for your help."

"I serve the Revolution," she intoned, and bowed her head as he left.

On the second floor Brand stopped to look over a huge display of domestic goods. There was Fang-fang lipstick, Pansy and Double Bull underwear, Horse Head tissues, Flying Baby toilet paper, White Rabbit candy, and Flying Pigeon bicycles among the many offerings. He smiled at some of the names, then looked at his watch. He'd supported his cover with a tour of export offerings, and later he might send a few faxes requesting quotations on various toys. Now it was time to visit the embassy.

Twenty-Three

WASHINGTON

As DARMAN GEROLD ENTERED the Assistant Secretary's office, IRVING CHENOW left his desk to shake hands, then indicated chairs by the coffee table. A tray held assorted sandwiches and condiments, beside it a thermal coffee jug. "Sort of spare," Chenow acknowledged, "but I seldom have the luxury of lunching out."

Chenow poured coffee while Gerold seated himself, and said, "Without being intrusive, may I ask how your daughter is?"

"Tired from the flight, of course," Gerold replied, and selected a turkey-on-rye sandwich. "So she's at a rest home in Alexandria for a while."

"Good. We're all hostages to our children's fortunes." He picked up a chicken sandwich and bit into it. After swallowing, he said, "A cable from Beijing embassy says young Peter Brand showed up there."

"I'll be damned! I know Mark'll be relieved."

Chenow nodded, then chuckled. "Peter arrived unexpectedly and forcefully—crashed a hospital ambulance through the gate and identified himself before the guards could throw him out. The young man is little the worse for wear and anxious to contact his father."

"Understandably. Of course he doesn't know Mark's in Hong Kong, but that's not a big problem. I saw Mark at the Manchu Hotel so he's probably still there."

"Then I'll cable the embassy to let Peter know. Shep Andersen's gravely concerned—he cabled—at the possibility of negative Chinese reaction. Asked for instructions on resolving the case—whether Peter should be handed back to the authorities. I cabled a reply saying hell no." He drank from his Haviland cup. "You see any of that traffic?"

"Been in meetings all morning, haven't seen any traffic at all." He wondered if Chenow had other business to discuss beyond the recovery of Mark's son. *My In box probably holds word from Whitbread with the same news.*

"Anyway," Chenow observed, "with the strayed recovered, it's a happy day for both parents." He ate more of his sandwich and set it down. "You indicated you'd briefed Mark on the gas warhead situation."

"Broad brush, no details."

"Well, there are more details now." He summarized what was known of the train collision and derailing near Pingying, and the likelihood that at least fifty-three persons had died from released gas. "Tommy Gray theorizes they were villagers drawn there by the crash."

"How could he tell?"

"Clothing," Chenow replied, "on undamaged bodies." He cleared his throat. "Support for the hypothesis comes from an unsuspected and previously untested source."

"Oh?"

"Peter Brand. He was at the hospital when bodies arrived and spoke with a nurse who gave him details of the crash site. As far as I'm concerned, that nails it down, so we no longer have just theory, we've got a pretty convincing case of lethal gas in missile warheads. Darman, I don't think we can just sit on the intelligence and pray it will go away. Higher authority has to be informed, and the sooner the better."

"The Secretary?"

Chenow looked at the wall clock. "Tried for an appointment all morning, but no luck. He was at the White House en route to Andrews. By now he's airborne."

"Undersecretary?"

"Brussels economic conference—G-7." He shook his head. "I'm tempted to get this to the Asia Group without delay but the Secretary vetoed that when I suggested it."

Gerold's mind was turning the problem around, searching for personal advantage in some quarter. Chenow said, "Your Director could do it, Darman; hell, he could convene the whole NSC."

After more consideration, Gerold said cautiously, "I suppose he could, but he'd want to know where national security interests are involved. What's your read on that?"

"Mutual defense treaty with Taiwan. It's never been abrogated, so if the ChiComs threaten or gas Taiwan we're ipso facto involved."

His words made Gerold uncomfortable. "I see that now," he told the Assistant Secretary, "and it's a pretty disturbing scenario."

Chenow nodded. "I don't believe this government should wait until gas missiles are on launchers aimed at the island. As I reminded the Secretary, the Cuban Missile Crisis could have been avoided if Kennedy had picked up the hot line to Khrushchev as soon as we confirmed nuke missiles were in Cuba."

"I agree, Irving. Who's our main man on this?"

"Tom Gray. But I think you should go with it."

He sighed. "Guess so. I'll have my in-house people synthesize everything, bring it all together and posit unassailable conclusions. Meanwhile, Gorgon will be bringing in frequent information . . ." He glanced at the wall clock. "I've got to zoom up to speed on this, Irving. Missed too much being away, but it couldn't be helped." He got up. "Thanks for lunch. I'll be in my office the rest of the day and probably a good part of the night preparing a position paper for the Director." He moved away, then turned back. "Anything to the rumor the Director's leaving?"

Chenow shrugged. "We've all heard the rumor." He smiled. "Why? Interested in the job?"

"Definitely," Gerold admitted, "and if it's appropriate, I'd appreciate you putting in a good word for me."

"If the opportunity comes," Chenow agreed, and saw his guest to the door.

As he walked back to his desk he thought, Darman isn't my idea of the ideal Director, but he's got intelligence experience, personal wealth, and social position, all rungs on the ladder. I'd prefer the President not install some retired general or admiral from the Pentagon. They bring too much service loyalty, tunnel vision, and geopolitical innocence to head the intelligence community impartially and usefully. And no more retired judges, puh-leeze, Mr. President. They don't make decisions easily.

So compared to some other possible candidates for the directorship Darman doesn't stack up too badly. And if my opinion is ever solicited, I'll support him as I said I would.

Too, once the Gorgon stuff is circulated a lot of important eyes will focus on Darman Gerold. How he works through the problem will very likely decide his future.

At his desk Chenow dictated a cable to Ambassador Andersen in Beijing, copy to the Consulate-General in Hong Kong. It asked that Peter Brand be informed his father was probably at the Manchu Hotel in Hong Kong, suggested Peter phone there, and asked the Consulate to check on Mark Brand's whereabouts. His secretary typed the form quickly, and as Chenow released it for transmission, he checked the Priority precedence box.

I want Mark back in Washington as soon as I can get him here, he said to himself. Win Hilyard's gone, in practical terms, and I need Mark to carry this China bolus before things escalate beyond recall.

BEIJING

AFTER THE TAXI LET Brand off at the embassy, he noticed welders repairing the grilled iron gates. He approached the Marine sentry box through a pedestrian opening, and got out the American passport he had brought concealed in the lining of his suitcase. The guard looked at it and asked, "Who do you want to see, sir?"

"It's a missing persons situation," Brand replied. "A consular officer, I imagine."

The guard nodded. "Just go in and the receptionist will give you a form."

"Thank you." Brand took a step and paused. "What's with the gate? Looks like a tank hit it."

"Some slopey, ah, Chinese driver let his car get out of control and smashed it." He grinned. "Too much mao-tai."

"Yeah, the stuff'll get you every time. Avoid it, Corporal," he cautioned and followed the paved walk to the entrance.

Inside, he showed his U.S. passport to the receptionist and was given an interview form. Others in the waiting area looked to be Chinese-Americans by their dress and use of English. Most of them, he thought, were probably seeking U.S. visas for Chinese relatives.

After completing the form, Brand returned it to the receptionist, who told him to take a seat, he'd be called in order, and gave him a plastic counter numbered 8.

Half an hour later the receptionist called his number, and Brand stepped through a security station and heard the detection bell ring. The guard said, "Please place any metal objects on this tray and go through again."

Brand placed coins and his switchblade on the tray and went through the device. The guard said, "We'll keep this knife for now. Claim it when you leave."

Brand nodded, and saw a woman beckoning to him from the hall. As he joined her, she said, "Follow me, please," and led him to a small interview room that contained a table and several chairs. After seating herself she said, "I'm Vice Consul McNamara, Mr. Brand," and looked down at the form he'd filled out. "You say here your son Peter was arrested in Canton—we call it Guangzhou now—and imprisoned in Beijing." Her gaze lifted from the form. "Also he may have escaped."

"There are indications," he said. "Government radio broadcasts, but I'm certain enough that I've come here to look for him."

"I checked the name, and all I could find was a State circular telegram advising us he was missing." She toyed with the pencil in her hand. "Beyond that I have no information for you."

"I see. Well, Assistant Secretary Chenow is an old family friend, and before I left Washington he assured me the embassy would do everything possible to locate my son and get him back to the States." He paused. "Possibly I should take it up with the Ambassador."

She considered the suggestion. "I don't believe Ambassador Andersen could help at this point"—she touched the telegram—"but he would probably see a friend of the Assistant Secretary before he leaves for Singapore. I'll ask his secretary." She punched three numbers on the telephone and spoke with the other party. After replacing the receiver, she said, "The Ambassador is at the residence preparing to leave Beijing. Sorry, sir," she finished, in tones that suggested to Brand she wasn't sorry at all.

"So there's nothing to be done, that it?"

"Not until we have more information."

"Terrific. Hasn't anyone from the embassy asked the authorities about my son?"

She looked down at the telegram again. "Marginal note shows inquiry made at the Public Security Bureau, negative results."

"How long ago?"

She showed him the penciled date. "About two weeks ago."

"And no return visit."

Her cheeks colored slightly. "This is a small embassy, not enough consuls to handle the visa load. We do as well as we can, but please understand your son is not the only American citizen missing in China."

"I'm sure of that," he said in a hard voice. "The host country has never accounted for the thousands of Americans they took out of Korea." He paused. "Was the Foreign Ministry asked about my son?"

"I don't know, doesn't say here."

"Well, who the hell would know?" His voice was rising, he had to control himself, not make an enemy of this bureaucrat. "Sorry," he apologized, "I'm under a lot of stress."

"I understand, sir, no problem. But I don't know who would know about representations to the Foreign Ministry." She thought for a moment. "Probably the Counselor—he does routine work for the Ambassador."

"Well, can I see the Counselor?"

"I'll ask." She called another office, spoke briefly, and replaced the receiver. "The Counselor is escorting a group of visiting congressmen on a trip to the Great Wall. But I'll try to find out if he can see you tomorrow."

"Let's do that," Brand said in a controlled voice. "I'll call you tomorrow—what would be a good time?"

"Oh—say, eleven o'clock. Let's see—the name is Brand and your son is Peter, right?"

"Right. I shouldn't have to cable Irv Chenow to get in to ask a simple question of a goddam counselor, but I'm perfectly willing to." He got up. "Do we understand each other, Vice Consul McNamara?"

"We do," she said curtly. "Good day, sir."

"Good day." At the door he looked back and said, *"Tsai-jien."*

"What's that?" she said sharply.

"Gaelic," he replied, and went out reflecting that the Foreign Service apparently had an inviolable rule against assigning speakers of a foreign language to the country where the language was spoken: German speakers to Tokyo; Arabic speakers to Scandinavia; Russian speakers to Peru; and the Agency was almost as bad. No rationale beyond the precedent of custom.

He regained his switchblade from the guard and went down the walk toward the ironworkers and welders. Must have been a big car to do that much damage, he thought, passed the Marine guard box, and walked to the taxi rank.

FROM AN UPPER WINDOW Peter Brand had been watching gate repairs when he saw a man striding away from the embassy entrance. The man's gait and squared shoulders reminded him of his father but it wasn't until the man turned and briefly showed his profile that Peter was sure. *"Dad!"* he shouted, tried to open the window, but it was bolted shut. "Damn," he grated in frustration. "Damn, damn, damn!" Grabbing the room telephone he dialed Whitbread's internal number, and when the COS picked up, Peter said shakily, "I just saw my father in the compound."

"No shit? You sure?"

"I'm damn sure. Can you go after him?" He peered out again and saw his father get into a taxi, the taxi pulled away. "He's gone," Peter blurted. "You've got to find him."

"Okay, take it easy. I was going to tell you the embassy got a cable for you saying your dad was in Hong Kong."

"Well, he's not there, he's here. Christ, I just saw him."

"All right, Peter, settle down. I'll find out what he was doing here, who he saw, where he's staying. We'll wrap this up real quick." The line went dead, and Peter sat on the edge of his bunk. So near and so damn far, he thought emotionally. That's been the story ever since I got to this damn country. And to see my father after all this time . . . Unbelievable. But he's here, thank God, and Jason will find and bring him back.

If the CIA can't do that, he thought bitterly, they ought to close shop and get out of business.

BEIJING

FROM THE HOTEL BRAND faxed identical inquiries to four toy manufacturers, and went out for lunch at the Fang Ze Yuan (Garden of Abundance and Color) restaurant, where he selected snowflake prawns, chicken puffs with sharksfin, and fruit jelly, from a multipage menu. As was customary, side dishes included steamed and fried rice, and soft rice-flour noodles. He enjoyed the spicy northern-style cooking as a change from blander Hong Kong-Cantonese fare, and in addition to unsweetened green tea, he drank a cold bottle of Tsingtao beer.

To settle his meal, Brand walked back to the hotel and slept until wakened by knocking at his door.

He opened it, expecting fax replies; instead he saw Yang, the eldest and largest of the three banditti. Yang bowed, Brand stepped aside, and Yang came in. Formally they shook hands, and Brand said, "Welcome, friend of my brother. Are you well? Was your journey a good one? Did Wo and San reach Beijing safely?"

After nodding yes to each question, Yang said, "We are staying in a small hotel on Sanlihe Road, a ten-minute subway ride from here." He gave Brand the hotel business card, "Room twenty-three."

"Good," said Brand. "Have you sufficient money for expenses?"

"Master Ning supplied our needs."

"Enough for bribes?"

Yang considered. "Perhaps additional money for that will be needed."

"Then let me know."

Yang looked around the room. "This may be the best in Beijing, but it is poor in comparison to Hong Kong."

Brand nodded. "These Mainlanders have much to learn from the rest of the world."

Yang grunted. "They are merely waiting until Hong Kong falls like a ripe plum into their waiting hands."

"Unfortunately so. After which we may expect to see the Colony decline in every aspect. Here"—he took a card-size photo from his wallet and gave it to Yang—"this is my son. Show it to your companions."

Yang studied Peter's features and put the photo away. "On the train we decided to divide the search as follows: Wo covers Lingyuan Special Prison to seek information from off-duty guards. San is to make inquiries of Gong An Ju men at a bar near their headquarters on Nan Chi Zi. As for myself I have taken responsibility to cover the *Meiguo dashiguan* on Kwanghua lu."

"I visited the embassy before noon," Brand told him.

"And I have just come from there. You saw the gate being repaired?"

"A Marine guard told me it was rammed by a driver who lost control of his car."

Yang smiled. "The entrance is watched by five policemen, as you doubtless saw. I thought the accident strange enough to share a bottle of mao-tai with one who was resting under a tree. He told me he had been on night duty when the incident occurred. He said a hospital ambulance crashed into the embassy compound, and though he glimpsed the driver only briefly, he thought the driver was not Chinese but European."

"You believed his story?"

"Why should I not? He had nothing to gain by lying. We were sharing a friendly drink, talking of other things as well."

"What happened to the driver?"

"He thought the embassy guards arrested the driver and took him away. He himself did not see an arrest, but heard of it from two comrades who did."

"That's very interesting," Brand remarked, "because when I was at the embassy the incident was not mentioned, nor did I hear of an arrested driver, Chinese or European." Still, he mused, it could have been Peter. "What was the driver wearing?" he asked.

"My man said he wore simple coolie clothing, not Western garb."

Brand nodded thoughtfully. To avoid capture Peter—or any fugitive—would disguise himself to blend with the locals. Before returning to the embassy and pressuring the Counselor, Brand felt he needed further information. "Tell Wo I want the name of the Westerner who escaped from Lingyuan. Tell San the same, and say he should try to learn if the Westerner was recaptured."

"I understand."

"I have plenty of money, so—"

"—I would dishonor Master Ning were I to accept it now. Later, it may be needed."

"Very well. I'm impressed by what's been accomplished in very little time." He smiled. "My brother chose well."

"We serve our master," Yang replied.

Brand said, "As you familiarize yourself with the embassy, consider possible ways by which a person could leave it without being seen." He paused. "Thinking, of course, of my son."

"I understand." Yang took the formulaic step backward, then halted and spoke again. "By chance, sir, are you expecting to see Cheong Wing-dah in Beijing?"

"No." The question made his body tense. "Why do you ask?"

"Because, as I neared the hotel entrance a few minutes ago, I saw a large black car pull up, and a man got out."

"Cheong Wing-dah?"

"No, sir. One of his men, an enforcer named Yu Min-sheng."

"What did he do?"

"Waiting for the elevator, I saw Yu go to the registration desk. Perhaps he was obtaining a room for his master."

Or inquiring for me, Brand thought, and said, "In Hong Kong Cheong made an indirect threat to me. He may be planning to pursue that threat—or he may have sent Yu on a business matter."

"It is widely known that Cheong Wing-dah supplies his galleries by smuggling ancient pieces, and does so by bribing officials who permit them to leave the Mainland."

"A profitable business," Brand observed, "but I don't want Cheong interfering with me. Ever since we were boys on Taiwan there has been bad blood between us." He paused. "His size and weight are an obstacle to travel, but it is possible he came to Beijing."

"And if he is here?"

"Recovering my son is more important than dealing with fat Cheong."

Yang left then, and Brand drank scotch with spring water while he reviewed all Ning's man had told him. Because he was registered as Thomas Lang he doubted that Fatso's men could locate him so he was not going to worry over that possibility. Of greater significance was Yang's tale of a European driver breaching the embassy gate and his possible arrest. Either the driver had been summarily ejected from the compound, or was being detained within the embassy. But if European, he would have been returned to his own embassy by now. If American . . . asylum would be granted. Unless—he stirred with the tip of one finger—unless the man was a fugitive wanted under Chinese law.

Useless to question Vice Consul McNamara; the Ambassador was away, and the Counselor of Embassy would not be available until tomorrow. He felt an impulse to phone Irving Chenow to get to the bottom of the puzzle, but that would break security. Already he had violated the terms of his special clearances by entering the Mainland, and while he regretted it, he felt then, as now, that he had no alternate choice. The clearances, the job, were trivial matters compared to his son's life and safety, which were beyond price.

How ironic it would be, he mused, if while gaining Mary, I were to lose my son.

Twenty-Four

Drawing a bottle of Cordon Rouge from the ice bucket, Nina Kenton handed it to John, who forced the cork with his thumbs until it popped out and hit the ceiling. Smilingly, John filled their champagne glasses and touched his rim to hers. "What shall we drink to?" he asked.

"Health and wealth, I suppose, not necessarily in that order."

John laughed and drank. His jovial mood reassured Nina, who had suffered agonies of uncertainty since telephoning him the bad news. It seemed only a few hours since their one-sided conversation, when he had given no indication of coming to Hong Kong. But that was John's odd way of doing things, she reminded herself, though she'd been rocked by his unexpected arrival at her door. After sipping, she said, "You wasted no time coming here."

"No. I felt it important to let you know it's not the end of the world. Too bad Brand eluded you, dear Nina, but he was an intelligence officer, after all, trained in evasive techniques."

Bending over, he kissed the back of her hand. "You're quite sure he went to the Mainland?"

"I asked the concierge. He found the taxi driver who took Mark to the airport for a two o'clock flight to Beijing."

"You did well," he said approvingly, "did even better to inform me promptly as you did."

"I knew you expected me to, John, and I've always tried to be truthful and follow orders."

"I know that." He sighed. "If Brand isn't caught and interrogated the situation remains basically the same, nothing compromised." He eyed Nina over the rim of his glass. "Of course, back in Washington you'll have to regain his confidence, but knowing you I don't feel that should be too difficult." He refilled their glasses. "I suppose you had no indication he was planning to leave."

"None at all. You told me to poison him, and I would have," she said firmly, "but now that it's not necessary I'd feel less nervous if you'd take the stuff back."

"Of course." He watched her take the clutch purse from the coffee table. She opened it and handed him the vial and pills he had given her in Washington. John put them on the table. "Feel better now?"

"Much." A thought occurred to her. "Suppose I can't patch up things with Mark—what then?"

"First, I have confidence in your ability to get what you want from any man. Second, if something unforeseen occurred—like Brand leaving GlobEco—why, I have plans for you. I'm considering your future even now."

"Then tell me," she teased, "I'm dying to know."

"Curiosity killed the cat."

"But I'm not a cat," she said coyly. "Please tell me, John."

"Later," he said, drained his glass, then drew her against him. Nina finished her champagne and circled his shoulders with her arms. They kissed deeply, and she felt his rod rising between her loins. He drew her dress top down and undid her bra. She stepped out of her shoes as he began to lick her nipples. Shivering in delight, she pressed his head to her breasts and felt desire spread out from her matrix. "The bedroom," she said huskily, and felt her knees go weak.

Undressing rapidly, she tossed clothing in a chair and lay back on the bed. John slowly removed his clothing and folded his things across another chair, Nina watching expectantly. His rod was fully erect, she saw admiringly, eager to tongue and fondle it. Never before had she really wanted him, but now her sense of gratitude and relief was making her truly excited. She reached for him as he joined her, parted her loins to accommodate his questing hand, and as she soared toward climax, she urged, "Now, John, right now. Do it, please do it before I die."

Instead of covering her, he got off long enough to roll on a condom. He'd never done that before, and she was too preoccupied with the burning in her loins to question him. And when he entered her she bucked convulsively and moaned, holding him tightly while he thrust and rammed and squeezed her buns until a hoarse gasp told her that he was coming, too.

For a while he lay heavily atop her, flattening her full breasts, until she murmured uncomfortably and eased out from under his weight. Coarse bastard though he was, she thought, he was one hell of a lover.

Rolling on his back, John stared at the ceiling, then sat up. "After that, we need a drink."

"Absolutely. God, it was wonderful." She saw him enter the bathroom, heard the toilet flush, and assumed he was disposing of the condom. Minutes later he came back from the sitting room with filled glasses and handed her one. "A night to remember," he remarked, and tilted his glass. Nina sipped until he said, "All the way."

So she swallowed the champagne, coughed, and blurted, "Tastes funny, must be flat."

"Not likely." He watched her expression change as a hand gripped her throat.

"Choking," she rasped, "help me," feeling pain like a knife in her heart. Her eyes were frightened, face anguished. Her legs and feet kicked and pounded the bed until suddenly she lay slack. John carried his glass to the bar and sipped more champagne. Then he washed and toweled the glass and set it carefully in the rack among the others. Holding the nearly empty champagne bottle, he returned to the bedroom. Her position hadn't changed, though her bladder had drained. After pressing her carotid he wiped his fingerprints from the bottle and rolled it against her open palm. Then he returned it to the bar top.

Next, he emptied the poison vial into the flushing toilet and dropped in the pills. He rinsed the vial and crossed the bedroom to where he'd left his clothing. He slid the empty vial in a coat pocket for later disposal and picked up Nina's scattered clothing. He hung her dress in the closet and arranged her underthings on the chair, under which he placed her shoes. Then he turned on the ceiling light and looked around. Her mouth was contorted in the rictus of death, one arm lay partway across a breast, the other paralleled her side.

As he dressed, he decided he was satisfied with the scene. By now stomach acids would have broken down the poison compound, leaving nothing for a medical examiner to ponder. Blood-alcohol index was explained by consumption of champagne prior to a lethal heart attack.

They'd find no semen in her vagina, no suggestion of an evening visitor at all.

In the bathroom he rinsed hands and face, dried them, and switched off the light. He buttoned his shirt, tied his tie, and pulled on his coat. Then for a moment he stared without remorse at the woman he had murdered, and said, "You failed me, Nina, became excess to my needs. In Washington you would have been a burden and a threat to my existence, so the end came here."

After turning off the ceiling light he left the bedroom and crossed the sitting room to the door. He opened it and polished the doorknob before stepping into the hall, toed the door shut behind him.

As he walked quietly toward the elevator he looked at his wristwatch. Good. Two hours to reach Kai Tak and board the return flight to Dulles International Airport.

The elevator opened, and he stepped in.

John, aka Oleg Tarnovski, ex-officer of the KGB currently employed as an independent contractor by the foreign intelligence service of North Korea, stood silently as the elevator lowered him to the lobby. He strolled unhurriedly toward the outside rank of taxis, reflecting that he had accomplished what had to be done efficiently and professionally. Overall, he would have been away from Washington less than twenty-four hours, a period in which, he told himself, no one would note his absence.

Except, possibly, the FBI.

Beijing

In Peter's small room—the sergeant-occupant was in Bangkok on R&R—Jason Whitbread said, "What with lunch-hour staff absenteeism and a general disinterest in my queries it took me a lot longer to get a fix on your father. Finally I checked the consulate visitor sign-in sheet, and there was your father's name. He was interviewed by Vice Consul McNamara, not the brightest of our employees, who confirmed your sighting. You were absolutely right, Peter. Your dad's in Beijing and he was here looking for you."

"Great, that's really wonderful!" Tears of happiness and relief misted his eyes. "Have you talked with him?"

Whitbread shook his head. "Not yet. He didn't tell McNamara where he was staying—she admitted she didn't ask. But the good news is he's coming back tomorrow to light fire under the Counselor on your behalf."

"God, I can't wait to see him."

"Of course." He stroked his chin. "Sort of a miraculous convergence but fully logical when you analyze it. You vanished in Beijing so your father came here—I guess he expected you'd try to reach the embassy." He studied Peter's taut face. "Did he suggest it?"

"Didn't know I was going to the Mainland, so he had no reason to. Anyway, where else was I to go? Believe me, I went over all the possibilities with Ah-peng. Oh—is there a way I can get money to her?"

"After you're safely home I'll use your map to locate her. Draw on funds sequestered for agent recovery—she'll have a better life, Peter, much better."

"Thanks," he said simply, relieved and assured by Whitbread's promise.

The COS rose from the chair. "Believe it or not I have things to do beyond rejoining father and son, so now that's pretty much taken care of I'll get back to my cloistered office and see what my overworked staff has been up to."

"Sure—and I really appreciate all you've done."

After the COS left, Peter poured a drink from the sergeant's bottle of Early Times, and knocked it back. After all this time it seemed impossible that he was going to be with his father tomorrow. Incredible, all of it. Before noon tomorrow he was going to watch from the window to see his father come in.

The ironworkers were finished repairing the gates, and stone masons were starting work on shattered masonry. Pretty sturdy ambulance, he thought, to inflict all that damage. If I'd been driving a compact car I'd be in a coffin now.

IN HIS HOTEL SUITE Brand read faxed quotations from toy manufacturers and decided they would make supportive pocket litter—if he was searched by Gong An Ju agents—so he folded them neatly into a coat pocket and considered how to kill the fifteen-hour interval before seeing the Counselor of Embassy. Too early for dinner, so he considered strolling around Tiananmen Square and the Forbidden City. La-li would want to know how he'd spent his time in Beijing, and he had no better thoughts for killing time.

Before leaving, he replaced his U.S. passport in the suitcase lining, and made sure the Canadian passport and travel permit were in his coat pocket. Then, dissatisfied with passport concealment he removed it and looked around for more secure stowage.

Using the tip of his switchblade, he unscrewed the metal back of the TV set, laid the passport inside, and screwed the back into place. Moderately pleased with the new cache, Brand made a short drink for himself and thought about La-li. He hoped her pregnancy was proceeding without incident, and that Peter would be home in plenty of time to marry her and assume the legitimate responsibilities of fatherhood. He looked forward to a splendid wedding for the couple, and weighed the possibility that Mary and Chu-li could be there, too. Major episodes in life, he thought, usually have an end purpose however obscured at the beginning. I went to Hong Kong to find Peter; instead I found Mary and the daughter I never knew. And he reflected that the framework of his organized and unexciting life was being recast as though by some inexorable force over which he had no control. Last month I had only Peter; now I have a pregnant future daughter-in-law, a daughter, and the promise of a wife. Who could have predicted it all? Somehow, everything will fall into place, I'm confident of that. So it was right to come to Beijing. No answers yet, but I sense motion, an invisible current of things developing around and beyond me. Listen to your inner voice, my father advised me, and until now I never realized how sound and prophetic were his words.

So thinking, Brand pulled on his coat and went down to Chang-An Boulevard, turned right and began walking in the direction of Tiananmen Square.

The sidewalk was crowded with homeward-bound workers, trucks and bicycles moved rapidly along the broad boulevard. Passing the display windows of a department store, Brand remembered his first view of Mary's Celestial Galleries, and how he had hesitated before going in.

At an intersection he waited for the light to change. Then a man spoke close to his ear: "Mr. Brand, a car will round the corner and stop for you to get in. If you do not, I will call police and have you arrested as an American spy."

WASHINGTON

THE VICE PRESIDENT of the United States received Assistant Secretary of State Irving Chenow in his second-floor office in the Old Executive Office Building next to the White House.

"Irving," the Vice President said, nodding, "you know these gentlemen, I believe."

Chenow acknowledged the Director of Central Intelligence, and Darman Gerold, both seated at a conference table that fronted the Vice President's desk. "Have a seat," the Vice President invited. "I believe there's enough coffee for everyone."

Chenow took a seat across from the CIA representatives and turned to look at his host. The Vice President looked older without his TV makeup, although, Chenow thought, he's barely fifty. And though he was not on close terms with the Veep—as he liked to be called—he had been in conferences with him several times before. Chenow remembered that the Veep had been governor of an Appalachian state, his name recognition and popularity deriving from several years as an American League shortstop and a plaque in Baseball's Hall of Fame. At his party's presidential nominating convention—where Chenow had also been a delegate—the then Governor delivered the final clutch of votes needed to win the nomination. His reward had been the Vice Presidency, a position jocularly considered to be a title that lacked a job.

"We're here," the Vice President said, "because of a potential-type situation that seems to be brewing in China." He removed a wad of gum and replaced it with a fresh stick of Wrigley's. Chenow recalled the Veep's trademark tobacco-chewing, a habit suppressed in public, but practiced in the privacy of his Observatory Hill residence. *De gustibus* . . . Chenow thought inwardly, and sat forward to catch the Vice President's further utterances. "A delicate kind of situation where we've got to step real carefully. By that, I mean this gas warhead business that's just come up. You're all clued-in, I surmise."

"Guess so," Chenow said, and saw Gerold nod.

"Now," said the Veep, "I don't for a damn minute think the Chinks, ah, the Chinese are plannin' to blast little ol' Taiwan back to the Stone Age—not that they couldn't do it—but because we got this mutual assistance defense treaty with the island, which makes the U.S.A. a player, like it or not. So, let's get that idea off the table right now." He looked at the three men in turn.

The DCI said, "We haven't worked through the National Estimate process completely, but Darman here feels we've got enough satellite and ground intelligence to reach a conclusion."

Gerold said, "I think Irving will agree there's no indication of a missile attack on Taiwan in the immediate future."

"That right, Irving?"

"Far as I've been briefed," Chenow replied. "Of course—"

"Hey, the future takes care of itself," the Vice President interrupted, "so let's not bring in the crystal balls." Again he scanned all three faces. "Anyone disagree with that?"

Gerold shook his head before saying, "I'm confident the satellite take will show where the warheads are going, giving us ample word before they're mated to missiles."

"Which," the DCI observed, "would put a different and more disturbing complexion on the situation. But for now—" he said before he was cut off by the Vice President.

"I'm not one for buyin' trouble, never have been. When I was playin' the national game I took every day as a fresh one, didn't look back on yesterday's runs, errors, or strikeouts. That's still a plenty good philosophy in my humble opinion. We're in this for the long haul, all of us, an' we got a full season to play before it's Series time again," said the Vice President.

Chenow found the sporting allusions difficult to interpret, but assumed the Veep was heading toward a summation.

"Now," the Vice President continued, "while our boss is out of town I'm sorta in charge, ex officio. And while I'm making no quick decisions, I think I'm speakin' the President's mind when I say what we really got here—pared down to rock essentials—is a public relations problem—you follow?"

Chenow did not, but said nothing, and noted that Gerold was giving worshipful attention to the unofficial President's words.

"By which I mean if word gets out there's warlike activity on the Mainland—never mind it don't come to pass—we got citizens with bigtime investments on the Mainland *and* Taiwan who'd get shit-scared and scamper like chipmunks with their money—like what happened in Germany when Hitler started growlin'. Neither the President nor I want a crowd of CEOs buggin' us for assurance everything's okay and they don't hafta run scared. Over there in China they'd get madder'n hell if we was to make charges, even leaks, of warlike intent—get my point?" The listeners nodded, waiting for the next pitch.

"Now, you gentlemen are all intelligent and successful in your lines of work or you wouldn't be sittin' here. We got to have balls-out secrecy from here all the way down to the last clerk-typist who handles classified papers because I don't want any bad China rumors gettin' out." He leaned back in his chair, jaws working his gum cud, until he said, "I can think of fifty, sixty up there on Capitol Hill who'd love to get hold of this situation and twist it to political advantage, maybe hearings even. The old so-called China Lobby's gone with the wind, but Taiwan's got plenty of sympathizers around this town, folks with big stakes in a peaceful Mainland and no menace to the island." He chewed briefly before saying, "Happens I chair the NSC ex officio, where we got a crowd of Eastern college bigdomes and staff workers, whose political persuasion the law won't let us investigate. I assume they're mainly loyal, patriotic Americans, but in every dugout there's chronic whiners and complainers who buck management any chance they get. I don't mean Agency heads, gentlemen, don't get me wrong, it's the toilers in the vineyard I tend to worry about. Some of them got friends, relatives working in the media, which ought to disqualify them from team play, but it don't. It's them I don't want in a position where they could sneak something damaging to their buddies in TV or the Associated Press. Moreover, I got a responsibility to keep the lid on things until the boss gets back." He eyed Chenow. "Your boss is there, too, right?"

"Right."

The Vice President paused before saying, "I want you all on board, everyone on the team roster, no bench-warmers, and agreed to keep this situation among ourselves." He spoke directly to the DCI. "Your folks can keep polishing that National Estimate, but I don't want anything going over to the NSC—until the President says so. And I don't think he'll be doin' that real quick. Now, I never traveled much, don't speak any language but English, the President neither. We're sort of home boys concerned with the welfare of these United States. That's our slogan, not Free Macedonia, Feed Uganda, which don't bring in votes, none of it. The President's more humanistic than I am, he's glad to send rice and beans to wherever natives are starvin' because he was a poor boy once, like me, and knows what a scant dinner plate looks like. The votes are in jobs, and the folks who make the jobs contribute hard money so we can spread the Administration's story where it needs to be heard. That's the long and short of it, gentlemen, so we're gonna lid the situation for the time being—by which I mean until the President resumes his high office as Chief Executive of the United States. He'll decide what's to be done—if anything—but until then I'd be glad not to hear about gas and warheads and Taiwan again. Do I make myself clear?"

The listeners nodded in unison. The Vice President smiled. "I appreciate y'all coming on short notice an' hearin' me out. Now, I got a Rose Garden ceremony to see to. Some junior agriculture breeder got himself a prize bull and I got to give him a blue ribbon."

Abruptly he laughed. "The kid, not the bull." He stood up in dismissal, as the three men filed out.

On the down staircase Gerold joined Irving Chenow, and when no one was nearby, asked, "Well, what's your take on the proceedings?"

"I think I struck out."

"Oh? I say he burned a red-hot liner through center field, three-base hit. Anyway, you had many dealings with the Veep?"

"Very few, and frankly I was surprised by his attitude. I don't get all the baseball jargon, but it's clear to me he doesn't want any talk about the issue."

"Clear to me, too," Gerold agreed. "In Langley we can polish the Estimate, but beyond that action's up to the DCI."

Chenow nodded as they reached the main floor, set in squares of black and white marble. "No need to stop Tommy Gray's surveillance, is there?"

"I didn't hear any such command, so I'm counting on Tommy to expand what he's already found. Still, it's sort of unheard of to keep the NSC in the dark. I mean—" he said hastily, "not that I'm criticizing the Veep, far from it, so my inference overall is he's proceeding with caution until the conductor gets back."

"Definitely. We've got a shared secret to keep secret."

"Right—oh, incidentally, Tommy has assigned a classified indicator to limit distribution of anything that deals with China, warheads, and gas. Good idea, too."

"What's the indicator?"

"Dragon Teeth."

"Appropriate," Chenow remarked, and saw the DCI beckon to Gerold.

"Gotta get back to the pickle factory, Irv, we'll be talking."

"I'm sure we will."

He followed the CIA officers down to the porte cochere, where their vehicles waited. During the short drive back to State Irving Chenow told himself that in a game of this sort with the nation's security at stake, an end run was definitely called for. And before he got out at the main State Department entrance he was mentally inventorying significant contacts at the Pentagon and listing who owed what to whom.

LATER THAT DAY DARMAN GEROLD used the private desk telephone to call the Arbor Vitae Center in Alexandria. After identifying himself as the father of a patient, he asked to speak with Dr. Hempill. The receptionist said, "I believe she is in therapy, sir, can you hold?"

Gerold was not used to phone delays, but he grunted assent and waited. At least, he reflected, I'm not assaulted with the refrains of old canned music, so he tapped his desk impatiently until he heard Dr. Hempill say, "Yes, Mr. Gerold, what can I do for you?"

"I'd like an appointment with you at your earliest convenience."

"Of course—but your daughter's treatment is barely begun."

He wondered if *barely* had special significance before saying, "I understand that, Doctor. But I have some thoughts I feel I should share with you."

"Oh? Concerning your daughter's—condition?"

"Exactly. Certain aspects of her past behavior you may not be aware of—actually I only recalled them myself, and they may have a bearing on her future. So—"

"I see. Well . . . can you come tomorrow at, say, noon? You won't be seeing the patient, of course, so I'll block out half an hour for you. Will that be satisfactory?"

"Entirely—and thank you, Doctor."

HE REPLACED THE RECEIVER and glanced at the desk photo of his present wife, Pauline. Early in their marriage she had distanced herself from his

children, especially Doreen, whom she occasionally described as beneath contempt. An active breeder of Palominos and thoroughbred
jumpers, Pauline spent much of her time supervising the country estate,
showing her mounts around the Eastern circuit, and attending equine
auctions. Gerold rode and rode well—Amy insisted on his "having a
good seat"—but he was indifferent to riding and declined to participate
in fox hunts held by Northern Virginia fancy. His usual excuse was
pressure of work, which was not entirely untrue. Pauline, however, was
an avid hunter around Warrenton and Middleburg, where her horseman-
ship was greatly admired.

After their marriage it turned out that his wife had little interest in
sex, though while he was courting her Pauline acted the avid practitio-
ner, eager for every opportunity to make love. She'd dissembled all that,
he soon came to realize, and he resented the way he'd been deceived
and deprived. Still, he'd never taken advantage of opportunities for
extramarital sex; one revealed misstep, and his career would be finished.

So, when the urge seized him he would assuage it privately, stimulated by erotic videos in his collection. On Asian travels Gerold had
acquired cassettes showing pubescent and prepubescent Thai girls and
boys together, or with adults. Though illegal the films were choice possessions, and he guarded them in a secret hiding place. In principle it
troubled him that the children were probably forced into carnal slavery,
but he rationalized the money paid the film vendors by thinking it
helped feed their bellies and prolonged their doomed and worthless
lives.

PAULINE STAYED at the Georgetown pied-à-terre—they called it—only
after a concert, play, or dinner party in town. When they entertained it
was usually at the Logos or City Tavern clubs, where they could host as
many guests as they desired.

In practical terms, he mused, the Georgetown house was his to
occupy as a bachelor would. So, after consulting Dr. Hempill concerning
Doreen's submerged psyche, and consonant with her progress toward
drug-free stability, he might discreetly suggest that Doreen live with him
as an outpatient in a transitional phase to determine how she accommodated to normal surroundings and parental care. He would assure her

psychiatrist that Doreen would be under his affectionate supervision for the therapeutic period and perhaps longer. Never before had he interested himself in his daughter's post-clinic care, and perhaps that was one reason for her inevitable relapses. Now, however, he perceived an opening to Doreen's subconscious that, carefully explored, could bring familial happiness to them both while altering the nature of their relationship forever.

The secure phone buzzed. He answered and heard Tom Gray saying, "I'm transmitting new pix, Darman. They show unmistakable signs of movement."

"South?" he asked.

"South. Hate to be the bearer of bad news, and I'm not above saying I'm a bit alarmed."

"I guess we all ought to be," he said with a grimace. "As soon as I have a chance I'll get back to you. Meanwhile, for your information the Veep has clamped a lid on Dragon Teeth distribution. Make a list of all witting personnel and fax it to me."

"The Veep, eh? Right away, sir," he said in feigned awe. "There's a fellow who can chew gum *and* walk bases while doing it."

"We'll talk later," Gerold told him and broke the connection.

If the situation was developing as Gray suggested, it could only get worse, and the Veep and the NSC were in for an unpleasant major surprise.

For a while Gerold thought back to friends and classmates from St. George's and Harvard he'd stayed in touch with over the years. Most of them had increased inherited fortunes substantially through bond trading, investment banking, and grain futures in the Chicago market.

Recently he had begun to consider soliciting their support for his DCI candidacy, and a related thought occurred. He could lock in support with a simple favor: informing a select few of a deteriorating relationship with Mainland China. The Veep had been absolutely right when he said capital always fled trouble. The friends he clandestinely informed would owe him reciprocal favors if his early advice enabled them to avoid disastrous losses from China or Taiwan holdings. Hell, they could even sell short and profit enormously when the market predictably fell.

That scenario, of course, was predicated upon providing them accurate and timely information they could act on before panic set in. As early as anyone in the intelligence community, he would know when zero hour approached; ample time to warn his friends—and political supporters.

Thumbing through his Rolodex, Darman Gerold extracted four names; two in New York, one in Chicago, the fourth, Paul Wembley, had offices in both Dallas and Baltimore. Gerold remembered Paul from Porker days, and decided to invite him down for lunch at the Georgetown house within the next few days. Paul, he recalled, had gone through two costly divorces and would undoubtedly welcome an opportunity to save certain investments while exploiting other opportunities. Besides, Paul belonged to the President's Club, a distinction conferred by heavy party contributions; guaranteed access to the Oval Office was one of its membership perks. Yes, he'd begin with Paul and pitch the others as time and opportunity allowed.

He knew he was contemplating a dangerous game even though he was not violating national security in an absolute sense. The secretive nature of his friends' business involvements convinced Gerold that they could keep their mouths shut; otherwise they'd have vanished in the dust long ago.

Hearing the click and hum of the printer, he got up and watched the latest Gorgon images come in.

Twenty-Five

BEIJING

NOT A CAR, BUT A GRAY-PAINTED PANEL VAN of indeterminate vintage and manufacture stopped. The side panel slid open, and Brand was nudged in. Bending over to keep from scraping his head, Brand sat on a wooden side bench and stared at the man seated opposite him as the van pulled away. "We meet again," he said. "How's the wrist doing?"

The man glared at him and pulled the sleeve cuff over a small bandage. Beside Brand, the man who had brought him said, "There is good reason for this as you will see."

"When will that be?"

"Quite soon. Meanwhile, you are in no danger."

"I'd like to believe that," Brand said wryly, and stared at the henchman he'd last seen on the high overlook. "Any comment?"

The man looked away.

So, Brand thought, it's going to be a silent trip. He envisioned a rice paddy where his throat would be cut, or some dank cell of the Gong An Ju. Another mile or so, and he began to reason that Cheong's men were neither going to kill him nor turn him over to the secret police. Vengeance would gain Cheong no face if executed secondhand. Assuming Cheong truly hated him—and Brand was willing to make that assumption—Fatso would do it himself, with witnesses attesting his bravery in the old Oriental tradition. Having reached that tentative conclusion, Brand folded his arms, smiled at the two henchmen, and closed his eyes.

The road grew bumpier, he heard the chuffing of a locomotive, the shrill whistle of a descending aircraft's jet, and surmised he was in the vicinity of an airport. The driver turned right, then left, and the road eased as the van slowed to take an incline. It leveled off on a smooth surface and the van came to a halt. "You get out here," he was told, and opened his eyes.

Stepping down to a concrete floor, he saw he had been taken inside a large warehouse. The center lane was wide, and on either side, stacked almost roof-high, were wooden crates and metal-strapped containers. Forklifts and front-end loaders were parked under the wings of a twin-engine executive jet. The fuselage was gleaming silver, wings and empennage brilliant green. Aft of the port wing a mobile loading ramp led up to a wide cargo door. The henchmen pointed to it without speaking.

Brand shrugged, began walking. So this was it, he thought. Nail me in a crate and drop it over the China Sea. Like the Count of Monte Cristo, thrown from the Chateau d'If in a weighted shroud. But Dantes had a knife to rip free; I'd need a power saw to get out of a crate, or the magic of Harry Houdini. He stepped onto the moving load belt and leaned forward to balance as he neared the open door.

At the top he stepped into the cabin and saw at the front end a wide upholstered chair. On it, wearing a robe of green and silver, sat Cheong Wing-dah.

"Welcome, old friend Mark," said Cheong, beckoning him closer. "I apologize for the way you arrived here, but I felt it the only way to preserve my security, and yours."

"I appreciate your concern," Mark replied, and sat in a cushioned chair. "It contrasts with my other drive in your limousine."

"True"—Cheong nodded—"and I have since regretted my impulsiveness. In truth I misinterpreted your contact with my wife, understanding now that in approaching me on your behalf she sought only to perform a service for one who had been close to her late honored father." His head bowed, burying his chin in a bulge of fat. "For that I humbly beg your forgiveness."

"The frankness and delicacy of your words disarm me. Only a rude barbarian from the northern provinces would be capable of denying so seemly a request."

"So," said Cheong, raising his head, "let the winds of fresh understanding disperse the past like the dead ashes of yesterday's cooking fire."

Brand set his palms together and drew them against his chest. "May it be so," he intoned. "We are all travelers on the Silken Road of Life, where purity of thought and deed alone are strong enough to ward off evil."

"As you say," Cheong replied, "and I reciprocate the sincerity of your esteemed and welcome words." He clapped his hands, and from the nearby galley a steward brought tea in ceremonial cups, handing one to each. Lifting his, Cheong said, "With this Hopei tea we seal a new understanding."

Mark sipped the unsweetened tea and returned the cup to the steward in exchange for a thimble cup of *bai-jiu*—rice liqueur. He and Cheong sipped together, after which Cheong said, "There, it is done in the traditional way. Now, perhaps a Western drink?"

"Scotch," Brand replied. "Will you drink with me?"

"Gladly."

While the steward prepared their drinks, Brand looked back

through the cargo opening and saw workmen moving and unstacking pallets with forklifts. Evidently a shipment was being organized. Turning to his host, Brand said, "I assume this godown and all it holds is yours, Wing-dah."

"It is so, and I think of it as my free-trade zone." He chuckled and his belly rolled like a wave.

"Sanctioned and protected by competent authorities."

"Of course. Like myself they value the rewards of capitalist enterprise."

Brand smiled as he took his scotch. "Underground enterprise." He sat forward. "Perhaps one of your 'facilitators' within the Gong An Ju would have information regarding my son."

"Before inviting you here I inquired about him." His plump hands spread. "Unfortunately your son remains on the list of prison escapees."

Brand sighed. "At least he hasn't been captured."

"Listen to me, Mark Brand. When your son is captured, and I am sure he will be, we will then know his precise location. From then on positive moves can be made to gain his release. When we spoke in Hong Kong I suggested I had means to deliver your son to freedom. Though I did not say so this aircraft can do that. Another reason I had you brought here." His hand pointed at the tall rows of stacked crates. "Here he could be hidden indefinitely, were concealment necessary. Then, at a propitious moment, he would be loaded aboard with other cargo containers."

Brand nodded. "I admire the soundness of your thought, the ingenuity of your plan." He paused. "But all depends on finding Peter."

Cheong nodded. "True, though I feel that is only a matter of time. And now that his name has been mentioned I want to say that I am fully prepared and willing to take all necessary measures to bring your son safely from the Mainland."

"You are ever-gracious, Wing-dah. How could I hope to repay your kindness?"

"Between brothers no request is too excessive, no assistance too difficult to render." He looked fixedly at Brand. "I have in mind a matter that goes back to our days on Taiwan, a hope that burned then and remains unfulfilled. Can you—think what it might be?"

"No."

"Then I will reveal to you that it concerns the Fang-tse brotherhood. I always believed that I was excluded from inclusion because of my late honored father's position in the Kuomintang and his intimacy with General Chiang Kai-shek. As you will remember, not all who fled to Taiwan after the final defeat were partisans of Chiang or the Kuomintang. Many were nonpolitical, or at least were never forced to choose between Generalissimo Chiang and Mao Tse-tung. My father's wealth and position in the new island government were resented, and brought hostility and antagonism toward him and his family. I felt that the Fang-tse declined to include me because of my father."

"Your late honored father, once Deputy Finance Minister of the Nationalist government at Chungking, was accused of looting and embezzling funds destined for Chiang's armies."

"No accusation or charge was ever proved, but the rumors and antagonism persisted. To this day, as we sit here friend to friend, I am convinced that I was a victim of slander aimed at my late father."

Brand considered. "That was long ago, Wing-dah, and much has escaped my memory."

"Let it pass. Nevertheless, I have long nurtured the hope of one day being accepted within the honorable brotherhood of the Fang-tse."

Brand nodded. "A goal beyond criticism by any man."

"So." He tented his fingers and his gaze lifted. "You were chosen young as an initiate because you saved the life of a member's son. Tsai Li-chen, I believe. And because of the healing works of your father, the eminent physician."

"Doubtless a factor," Brand conceded.

"So what I am going to suggest, with all possible delicacy, is that, were I able to deliver *your* son, as you saved the son of another, that act might establish my candidacy for membership in your noble clan."

"I would think so," Brand responded, and paused before saying, "Nevertheless, I have understood that Worshipful Master Leong drinks jasmine tea in the palaces of our celestial gods."

"That is regrettably so. His passage to immortality took place some years ago."

"His successor would have to be consulted."

"Of course. But in Hong Kong there are Fang-tse brothers who would support my candidacy were you to advocate it. I number Shek, Li, Ning, and Wong among them, and there may well be others who migrated from our island." He breathed as deeply as his envelope of fat allowed. "Of them, only one conducts a legitimate business. The others are engaged in extortion, prostitution, and the making of degenerate films. But were I admitted to your brotherhood, I would offer them participations in all my profitable businesses without restriction."

"Your exceptional offer would be a powerful persuasive," Brand remarked, and finished his scotch. "On my return to Hong Kong I will willingly consult them on your behalf, not failing to mention your proffered aid to me and my son."

"My gratitude will be eternal. Now, it has been many years since I glimpsed the sign of the brotherhood. As a final request, may I see yours?"

Brand removed his coat and rolled his sleeve to the shoulder. Approaching Cheong, he displayed the clan tattoo. Cheong stared at it, said "Thank you," and Brand rolled down his sleeve.

"In return, may I ask how I was traced to the Beijing Hotel?"

Cheong shrugged. "In Hong Kong the *Luxingshe* is not immune to *zha gu*," he said, smiling, "delivered *zou hou mein*." Through the back door. "You were followed to the travel office from the Manchu, and your travel identity, destination, and hotel revealed." He spread his hands. "Through *guanxi*, connections that the brotherhood may find useful."

"Undoubtedly," Brand responded. In the West he would now summarize the understanding, but in the East where subtlety permeated all negotiations, a hard, firm statement was unneeded and discourteous. The bargain was simple: Cheong's admission to the brotherhood in exchange for rescuing Brand's son.

I'll grit my teeth when I propose him, Brand thought, but to get Peter safely back I'd kowtow, grovel, and lick his feet.

"So that no misconceptions remain between us," Cheong said, "please visit our Celestial Galleries whenever you choose. My wife will be interested to hear of your unusual life since leaving Taiwan, and my daughter will be pleased to know that her grandfather, Museum Director Chen, was held in high esteem by a foreign scholar."

"Thank you," Brand said, "though when my son is free we will not linger in Hong Kong." Rising, he backed away, murmuring appreciation for Cheong's courtesy, and walked down the cargo conveyer to the floor.

His escort met him at the bottom and said, "I will accompany you to your hotel, or you may ride alone."

"Alone," Brand said, and got into the van beside the driver.

A broad steel door swung open and the van rolled down the incline into what Brand saw was a railroad marshaling yard. He noted the return route with its twists and turns until the van merged with light traffic on Chang-An Boulevard as it flowed toward his hotel.

Walking to the elevator, he realized he had gone through an astonishing episode he had never dreamed possible. No longer two scorpions in a bottle, he and Cheong were now joined in a solemn bargain that could lead to consummation of their hearts' desire.

If, he mused, Cheong's enmity is truly gone, and he delivers Peter safely home.

Twenty-Six

WASHINGTON

MORNING STAFF MEETINGS CHAIRED by the Deputy Director of Central Intelligence lasted a minimum of an hour, and could go on until the D/DCI was satisfied he'd heard everything about everything going on around the world. In his late sixties, the Deputy Director was a tall man with a barrel chest and muscular shoulders, easily recognizable in a crowd because of his abundant white hair. Vice Admiral USN (Ret.) Logan "Buck" Doremus had acquired his nickname as a famed Naval Academy fullback whose ball-carrying trademark was bucking an opponent's defensive line. And within the Agency it was often remarked that he really should have worn a helmet while playing.

In an agency where preparation and dissemination of classified paper was routine, Buck Doremus demanded verbal communication from subordinates, even if that required their reading aloud an entire document while he tapped a pencil rhythmically on his desk. Generally, though, senior staff officers taking their turn for the briefing stood and summarized whatever significant information they thought should be conveyed. That was normal recitation procedure at the Naval Academy, Doremus frequently reminded his listeners; it worked for him then, and he wasn't about to change it now.

The overall result of prolonged staff meetings and verbal summarizing was to keep senior officers from desks, where they were needed, with consequent resentment over losing precious time.

To Gerold, the Chief Reports Officer whispered, "I think the son of a bitch can't read, he acts like a dyslexic. Or maybe the Academy didn't offer farm boys remedial reading."

Gerold smiled. "You're probably right on both counts, Chet, but don't quote me."

"Cross my heart."

Gerold listened vaguely to a summation of renewed ethnic bellicosity in the Mideast, and when it came his turn to rise and recite, Gerold surfed easily through overnight events in Korea, Thailand, Vietnam, and Cambodia without notes, while the Deputy Director nodded approval.

Resuming his chair, Gerold glanced at the wall clock; his monologue had taken just six minutes, thanks to no questions from Buck Doremus. At ten-twelve, the Deputy Director dismissed his briefers, who gathered their papers and left as expeditiously as possible.

Gerold's office was on the floor below the D/DCI's, and as he passed through the reception area he told his secretary to hold calls for later response. At his desk he used his personal telephone to call Paul Wembley in Baltimore, and after a short wait he heard Paul's voice and invited him to lunch at the Georgetown house the following day. "Great idea," Paul said. "Just the two of us?"

"Right. I think you'll be pleased to hear what's on my mind."

"Hope it's devious. One o'clock you said?"

"Vodka marts will be waiting."

He made a notation on his private calendar, then called Fred Postlewaite and Darcy Whiting in New York, inviting Fred to breakfast at the Union, Darcy to lunch at the Racquet and Tennis two days hence, not revealing what he had in mind.

It was too early to reach Sonny Simpkin at his Chicago office, so Gerold jotted a reminder to try later.

In the time remaining before he had to leave for Alexandria, Gerold received two regional desk chiefs, signed and released proferred cables after brief scanning. He left with them, after telling his secretary he had a medical appointment to keep and would be back by one.

After gaining the Beltway, Gerold drove south and east into Alexandria, slowing to turn between brick posterns over which an arch of iron grillwork spelled Arbor Vitae Clinic. To one side of the blacktop access road signs invoked slow speed and silence.

As he neared the parking area he looked up at the four-story Georgian Colonial building, noting, as he had before, that all the windows were barred. Before leaving his car, he sat for a few moments considering approaches calculated to gain optimum responses from Doreen's psychiatrist. Then he thought, Why limit myself to one? and went in to the receptionist.

Dr. Hempill received Gerold in her book-lined office, greeted him from behind her desk, and opened a thick file. Gerold took a seat near the therapy couch and said, "I appreciate your seeing me on short notice, but I'll be out of town for a few days and wanted to confer before leaving."

"Of course, sir. You mentioned—"

"Before that, Doctor, what's Doreen's medical condition—I mean, is she by any chance pregnant? Infected with any venereal disease?"

"The medical staff says no to both your questions, though I would not have been surprised to the contrary considering the sort of gypsy life she's been leading."

Gypsy, he thought, that's one way of gilding it, and said, "That's very good news. So her treatment will focus on detoxification."

Dr. Hempill nodded. "Parallel to which is, of course, the psychological therapy—as you doubtless recall, our clinic's approach to patients is holistic."

"Which I thoroughly approve. Doreen is—how shall I put it—stabilized?"

"Rather in the initial phase toward stabilization. Methadone therapy, I think you know, suppresses the worst symptoms of heroin withdrawal. Just before you arrived I looked in on Doreen and found her tranquilly watching television."

Gerold affected a sigh of relief. "That's an improvement right there."

Dr. Hempill turned a file page and said, "She ate a good breakfast and will be encouraged to consume normal amounts of food. Gradually her stomach, somewhat shrunken from abstention, will signal its needs. And we will watch her weight very carefully. Her medical consultant recommends a gain in the area of twenty pounds."

He visualized a restored, sleeker Doreen with fuller breasts and curvaceous bottom, but it had been a long time since her figure had been indisputably feminine. Along with other things, that would develop in time.

He wiped perspiration from his upper lip and said, "Because I don't want the clinic to become her revolving door, Doctor, I've been searching my mind for background that might be useful in your counseling."

She picked up a ballpoint pen and poised it above a lined pad. "I'll be most interested in your thoughts, sir."

"Ah—whatever I say is treated confidentially?"

"Of course. As a codependent of your daughter."

"Well, as a lawyer I wanted to make sure." He managed a bleak smile before saying, "Doreen was shattered when her mother and I divorced, she was fifteen at the time, and I trace her alienation back to that early trauma."

"I believe her psychological history confirms it."

"For a time—far too long—I myself was rudderless. Tried to sublimate feelings of hopelessness and abandonment by burying myself in my career. That left very little time or thought for Doreen, and it's obvious to me that she couldn't come to terms with losing her mother, and being ignored—it seemed to her—by her father. A double blow on an adolescent mind." He looked away, snuffled, and blew his nose.

Dr. Hempill said, "It's a shame we didn't have this talk two or three years ago—before your daughter reached the, ah, depths, behaviorally speaking."

"I know, I know, my fault entirely. And I realize my reaction was totally wrong. Her behavior was an embarrassment, and I reacted by resenting her. My present wife—her stepmother—is totally alienated from my daughter, won't have her around the country estate, doesn't want to hear about her. I—I'm afraid I accepted that attitude—I guess I felt having lost a wife, and having a daughter I couldn't communicate with in any useful way—I made some sort of internal decision to preserve what I had, my second marriage."

Dr. Hempill nodded. "Not unusual to see children slip through the interstices of a parent's second marriage. I know from what Doreen's said during past clinic stays that she dislikes and resents her stepmother."

"She's said vile, fantastic things to her, which only increases my wife's dislike for her stepdaughter." He paused lengthily before saying, "Doctor, one of the possibilities that has occurred to me is that my daughter may consider my wife as a rival."

"Rival—for—?"

"Simply put, my affections is one way of saying it."

"You mean, Oedipal reversal—father fixation."

His face brightened. "Yes, yes, I think you've hit on it, Doctor." He smiled enthusiastically. "Could you explain that a little?"

She smiled tolerantly. "In simple terms many girls, usually in adolescence, regard a father's second wife as an obstacle to the paternal affection they feel entitled to. They fantasize that the remaining parent—the father—owes the daughter the entirety of his love and affection, which they feel entitled to claim. The second wife, stepmother, is regarded as an intruder, and when the father continues to enjoy life with the second wife the daughter feels cast aside, her claim to affection cruelly ignored by her blood parent. The typical reaction, which Doreen manifests quite frequently, is to attitudinalize hatred to father and stepparent. Such an attitude is often accompanied by outrageous attention-getting acts calculated to damage both parents—in the subconscious—or conscious—hope of destroying the marriage. Such young females fantasize that, lacking a wife, the father can then focus his full love and attention on the child." She tapped her pen on the pad. "The adolescent mind being what it is: filled with fears, apprehensions, hormonal stimuli, and socially unsanctioned ideas."

"Socially unsanctioned?"

"Daughter becoming substitute wife. The lover of her father."

Gerold frowned until Dr. Hempill said, "I don't want you to think that concept necessarily reflects Doreen's view of the way she regards you, your wife, and herself. And you probably don't realize that religious and state-proscribed incest, while viewed with horror in the Judeo-Christian West, is—one might say—commonplace in societies that outnumber our Western civilizations by an enormous ratio. In ancient Egypt, and I cite only one example, incest was not only religiously condoned, but the practice enabled ruling families to propagate their line without genetic adulteration. Of course, over thousands of years inbreeding weakened and eventually ended the Pharaonic line. And the Borgias of Italy freely practiced in-marriage, probably for much the same reasons the Egyptians did. Africa . . . well, I could go on, but the point I want to make is that father-daughter, mother-son, and brother-sister sexual relationships are far from uncommon in large portions of the globe. As for the animal kingdom, mating occurs without regard to consanguinity. It is a natural occurrence, Mr. Gerold, and humans are not developmentally distant from animals."

"Why," he exclaimed, "I never thought of those things, but you've opened my eyes." For a time he was silent, studying his hands on his lap. Then he said, "Without really being able to define or comprehend some aspects of Doreen's past behavior, I found certain incidents troubling me, and decided I ought to reveal them to you." Swallowing, he licked his lips.

Dr. Hempill said, "Please speak freely, sir. We both have your daughter's best interests at heart."

"It's difficult to put into words, Doctor, but you saw how she was dressed—or undressed—when you arrived to bring her here. Earlier I'd rebuked her, and that provoked a venomous tirade. Frankly, I was relieved and grateful when you drove her away. Doctor, I know I shouldn't have had angry feelings, and while I was driving to my office I felt ashamed of myself."

"Natural reaction," she observed, and turned several pages in Doreen's file. "Shame is a negative emotion that blocks assimilation of positive ones." She leaned forward. "Tell me, sir, if positive thoughts then formed."

"They did," he said with a nod, "but it was a struggle to pierce the negative veil. I began by attempting to discern an explanation for her morning nudity. Bad enough in my presence, but the houseman observed her, too."

"It seems quite obvious she did that by design, for shock effect, knowing it would gain your attention."

"Realizing that, I discarded my initial thought, which was of a willful, malicious act. And for the first time in a long time, I felt a degree of sympathy for her. Then I began visualizing Doreen as a newborn baby, as a kindergarten child, as a shy girl on the verge of adolescence . . . inconsolable over the divorce. Even as I criticized my incomprehension, my thoughts traveled back to sporadic incidents that disturbed me at the time but which I dismissed as innocent." For a while he was silent, his mind searching for the best way to continue.

Finally Dr. Hempill said, "I sense that your subconscious is attempting to block out those, ah, episodes which your conscious mind is perceiving in a new and different way."

Slowly, Gerold nodded. "This is very hard to say, Doctor, very embarrassing to verbalize . . ."

"Compose yourself, and let it flow. Closing your eyes may help . . ." She left the suggestion unfinished, but Gerold closed his eyes, ending the necessity of looking into hers.

"We've always had large family houses, some with swimming pools, some with oceanfront beaches—summer places. I specify large houses meaning bedrooms with bathrooms, and guest rooms—guest houses, too—because private rooms and baths confer privacy on occupants whether family members or guests. So it irritated me to catch sight of Doreen traipsing nude down the hallway, or glimpse her naked in her bedroom through a partly open door. Showering nude after a swim, then stretching out on a mattress or float to tan her body. I accepted the incidents as carelessness or nonchalance and asked her to be more modest." His eyes opened so he could judge the psychiatrist's reaction.

She was writing rapidly, and looked up when he stopped. "I'm not sure that was the most productive reaction."

"No? What should I have done? I didn't want my daughter bare-assed around the house or the pool, where friends often came for a plunge and a drink." He shook his head. "What would have been your advice?"

"I can't form an opinion on that until Doreen and I have discussed those episodes; you see, I must get at her perspective, determine what she was trying to accomplish by behaving in ways you reacted to negatively."

Somewhat sharply he said, "So you can't suggest now what I should have done then, contemporaneously?" That's second-guessing, he thought, ex post facto chicanery. Today we know George Armstrong Custer shouldn't have deployed his troopers as he did, but at the time there was no one around the Little Bighorn to advise him.

"What I *can* say," the doctor responded, "is that based on Doreen's history and on the things you've been revealing, I think she was exhibiting herself in a conscious or unconscious way."

"Why would she do that?"

"To possess you."

Gerold stared at her. "Possess?"

"Seduce is a word more appropriate to her subconscious thinking. You were a single male, the only one she could depend on, gain comfort from—and she was a nubile young female." Hempill shrugged. "To me the conclusion is obvious. She is fixated on her father and uses narcotics to block out desires her conscious mind may be unaware of—or unwilling to accept."

"Good God," Gerold said with a horrified expression. "I don't know what to say, and now I'm more disturbed than ever. I've treated my daughter badly, created a family situation she had to flee before it destroyed her." Then reflectively, he said, "And nearly destroying herself. God, how misguided I've been!"

"Misguided, yes, and misdirected, through incomprehension, no volitional fault of yours, so you must not be harsh on yourself." She smiled sympathetically. "I feel we are closer now to the root of the problem than ever before, and that's a breakthrough. A real accomplishment." She made several notations on her pad and set aside the pen. "I feel I should warn you against harboring any sense of guilt or shame. A situation not of your making arose, and you dealt with it as you thought best—subjectively. Now, with a clearer understanding of your daughter's psyche, I'm quite sure that a man of your considerable intelligence will act quite differently."

"I hope I'll be able to turn things around," he told her, "by viewing my daughter as a victim of circumstances over which neither she nor I had any control. She acted out of—instinct?—while I reacted blindly."

"Conventionally." Hempill nodded, and Gerold sat forward.

"Doctor, from now on I'm going to replace criticism, sarcasm, and rebuke with tolerance and kindness. Show Doreen gradually, if necessary, that she is loved and esteemed and that the past can be buried."

"Excellent," said the psychiatrist approvingly. "Words that you spoke spontaneously . . . yes, a breakthrough indeed."

"In that regard, and since my daughter will not be living here forever, I want to offer a suggestion you may approve or not." He breathed deeply, this was it. "Without dissecting my marital situation, the fact is that I live mostly in the town house, whereas my wife's life is focused on the Upperville estate with its spaciousness, horses, and related obligations. Only occasionally does Pauline stay overnight in Georgetown, so in effect I live alone, except for the houseman who cooks and runs things." He paused. "At a time of your choosing I would like to have Doreen with me, at first on an outpatient trial basis, then independently as her progress permits. For unless we are in frequent contact there is no way I can demonstrate the affection I truly feel for her."

Musingly, the psychiatrist said, "She balks at our restrictions here, so perhaps a measure of freedom in a semicontrolled family environment would bring her more rapidly to normalcy. Of course, before I acceded to such an arrangement I would want to have confidence that her addiction was cured."

"Of course."

Dr. Hempill stood up. "I have another appointment, Mr. Gerold, but we should talk again soon. You have given me a good deal to consider, potentially fresh openings into a heretofore closed and hostile mind. I see a new framework for therapy, other directions never traveled before. All other things being equal, and after I consider all relevant factors, I think I will be able to recommend the change you suggested. But—that is only my tentative conclusion."

Gerold got up. "Thank you, Doctor."

"Credit yourself, please, and do not subject yourself further to useless feelings of guilt and self-criticism. The mind is a fragile thing, and if we work together, sir, I am cautiously optimistic that Doreen can become the daughter you always wanted her to be."

"My fervent desire," Gerold said, and left.

INSTEAD OF DRIVING back to Langley, Darman headed into the District. There were urgent matters to go over with Tom Gray, some bearing on the likelihood of an imminent threat to Taiwan. As point man on Dragon Teeth, Gray was in optimum position to predict the future course of events, and Gerold planned to exploit the situation to advantage.

Besides, he told himself, I think I did rather well with the doctor. Got everything I wanted from her without having to admit my degree of personal responsibility for Doreen's decline. And left with an expectation of better things to come.

If Hempill agrees Doreen can live with me, Pauline will be in no position to buck a medically endorsed change. She'll have to go along with the situation, accept it as a design for living. And all three of us will be a hell of a lot happier than we've been before.

At the GlobEco building, Gerold turned into the rear parking lot, went up the steps into the marble-floored lobby, and showed his pass to the guard. Upstairs in Brand's office, temporarily occupied by Gray, Gerold reviewed the latest Gorgon surveillance images.

The sequence showed the warhead-laden freight train moving in the direction of a military airport south of Beijing. "So," Gray said, "looks like they're going to fly the warheads to their assembly destination."

"So it seems."

"Alternate transport I hadn't considered before."

"Nor I," Gerold admitted. "Write it up and transmit it to me with the photos. The Director ought to see them today."

"Hearing and obeying," Gray said sardonically. "And you've checked the Bigot List?"

"Yes, and it's frozen. There's the Veep, SecState, the DCI, Irv Chenow, you, me, and some NRO bean-counters who don't know the significance of what's being collected."

"Two more," Gray said.

"Who?"

"Mark Brand—you briefed him in Hong Kong—and his son."

"Peter? Right—he saw the results of the gassing." Gerold frowned. "When he shows up he'll have to be sworn, warned, and silenced. Can't have him leaking to his slopey girlfriend."

"Good precaution," Gray said. "Anything else?"

"You notify me first on any developments, not Chenow, me."

"Got it."

Gerold smiled toothily. "Turns out your move here was beneficial beyond expectation."

"Sure was," Gray responded, "and I'm much obliged."

"So I'm counting on you continuing the exceptional work you've been doing. If Dragon Teeth turns into a real fire storm we'll be the ones credited with early warning signals. The Administration will owe us, Tom."

Or dispose of us, Gray thought, and watched Darman leave.

He doesn't really care about the possibility of a million Taiwanese being gassed, Gray thought disgustedly. All he wants is credit for telling our superiors it could happen.

From a lower desk drawer he pulled out a pint of Crown Royal and swallowed lengthily. The smooth rye soothed his throat and eased the tiredness he felt most of the time. Week by week Lila's physical deterioration continued, and caring for her night after night was dragging him down. The end was inevitable, the only question, how long.

Meanwhile, the eruption of Dragon Teeth was making nearly impossible demands on him, and he wondered how long he could maintain the pace. He'd only been scheduled to fill in while Mark was in Hong Kong, and now Beijing Station reports that Mark is in Beijing.

Hope he brings Peter back soon, he's needed here before I collapse, Gray thought as he cached the bottle out of sight, and turned to watch the latest NRO feed come in.

Twenty-Seven

BEIJING

MARK BRAND LOOKED DOWN from his sixteenth-story window at smoothly flowing traffic on Chang-An Boulevard, and turned back to Yang, who had come early with a report.

"So what we have," Brand said, "is Wo confirming a Western prisoner escaped from Lingyuan, and San saying his Gong An Ju drinking buddies haven't heard of the man's recapture. And the fugitive remains nameless."

Yang nodded. "Evidently the identity is known to only a very few officials, who rank well above San's contacts."

Brand returned to the chair beside Yang. "Naming the man would be an admission they haven't made, and may not make. So long as they don't, they retain a full range of decisions. Did you learn anything from the embassy police guards?"

"Only that, with the gates repaired, nothing unusual is taking place. In and out traffic normal."

"Do the police inspect what goes in?"

"If a Chinese driver has a cargo of boxes large enough to hide a man the police will search the truck."

"Thoroughly?"

"Depends on the policemen on duty. Some are more motivated than others."

"And trucks leaving the embassy compound?"

"Less attention is given their contents. Of course, those vehicles marked as belonging to the embassy are passed without search."

"Indicating Peter is still in hiding." He looked at his watch; too early to phone the Vice Consul. "Yesterday," he said, "I was taken to see Cheong Wing-dah at a godown large enough to house a jet aircraft. Cheong offered to fly my son out of China if I can get Peter to the godown."

Yang's expression registered astonishment. "Cheong will do that for you?"

"He wants something from me, something he craves and which I am willing to provide—if he fulfills his part of the bargain."

Yang said, "Your judgment is far superior to mine, honored brother of my master, but without disrespect permit me to suggest that Cheong is not to be fully trusted."

"I value your advice," Brand replied, "and will take all possible precautions. For it is not within my experience that a tiger can easily change his stripes. So I have made this map of the route to the godown. I assume Cheong's merchandise arrives from gravesites by train, the cargo is crated and stored in the godown, and loaded aboard his green-and-silver aircraft. There must be an airstrip conveniently near, but I did not see it."

Yang studied the map, asked about landmarks, and folded the map into his pocket. "If Cheong acts in good faith," he observed, "then your son will have to be transported only from the embassy to the godown."

Brand nodded and Yang got up. "I will trace the route so that when the time comes we will be able to follow it without delay."

Brand said, "I am pleased with what you have accomplished, and anticipate a favorable conclusion to our mission." With that, he dismissed the leader and reflected that he could not stay in Beijing much longer before his cover story began to wear thin. So far he had come up with a string of negatives and had nothing positive to build on.

After breakfast Brand went to a public telephone off the hotel lobby and called the American embassy. When Vice Consul McNamara spoke, Brand asked if he had been given an appointment with the Counselor. "No, sir," McNamara replied. "From now until late afternoon the Counselor is attending a Trade Office luncheon for a group of American businessmen."

"Damn! When *can* I see the Counselor?"

"That may not be necessary, sir. Our First Secretary is interested in your son's case, and—"

"Interested?"

"He saw your name on the visitor list and asked to be informed if and when you returned."

"Good. I'll come now. Oh, what's his name?"

"Sorry, sir, we don't mention names by telephone."

Understandably, Brand thought, and said, "I'd appreciate your telling the First Secretary I'm on my way."

Fifteen minutes later Brand was in the embassy reception room. As she had yesterday, Vice Consul McNamara guided him to an interview room, opened the door, and said, "I'll tell the First Secretary you're here," and left.

Within a few minutes, a thin, sandy-haired man came in and closed the door behind him. "Mr. Brand?"

"Yes."

"I'm Jason Whitbread." They shook hands and Whitbread sat across the table from Brand before saying, "I'm happier to see you than you can imagine. Got any ID?"

Brand slid the Canadian passport across the table. Whitbread opened it, glanced at photo and name. "Where'd you get this?"

"Darman Gerold."

"Good enough for me," he remarked and returned the passport, "since he's my chief."

"Then you're COS."

Whitbread nodded. "And I'll be plenty relieved to get your son off my hands."

"Peter—he's *here?*"

"He is, sir, and we've been keeping his presence need-to-know for reasons you'll understand."

"Where is he? When can I see him? How is he?"

"He's fine, especially considering he rammed an ambulance into the compound. Gained some weight after—but let him tell you. Right now he's in borrowed Marine quarters—saw you leave the embassy yesterday so he's been expecting your return. Since we're keeping his presence known to only a few people—not wanting the Chinese to start demanding him—you can see him in his room."

Brand stood up. "Let's go."

"In a moment. Peter's gone through a lot, I admire the way he's handled himself and managed to pick up some interesting intelligence along the way. I'm sure you're proud of him, and you have reason to be. The Ambassador wasn't at all pleased by Peter's arrival, and his first impulse was to hand him over to the Chinese."

"Typical," Brand muttered.

"The Counselor also regards Peter as a potential obstacle to swell relations with our hosts but he's a creature of the Ambassador, a high-salaried gofer, not an independent thinker. Fortunately, a cable from Assistant Secretary Chenow instructed the embassy *not* to deliver your son into the hands of his enemies, and that quashed the Ambassador's appeasement instincts. So"—he breathed deeply—"I've assumed responsibility for Peter."

"Glad you did. Does the Ambassador know why Peter went to Canton, how he came to be arrested?"

Whitbread shook his head. "Wasn't necessary. And I wasn't looking forward to admitting Agency responsibility for another no-brainer. Anyway, your son's here, but getting him out is a problem. We're in a holding pattern, a limbo situation until there's a fail-safe solution." He paused. "Any ideas?"

"Some," Brand told him, "and we'll cover them later. Right now, I want to see my son."

"Just follow me."

* * *

AFTER HUGS AND TEARFUL EMBRACES, father and son sat down and looked at each other. "Hard to believe you're here," Brand said.

"Hard to believe *you're* here," Peter echoed, and they both smiled.

Brand put his arm over Peter's shoulder and said, "You did all the right things to survive, but if you love your family, for God's sake don't do favors for the Agency again."

"I won't, and that's a promise. Besides, I had expert help along the way or I wouldn't be here. Around dawn a few hours after I escaped an old woman found me. Her name is Ah-peng and she was my savior." Then for the next half hour Peter described all she had done for him; hidden and fed him, guided him to Beijing, and felt tears well in his eyes at the memories. "She was my grandmother," he said emotionally, "the grandmother I never knew."

Brand nodded. "I understand." He looked around the small room. "You comfortable here? Feeling okay?"

"Yes, but I don't want to stay here forever."

"Won't have to. In Hong Kong I looked up some Fang-tse brothers, they've done everything possible to get information about you. Even sent three cutthroats here to scour the city for the 'escaped Westerner,' reliable men." He told Peter about his meeting with Cheong Wing-dah and Cheong's aircraft, and Peter's expression brightened.

"God, I wish we were flying home right now. Seems like I've been away months, years. Have you seen La-li?"

"We were in touch until I left Washington. Peter, I hope you're serious about that young woman, because she's pregnant with your child."

"Oh, Dad," he said, "oh, Dad, what wonderful news! When I talked with her she didn't mention it. Why not?"

Brand shrugged. "It's the way of Chinese women, always has been. She may have felt uncertain how you'd feel. Anyway, I expect you to marry and give my grandchild our name."

"Of course I will. I—I—everything's happening so fast." He turned away and Brand saw his shoulders shaking. "All right, son," he said, "take it easy, everything in good time. Maybe I should have waited, but I'd have been uneasy withholding the news."

"Oh, no, I'm grateful you told me."

Brand said, "When we get back to Washington we may find ourselves without jobs."

"Oh, I expect to be canned for absence, but—you?"

"I violated my clearances coming to the Mainland."

"Isn't that just a bureaucratic stipulation you can—"

Brand shook his head. "I broke rules and expect to take the consequences." He touched his son's hand. "Had to look for you, hopeless as it seemed."

Peter stared downward. "If I'd even thought I'd be captured I wouldn't have gone to Canton. Wouldn't have put you through all this. Dad, I can't tell you how sorry I am, and I don't know how I can ever make it up to you."

"By being a good husband and father. And prison is punishment enough—more than enough." Getting up he gazed down into the compound, at the repaired gates and Marine sentries. "What's past is past, as Wing-dah said. Now we have to get you out of here, and home."

WASHINGTON

TOWARD THE END of his luncheon with Paul Wembley, Darman Gerold broached the motive behind his invitation. "Figures from Commerce indicate you've invested close to four million in Mainland China industry."

"About that," Wembley agreed. "Bicycles and auto parts manufacture—built the factory from scratch. Computerized assembly line makes it the most efficient producer on the Mainland." He turned a cognac snifter in his hand.

"And—what?—two million more invested in Taiwan?"

"Right. Modernized a shipyard in Keelung, projected profitability in another four months." He let ash fall from his panatela. "Cruise ship refitting and tanker overhaul." He smiled. "Looking for a place to invest dormant capital?"

"Not really. What I have in mind is protecting yours."

Wembley sat forward. "Before investing, I commissioned studies to guarantee political stability both places. By any chance are you suggesting those studies were wrong?"

"At the time, they were valid, Paul, but political dynamics change."

"I see," he said thoughtfully. "Like a break in relations with Beijing? Not over that human rights bullshit, I hope."

Gerold shook his head. "Getting to the point, there are growing indications China is getting ready to act on long-standing threats against Taiwan."

"Good God!"

"Even if there's no actual invasion, Chinese aggressive preparations and Taiwan's defensive response would play hell with your interests in both countries."

"Damn right! I know you've got access to the best sources there are, so I don't question them. So if you were me, would you start liquidating now?"

"Premature, Paul, but the situation is serious and I don't want my friends to get hurt. So I thought I'd speak frankly with you and a couple of others, who'll remain nameless. Give you some time to plan ways to get out without loss."

"I'd need every damn day, too. How much lead time can you give me?"

"Depends on White House reaction. With the President away I've been in meetings with the Veep who knows the situation but is just stalling and not saying or doing anything until the President returns. So far, the early warning indications haven't gone to the NSC, by direct order by the Veep. Now, you and I know how far the Administration has gone to placate China, keep trade moving for the sake of U.S. jobs and investments, but we're locked into a mutual defense treaty with Taiwan that can't be ignored."

"Jesus, you're suggesting we'd be dragged into a war with the Mainland?"

"That's worst case, Paul. But if the U.S. merely *warns* China to keep hands off Taiwan the financial repercussions will be enormous."

"Shit yes, I'd probably be wiped out." He shook his head. "A Swiss-Swedish consortium has been nosing around, expressing interest in my Mainland operation. And a Hong Kong banking group wants to buy into Keelung." He eyed Gerold. "Guess it's not premature to sound them out, right?"

"Not if done with your customary delicacy. But for God's sake don't indicate your true motivation."

"Hell, no, think I'm nuts?"

"Or mention me and the Agency to anyone—not even in your sleep."

"Goes without saying." He drained his snifter, set it down. "Listen, Darman, I'm damn grateful you warned me, everything's top-secret confidential between us. I'm going to take a few preliminary steps involving my lawyers only. My shares are privately traded, so I don't have to notify the SEC," he said, thinking aloud. "The Swedish-Swiss consortium is represented in New York so I don't have to travel to Zurich. Hong Kong bankers, too. Can you give me any idea how much lead time I'll have?"

Gerold rubbed his chin. "State and Defense will argue the situation in the NSC before reaching a position for the White House. After that, the President will call in his political advisers for their input." He shrugged. "Minimum two weeks, maximum four. Unless, of course, the White House issues an Executive Order banning trade and financial exchanges with China and Taiwan. That could come anytime. And I wouldn't be surprised if the President interposed carriers between Taiwan and the Mainland to forestall invasion."

"Yeah, that's about the way it would go," he said unhappily, "and China could bomb the shit out of Taiwan without challenging us directly." He sighed. "I thought you'd invited me for a look back at old times in the Yard, never expected dire warning. Okay, you've done me a big sub-rosa favor I'll never forget. Anyone but you I'd pay twenty-fifty thousand dollars for the tip, but you don't need money. Is there anything I can do for you?"

This was it, the crux of the whole thing. Darman smiled inwardly. "Possibly," he replied. "There are rumors our esteemed Director is leaving the Agency. If you felt it appropriate you might mention me favorably to the President as a qualified replacement. Your endorsement could go a long way, Paul—but only if you felt it the right thing to do. Understand, I'm not suggesting a quid pro quo, but since you asked me, I can't think of anything more helpful you could do."

"And I will, Darman, believe me, I will. When's the President returning?"

"Should be the next few days." Gerold smiled. "Unless he takes a Bangkok side trip to get laid."

"A real ass-hound," Wembley remarked, "when the missus ain't around." He stubbed out his cigar and stood up. "An earthy guy who knows how deals are made, not an ivory-tower creep like Wilson and Carter. Okay, Darman, thanks for an excellent lunch, and I'll expect to hear from you."

"You will." They shook hands, Darman showed him to the door and walked with Wembley to his waiting limousine.

"Stay well," Wembley said, and got in. Gerold saw him reach for the cellular phone as the limousine pulled away.

One down, he thought as he walked back into his house. Three to go.

THAT EVENING HE FLEW to New York, signed in at the Harvard Club, saw a Broadway musical, and had late supper at the Four Seasons. Freddy Postlewaite met him for breakfast at the Club, and Darcy Whiting joined him for lunch at the R&T. Repeated calls to Sonny Simpkin brought information that the Chicago grain trader was sailing with his family between San Diego and Honolulu and was out of touch with his office for the next several days. Gerold left his name and a request to be called.

On the afternoon flight to Washington, Darman reviewed the day's accomplishments with satisfaction. As with Wembley, things had gone well with Fred and Darcy. Both showed deep appreciation for Gerold's offer of inside information and vowed in return to act as his advocates with the President.

Driving from National Airport, Gerold decided on an early session with Tom Gray next morning, after which he would go to Upperville and enlist Pauline in planning a series of dinner parties whose guest lists would comprise members of the Senate Foreign Relations and Intelligence committees, presidential advisers in and out of the Administration, the Vice President, and of course Irving Chenow.

Some sort of limited war with the Mainland might come, he reflected, but by then he might be DCI with influence over its outcome. It was a pleasing prospect, he mused, becoming one of the most influential figures in Washington, and Pauline would enjoy her enhanced position to the hilt.

A turnoff sign to Alexandria reminded Gerold of Doreen, and he wondered how long it would be before his reoriented daughter could join him in their Georgetown home.

HONG KONG

FROM THE *SOUTH CHINA MORNING POST*:

American Socialite Dies in Hotel Suite

The body of Washington socialite Nina Kenton was discovered in her suite at the Manchu Hotel by room servants. Mrs. Kenton had occupied the suite for several days, hotel management confirmed, while visiting the Colony on a shopping and sight-seeing trip.

The Crown Coroner stated that Mrs. Kenton's death was due to natural causes, specifically a massive heart attack.

The whereabouts of her only son, Gareth, are not known at this time, and he is being sought for notification by Colony and Washington authorities. The American Consulate-General is responding to inquiries, and requests the public's assistance in locating the surviving son.

Twenty-Eight

BEIJING

BRAND AND PETER WERE at a conference table in the office of the Beijing Chief of Station. He sipped coffee and said, "Since this is a brainstorming session I'm open to almost any idea how to get the fugitive out of here. Mr. Brand?"

"It's about seven miles to Cheong's godown," Brand replied, "but the first hundred yards from the embassy could be the worst of it, thanks to the ever-vigilant police." He smiled. "Any chance of leaving in an embassy car?"

Whitbread considered. "Not impossible. What have you got in mind?"

"Deception," Brand told him. "Keep the police busy inspecting a suspicious-looking truck, while an embassy car goes through uninspected." He looked at his son. "You in the trunk."

Whitbread said, "You've considered the inadvisability of an embassy vehicle entering the godown."

"I have. A few blocks from here we could switch to another vehicle for the rest of the way. The embassy car returns to the compound, and all is well."

"Where will you get the second vehicle? Cheong Wing-dah?"

Brand shook his head. "That's my problem—I'll get wheels." If Yang and his men can't steal a van, he thought, they aren't the accomplished criminals I think they are.

Whitbread asked, "You'd do this by night?"

"After nightfall—not so late as to be suspicious—but dark enough that changing vehicles won't be noticed."

Peter asked, "Can we be sure the plane will be there?"

"I'll check at the godown. If Cheong's going to back off from our agreement, now's the time to know."

Peter said, "Agreement? What kind of agreement, Dad?"

Curtly, Brand said, "Personal, between Cheong and me. Jason, what's your opinion?"

"Sounds good. All I have to do is lend a car for an hour or so, you handle the rest."

"Not quite. You have to ready the deception truck."

"Right. Very important." He scribbled a note and looked up. "Timing?"

"If the plane isn't here, it could take a day getting here. But if the plane's still here we could plan on tomorrow night."

"And you'd fly to Hong Kong."

"That's the plane's home base."

Whitbread smiled. "I ought to get to know some of your contacts. Too often I feel I'm isolated on an island of ignorance."

"I remember the feeling," Brand remarked, "and you get out or get used to it. My troops can't pass an Agency background check, but you've already gotten an A-1 report from a novice informant." He glanced at Peter.

"True," Whitbread said, "so you know about the freight train and the gas missiles."

Brand nodded. "Gerold had breakfast with me in HK, gave me a prelim. At that point the trains hadn't collided."

"I think of lethal gas and I get a very bad feeling. Doesn't seem likely the Chinese are planning to use it on the Mainland. They deploy tanks and machine guns for crowd control."

Peter said, "Maybe they're tired of waiting for capitalist Taiwan to collapse. Gas the population, and take over without firing a shot."

"I've thought of that," Whitbread said, "but the thought is too damn awful. Anyway, Peter, you have a knack for this business, and if you want to sign up, I guarantee you won't have to spend time at the Farm in basic training."

Brand said quickly, "Not a chance—he's got a child on the way, a family to take care of."

"Congratulations," Whitbread said. "As your father may have intimated, families can be a drawback in this business."

"He has," Peter responded. "Besides, I didn't do awfully well first time out."

Whitbread shrugged. "You followed instructions, that's all we can reasonably ask. And you more than made up for that with your hospital report."

"Not to mention prison time and survival in a hostile land." Brand got up. "Since Peter can't go out dining with me, save me a place at the mess table, will you? I'll be back later."

With a smile Peter said, "Be careful, will you? This can be a tough town."

"From the mouths of babes," Brand sighed, and left the embassy.

In his hotel room, Brand watched TV and read magazines until Yang the Elder came. Then he told him what he wanted the three of them to do.

Washington

After returning from Hong Kong Oleg Tarnovski slept eight hours to recover from jet lag, shaved, dressed, and took a taxi to the apartment building where Nina Kenton had lived, checking for mobile surveillance along the way.

From a public phone at Dulles airport Tarnovski had phoned his San Francisco contact a one-word message: *Done.* Now he had to go through the apartment and clean out any traces that could compromise him. He was thinking of her message machine, address books, tape recordings, cached money, checkbooks, possibly a diary, the usual legacies of the newly dead.

As he fitted his key into the door lock, he reflected that he had enjoyed himself in the apartment, a few good meals, excellent wines, and average sex. But, he thought as he moved inward, you can't expect to have it all.

It surprised him that a table lamp was lighted. Then he reasoned that Nina must have left after dark. He folded his coat over the back of a chair and rolled up his shirtcuffs. He opened the message machine and removed the tape cassette. At her writing desk he pocketed two address books and leafed through a box of personal stationery. No half-written letters. The ornamental wastebasket held crumpled papers and envelopes to be disposed of before he left. An estate-size checkbook showed a balance of three thousand and change. Too bad he couldn't liquidate it, because the cash would give him a good weekend in Vegas. But when the police went through the apartment, they'd notice a missing checkbook, too large for a lady's purse. Briefly he considered collecting her mail from the lobby box, but the police could notice that, too. Besides, her bills and incoming letters didn't concern him, just anything outgoing that hadn't been mailed.

Methodically, he went through each desk drawer and found nothing incriminating. Poor old bitch, he thought, she didn't take the elementary precaution of hiding something to save herself from me.

He turned on kitchen lights and looked back at the living and dining rooms, visually checked china stacked in the glass-paned cabinet, then went through drawers that held silver service bought with his money. He'd spent tens of thousands of dollars setting up and maintaining Nina, and she had never produced for him—if you could even count that throwaway stuff on China's Kunlun range. Hadn't been able to keep Brand from the Mainland, the final straw.

He emptied three table vases and a roll of currency tumbled from the third. Hundred-dollar bills, he'd count them later.

Kneeling in the kitchen, he checked among pots and pans under the sink. Nothing. Nothing in the double ovens, either. The refrigerator held wilted lettuce, a few vegetables, bottles of soda and mixers, an open container of acidophilus. Tarnovski grimaced; she'd never have to worry about gas pains again.

He opened the freezer side and removed sealed microwave dinners before taking out ice cube trays. One of the four showed an opaque layer beneath the translucent ice. At the sink counter Tarnovski broke it out and found a plastic bag containing jewelry and six hundred-dollar bills. Now we're getting somewhere, he told himself, refilled the tray with water, and slid it back with the others. After wiping the plastic bag dry, he shoved it in his trouser pocket and mounted a chair to check cabinet tops. Nothing but dust and a few dead roaches. He replaced the chair and decided the bedroom and bathroom were next. Months ago he'd installed a hidden video camera in Nina's bedroom to record her occasional couplings with Brand. The camera could stay, but the cassette had to be removed. Very important, he told himself as he switched on the bedroom light.

And froze.

Sitting on the bed were two men with drawn guns. Tarnovski's reflex was to turn and run but he quickly realized flight was hopeless. Whoever they were, they could drop him before he was a yard away.

"Who the hell are you?" he demanded in feigned outrage.

"FBI," the gray-haired man snapped and held up an ID carnet with his free hand. "Special Agents Hoffman and Gearing. You're under arrest for burglary, robbery, and the murder of Nina Kenton."

His knees went liquid. "I—I pay the rent here, this is my place. I'm an American citizen and you can't arrest me on a lot of trumped-up charges. Now get out."

"Doesn't work that way." The agent produced handcuffs and clamped them around Tarnovski's wrists. "First, the lease is in the name of Nina Kenton—the late Mrs. Kenton. Second, you're not an American citizen. Your name is Oleg Vasilievich Tarnovski, and until now you've been working for a foreign intelligence service. Third, you murdered Mrs. Kenton in Hong Kong."

"Prove it," he snarled.

"Easily done. You've been surveilled for weeks. In Hong Kong Special Branch agents tailed you to the Manchu, tailed you back to Kai Tak. Her body was found while it was still warm. The Brits wanted to hold you for murder, but we persuaded them to let you come back." Standing, he stretched and yawned. "Thought you'd get here sooner for cleanup." From the bed he picked up a videocasset'e. "Looking for this, Oleg? A case can be made for blackmail conspiracy on top of everything else. Now sit down—floor's fine—and listen carefully."

Tarnovski grated, "Whatever happened in Hong Kong doesn't concern the FBI."

The seated agent said, "Until recently that might have been true. Since then new antiterrorist laws were passed giving us jurisdiction over crimes against U.S. citizens anywhere in the world." He grinned. "Including Hong Kong."

"Also," said the standing agent, "your call from Dulles to San Francisco was intercepted. 'Done' meant murder accomplished to your controller—and of course we know who he is and where he is." He stared down at the Russian. "We have all the cards, Oleg, and you have nothing, zilch, zip, nada. Understand? You're facing execution or at best life without parole in the kind of hard-ass prison we like to send guys like you."

Tarnovski licked lips suddenly gone dry. "I want to see a lawyer."

"Yeah? Listen, *tovarich,* Yakov the comedian you're not. Seeing a lawyer gets things on paper, complicates a bad situation beyond recall. Whereas, if you're as intelligent as we think you are, you'll recognize an opportunity to possibly turn the situation to your advantage."

Looking up at their faces, Tarnovski realized he had nowhere to turn. He drew up his knees and rested his chin on them. "What do you have in mind?"

Special Agent Kevin Hoffman looked at his partner, Chris Gearing, and smiled. This piece of Russian shit was going to earn his freedom every fucking day for the rest of his putrid life.

Washington

Tom Gray watched Darman Gerold studying the latest Gorgon take under the illuminated magnifier and said, "The freight train reached Heijian airfield last night. So far, the warheads haven't been unloaded."

Gerold turned off the light and sat across from Gray's desk. "That's good, isn't it?"

"Good? They're probably waiting for one of their big cargo planes to come in. Then the warheads can be loaded in three or four hours. So it's not really good, Darman, just a temporary delay."

Gerold considered the situation before saying, "Guess I better update the DCI."

"When's the President due back?"

"Sometime tomorrow. With the Secretary of State and National Security Adviser."

Gray grimaced. "They'll find tough decisions waiting. Incidentally, Irv Chenow is asking for an update."

"Can you put him off?"

"I can try."

"Do that. Irv can be a loose cannon."

Gray frowned. "Meaning?"

"Maybe going public, forcing the Administration's hand."

"I don't think Irving would do that, Darman. He's too close to the President to embarrass him."

Gerold shrugged. "Never know. Anyway, the less he knows for now the more comfortable I'll be. After tomorrow he can get Dragon Teeth info from the Secretary on a need-to-know basis."

Gray sighed. "So be it. But the NSC should have been alerted days ago."

"Agreed."

"And I'll be relieved when Mark gets back to share the load."

"Reminds me," Gerold said, "Beijing Station sent a back channel saying Mark showed up at the embassy and found his son."

"Great! When are they coming back?"

"The problem is getting Peter out from under the noses of the Chinese. And when Mark finally reports in he'll have some explaining to do to our Security mandarins. It's not unlikely his Gorgon, Paladar, and Special Intel clearances will be lifted."

"Because he went to the Mainland?"

Gerold nodded. "Can't blame Mark, but rules are rules. You live by them, so do I. Mark broke them knowing the consequences."

"I'd say the immediate national interest requires Mark back on board with full clearances. He got your daughter back, Darman, so you ought to intervene for him now."

"If it comes to that," Gerold said, irritated by Gray's reference to Doreen. In Hong Kong Mark had taken sexual advantage of his daughter, a helpless addict, and every mention of his name was a bitter reminder.

Gerold said, "I'll take these photos to the Director and hope they reach the NSC." He got up and placed them in an envelope. "I appreciate the way you've been keeping me current, Tommy."

"It's all in the national interest," Gray responded, and watched Gerold leave. Not a man for crisis management, he thought, or anything demanding tough decisions. Thank God Mark finally has his son; the only good news I've had since he went away.

Twenty-Nine

BEIJING

DUSK.

In the shadowed rear of the embassy compound Brand and Whitbread supervised loading of the decoy truck. Four coffin-size crates were nailed shut and banded to hold rugs, carpets, bedding, toys, kitchenware, and file boxes to resemble a shipment of household effects returning to the USA. The driver was a Portland-born Chinese-American Marine Private named Frank Yuan, who was in civilian clothes.

"Okay," Whitbread said as Private Yuan closed the tailgate, "we're close to showtime so tell me what you're supposed to do."

"Aye, sir," Yuan responded. "On your signal I drive to the gates, proceed through, and turn left on the street."

"Slowly, very slowly," Whitbread prompted, "like you were trolling bait. If the police don't stop you, stop anyway and go round to the tailgate. Make like you thought you heard crates shifting."

Yuan nodded. "One or two of them will come around and start asking what's in the crates. I say I don't know. They'll tell me to open the crates and I point out I don't have a crowbar or a band-cutter." He grinned. "They might have to send to Shanghai for tools."

Whitbread smiled. "Go on."

"While they're deciding what to do I pass around cigarettes, friendly-like, invite them to swig mao-tai. By then your car with diplomatic plates and fender flags will be out of the compound." He paused. "You clear this with Gunny?"

"I asked Gunny to lend me a good man for a couple of hours. He didn't ask what for and I didn't tell him. What you get out of it is a letter of appreciation for your file. Okay?"

"Okay, sir. Well, guess I'll mount up and stand ready."

As Yuan got into the cab Whitbread turned to Mark Brand. "Any comment?"

"Sounds A-okay." He looked at his watch: seven-thirty. "By now the van should be in place. Let's check with Peter."

Together they walked back to the embassy garage, where Peter waited in darkness. Whitbread unlocked the trunk of the Mercury sedan and lifted the lid. To his son, Brand said, "You won't be there long, Peter."

"I know." He went over to Whitbread, and said, "I'm very grateful for everything you've done, sir. Thank you."

They shook hands, and Whitbread said, "Glad I had the opportunity to help make up for an Agency mistake. Like your father, I'm old at the game, but this is my first personal involvement in E&E and I kind of like it. But since we won't see each other real soon my final request is to avoid mentioning my name. Okay?"

"Okay." Peter nodded, and climbed into the trunk. Before the lid came down he asked, "What if the plane's not there?"

"It had better be," Brand said, "but if not, we'll stay in the godown until it comes."

"Let's hope," Whitbread remarked. "I'd just as soon not go through all this a second time."

"Hell," Brand said, "it's now or never, so get behind the wheel and drive." He pulled down the trunk lid and motioned Whitbread to start the engine. Then he walked to the truck and signaled Yuan to get moving. He waited until the gates opened and the truck was passing through before getting in beside Whitbread. They watched policemen wave Yuan's truck to the curb and then Whitbread steered the sedan through the gates and turned away from the halted truck. Focused on the truck, the policemen hardly glanced at the embassy vehicle as it drove away. Brand said, "Hang a left there to get out of sight. Go four blocks and turn right. Anyone following?"

"Not that I see, and I've been checking the mirror."

Yesterday Brand had shown Yang the rendezvous point, and Yang said he'd either steal or rent a van for the evening, no problem.

The real problems, Brand mused, concerned aircraft readiness, and the possibility of Cheong Wing-dah's welshing on their deal. Still, he was resolved to fly Peter out of China that night whatever the obstacles.

Beside him, Whitbread said, "I don't suppose you're carrying a piece."

"No."

"So, just in case—reach into my pocket, will you?"

Brand felt around and encountered cold steel, drew out a black .380 pistol.

"Full magazine," Whitbread told him, "one in the chamber. Hope you don't need to use it, but if you do—well, it could be useful."

"Thanks for the loan."

"My personal piece," Whitbread said. "When I'm on home leave I'll pick it up from you."

Brand pocketed the pistol and stared ahead. "Get ready to turn," he instructed, and saw Whitbread nod. A police motorcycle came toward them, headlight on, but stayed close to the curb.

Whitbread made the turn and said, "So far, so good. How much farther?"

"Five blocks. It's a dark area, and quiet. Old pre-Revolution houses now occupied by Party elite."

"Under their noses, eh? Nice touch."

Brand smiled. "Pure chance," he admitted, "so we work with what we got."

He was looking ahead, wondering when Yang's van would come into view, when Whitbread said, "Would you mind having Peter debriefed about the hospital incident? Not often the analysts get a chance to query a live, on-site agent."

"I'll suggest it to Gerold," he said tensely, not wanting to think that far ahead, just concentrate on the next few minutes.

Headlights bored through the darkness, the rendezvous point couldn't be far away, then they passed it and Brand realized the van wasn't there. His watch showed seven forty-eight. "*Shit*, no van, dammit."

"What now?" Whitbread asked calmly, Brand peering back out of the rear window.

"Circle the block and come back. If it's not there, we'll drive farther away and try in fifteen minutes."

On the next pass, no van. Brand gritted his teeth, and saw a man walking toward them. "Easy," he said to Whitbread, and then the headlights illuminated Yang. "Pull over," he said, "and we'll see what the trouble is."

Rolling down the window, Brand hailed Yang who came to the car apologies on his tongue. Brand cut them off as Yang explained they'd had a flat tire and Wo and San were changing it. "Get in," Brand told him, "we'll make the exchange there."

Yang guided Whitbread to where the jacked-up van stood at curbside. Wo was tightening the wheel nuts while San began cranking down the jack. The old van, Brand noticed, had a bakery sign on it, the sides showed rust amid patches of varicolored paint.

Whitbread drove just beyond the van and backed up to it. Brand got out and opened the van's rear doors, then unlocked the sedan trunk. He looked around before telling Peter to get out and into the van, and closed the doors. Then he returned keys to Whitbread. "Thanks again, Jason. End of the line for you."

"Glad we found them," the COS said. "Have a good flight, both of you." He pulled away, and for a moment Brand watched his taillights recede, then got into the rear of the van with Peter. Wo joined them, while San took the seat beside Yang, the driver. The engine started, cylinders chuffed, and the van moved ahead.

Brand's face was damp with perspiration. He put his arm over Peter's shoulders and said, "The worst is over. Only one more stop before we're airborne." He looked at San, who was smiling, gave him the thumbs-up, *ting-hao* sign, and Peter did the same.

I've got my son and an aircraft, Brand said to himself, so the Mainland problem is solved. After we get home I'll take Peter to Simon's place for some family fishing and then I'll probably return to Hong Kong for Mary and Chu-li.

As THE VAN NEARED the city's outskirts, Brand told Yang to pull over and stop the engine. When there was quiet inside, he said, "The situation is this: I made a deal with Cheong Wing-dah whereby he's to fly us out of China. We drank Hopei tea, and ritual *bai-jiu* to formalize the understanding. His aircraft should be either in the godown or at the airstrip."

Yang said, "Forgive me, sir, but may I ask—do you trust Cheong?"

"I want to believe he'll carry out his part of the bargain, but we've never been friends, and that worries me. On Taiwan, when we were young, we disliked each other. Later, he married a woman I should have married, and when I saw her again in Hong Kong it disturbed him. There was a threat to my life that Cheong apologized for, saying it was a misunderstanding. Only then did we drink the ceremonial cups. He wants something from me that only I can deliver, so the question is whether Cheong wants it enough to keep his bargain."

Peter said, "Dad, you had a sweetheart on Taiwan?"

"After your mother's death, when you were very young. Eventually you'll meet her." He turned to the others. "If Cheong is at the godown or on the plane it is necessary that I appear to trust him. But I want all four of you to understand that the situation could change very quickly and I want you prepared for that."

Yang nodded. "Not trusting Cheong, I acquired weapons."

"Good. My son is not armed so I expect you to protect him. The purpose of my going to Hong Kong, then Beijing, was to find my son and get him safely from the Mainland. That he reach freedom is much more important than what happens to me."

Peter interrupted, "But, Dad—"

Brand held up his hand. "My decision, no argument."

Peter looked silently at his hands.

"With that understanding," Brand said, "we'll continue on to the godown. They won't be expecting you three, but if there's a rifle platoon waiting it won't make much difference. Start the engine."

The van crossed railroad tracks and moved into the marshaling yard. The broad door of the godown was dimly lit. The van moved up the incline and stopped. Brand got out and knocked at the side entrance door. A view slot opened and eyes stared out at him. Brand said, "Open up, quickly." The slot closed and Brand stood beside the van while the main entrance door rolled aside.

The green-and-silver aircraft was parked near the door, cabin lights on. The rear of the godown was unlighted. Not a good sign, Brand thought, but walked inside, and told Yang to pull up by the loading ramp. The henchman Yang had called Yu Min-sheng strolled over and said, "Everything is in readiness. You and your son may go on board."

"Excellent." Brand walked to the van and spoke to Yang. "Peter and I will board first. Back the van a few yards and wait before coming aboard. Peter, let's go."

Together they walked up the loading belt into the cabin, Yu came behind them. As they stepped into the aircraft, Brand saw Cheong seated on his simulated throne, raising his hand in greeting. To Peter, Brand said, "Our host, Master Cheong Wing-dah, my friend. Go to him and make known your thanks." He bowed in Cheong's direction, and became aware of movement in the rear of the cabin. Without changing position, he looked down at Yang in the van.

Cheong said, "It gives me great satisfaction to see father and son together. That you have overcome great obstacles to arrive here does credit to you both."

"Thank you. We look forward to our journey."

"Doubtless you do. It will be a short one for you both."

His tone tensed Brand, who realized that three men had come stealthily behind him. Peter moved away from Cheong, alarm on his face. Brand looked at the three men and saw one holding a pistol. "Fellow travelers?" he asked, and saw a smirk above Cheong's fat jowls.

"Officers of the Gong An Ju with whom I have done much business. I am repaying their favors by returning to them an escaped prisoner and an American spy. You see, Brand, I wanted a way to dispose of you, and here is more convenient than Hong Kong, where your Fang-tse brothers could intervene or take revenge. Besides, these officers are doing no more than their duty after I pointed out the way."

"Very clever," Brand retorted. "I suppose we're to go with them now?"

The man with the pistol said, "Down the ramp, both of you."

Followed by the three officers, Peter and Brand started down the ramp and Brand saw Yang's face replaced by the muzzle of a gun. It spat flame twice, the gunman behind Brand fell off the ramp, another dropped forward, and the third tried to climb back into the plane before Yang shot him twice.

The van's doors slammed open, and Wo and San came out, guns in their hands. From the side, Yu Min-sheng fired at them, hitting the van. Wo turned and dropped Yu with two quick shots. San came to the ramp and kicked the pistol from the officer's hand while Brand toed the third man's body from the doorway. It dropped on the concrete floor.

Then Brand, borrowed pistol in hand, strode forward and covered Cheong, whose face was a mixture of shock and fear. Something gurgled in his throat, but no words came out. Brand said, "We're flying out of here, and if you move from that chair I'll drill your fat guts and watch you bleed to death." He opened the cockpit door and showed pilot and copilot the pistol. "Master Cheong says we leave now. Start your engines."

"But—but there is no tractor to pull us to the airstrip," the pilot protested.

Brand shoved the pistol against his skull. "Get us there or you're a dead man."

The copilot flicked ignition switches, and the jets began their accelerating whine. Still covering the pilots, Brand called Peter to have Yang open the big godown door completely, then board the plane with San and Wo.

With one hand he got out his switchblade and with the other tossed his pistol to Peter. "Cover the pilots," he told Peter, "while I have a talk with our host."

He came up behind Cheong, grabbed his hair and jerked back his head, trailed the knife edge across his throat. "You like having others do your killing, while I prefer doing it myself." The knife point pricked throat flesh enough to draw drops of blood. Cheong squealed and writhed in his chair. Brand trailed the knife point down from throat to chest and stomach, severed the silk cord that served as a belt for his gown. Brand looped the cord around Cheong's throat and tied it to the top rung of the chair.

Cheong puffed and panted, features contorted in fear. "Don't . . . kill . . . me," he pleaded, "I'll . . . make . . . you . . . wealthy."

"I've got enough money," Brand snapped.

"Then . . . I'll . . . give you . . . Chen Ling-mei."

"Who says I want her?"

Cheong blinked. "Then take Chu-li. She is beautiful, educated, she will make a perfect concubine for you."

Brand struck his face hard. Cheong shrieked and blood flowed from his damaged lips. "For your miserable life you'd make a whore of your daughter," Brand snarled. "You really don't deserve to live." He tightened the garrote, and Cheong's face reddened and purpled before Brand eased the tension. "I thought you might drop me in the China Sea, but I should have figured you saw me as trade goods." He grunted, saw Yang, Wo, and San enter the cabin behind him. The cargo door slid shut and the plane began to move out of the godown, wing lights flooding the incline. He beckoned to Yang and said, "If this son of a leprous sow moves, shoot him in the belly."

"Yes, honored sir."

Brand went into the cockpit and strapped himself in the empty radioman's chair. He pushed the pistol muzzle against the back of the copilot's neck. "Have you got flight clearance from the authorities?"

"Yes."

"Destination?"

"Hong Kong."

"Wrong. We're flying to Taiwan." He looked down at the navigational chart on the fold-down desk. "Follow the normal Hong Kong course as far as—Nanjing. That's about six hundred miles. From there head gradually east to leave the coast north of the Taiwan Strait. Got that?"

"Yes, sir," they replied.

"Is there a control tower at the airstrip?"

"Yes, but there's no air controller after dark."

"Good. So I don't want to hear you talking to someone who's not there. From now on, radio silence. If there's a fighter challenge I'll tell you what to say. Understood?"

Both men nodded.

"I have nothing against you men, you've worked for Cheong Wing-dah but now you're working for me. Do as I tell you and you won't be harmed."

The plane was trundling over level ground, and Brand could make out the dark ribbon of an airstrip ahead. When the plane reached the near end the pilot braked and ran up the engines while he went over the preflight checklist. The fuselage vibrated until the copilot released the brakes, and the aircraft moved forward, gathering speed until it lifted from the ground. The pilot banked to the east, gaining altitude above the lighted city, until at fifteen thousand feet he leveled off and locked the autopilot on their southward course.

Brand left his seat then and opened the galley, found scotch, cognac, rice wine, and *bai-jiu*. After pouring scotch for himself and Peter, Brand invited his three brigands to join them. With Cheong motionless in his ornate chair, Brand thanked them and drank to their health.

Peter said, "The way everything happened—incredible. I was more scared than I've ever been, but I knew somehow you'd work things out, get the upper hand." He breathed deeply. "Finally I'm going home."

Brand touched his glass to his son's. "Yes, Peter, we're going home."

After a few moments Peter asked, "Why Taipei instead of Hong Kong?"

"Cheong has agents all over the place, point one. Point two, the British can be sticky about air hijacking, which is what we've done. And I don't want to get into a pissing contest with Cheong over who did what to whom." After a pause he went on. "I still have a few contacts on Taiwan. If I can reach them they'll lend a hand." He smiled at Peter. "Satisfied?"

Peter smiled, too. "Yes, ever-wise, honored father from whom I have much to learn."

* * *

FROM TIME TO TIME Mark checked course heading to keep the pilots honest, and saw that his men were settled comfortably in cargo space. Wo relieved Yang watching Cheong Wing-dah so Yang could sleep awhile. All had been under heavy stress accented by the firefight, and Brand was glad to see them relaxing as the plane droned on.

An hour and a half into the flight, the copilot came to the cockpit door and said, "Coming into Nanjing air control space. They've got us on radar. No radio yet."

"Start turning for the coast," Brand instructed, "I want to pass well south of Shanghai," and checked the new heading.

Cheong seemed to be sleeping, so Brand went back to where Peter lay sprawled on the deck and saw his son's eyes were open. "Can't sleep?" he asked. "Everything's under control."

"I know that, but I've been thinking about Cheong's wife, the lady you should have married long ago." He hesitated. "Have you any plans?"

"I have," he admitted, "and we'll discuss them another time, when things are more tranquil." He started to leave, but Peter held his hand.

"I just want you to know that whatever you do is okay with me. I'm grown, Dad, not a factor anymore."

Brand smiled and walked forward, intending to monitor the pilots in case they got a radio query from ground or air. He was nearing Wing-dah when he saw the glint of metal in Cheong's hand, ducked to the right, and heard a gunshot. The bullet caught him below the left shoulder, and Wo fired at close range to keep Cheong from shooting again. Cheong yelled as the bullet slammed into his chest, and Wo slapped the weapon from his hand. It clattered to the deck, and Brand saw it was a two-shot derringer, a lady's firearm, lethal if fired into heart or head. Brand clamped his right hand over his wound, felt warm blood. By then Peter was beside him, his face distraught. Wo bowed low before him, intoning apologies until Brand said, "My fault, I should have searched him," and pulled off his coat. Peter gasped at his bloody shirt and Brand said, "Make a tourniquet for me." He gazed down at Cheong and muttered, "Oh, shit!" Bloodstains widened across the silk fabric covering his chest. Breath rattled in Cheong's throat, he coughed violently and blood spewed from his mouth. Wo must have severed an artery, he thought, or nicked the fat man's heart.

Peter freed the silk cord from Cheong's neck and tightened it around his father's upper arm. "Jesus, Dad," he said shakily, "he could have killed you."

"He tried. Now get me a drink—and one for yourself."

Peter returned with the bottle and Brand lifted it and drank. Peter did the same and looked at Cheong. "Will he die?"

"Think so," Brand replied. "Pour a little of that stuff on the wound." He set his teeth as the alcohol scorched raw flesh, blinked, and passed his hand back and forth before Cheong's eyes. No movement. He went to the cockpit and checked course heading before taking the radioman's seat. Both pilots looked back at him. Brand snapped, "Keep your eyes on your work." He loosened the tourniquet and let blood flow again.

Damn, he said to himself, I should have known he'd try something, but things were going so well I ignored him. Never make that mistake again.

From the doorway Peter said, "Anything I can do?"

"Look up Taipei air control frequency and set the radio dial. When the tower calls, say we're short of fuel, have to land."

"Ambulance?"

Brand shook his head. "Take a truck to move Cheong, and I can walk."

Peter tightened the tourniquet. "You're still bleeding."

"Don't worry about it."

"Dad, I don't think we ought to land with Cheong's body."

He nodded. "You're right. Tell the pilot to slow so we can open the cargo door. Our friends can shove him out—that damned chair, too."

"Will do."

"I'll say I shot myself fooling with a gun. The four of you will confirm it."

Peter glanced forward at the pilots. "What about them?"

"They can go on to Hong Kong or back to Beijing, I don't care either way." He was feeling a little giddy. "Take care of things."

Peter leaned forward between the pilots and spoke to them. Brand felt the plane's speed decrease. When the cargo door opened bitterly cold wind blasted in. Peripherally he saw Cheong's body dragged to the open doorway. When he looked again, body and chair were gone. The door slid shut, the cabin began to warm.

Brand dozed then, wakened by the jolt of landing. Looking out, he saw Taipei's control tower. The aircraft taxied toward the terminal and when it stopped Brand stood up. Steadied by Peter, he walked to the door and waited until a mobile staircase arrived. Then all five of them went down to the tarmac.

Home again, he thought drowsily, back where I spent the best and worst years of my life. Tongue thick, he said to Peter, "I never should have left."

Thirty

WASHINGTON

ASSISTANT SECRETARY OF STATE Irving Chenow's luncheon guest was the Air Force Vice Chief of Staff, Lieutenant General Bruce Barlow, whose son Chenow had defended in federal court three years ago. At the time, Ben Barlow had been a junior broker in a Chicago brokerage firm whose senior partners accused him of embezzlement, insider trading, and account churning. Chenow had taken the case mainly out of sympathy for a young man he felt was being made a scapegoat to conceal his seniors' defalcations, misfeasances, and deceptive practices. Not only had Chenow convinced the judge of Ben Barlow's innocence, but his trial strategy resulted in federal indictments against the conspirators.

General Barlow had sat through the two-week trial, and when his son's innocence was proclaimed, wept joyfully and told attorney Chenow that he stood ready to perform whatever future service Irving Chenow might require.

They were lunching on the patio of Chenow's Potomac Falls home outside the Beltway where, Chenow reckoned, they could converse in absolute privacy.

Bruce Barlow was a handsome man of angular jaw, piercing gray eyes, and leonine white hair. He was, Chenow thought, a near-perfect image of what every service cadet aspired to become, and the Air Force wisely exploited his commanding presence, deep voice, and considerable intelligence at congressional hearings where Air Force budget matters were under review. But Chenow knew his guest was more than a charismatic figure in Air Force blue. Barlow had flown fighters in Korea and Vietnam. There his F-5 had been shot down, and Barlow endured and survived close to two years at the Hanoi Hilton before the war ended. Service prior to his present post had been as Director of the National Security Agency, the government's code-making and code-breaking agency. The NSA also conducted related activities too sensitive for the ears of any but a few congressional insiders.

After a second martini, and a cup of clear bouillon, Barlow said, "I know you're around town, Irving, but I never get to see you. Oughta get out more."

"So Vivian tells me. How's Ben doing?"

"Pretty well. Got a second child, lives in Oak Park, and sells computers. Blacklisted in the brokerage fraternity because he testified against the bastards who framed him." He set down his spoon. "But you didn't invite me all the way out here to ask about Ben."

"No, but I'm interested in him." Chenow smiled. "Once a client, always a client."

"So, what's on your mind? Want a free flight to Rio, say the word and I'll lay it on."

"Thanks, Bruce, but it's a little more complicated than that." He paused. "I wonder how much national intelligence you get to see."

"Probably less than you—my job is, well, largely ceremonial except when the Chief of Staff's away. Then I see a pretty good slice of the take."

"But nothing like what you saw at NSA."

"True. Of course I don't need it in my job."

Chenow stayed silent while the maid removed their first course and brought plates of medium-rare lamb chops with new peas and *rissolé* potatoes. "Recently," he said, "I was being shown some very interesting and disturbing satellite pictures, now I seem to be cut out of the loop. Among other things the Vice President clamped a lid on dissemination pending the President's return."

"Well, he got back last night."

Chenow nodded. "My hope is he'll take remedial action promptly—it's late in the day if a tragedy of almost unimaginable proportions is to be averted."

Barlow frowned. "Irving, nothing in any way resembling that description has come to my attention, so I guess you better tell me what it is."

Chenow described the apparent mating of Chinese IRBM warheads and lethal gas, related the freight train's collision and derailment, and the death of villagers near the smashed warheads. "At that point," he said, "the intelligence flow ended for me."

"Jesus Christ, what the hell's going on over there?" Barlow exploded.

"What few indications there are strongly suggest the warheads are being moved south. There's an army missile base at Leping inland from the coast, about two hundred miles from Taiwan." He eyed his guest. "As the missile flies."

Barlow shook his head. "Is there a National Estimate covering the situation?"

"Last I heard CIA was preparing an all-source Estimate, but the DCI isn't able to release it to the National Security Council without presidential approval."

"The whole thing sounds damn incredible—I mean, I believe every word you've told me but why is red-hot stuff being withheld from top echelon?"

"I've got a one-word speculative answer: trade."

"Trade with China? Damn, Irv, educate me."

Chenow swallowed a bit of lamb, washed it down with a sip of Beaujolais. "The Veep put it succinctly. Trade with China means U.S. jobs, a lot of them. And jobs translate into votes. The economy, as you may have noticed, has taken some rough hits including military base closings leaving a lot of workers jobless—and angry. The Administration has all along been doing its damnedest to keep things smooth with China, not ruffle their feathers. My inference is the Administration prefers not to take notice of potential Chinese belligerence and hope they'll change their naughty ways."

"In Korea," said Barlow bitterly, "I flew against some of those Chinese bastards. Didn't like them then, don't like them now. Ol' Dugout Doug was right, y'know. Drop a couple of A-bombs on the cocksuckers and terminate the problem." He seemed to lapse into a reverie. "But Give 'Em Hell Harry didn't have the guts for it. So we fought a limited engagement out of deference to our European allies, never ventured north of the Yalu, and lost fifty-five thousand young Americans. Irv, it still makes my blood boil. And when I was a Cong prisoner in their stinkin' tiger cages I still thought about China and Korea, and concluded if we'd won that one, we wouldn't have had to go into Vietnam and lose a hundred, two hundred thousand more." Face flushed, he looked away. "Ben wanted to go to the Academy but I was against it, having seen how our politicians get us into wars they won't let us win. Private thoughts, Irving. I'm sick of Washington, politicians, intrigues, and all the rest of it. Can't wait to put in my papers and take off my suit."

"I always thought you were a contender for Chief of Staff."

Barlow laughed thinly. "Thought so myself years ago, but—got time for a story?"

"Of course."

"While I was a prisoner in North Vietnam my wife figured I'd never get back and started acting like a single girl, a swinger. Bedded half the Andrews Officers Club, I heard. When I finally showed up she kept her adulteries furtive but they came to light anyway, and I figured it was one thing for her to sleep around if she thought she was a widow, but when she knew damn well she wasn't—well, I wouldn't put up with it and we divorced."

Chenow nodded understandingly. "And you remarried."

"Very happily, I'm glad to say. But the upshot of all that is my seniors felt I hadn't played the Air Force game, and I was given to understand that the top prize would never be granted me."

"I guess I don't understand."

"Irv, my first wife, the one I divorced, was a general's daughter. And you don't embarrass a general's daughter or the general by divorcing her." He shrugged. "That's how it is. Oh, I'll get my gravestone promotion fourth star, but no further advancement. This assignment is my last. I've shed blood for my country, served it well, and now I'm ready to go fishing."

"I understand."

Barlow resumed eating, and after a while said, "Bottom line—you think Taiwan's in danger."

"I do. Assuming the missile warheads can release sarin or Tabun gas on impact, the island's population could be exterminated in a couple of hours. Chinese troops could cross the Taiwan Strait and stroll in at their leisure. The U.S., the U.N., and the rest of the world would be confronted with a fait accompli. Another man-made Holocaust, Bruce, a scenario that agonizes me."

"A terrible thought," he agreed, "but surely the President won't back off from warning the Chinese once he understands the situation and its possibilities."

"Who knows?" He spread his hands. "And why wait?"

General Barlow sucked in a deep breath. Sunlight glinted from his chest medals. "What's to be done?"

This was the moment he'd been maneuvering toward. Exploiting it, Chenow said, "I know the old U-2s are mothballed, but I guess you've got a few Blackbirds stashed here and there around the world."

"SR-71s." Barlow nodded. "Fastest, highest-flying aircraft in the world, bar none. You thinking of a photo-reconnaissance run?"

"I am, Bruce. It would accomplish two things. One, we'd get better target definition from Blackbird cameras than from satellite pictures, and we need the kind of indisputable proof that only lower-level photography can provide. Two, a Blackbird photo run doesn't violate any current Administration orders. I suspect you can order it as part of routine Mainland coverage." He paused. "Can you?"

After hesitating, Barlow nodded. "Take a little doing, a detour here and there, but I can have it done."

"Wonderful."

"Show me the area you want covered."

Chenow bent over, opened his briefcase, and extracted a small-scale map of East China on which he had outlined a long narrow oval that straddled the line indicating 118° East Longitude. He pointed out the Yangyuan warhead factory and Zhuolu chemical plant to the north, the Leping army missile base at the southern end. "Six or seven hundred miles, roughly."

Barlow smiled. "Flying at thirty-five miles a minute, the bird covers seven hundred miles in twenty minutes. And from seventy thousand feet the photos will look like you took them in your own backyard. You can read the numbers on the warhead casings. Good enough?"

"Plenty good enough." He sighed, felt his palms slick with perspiration, but tenseness was wearing away.

Barlow said, "We've got Blackbirds—on Okinawa, Luzon, and Atsugi that can do the job. I'll tell the Assistant Chief of Staff A-2 to get birds aloft, have the product transmitted to me. Eyes Only."

Chenow cleared his throat. "Is he likely to ask why?"

"He better not. At the Academy we were drilled that only three responses to a superior are permissible: Yes, sir; No, sir; and No excuse, sir."

Chenow smiled. "Not quite what we learned in law school, but each profession has its own customs and rules."

"Right." He glanced at his wrist chronometer. "From the time I get back to my office I'd say a Blackbird will be airborne within four hours. This will *really* be a black flight." He looked at his host. "One thing you haven't told me: When you have the photos, what do you intend to do with them?"

"Go public."

General Barlow stared at him. "Go . . . *public?*"

"Unless the President acts first. No other way to warn off the Chinese, and force the President to do the right thing."

"Jesus, Irv, you've got a wagonload of guts hid in that little frame of yours." He chuckled. "I shoulda known that, the way you fought for Ben. Anyway, in for a shilling in for a pound."

"If the heat gets to you, blame me."

"Don't like snitches, Irv, and I'm not one. Hell, we'll try to do the right thing, and take what comes." He pocketed the map and got up. "Hate to leave this splendid meal, but it's dark in the target zone right now, and I want coverage there starting at dawn."

"Bruce, I don't know what to say other than I'm grateful."

"Save thanks till later." He drained his wineglass. "Knew you could count on me, did you?"

"I hoped I could."

"Hoped. Irving, listen up. You saved my son, and now you're giving me an opportunity to maybe save a whole race of people. In retirement that knowledge is going to mean a hell of a lot more to me than one more medal, one final star." Turning, he crossed the patio, went down the brick steps, and strode toward where he had left his car.

Chenow sat at the table staring at Barlow's empty chair. They're not making them like him anymore, he mused, so have I done right involving him? Am I doing the right thing for our country? He picked up his briefcase and rose. We'll see.

TAIPEI, TAIWAN

MARK BRAND ADJUSTED the motorized recliner so he could better see Philip Lichter, Taiwan Chief of Station, who asked, "How you feeling, Mark?"

"Better, considerably better." He looked at the needle in his arm through which his veins were receiving a flow of plasma and antibiotics from plastic bags above and behind his head.

They were in the Soong House, a lavish lodge maintained by the Agency for VIP guests ever since the late Gimo rented it to the CIA for a dollar a year. The Soong family wanted it back, but the Agency was not inclined to accede and violate long-standing tradition. So the house was maintained in immaculate condition, and fully staffed with aging servants from the Mainland.

"Have you talked with Peter?" Brand asked.

Lichter shrugged. "Tried to, but he corked off. Sleeping in his room."

Brand nodded. "Good. He's gone through a lot."

Lichter grunted. "Perhaps in time I'll be made privy to some of what the hell's going on around here."

"Possibly." Brand smiled, and gazed at the COS. Philip A. Lichter, Ph.D., was slightly over forty. He wore thick lenses and a full, well-trimmed beard appropriate to his scholarly background.

"Good of you to think of me," Lichter said sarcastically, "when you brought in unannounced your son and yourself, three dangerous-looking individuals I'd type-cast as Kowloon cutthroats, and the pilots of a stolen plane."

"Well, you responded to the situation with alacrity, got me stitched up, and my companions bedded down. I really appreciate it."

"Let me tell you, the airport staff was reluctant to let you go until I said I'd take personal responsibility for the lot of you."

"Whatever that means. Listen, Phil, you continue clinging to that by-the-book bullshit and they might make you Director."

"Oh, sure. And though I haven't notified headquarters, you and your traveling companions arrived here in the dead of night, violating Taiwan airspace and operating procedures—you with a gunshot wound to flavor the drama—not a Taiwan visa among you, to say nothing of a passport shortage—"

"I've got two of them—Peter can use one."

"—and the local authorities I have to deal with want all of you off the island, and fast. Now, I don't have any real hope I'll learn the truth of this episode from you, but I have to cable headquarters something pretty damn soon." He opened his mouth and with his thumbnail tried to dislodge a foreign object between two upper teeth. Failing that, he said, "My problem is this: What do I say to headquarters?"

"Anything you like. Darman Gerold will be relieved to learn my son and I are in safe hands."

"Gerold?" One hand ran through his bushy hair. "He's behind this?"

"Where do you think the Canadian passport came from?"

"TSD?"

Brand nodded.

"Be damned. Didn't know you were still with the Agency . . . but that alters the situation."

"Need-to-know basis, Phil. Heavy secrecy." He breathed deeply. Stress and loss of blood had drained his energy. "On that basis I'll tell you this is the penultimate page of an extraction operation. My son serviced a drop in Canton—a hot drop as it turned out—and got arrested. Secret trial in Beijing and a long prison sentence. He broke out of prison, and I went to Beijing to bring him back."

Lichter stared in astonishment. "Then your son's an agent."

"Co-opted as a Legal Traveler by Applegate's shop."

Lichter nodded thoughtfully. After a while he removed his glasses and polished the lenses. Replacing them, he said, "What about the plane? The pilots say you hijacked it."

"They need counseling," Brand told him. "But as to the plane it was made available by a Taiwan-born fellow named Cheong Wing-dah.

He came along to make sure everything went well, but no one realized he had a pathological case of claustrophobia plus acrophobia. Partway here Cheong ran screaming to the cargo door, opened it, and dived out." Brand rolled his eyes. "You can imagine the impact on the rest of us, how the death of our benefactor zapped our morale. Well, in Cheong's absence someone had to take charge so I told the pilots where to go and what to do." He shook his head. "Didn't realize the air crew was going to get unnerved and hysterical, so we can discount anything they say." He paused. "Pending counseling."

"What a hell of a story! And they said nothing ever happens at Taiwan Station."

"Don't even think that, Phil, you're in the thick of the action so be proud of it. In fact," he continued musingly, "before long you'll be notified of Mainland developments that could threaten this happy isle."

"No shit? The long-awaited invasion?"

"Maybe worse—but that's not for me to reveal." He smiled. "Need-to-know, sorry."

Lichter thought it over. "Okay, whatever the future holds, I'll handle it. Right now I've got to smooth things over with the locals. They want to expel all seven of you and keep the plane."

"I'll go along with expulsion. As for the aircraft, I assume it now belongs to Cheong's widow. Like her late husband she was born here and enjoys certain Taiwanese birthrights—including possession of private property. The plane can stay here until Madame Cheong decides what to do with it. The pilots, though—they're in unstable condition. Ought to be detained here for maybe a week's orientation. Can you manage that?"

"No problem. What about the rest of you?"

"We'll fly commercial from here to Hong Kong. After that, back to the Beltway."

Lichter nodded, looked at the tubes running into Brand's arm. "When do you want to leave?"

"Tomorrow afternoon okay?"

"Under the circumstances I feel I can justify flying you to Kai Tak in Station aircraft."

"Even better," Brand said appreciatively. "Meanwhile, I suggest you let Gerold know Peter and I arrived safely from the Mainland and anticipate onward travel over the next few days. No details."

"Sure, that covers my ass."

"Transmit routine precedence, LimDis, info Briggs Dockerty and Jason Whitbread. They'll welcome the news."

"Okay, Mark. I was a little pissed off to be yanked out of bed, but now that you've put me in the picture I'm glad to be part of it." He got up from his chair. "The doc'll be by for a look-see after breakfast." He frowned. "You didn't say how you got the bullet wound."

"It's embarrassing. Fooled with a loaded pistol, not mine, and took a round in the arm. Not proud of it, Phil, so I'll thank you to keep it quiet."

"Whatever you say. See you in the morning."

He watched Lichter leave the dimly lighted room, and reflected that things had gone better than anticipated. The Station plane would land at Kai Tak and park in the crowded General Aviation area. Yang, Wo, and San would vanish, while he and Peter put up at the Hilton where Nina was not likely to be.

He thought of telephoning Mary, but decided to see her at the gallery instead. It was his obligation to tell her of Cheong's death, introduce Peter to her and Chu-li, and begin making plans that would bind them together for the rest of their lives.

After a while, a jacketed houseman came silently in, saw Brand was sleeping, and left as silently as he had come.

Thirty-One

ATSUGI AIR BASE, HONSHU PREFECTURE, JAPAN

AT 0215 HOURS, PREFLIGHT CHECKS having been completed by ground crew and rechecked, pilot Lt. Col. Keith McAwley, USAF, received a short weather update and signaled his recon officer, Major Burt Sampas,

USAF, that it was time to get going. In bulky pressure suits they climbed parallel ladders into their respective cockpits and heard external clanking that signified fuel being added to top off the tanks.

In his forward cockpit McAwley punched course headings into the computer guidance system that would control the aircraft through most of the estimated four-hour flight. He put on his helmet, plugged in radio earphones, and spoke to Sampas. After hearing Sampas's voice, the pilot called tower control and learned that no aircraft were in the vicinity of Atsugi, some forty miles west-southwest of Tokyo. "Ready," he said and closed the hatch, feeling the towing tractor's tug as it drew the aircraft out of the hangar.

Like all SAC pilots privileged to fly his aircraft, McAwley knew that it had been designed by Kelly Johnson, the Lockheed genius who created the slower, now obsolete U-2 in a bygone era when photo coverage of the Soviet Union was critical to national defense. Only two U-2 aircraft had ever been shot down; one over the USSR, the other over Cuba as the Soviet missile crisis was heating up.

Since then, satellite coverage of target countries had diminished but not eliminated the need for manned aircraft, such as the one he was preparing to fly. Satellites were tireless, required no fuel or landing bases, and were immune to interception. Yet, sharp as satellite cameras were, their distance from photo targets left a definition gap that manned reconnaissance aircraft could fill.

McAwley felt forward motion stop, heard and felt the tow tractor disengage, and realized he had reached the flight line.

Powered by two Pratt & Whitney JT11D engines delivering thirty-two tons of thrust, the SR-71 could fly at two thousand miles an hour at eighty thousand feet. Above a hundred thousand feet it could exceed Mach 3.

"Ready?" McAwley asked.

Sampas replied, "Ready, man. Just bring us home, okay?"

"That's a promise." He flicked on the burners and the fuselage shivered while brakes restrained it against the twin jets' enormous thrust. He watched the digital readings until takeoff power was reached, released the brakes, and the matte-black fuselage catapulted forward, its incandescent jets spewing flames like the snouts of a fire-snorting dragon.

Despite max fuel load, the SR-71 lifted quickly off the runway, and

McAwley pulled it into a steep climb that would have stalled a less powerful bird. One eye on the altimeter, he glimpsed the distant lights of Tokyo under the stubby wing. At ten thousand feet, he killed the afterburners and notched the airspeed forward beyond Mach 1, where it stayed until the altimeter registered fifty thousand feet. The computer turned the still-climbing aircraft westward on a course heading of 253° true that would take it to the Initial Point far above the northern border of China and Mongolia. Then it would descend to fifty thousand feet and begin the recon photo run.

This was a special mission, McAwley knew, ordered by Headquarters USAF rather than by the Strategic Air Command. He had just arrived with his family at their summer bungalow outside Kamakura when his beeper sounded, and he knew that the family weekend was not to be.

Not for seven months had he been ordered to make a run over China; his normal coverage was North Korea and the Kuriles, so something must have come up requiring high precision coverage of a specific segment of the Mainland.

Here in the tropopause the SR-71 was well above earth's weather patterns, the temperature a steady minus seventy degrees. The sky was indigo, pierced by stars brighter than diamonds. McAwley loved the pure joy of high flight that let him feel one with the endless universe.

The console's instrumentation was A-okay. In place of bombs, the aircraft's belly was jammed with video cameras and electronic gear to make them function when the photo run began.

At a hundred thousand feet the spy plane leveled off and accelerated to nearly Mach 3 in the frictionless atmosphere. From astern, had there been human observers, the twin jets were pale pink dots against the night's deep indigo as the Blackbird flashed like a missile through the night.

WASHINGTON

THE PRESIDENT HAD CALLED a morning meeting in the Roosevelt Room of the White House to avoid his appointments secretary listing the attendees.

Excluding the President, seven officials were present.

At the President's right was the Secretary of State, next to him the National Security Adviser. On the President's left were the Secretary of Defense, the Director of Central Intelligence, the Chairman of the Joint Chiefs of Staff, and Presidential Counsel Jerry King, who had arrived tardily and gained a glare from the President who, he thought, looked tired from his Asian trip, and in a lousy mood.

Without preliminaries the President said, "I've been informed of a development in Mainland China that appears to contain potential elements of a really bad situation that can involve our national security interests up to and including combat with the Chinese." He looked around the table. "How many know what I'm talking about?"

The Secretary of State, the Veep, and the DCI raised their hands.

"Only three? When I leave town doesn't word get around where it ought to?"

The Vice President cleared his throat. "Pending your return, sir, I felt it best to restrict knowledge of the subject. My purpose was to prevent premature leaks so that you would be able to review the entire situation including options."

"Good idea in principle," the President responded, and eyed the Secretary of State. "You were with me, so like me you were out of the info loop. The Deputy Secretary of State?"

"Brussels, Mr. President, heading our delegation to the G-7 conference. In his absence, the Assistant Secretary of State for Asian Affairs, Irving Chenow, represented State's interests."

"Irving, eh? Probably did his usual thorough job." Having tossed a small bouquet to the absent Chenow, the President looked at Vance Jordan, his National Security Adviser. "Any of this China stuff reach your sacred precincts?"

"No, sir."

The President leaned forward and set his elbows on the table. "Any idea why not, Vance?"

"Apparently there was an embargo on the information."

"I see. You mean a communications breakdown?"

"Actually, sir, I mean the NSC was cut off."

The President sighed, faced left, and spoke to Defense Secretary Billings. "How about your shop?"

"Same situation, I'm afraid, sir. I checked with Joint Chiefs Chairman Sosnowski before coming here. He didn't have a clue."

General Sosnowski nodded concurrence, and the President tapped the table irritably. Counsel Jerry King said, "Me neither, sir."

The President shook his head in wonderment. "To me it's incredible that of you seven gentlemen only three had knowledge of this potentially disastrous situation. Apparently the bad news was piling up for my return. Now, I'm not going to take time to brief those of you who don't know about Dragon Teeth. Instead, I strongly recommend you read the National Estimate prepared by the Director, and become familiar with the background of the China problem we face." He lapsed into silence, broken only by the muffled ticking of an antique grandfather clock acquired by Jackie when she refurbished the White House. "I'm going to ask some questions," he said, "and I want only straight answers. Starting with this: Will the Chinese launch gas missiles against Taiwan?"

Defense Secretary Billings said, "Haven't the faintest, not having read the NE."

The DCI said, "Yesterday a cargo aircraft delivered about forty missile warheads from the Beijing area to an army missile base inland from Taiwan. Based on ground intelligence we believe the warheads contain binary compounds for lethal gas."

"To repeat," the President said impatiently, "will the Chinese use them?"

"I don't know, sir. Intentions are the hardest area to judge."

Chairman Sosnowski said, "I'll ask NSA for a readout on any Chinese radio traffic that could provide indications."

"Good. Do that, and fast."

The Secretary of State said, "The Chinese may be bluffing, Mr. President."

"Of course—they're among the world's best bluffers. But why would they set something that serious in motion if it's only a bluff? And who are they bluffing? Us? The Taiwanese? I don't get it."

The Director said, "I'm puzzled why the Chinese would do all they've done in a comparatively open fashion. They know we have satellite coverage, know we run Blackbird reconnaissance flights. Why so little concealment?"

"Exactly," said the Secretary of State. "Tending to bolster the bluff theory." He looked around with a pleased expression.

"Or possibly," the President remarked, "the Chinese don't give a fuck for us or anyone else. Let's not exclude *that* from our thinking." His gaze fixed on the Vice President at the far end of the table. "You had a handle on this from the onset, so presumably you know as much as anyone present. After the meeting I'd appreciate you sharing your thinking with me."

"Of course, Mr. President."

Several of those present smiled inwardly. The President was going to take the Veep to the woodshed.

"So," said the President, "there's no consensus on Chinese intentions. They go to the trouble of making gas warheads and flying them to a launching base within easy range of our treaty partner, Taiwan. Am I to suppose they plan to let the missiles just sit on their launchers until they rust away? Why would they do that? If they're in a bluffing mode, I ask again, who do they hope to bluff?"

None of the officials responded.

"Okay," the President said after a long, silent pause. "Let's stop talking about bluff—the word's abused its welcome. I think our thoughts should concentrate on a posed threat—like a drawn pistol."

Unbidden, General Sosnowski said, "I have something of possible relevance to the situation. Only an hour ago I was informed that one of our Blackbird photo reconnaissance aircraft was shot down."

"Damn!" The President's fist slammed the table. "Where?"

"Just off the East China coast."

The DCI looked astonished. He turned to the Secretary of Defense who shrugged and muttered, "Knew nothing about it."

The Secretary of State's face whitened. "What was it doing there?"

Sosnowski said, "As far as I've been able to determine, the Blackbird, out of Atsugi, Japan, was making a north–south run not far from the China coast. A signal confirmed the run was completed and the Blackbird was turning back toward Japan. A satellite caught the flash of an exploding aircraft, and the Blackbird never reached Atsugi."

"My God!" the President exclaimed. "Did a Chinese fighter intercept it?"

"I doubt it, sir. The Blackbird is faster than any fighter aircraft in the world. So, either the Blackbird was hit by a missile, or for unknown reasons it exploded."

The President grimaced. "This hasn't been an easy morning, and I sense it's going to get worse. Have the Chinese said anything?"

"No, sir," the Secretary of State replied. "At least not yet."

"Will the Chinese have wreckage to point to like the Soviets did with that U-2?"

"Apparently what was left of the plane fell into the sea."

"So," said the President, "we have egg on our face again. And whatever the rationale for the Blackbird flight—and I'll want to hear about it—the photos it took disappeared with the plane."

"No, sir," the Secretary of Defense said. "There was so much time lag between photo taking, film development, and product receipt that the Air Force last year developed a system of electronic video cameras that record images on tape just as in the old film system. The big improvement is this: As the cameras record, the images are transmitted simultaneously to a Delos communications satellite that relays them—I hardly understand the process myself—to a dedicated receiver. On Okinawa, probably, or directly to NRO, or the Pentagon."

"I'll be damned," the President exclaimed. "Why didn't someone tell me about this?"

Adviser Vance Jordan said, "Technical stuff, sir, nothing to bother you with."

The President eyed him coldly. "Sounds like a tremendous technical leap to me, and I want to know about those things, okay?"

"Yes, sir."

"Now," the President continued, "assuming the coverage was transmitted before the plane went down, it seems fair to presume it's somewhere and can be retrieved? Even put to use?"

"I'm fully sure it's locatable," the Secretary of Defense responded, "and NRO is probably interpreting it even now."

The Secretary of State said, "While you fellows are beating the bushes for that good stuff, I'd kinda like to know who authorized the overflight, and why. Seems strange to go baiting the Chinese when we've been bendin' over backward to keep 'em happy. At the least, the timing seems—how shall I put it?—unfortunate." Pausing, he sat back in his chair. "Time was when my office cleared reconnaissance flights over foreign territory, and I don't rightly recall when the practice stopped."

"I can brief you on that," the Defense Secretary rejoined, "but let's not take everyone's time with it."

The President smiled thinly. "I suspect the overflight was conducted to give us more information on the Dragon Teeth situation. But since the Vice President has told us the existence of the problem was known to only a handful, who instigated the mission? I want to know by day's end."

"Had to be a leak," the DCI said flatly.

Chairman Sosnowski said, "Blackbird overflights are controlled by SAC, so it won't be difficult to determine authorization."

"Good," the President said. "Then we can start to find out the rationale." He breathed deeply and stared at his hands on the table. "If the Chinese protest the overflight, I suppose we can say the plane strayed off course, sorry and all that."

The Secretary of State nodded approval. "Good tack. Keep 'em in good humor."

Ignoring his offering, the President said, "Tomorrow, same time, I want you all here and thoroughly familiar with the National Estimate so options can be considered. Today, Vance, you're to distribute all available Dragon Teeth information to the NSC. Hand-carry packets to each member and get signed receipts. This is strictly need-to-know, and I don't want—I mean *any*—word escaping authorized channels." He paused. "Too many damn cowboys around—apologies, Mr. Secretary, no offense intended—and it's of crucial importance the Chinese don't become aware we know about their damn gas missiles. Could provoke them into firing them, and I'd be under all kinds of pressure to bomb Beijing. In fact," he ruminated, "the mere rumor of trouble between China and Taiwan, and China and us *over* Taiwan, would give us an economic hit we absolutely cannot afford to take. Only two days ago in Singapore the Secretary of the Treasury was telling me the economy's headed for a downturn, and I sure as hell don't want to see it turn into a plunge. Which could be the case if this Dragon Teeth megillah is even hinted at." He looked at his watch. "Hermetic secrecy, understand? Okay, I'll see you tomorrow, by which time we all should be a hell of a lot better informed."

All present except the Vice President got up and filed from the room. The President glanced at him, said, "Oh, you, yeah, I wanted a private word with you," and beckoned him to the head of the table.

While the Veep remained standing, the President said, "In my absence, and I put this frankly and charitably, you acted like an ignorant asshole. I find it incredible that a man of your intelligence and familiarity with government just sat on intelligence information that any idiot can see is crucial to our national security, not to mention the security, maybe even the survival, of Taiwan. So tell me, when you forbade distribution to the NSC, didn't anyone object?"

"No, sir, not as I heard," the Veep replied stiffly.

"Any discussion?"

"No, sir."

"And I'll bet you didn't invite any. All right, I've had my say, you've heard me. Now I want to know what factor or factors decided you to withhold Dragon Teeth intelligence from those who could best evaluate and maybe use it?"

"May I sit down, sir?"

"Sure, have a seat." The President kicked back from the table without taking his gaze from the Vice President.

"I did it for you, sir."

The President stared at him. "For *me?* You crazy? Too long in the desert sun? You better explain that."

"The whole government, not excluding the White House, leaks like a sieve. By keeping everything under tight wraps while you were gone, I managed to keep the bean-counters and typists and copiers from learning about it, and maybe opening up the can of worms. Like you said yourself premature word could sink the market and the economy, and as I've heard you say five hundred times, trade means jobs, and jobs translate into votes. We got billions in trade with China, I don't need to remind you. If the Chinese hear rumors like we know about their damn gas warheads, they'll close up tighter'n a bull's ass in fly-time, and this Administration will face a lot of questions, like, what are we gonna do about it? Gonna save Taiwan, or sit on our hands and let twenty million people be gassed to death." He shook his head. "You came down hard on me, Mr. President, and I don't think I deserved it. There's renomination and reelection ahead of us and all I was tryin' to do for a few days there was keep the lid on the situation. Well, you're back now, you're in charge. Vance'll get the NSC off its collective ass and come up with action options for you. Whatever you decide, I salute an' run up the flag. I'm loyal to you, and I'm loyal to this country that's done so much for this country boy, and I want to see its greatness expand without the loss of a single soldier on the Mainland or Taiwan."

Dryly the President said, "Thank you, sir, but spare me that excerpt from your standard speech. Greatness is okay, but I'm not sure the country boy stuff is appropriate for modern times, modern thinking. Here and abroad people could begin looking at us as shit-kicking farmers lacking education and talent to govern."

The Vice President said, "We ran and got elected on a down-home populist ticket."

"Right. Populism is fine and we'll trot it out again—once every four years is about right. Like whiskey it has beneficial effects but shouldn't be abused. The opposition would love to depict us as barnyard buffoons, and we can't afford that image."

"No, sir," the Veep said reluctantly.

"Getting back to the main issue, we've started off losing a billion-dollar aircraft and two skilled Air Force officers. Whether the sacrifice is worth anything depends on what those dedicated young men sent back before being blown to bits. As of today I'm issuing an Executive Order canceling all manned spy flights until further notice. Meanwhile, I'm going to find out how those pilots got where they were, who sent them. Full info. But if we're lucky maybe only the widows will learn their husbands were destroyed photographing China." He ran one hand over thick, razor-cut hair. "Maybe I'll call Chairman Deng and tell him to dismantle those gas missiles. Maybe we'll launch a couple of cruise missiles to knock them out. Maybe we'll simply wait to see how the China scenario plays out. I don't know. I need time. Time to hear the full story, learn the options, and make decisions. Until I've accomplished that any leaks will be treated as criminal offenses, espionage, subversion, conspiracy—whatever." He got up and the Veep rose beside him. "You did an excellent job keeping the situation bottled up. So until we're past this Dragon Teeth crisis I'm putting you in charge of security as it relates to our concerns. No measures too extreme. Stay away from the NSC, let Vance Jordan chair it. Now, I'll be spending midday in New York speaking to the Business Council, with a fund-raising reception afterward. I'll study my speech on the plane. You get busy."

The Vice President said, "So I understand you—I'm in full charge of Dragon Teeth security."

"That's it." The President walked to the door, opened it, and looked back. "Have a good day."

Thirty-Two

HONG KONG

DURING BREAKFAST IN THEIR Hilton room, Brand said, "Peter, this is going to be a memorable day for you, for both of us."

"Right. First day back after my wretched Mainland adventure."

"More than that."

"Of course—I'm to meet Cheong's widow."

"Well, let's not think of Mary as someone's widow. Think of her as the girl I loved and left on Taiwan. Long story, Peter, but it all comes together today." He started to lift the coffeepot, winced, and set it down.

Peter picked it up and filled their cups. "How's the arm?"

"Better than yesterday. But call the desk and have the hotel doctor sent up—I think the bandage needs changing."

While Peter was at the phone, the door buzzer sounded and Brand admitted a short man with bristling red hair and a red mustache. "Morning, sir," he said, "Jamie McPherson at your service." He opened a satchel and spread sample swatches across the bed.

Peter replaced the receiver and said, "Within half an hour."

"Good. Peter, meet Mr. McPherson of the house of McIntosh, an estimable tailoring establishment well known to your grandfather and me."

"My pleasure, sir," McPherson said, shaking hands with Peter. "Your father looks a bit worse for wear, but how is the good doctor these days?"

"Active as always," Brand responded, and began going over samples with Peter. They selected flannel and worsted suitings, Shetland and Donegal tweed for jackets, and submitted to the tailor's painstaking measuring. After that, Brand said, "We'll need a white and blue shirt each; gray, black, and brown stockings."

The tailor eyed him over half lenses. "Over-the-calf length, no doubt."

"No doubt."

McPherson consulted his watch. "I'll have your suits here by five o'clock, jackets and slacks tomorrow. Will that be satisfactory?"

"Entirely."

He folded the tape measure into his pocket, replaced swatches in the satchel, and said, "Good to see you again, sir, it's been a few years. And my respects to the good doctor."

Peter let him out and said, "Dad, we need shoes."

"There's a shop off the lobby. We'll check it on the way out." He paused. "Incidentally, that borrowed suit you're wearing looks like it was dragged the length of the Yangtze."

Peter smiled. "It does, doesn't it. Shall I send it back?"

"When McPherson returns, give him the suit and tell him to duplicate it in a better quality material. What's the sergeant's name?"

"Bailey."

"Give McPherson his name, and he'll ship it to the Beijing embassy."

"Great idea." Peter answered the door buzzer and let in a round-faced, bespectacled gentleman with a physician's bag. "Mr. Brand? What can I do for you, sir?"

With Peter's help, Brand got off his shirt and heard the doctor whistle. "Still bleeding, eh? How long?"

"Couple of days. I was patched up in Taipei."

"I'm Dr. Lau Ye Chai. Be seated and we'll see what's to be done."

After cutting off bandages, the doctor whistled again. "Gunshot wound, eh?" He pressed the stitches until Brand yelped.

"How long since you had an antibiotic?"

"Yesterday afternoon."

"I'll give you another shot before I leave. No evident infection, but then we don't want any, do we?"

"We don't."

Peter smiled. "Definitely not," and watched the doctor change the bandage, then stick a hypo in his father's thigh.

That done, Brand rubbed the smarting area and said, "I'd be grateful for some pain pills."

"Absolutely." Dr. Lau counted six capsules into a paper envelope and closed his medical bag. He whistled as he made out his bill.

Peter paid him, and the doctor left a professional card before departing. Peter asked, "How do you feel now?"

"No worse. I heard you talking with La-li last night. How is she?"

"Says she's over morning sickness, but had to quit her job. Grandfather keeps in touch with her."

"Said he would."

"Dad, you've been great through this whole thing, and I—"

"You've been pretty great yourself so it balances out. Okay, look up the number for Celestial Galleries and dial it for me."

After taking the receiver from him, Brand heard the soft voice of Chu-li and said, "Good morning, Chu-li, Mark Brand calling for your mother. Is she there?"

"Not at the moment, sir. Oh—you're in Hong Kong!"

"With my son. And we—"

"But that's wonderful! I'm so anxious to hear about it—you're both safe and well?"

"We are, and looking forward to seeing your mother. Ah—Chu-li, could you give us a convenient time when we can come by—and pay our respects to you both?"

"Let me think—I'm alone at the gallery while Madame—Mother, that is—went Kowloon-side to see some antiquity dealers. So I can't say when she'll be back."

"Then, perhaps you'd call me later at the Hilton. Room 923."

"Of course. And—I'm thrilled that you found Peter. We—we worried about you."

To Peter, he said, "They'll call later. Now, see if you can raise Briggs Dockerty at the consulate."

HALF AN HOUR LATER Dockerty arrived, and after introducing him to Peter, Brand said, "I bring greetings from Jason Whitbread and Phil Lichter. Collectively they did a lot toward bringing Peter back."

"Good to hear." Dockerty slumped in an overstuffed chair and studied Peter. "Someone owes you a shipload of apologies and I'll start with me. On behalf of the Station I deeply regret that fucked-up mission, and all that happened to you as a result."

"Thanks," Peter said politely. "There were plenty of times I thought I'd never see my father again."

"Well, you have, and he's here—but not in prime condition, I see—if the bandage means anything." He peered at Brand's arm. "How long you going to be around?"

"Couple of days, why?"

"Got a NIACT Priority from Darman slugged DRAGON TEETH. Know what it means?"

Brand shrugged. "What's the text?"

"Headquarters wants you both sworn not to reveal anything you learned on the Mainland."

"Isn't that a little strange? I thought your office would be salivating to debrief Peter."

"Normally, yes, but I guess headquarters wants the privilege. Anyway, I brought papers to sign—if you don't mind." He took folded sheets from an inside pocket and laid them on the coffee table. After scanning the typed oath, Brand set it down and frowned. "No period mentioned, so it could be perpetuity."

"Headquarters framed it, not me."

"Besides, Peter's a civilian. He has no obligation to comply with the Agency's whims."

"But I suspect you do."

"I also suspect I'm in bad odor with the powers that be. Can't very well defend myself if I can't mention Mainland happenings."

"I suppose not. What do I tell Darman?"

"Tell him Peter's not going to sign anything, and as for me I'll consider the proposal and discuss it when I return."

"Fair enough." He refolded the papers and returned them to his pocket. "Last time we met we had Darman's problem daughter on our hands. Wonder how she's getting along."

"He was going to have her detoxed and rehabbed, not that it hasn't been done before. Incidentally, Peter's passport was lifted by the Gong An Ju, so he needs one to travel on. Can you take care of it—like maybe today?"

"Why not? A fax to State, a return fax to the consulate, and it's done."

"Good. While on the subject, I suppose the Agency still has a bloc of immigration permits for worthy foreigners?"

"I guess. Haven't had to apply for any since I've been here."

"But you could."

"I could—based on what?"

"My word."

Peter glanced at his father but said nothing. Dockerty said, "I might have a problem with that if you're thinking of your villain-friends."

"No. Otherwise—?"

"I can probably squeeze it." He eyed Brand's bandage again, pursed his lips, and said, "I'll send the passport when it's ready."

"Many thanks, Briggs. All things being equal we'd like to fly back tomorrow night or the night after."

"Shall I tell Darman?"

"Rather you didn't. After what we've gone through—particularly Peter—we need some time and space to get things together."

"Understandable." He shook hands again with Peter and left the room.

Peter said, "He seems pretty efficient, Dad."

"Within limits," Brand remarked, and sent Peter down to buy shaving gear.

IT WAS NOON BEFORE Chu-li called back. "Mother suggests we dine together this evening—unless you have plans."

"None at all. Where will we meet?"

"At the gallery. Our apartment is adjacent to the office, so just come at six. She's very anxious to see you—and meet Peter—and so am I. She said she hasn't seen him since he was a toddler."

"He's grown," Brand said with a smile, "and soon to be married." He paused. "A Chinese girl, by the way."

"Really—that should please her." Chu-li's voice lowered. "I know my father offered to help you on the Mainland—we wonder if he did."

"Yes, Chu-li, and I'll tell about it at dinner."

"I'm very glad of that," she said, "because . . . well, you know how concerned I was before you left."

"I know," he said, suppressing emotion, "and I'll never forget it."

Leaving the telephone, he looked at Peter. "Dinner at six. We need to send flowers, or whatever the lobby boutique suggests for the occasion."

"I'll take care of it," Peter volunteered, "and I don't envy you having to tell Mary her husband's dead. And Chu-li—won't be easy for her." He put one hand gently on Brand's shoulder. "Losing you would be more than I could bear."

"I hope we always stay this close," Brand said, "because there's a special bond we share."

AT FOUR O'CLOCK A consulate employee delivered Peter's replacement passport. Peter signed the passport and receipt and said, "Thank you, and thank Mr. Dockerty."

At five o'clock a porter wheeled in a rack of clothing, followed by Jamie McPherson, who rubbed his hands together and said, "We prefer our clients have at least one try-on fitting, but I thought speed more important. Any needed alterations can be managed tomorrow."

Peter got into a new shirt and then the oxford-gray flannel suit. McPherson pinched it here and there and said, "Not perfect, but we did well on short notice. Mr. Brand?"

Brand tried on a matching suit, wincing as his arm went through the left sleeve. McPherson said, "I make the same observation, sir, but it should do for the evening."

"And do very well," Brand said, and saw McPherson lift a hanger of neckties from the rack. "You didn't mention these, but I brought along an assortment."

"Simply forgot," Brand said, and selected two repps for himself and a conservatively figured silk on dark blue background. "We're very pleased, Mr. McPherson. Thank you for your thoughtfulness."

McPherson transferred the other suits to their closet rack, shook hands with both Brands, and left.

When they were dressed, Peter said, "It's good to have my own clothing again. I really didn't look forward to meeting my future stepmother in the sergeant's rags. First impressions are important."

"Very. How do I look?"

"Like Cary Grant. Ready? Let's go."

*   *   *

A HOTEL LIMOUSINE TOOK THEM to the gallery, which was closed for business, but through the glass door Brand could see Chu-li waiting inside. That's my daughter, he thought in a surge of pride, and rapped on the door.

She came toward them, wearing an ankle-length gown of iridescent silk, a jade-link necklace, and hair swept back from her forehead and gathered behind in a French braid. Peter gulped. "My God, Chu-li?"

She unlocked the heavy door and stood aside, locking it when they were inside. Peter gazed around in awe until his father said, "Chu-li, my son Peter."

Bowing politely, she said, "I am very pleased to make your acquaintance, sir."

"Peter, please."

Chu-li said, "We can talk in the apartment; let's not keep Mother waiting."

So they followed her through the gallery, and up the staircase to the second floor. She led them through the office to a teak door carved with Chinese symbols and opened it.

Beyond lay the marble-floored foyer, whose centerpiece was a fountain whose pool rim followed the graceful curvings of the traditional axe-head form. Water issued from the jaws of a stylized green celadon dragon and fell on the pool surface, below which could be seen the moving colors of carp and goldfish. The scent of jasmine hung in the cool air.

"It's beautiful," Brand said, "did you design it, Chu-li?"

"Mother and I together." She turned and Brand saw Mary coming through a doorway to greet them.

She was dressed in white silk, smock over trousers, and went directly to Peter. On tiptoes, she kissed his cheek and said, "I remember you when you could barely walk, Peter. You were a beautiful boy and you've become a handsome man."

Peter blushed. "Thank you—shall I call you Mary as my father does?"

"Please do. And I am so happy and grateful that you returned safely to your father's side." She glanced at Brand. "We are very old friends, you know."

"My father has spoken of you."

"Mark, the flowers are beautiful."

"Peter chose them."

"Your taste is excellent," she said, and took Brand's hand. "Let us drink to your safe return." She led them through the doorway into a large living room furnished with Chinese pieces upholstered in white and red. She spoke to a female servant, then to Brand. "In Taipei, I remember we drank tea mostly, and wine."

"Very little wine," he said, "and then on occasions when your revered father played host." He noticed that from the side, Chu-li was watching Peter. "Now," he said, "if there is wine I would welcome it."

They sat around a low table of polished rosewood, and lifted jadeite cups to each other's health. Then Mary said, "Chu-li said that Cheong Wing-dah assisted your escape from China. If that is so, Mark, I am very pleased that I asked for his help."

"So am I," Peter said.

Brand added, "Without it we wouldn't be here."

Mary reached for Peter's hand and held it. Brand set down his cup and said, "There is no easy way to say this, but there is virtue in brevity. Cheong Wing-dah died during our escape."

Mary's face was impassive, but Chu-li's hand covered her mouth as tears streaked her face. "Oh, Mother," she gasped, "oh, Mother," and left the table. Brand saw her slump against the wall, shoulders shaking.

Leaning forward, Mary said, "I leave to your discretion how much you tell me, but I ask this, Mark: Did you kill him?"

"No," Brand said, and Peter echoed the word.

"The rest is unimportant. At another time you may tell me more if you care to. Meanwhile"—she looked at her daughter—"what shall I tell Chu-li?"

"Say Wing-dah's heart gave out while aiding our escape."

"I don't mean that, Mark—you know what I mean." She glanced at Peter. "Does he know?"

Brand shook his head.

Peter said, "What don't I know?"

Mary breathed deeply, called Chu-li to return, and said, "There is no longer reason to withhold my secret."

Dabbing her eyes, Chu-li asked, "What secret, Mother?"

"Your parentage, child. Long ago in Taipei Mark and I were lovers.

Yes, it is true. We loved each other deeply, but he was called away by his government, and"—she hesitated—"I found I was with child."

"Mother!"

"We are all creatures of destiny, my honored father often said, and subject to the whims of the gods. My father arranged marriage with Wing-dah, who had long desired my hand, and who never knew you were not his child. Chu-li, beloved daughter, Mark is your father, and Peter your brother. Dry your tears, and kiss your father as a daughter should. Greet your brother as a sister should."

"Mother—why did you wait so long to tell me? Why now?"

"Wing-dah would have killed us both had he known the truth. And it would have done good for no one if Mark had not returned from the Mainland. That he has, and with Wing-dah among the Immortals, the time was ordained."

Dutifully, Chu-li approached Brand, who stood and took her in his arms, tears welling from his eyes. Then his daughter turned to Peter and embraced him.

Mary said, "As to Wing-dah's death, I will not pretend a sorrow I cannot feel. My daughter knows his brutality, his villainy, and I urge her not to mourn. The four of us are together as we should be, and I see nothing but happiness for us all."

To Peter, Chu-li said, "You didn't know, either?"

"Not until now, sister."

The word made her smile. "To think I have a brother. Oh, I'm so happy. And a man I respected and admired is my real father."

Mary, too, was drying her eyes. "We have much to go over, and dinner waits. But before we dine, how long will you be in Hong Kong?"

"Another day or two," Brand said, taking her hand. He kissed the tip of her nose and Mary said softly, "I remember so well the way you did that when we were young."

He nodded. "I haven't mentioned it to Peter, but I've been thinking he and I should go into business together."

"Where, Father?"

"Here. And after the Chinese take control, we can go to Taiwan. If Mary and Chu-li agree."

"Wherever you say," Mary responded. "It is the duty of a wife to follow her husband wherever he may go."

Peter and Chu-li exchanged glances before Peter said, "I want La-li at your wedding. Will there be time before our child is born?"

Brand nodded. "We'll go back to Washington and take care of things, return here with La-li." He seated Mary at the head of the dining table and sat at her right beside Chu-li. Peter sat at Mary's left, noting the flowers he'd chosen were the centerpiece.

"You have a good solicitor?" Brand asked Mary.

"A good one, yes. Why?" She picked up ivory chopsticks as a maid offered the first course.

"Cheong's plane is at Taipei. Since you won't be smuggling, I suggest you sell it. Did Cheong have a will?"

"He left everything to Chu-li."

Her head bowed. "I never thought he cared for me."

Mary said, "What little affection he had was for you, my very beloved daughter, and we will protect your inheritance."

"And for that," Brand said, "you'll need a team of solicitors."

Mary hesitated. "Can Cheong's death be verified?"

"With witnesses."

She lifted her wineglass. "To us, then," she said. "To us, to Peter's wife-to-be, and their coming child." She turned to Brand. "I loved you all my life. I never loved anyone but you. I love you still."

"I will always love you," Brand vowed, and kissed her lips. "Forgive me all those wasted years."

Peter said, "I'm so happy for you, Father."

Chu-li said, "Mother, my happiness is the equal of yours." She lifted Brand's hand and kissed it. "Father," she whispered. "My father. I never believed Wing-dah could have sired me so I dreamed of a father like you."

At that she began to cry again, but Brand said, "No more tears on this happiest occasion." He kissed the top of her head and held her until she could dry her eyes. To Mary, he said, "I'll leave you one more time, then never again."

"While you're away I'll miss you more than ever. Please don't stay long."

"I promise," he said.

Peter said, "I promise, too."

Thirty-Three

A CALL FROM GENERAL BARLOW knotted Irving Chenow's stomach and he felt a sudden chill. "Irv, I assume your phone's relatively secure, no eavesdroppers."

Chenow swallowed. "None I'm aware of."

"Good. Losing the Blackbird energized the White House, and the Vice President is investigating the whys and wherefores of the overflight. The Veep's brought in Air Force Special Investigations and they're climbing the information tree."

"Toward you?"

"Toward me. Atsugi referred them to my A-2, and he'll point to me."

"I'm sorry, Bruce."

"Calculated risk. Might have gotten out clean but the Blackbird loss changed everything. I'm damn sorry about those pilots, but coverage transmitted during the overflight may save a lot of American lives."

"That's my hope." His mouth was dry. Swallowing was difficult. "Is there an out for you?"

"Not really. The CD and videotape I sent you—got them in a secure place?"

"I have."

"Good. When I'm asked about the coverage tape I'll surrender my copy and pray it's seen in the White House. There'll be no mention of yours."

"Bruce, I—" he began, but General Barlow broke in.

"Realistically, my time in office is extremely limited. I don't think we'll be talking again soon."

"I understand. Count on me to follow through."

The line went dead. Chenow stared at the telephone before replacing it. Watching the tape last night shocked him. At Leping the warheads were being mated to missiles, whose launchers were already pointing at Taiwan. And when the tape ended Chenow thought of it as a message from the grave. Graves. An unmistakable call for immediate action by the President if Taiwan was to be spared.

He dialed Tom Gray's GlobEco office and when Gray answered, Chenow asked, "Anything new on that subject of common interest?"

Gray hesitated. "Nothing, why?"

"I thought maybe the satellite picked up that Blackbird being downed."

After a pause, Gray said, "Irv, I can't talk to you, orders from on high. But I thought you might know who ordered that overflight."

"Seems to be a mystery," Chenow responded, "but maybe you can tell me if Mark's in Washington."

"Still in Hong Kong—with Peter."

"Glad they're safe. Tom, perhaps you can tell me this: is the NSC on top of things?"

"Should be. Apparently the President lifted the Veep's embargo, so there ought to be a normal flow."

"That's encouraging," Chenow said, and hung up.

There was still a possibility the President would take preemptive action, he told himself, and he wouldn't have to use the contents of the envelope he'd entrusted to Vivian. He felt badly about Bruce Barlow's future, but Bruce had reached the end of the career line anyway and was philosophical about it. And a man who'd endured what Barlow had as a Cong prisoner wasn't likely to be shaken by Air Force gumshoes.

His next call was to Darman Gerold, whose tone of voice was cautious. "Irving, don't blame me for present restrictions. They're ordered by the DCI."

"Okay, I understand. But maybe you can tell me this: did the DCI get your position paper and the NE to the NSC?"

"I believe so, but I can't talk about it. I'm up to my ass in security types trying to find out if the Agency ordered that doomed overflight."

Chenow smiled thinly. "I sort of thought *you* had."

"God, no. Listen, when things calm down I'll call you." He hung up and Chenow thought, By then I may not be here.

Worse than useless to ask the Secretary of State what was going on decision-wise, but Chenow wanted to be absolutely sure the Administration wasn't going to act before he was forced to. How long will they mull it over? he wondered. The Chinese could launch their missiles anytime. The question was, Would they? And when?

THE VICE PRESIDENT ENTERED the Oval Office carrying a VHS cassette. The President ended a phone conversation and looked up at the Vice President. "Well?"

"The overflight order was issued by General Barlow, Air Force Vice Chief of Staff."

"Bruce Barlow? I'll be damned. Why'd he do it?"

"Wouldn't say. But he turned over the Blackbird's surveillance coverage." He tapped the cassette.

"Anyone seen it?"

"Apparently not. He said it was conclusive evidence the Chinese are ready to launch against Taiwan."

"Then we better see it. All right. I want everyone here who was at yesterday's meeting. DCI, Billings, Vance Jordan, Sosnowski, and of course the Secretary of State."

"Jerry King?"

"No. Leave the tape with me."

"Yes, Mr. President." He went out and told the President's secretary to convene the meeting as soon as possible.

The President stared at the cassette as though it were a venomous snake. Damn the Chinese anyway! Cause nothing but grief wherever they stick their flat noses in. And I've bent over backward to keep them happy, in line. Peaceful. *Shit.*

AN HOUR LATER THE DCI activated the President's VCR and images appeared on the large screen. "Coverage was run from fifty thousand feet," he said, "but magnification brings objects as close as a thousand feet. What you're seeing now is the plant that manufactures chemical warfare gas, there's the rail line leading to the warhead factory where previous coverage showed loading. A little farther on we see—looks like wrecked freight cars off the rails—there was a head-on collision there, and of course the gassed corpses have been removed.

"Now the Blackbird is heading south toward the army missile base. I'll fast-forward to get there."

Terrain images sped across the screen until the DCI said, "Nearing the missile base. Just beyond the airstrip you see the launchers. One, two—that's four ready missiles on the launchers. Over there on the right they're bringing missile bodies and warheads together."

He froze the frame and the President asked, "How many missiles would it take to kill off the Taiwanese?"

"We don't know, sir, for two reasons. One, the kind of gas. Our analysts say either sarin or Tabun, both extremely lethal. Two, whether the warheads are to explode on ground contact, or in the air above targets." He paused. "Actually, they could do both." He released the frame and presently the base passed from view. A few moments later the tape ended in a jumble of black and white.

"That it?" the President asked.

"Yes, sir. A few minutes later the Blackbird was destroyed, undoubtedly by a ground-fired missile."

The President sucked in a deep breath. "So the Chinese knew the base was being surveilled."

"Yes," the DCI responded, "but they have no way of knowing we have the coverage."

"Why not?"

"They have to assume the Blackbird was carrying conventional film cans that went down with the plane. Not even our allies know we instituted real-time electronic transmission."

The President said, "I'm tempted to call Chairman Deng and tell him to lay off. What's the group consensus?"

As senior Cabinet member, the Secretary of State spoke first. "There are advantages and disadvantages to such a personal approach. The advantage is receptivity on the part of Chairman Deng to an overture by the President of the world's most powerful nation. Shading that is the undeniable fact of the Chairman's considerable age and apparent diminishing faculties—meaning he could not respond directly to the President, but would have to consult with members of his ruling clique.

"Such consultation could mean delays of unpredictable duration during which the internal political dynamics could adversely affect the Chairman's power to take action.

"An obvious disadvantage to direct communication between the President and the Chairman is alerting the Chinese to the fact that we possess knowledge of their presumed intentions as regards Taiwan. In turn that could accelerate their commission of a hostile act against what they consider a province of Greater China. Contrariwise, they might—facing the reality of our awareness—decide to abandon their plans."

He seemed to have concluded, so the President said, "Seems to me any schoolboy—or girl—could have figured out as much. I'm looking for guidance, gentlemen. Give me something tangible."

The Secretary of Defense said, "Well, we certainly don't want to go to war with China over Taiwan or anything else. Yet the Chinese have always regarded Taiwan with covetous eyes and having gone to the trouble of assembling missiles and preparing to launch, I feel it safe to assume that they are probably ready to do so. I agree with the Secretary, however, in the sense that direct contact between the two heads of state is not likely to be productive—in terms of our national interest."

National Security Adviser Vance Jordan said, "I believe Orientals operate on a bilevel duality. They show one thing while covertly maneuvering to gain another. At this point—and I realize we're faced with a constricting time frame—perhaps our Ambassador in Beijing could ask the Chinese Foreign Minister what it is they truly want."

"Not a bad idea," the President remarked, "but again there's the problem of timing. The Foreign Minister can simply be unavailable to Shep Andersen until after the dirty deed is done."

The Chairman of the Joint Chiefs said, "If you feel the prospects for quiet diplomacy are poor, Mr. President, we might want to move two or three of our carriers close to Chinese waters, and let our attack subs be seen on the surface. That should give them pause for further thought."

"And they could take the position that such movement represents provocative action and proceed with the gassing of Taiwan." He looked at the DCI. "What's your opinion?"

"Sir, as you know, the Agency attempts to stay out of policy matters. All I can say is that satellite and Blackbird coverage have established the launch-readiness of gas missiles. I can't venture an opinion as to whether they'll actually be used."

General Sosnowski said, "NSA reports no unusual military traffic between Beijing army headquarters and the Leping missile base."

"Wouldn't have to be any," said the DCI. "They can fly orders back and forth in a couple of hours. And may have done so."

The President grunted. "And the longer we hold in this limbo mode, the more likely there'll be leaks." He faced Sosnowski. "I want General Barlow disciplined for violating White House orders."

General Sosnowski thought it over. "What orders, sir?" he asked meekly.

"Why, mine," said the Vice President. "I ordered a complete blackout on the China situation, and General Barlow took independent action to . . . to verify the intelligence we had."

Defense Secretary Billings said, "Under present circumstances I suggest that any disciplining—or attempted disciplining—of General Barlow be held in abeyance. For one thing, he's put in papers for immediate retirement. Also, he hasn't leaked any information I'm aware of. In fact, he held it personally—I mean the tape we've just seen. If Barlow is sanctioned for doing things we'd rather not see in the press, he'll be seen as a scapegoat, and I'm sure we want to avoid that at all costs."

"Nevertheless," said the President irritably, "he's got to be guilty of something. If your department can't pin something on him I'll have the Attorney General find something appropriate. Mutiny, maybe. Rebelliousness, disrespect to the office of the President. There have to be a dozen ways to punish him. And of course, he's responsible for losing our Blackbird and two officers." Looking around, he sensed a lack of concurrence among his advisers, shrugged, and said, "Well, back to subject one. Any further thoughts? Fresh ideas?" Hearing no voices, the President said, "I've concluded that phoning Chairman Deng is not likely to accomplish anything but warn the Chinese we're on to them. Agreed?"

All heads nodded, and the President turned to the Chairman of the Joint Chiefs. "Like all nations we enjoy freedom of the seas. If we want to sail our carriers off the China coast that's our right. If we have nuke subs conducting maneuvers in sight of the Mainland that's also our sovereign right." Again he looked at his advisers. "Any nays?

"Good, we finally accomplished something. General, see to the subs and carriers, will you? With the Secretary's approval, of course."

"He has it," Billings said, "in advance, so as not to delay."

"Meanwhile," the President said, "I can't overemphasize the necessity of maintaining full security. I suggest tapping General Barlow's phones, and if it seems he's prepared to blow, put him under house arrest." He smiled thinly. "Apologies can come later. But I need freedom of action for the foreseeable future. Am I understood?"

"Yes, Mr. President," they chorused, and the President motioned the Vice President to stay behind. When the Oval Office emptied, the President said, "Get that tape over to the NSC. You did a damn good job getting it, and you can look forward to chairing the NSC in the near future." He watched the Veep extract the cassette from the VCR and said, "Any leak problems?"

"None. And on the chance that diplomatic personnel in Beijing and Taiwan may inadvertently have come into possession of critical information, I've banned all homeward travel from those posts."

"Good thinking," the President said, and waved the Veep goodbye.

It may still come to war, he mused, but I'm doing everything I can to avoid it.

While saving Taiwan from extermination.

Getting up from his desk, the President stretched and thought, If I can do all that they ought to award me the fucking Nobel Prize for Peace. And that would guarantee my reelection.

Thirty-Four

HONG KONG

MARK BRAND AND PETER were hosting a banquet at the Shing Hong restaurant for Mark's Fang-tse brothers and the three men who had served them so well from Beijing on. There was Eddie Wong, Sammy Lu, and

Tommy Ning, as well as Yang, San, and Wo who were ill at ease until mao-tai relaxed them enough to join in the celebration.

Brand had wanted Johnny Shek to be with them, but Johnny was in Macao visiting his father.

There had been course after course of Peking duck, crab with black bean sauce, snow mushrooms, soft and fried noodles, giant prawns sautéed in ginger sauce, melon soup, spring rolls, and dumplings. To Peter the dishes seemed endless, and when he could eat no more, he shoved back his chair, patted his stomach, and belched happily. Gradually the others set aside their chopsticks while waiters refilled wine cups gone dry. Brand got unsteadily to his feet, lifted his cup, and said, "Want to thank every one of you, my brothers, for everything you did to rescue my son. I especially thank your loyal followers Yang, Wo, and San for aiding our escape. When trouble threatened, they were alert and solved the problem. True, we lost a passenger, but I saw no long faces of regret."

Everyone laughed at the reference to Cheong's death.

"Soon," Brand continued, "we leave for Washington, where we will stay only long enough to wind down our affairs. Then I will return to Hong Kong, and I want you to know that Chen Mei-ling has consented to cut short her widowhood in order to become my wife."

Cheers broke out, Peter clapping loudest. He got up, steadied himself on the table, and said, "All my life I will be under obligation to each one of you. You have my eternal thanks." Tears welled in his eyes, he wiped them away, tried to continue speaking but found his throat too choked, and sat down.

Brand put his arm around Peter's shoulder and hugged him, then got to his feet once more. From an inside pocket he drew out three envelopes filled with HK dollars, and gave them to Yang, San, and Wo. "Money cannot purchase friendship or loyalty," he said, "but it can move aside obstacles to the enjoyment of life." The men looked uneasily at Tommy Ning, who gestured that they should accept Brand's gift. That done, Brand said, "Long years ago when I was accepted into our noble Fang-tse clan I never thought that one day I would turn to my brothers for the kind of help that only brothers can provide. But I did, and together all of you brought me out of dismal darkness into shining light, and as my son said, my gratitude, too, is eternal."

All six Chinese rose and cheered and clapped resoundingly.

Taking Peter's arm, Brand said, "And now we must take our leave of you. But I promise we will return ere a new moon touches the mountains of our beloved Taiwan. Peace, love, strength, health, and prosperity to you all."

They made their way from the banquet hall, down the staircase, and into the waiting limousine. Sitting beside his father, Peter said, "It was wonderful, all of it." He looked out of the window at the lights of the Peak and the harbor beyond. La-li had never seen Hong Kong, he reflected, but she would see it soon and become part of a family he never knew he had.

Brand said, "Do you think it troubled Chu-li that I stayed over last night?"

Peter shrugged. "She said nothing to me. I think she's so glad to find you're her father that you can do nothing wrong."

Brand smiled. "And you?"

"I think you are a very fortunate man. I'll stay in our room and tell the driver where to take you, okay?"

"Okay. Our flight leaves tomorrow night after dinner. I know you're eager to be with La-li again, but I'd rather not go back to Washington." His tongue was thick from wine, and he anticipated a dreadful hangover in the morning. "Still, I'll be able to find out from Tommy what's been happening while I've been away."

PART
FOUR

Thirty-Five

WHAT ALERTED DARMAN GEROLD to the changing situation was a State Department telegram to Beijing and Taipei banning homeward travel by all post employees pending further notice. The final sentence stated that it was hoped the ban would end in the near future.

Gerold had seen similar telegrams before, the usual reason being budgetary restrictions. But funding shortage was not mentioned this time, and as Gerold studied the text for possible clues he saw that the message had been drafted in the office of the Secretary of State and released for transmission by Assistant Secretary Irving Chenow.

He called Chenow's office, and when the Assistant Secretary responded, Gerold said, "Irving, I'm a little puzzled by that telegram banning homeward travel by our people."

"So am I," Chenow said curtly.

"Can you elucidate? My people are involved, too."

"Darman," Chenow said, an edge to his voice, "you and Tommy made it plain you're under restriction not to talk to me. Far as I'm concerned, that's a two-way street."

"Look," Gerold said uneasily, "I didn't order the cutoff, don't blame me. I only follow orders. You signed the telegram."

"I didn't originate it, I released it—big difference."

"That's true, but the Secretary must have had reason to issue the prohibition. Last two mornings the DCI has been at White House meetings, so something unusual must be up. Was the Secretary there, too?"

"He doesn't confide in me," Chenow said dryly, "and I don't schedule his appointments."

"I understand that—but aren't you at all curious?"

"I try not to be, Darman. I don't even speculate."

"Well, I'm speculating it somehow concerns that code-word subject we were discussing."

"We were discussing the subject until I was cut off—remember?"

"I know, Irving, and I'm sorry about that, but it's none of my doing. Please understand I had no responsibility. Now we've lost a Blackbird, a spy plane on an intelligence run, and I feel there's a connection between that tragic incident and your travel telegram. If things are heating up over there I ought to know about it—so should you."

"Well, I haven't heard anything either way. My guess is the basic subject is under discussion at the NSC, where it should be."

"Logical assumption. I suppose they're also considering how to respond to the Blackbird loss. As far as I know the Chinese haven't made an issue of it."

"Your ignorance equals mine," Chenow remarked, "and I assume in due course we'll be told what's going on. If there's nothing else, Darman, I've got a visitor waiting."

"Sure. Always good to talk with you." He replaced the receiver and tried to make sense of the situation. If Dragon Teeth was coming to a head he had to inform Paul, Fred, and Darcy, and timing was critical. Too early to warn them? Probably. But maybe something corroborative would come in during the day.

Last night's dinner party at the Logos had been reasonably enjoyable, he thought, and Pauline had been a gracious hostess to three senators, four congressmen, and the chairman of the President's political party. All with their wives. He had refrained from discussing the object of the evening—his claim to the directorship—feeling it was sufficient for the present to show himself in a good light so he would be favorably remembered by the invitees. Afterward, Pauline declined to overnight in Georgetown, saying she had to take the road early with a four-horse trailer to attend a show near Richmond. Before she drove away they agreed on a date for tented dining and dancing at the estate, three weeks hence. Pauline suggested twenty or thirty couples, the guest list to combine Darman's power choices with her horsey friends. A mix of the influential and the affluent.

Ray Applegate, the China Desk Chief, came in with three cables for Gerold to release. After scanning them, Gerold signed off and said, "What do you make of that State travel restriction?"

Applegate shrugged. "Budget shortfall?"

"Didn't say so."

"Maybe it concerns the downed Blackbird."

Gerold nodded thoughtfully. "Been thinking along the same line. I'm not suggesting there's trouble ahead, but if indications crop up we need to get our people to a safe place. Like Hong Kong."

"Right. Incidentally, I got a Routine from Briggs Dockerty. Mark Brand and his once-missing son are flying back."

"They are? When?"

"Tomorrow, I guess."

"Wonder why Briggs didn't honor that travel ban?"

"Probably because the son isn't an employee, and Mark works for GlobEco."

"I see. Well, I'll be glad to welcome Mark back, though I'm sure Security will want to talk with him."

Applegate nodded. "And I want to schedule a full debriefing for Peter. My shop, plus a few China analysts. That okay with you?"

Gerold nodded. "Meanwhile, get a fix on their flight and arrival time. Mark might appreciate being met."

Mark and Hong Kong combined in Gerold's mind to equal Doreen. He was eager to have her home, and placed a call to Dr. Hempill at the Arbor Vitae Clinic. When the psychiatrist answered, he said, "I wonder if you could update me on my daughter's condition?"

"Why, Mr. Gerold, I can, gladly. In fact, I have a reminder to call you today with an interim report. Just a moment while I find my notes. There. Well, she's doing much better than anyone expected. Seems to be well adjusted to her environment, and apparently quite grateful for the things you sent her: pajamas, dressing gown, underthings, frocks, slacks, shirts . . . she was quite delighted, even asked me to convey her appreciation." The doctor chuckled softly. "Doreen is eating so well that I suspect she will need larger sizes very soon. Isn't that splendid?"

"It is."

"And I must mention the birthday flowers and candy you sent her. Doreen said you hadn't remembered her birthday for years."

"Unfortunately true—but she was seldom around on those occasions. Well, I'm glad parental attention is having positive effects."

"Indeed they are. Formerly Doreen refused beauty care, but now she let the coiffeur give her a new hairstyle, and the manicurist attended to her hands and nails. I think you will be most pleasantly surprised at the transformation."

"I'm sure I will be." He felt a stirring in his crotch. "And detoxification?"

"Responding very well. I feel we will be able to act on your suggestion of treatment on an outpatient basis much sooner than anticipated."

"Wonderful news, Doctor. Does Doreen know of the outpatient suggestion?"

"She does. Only yesterday I broached the subject with her and she reacted receptively. Of course, she's not overfond of her stepmother, but perhaps that potential conflict could be avoided."

"It will be. As I mentioned before, my wife and I lead essentially separate lives so there won't be a suffocatingly critical presence around Doreen."

"Excellent. We're planning to suspend methadone therapy in the next few days, then monitor her carefully."

"You'll let me know?"

"Of course. Oh, I should add that Doreen is taking our exercise classes and enjoys them."

"Like—Jazzercise, if that's the word?"

"Exercise to music. Yes. Your call was timely indeed, and do feel free to follow up at any time."

Hanging up, Gerold licked dry lips. Into his mind came a vision of a healthy, well-formed Doreen in a diaphanous gown, flowing toward him in slow motion, arms outstretched. He closed his eyes, remembering Amy's unusual and innovative taste in couture. She would delight in dressing Doreen in fashions designed to enhance the most attractive features of her figure. Well, he had ideas along those lines derived from Amy. He opened his eyes again. With Doreen safely home and sharing a new rapport they could visit salons together and make selections pleasing to them both. Which Mark Brand would never see.

Brand. He would have to be warned to say nothing of his Mainland experiences, whatever they were. The son, too. Both were subject to the Veep's restriction until after this Dragon Teeth business was over and done with.

He decided to visit Tommy Gray at GlobEco and extract whatever information Tommy had that could shed light on the developing situation.

As he drove across the river into Washington, Gerold reviewed all that Dr. Hempill had told him. Everything was proceeding excitingly well, and the only possible obstacle he could foresee was the untimely arrival in Georgetown of Fitzhugh. Gerold seldom thought about his son, who had left for Alaska to work cleaning up the *Exxon Valdez* oil spill. By now, he reflected, that job would be finished, though Fitz was probably working elsewhere in Alaska. Bartender, maybe, or waiter—some menial, life-sustaining job incongruous to a privileged background. Fitz had dropped out of St. Alban's before graduation, and to all intents and purposes disappeared. It troubled Gerold to recall the childhood closeness of Fitzhugh and Doreen. At times they had been inseparable, he remembered, double-dating together and enjoying adolescence to the full. He didn't want Fitz to appear out of nowhere and claim board and lodging privileges. Because after Doreen was fully integrated into his life the last thing he wanted in their Georgetown home was competition.

Washington

In his Pentagon office, Lt. Gen. Bruce Barlow, USAF, was clearing out desk drawers and removing family photographs, which he gazed at before placing gently in a carton. His aide, Maj. Ernest Findlay, came in and said, "General, I have a message for you."

"Spit it out, Ernie. Don't keep me waiting."

"Sir, the Chairman wants you in his office."

"General Sosnowski?"

"Yes, sir. As soon as possible."

"Say why?"

"No, sir."

Barlow placed the last of his photographs in the carton and squared his shoulders. "Likely a final chewing out."

"Doubt that, sir. Probably a well-deserved decoration."

"Thanks, Major. Won't be a Good Conduct medal, that's for sure."

Major Findlay smiled. "Shall I accompany you, sir?"

"Thanks, but I'll walk the last mile myself." He paused. "I made out your Fitness Report—seen it yet?"

"Yes, sir. I appreciate all the good things you said."

"Well, you'll make light colonel next promotion round. You can bet on that." He glanced around his office for a last look before leaving. Pretty bare, he thought. The walls remain but the occupants come and go, like replaceable parts. Tossed out like old air filters.

He strode to the door, passed through the reception area, and walked along the ring until he was at the guard-flanked entrance to the office of the Chairman of the Joint Chiefs of Staff.

Inside the waiting area, an eagle colonel stepped forward and said, "General, go right in, sir."

"Thank you." He opened the oak door lettered in gilt with the Chairman's full title, and saw General Sosnowski rise from behind his desk. Barlow came to attention, saluted, and stood at attention.

"At ease, Bruce. Packed and ready to go?"

"Yes, sir, General."

"You're still on active duty, you know."

"Until seventeen hundred hours today."

Sosnowski picked up what Barlow realized were his retirement papers and waved them before replacing them on his desk. "A bit premature, don't you think?"

"No, sir. Under the circumstances I felt it in the best interests of the Air Force—and myself."

"I haven't approved your retirement application, and the Secretary can't sign off until I do."

"Is that fair, sir?"

"All things considered I think it is. Have a seat and listen to what I have to say—in complete confidence, understand?"

"Yes, sir." He sat across from the Chairman and folded his hands.

"This morning at an early hour I was summoned to the Oval Office. The surveillance tape you commissioned was shown to me and appropriate members of the Cabinet—and the President. The effect on all present was profound, though reactions were not unanimous."

"Meaning what, sir?"

"Be patient, let me tell this my own way."

"Sorry, sir."

Sosnowski managed a tight smile. "I don't like hearing officers of general rank saying they're sorry until they have good reason to be."

"I assumed I fit rather easily into that category."

"Bruce, dammit, don't be so hard on yourself." He paused. "I think some high-ranking civilian persuaded you to run that Blackbird surveillance, because I doubt you'd go off on a singleton tangent and do it by yourself. You had no motive. And, as far as I know, you had no classified background information that would have suggested the immediate need for a Blackbird run. Now, I'm not asking who got you to do it, because the President hasn't asked me, and you'd either have to refuse to answer, or lie. And you're far too fine an officer to do that. However," he continued after a deep breath, "there were a few at the meeting who demanded you be disciplined for issuing an unauthorized order, defying higher authority, and so on." He shook his head. "After a certain amount of back-and-forth discussion none of the participants could come up with a violation worthy of the name. I was pleased to point out that, as far as anyone knew, you hadn't given intelligence information to a foreign power or to any unauthorized person. There was some grumbling about that observation, but the issue faded away because the President seemed to like my suggestion of cruising a couple of carriers off the China coast and letting the Chinese watch some nuke subs at play." He smiled. "Like whale watching."

Barlow said nothing.

"I haven't seen Gorgon surveillance take on the Leping missile site, but I assume their state of launch readiness is advancing. The tape you're responsible for acquiring shows four launch-ready missiles, and by now there may be more."

"Very likely," Barlow remarked.

"Okay, that's background to what I have in mind. Carriers are moving from Subic Bay toward the China coast. We already had four attack subs stationed between the Yellow Sea and the East China Sea so detailing a pair to play war games was no problem. However, my reading of the Chinese—and I fought in that Korean 'police action' just as you did—is that the Chinese are very good at bluffing, but don't take it well when the coin is turned. You concur?"

"Yes, sir, I do."

"Good. We may shortly have a meeting of minds. Now, if we agree that the military display I just described is insufficient to dissuade the Chinese from attacking Taiwan, what's left for us in terms of ending the threat?"

"Take out the missile site."

Sosnowski nodded. "*And* the chemical warfare plant. Right?"

"Right, sir."

The Chairman gestured at a large Mercator map on the near wall. "I try to think ahead of events, believing preparedness is an essential ingredient of strategy. That was drilled into me at War College, and when you were there I assume you were similarly indoctrinated."

"Yes, sir, I was. Two classes after you."

"Now, let's suppose for theory's sake that at the highest level of government a take-out strike is authorized. Forget the subs and carriers, they're just for show purposes. Where would you launch a strike from, and what means would you employ?"

"With permission, sir." Barlow rose and went over to the map. After a few moments' scrutiny he said, "Taiwan would be easiest because it's nearest to target. But since this is to be done clandestinely to preserve deniability, I'd say it comes down to aircraft leaving from Luzon or Okinawa."

Sosnowski nodded. "What type aircraft?"

"B-1 carrying Tomahawk missiles escorted by two F-117 Stealth fighter-bombers."

"Can you expeditiously arrange mission readiness?"

"Yes, sir."

"Very good. General, I'm ordering you to undertake such necessary actions as may be essential to the successful execution of the mission just described. The sole limitation is that responsibility be deniable on the part of this government."

"Understood, sir, and thank you."

"Inasmuch as paper trails are damning I don't want any radio or pouch communication on the subject. Your authority is VOCO. Any resistance, the Field Commander can call me direct."

"I assume participating aircraft are to remain in mission readiness until such time as I receive launch authorization from you."

"Exactly. I've got a plane on standby at Andrews for you." He paused. "Launch signal will be 'The tree fell' or something similar. You stay at the base until the mission is executed, or alternatively, you're recalled. Where will you be?"

"I'll check a computer printout to tell me where suitable aircraft are. I think all three should fly together, no meeting up after dark, thirty thousand feet above the China Sea."

"All right. Given the President's apparent state of mind, I think you should be prepared to execute the mission shortly after reaching either Okinawa or Luzon. Unless the Chinese launch first, in which case we're all of us royally fucked."

"Right, sir." He looked at his watch. "You haven't forbidden me to fly on the mission."

"That's right. I haven't forbidden you to fly the mission. Maybe the thought will occur to me two or three days from now. Good luck, Bruce." He extended his hand and General Barlow shook it.

As he walked Barlow to the door, Sosnowski said, "One final word—a personal one. I know all about the divorce that handicapped you in some dinosaur minds. So I want to say it was bullshit then, and it's bullshit now. For my part, should the opportunity present itself, you'll have my recommendation for the top post—and a fourth star while you're alive to enjoy it. Meanwhile, not a word to anyone, your aide, your lovely wife, no one. Say adios and disappear."

"Yes, sir, I'll do my absolute best."

"I know you will. Now, get moving."

General Barlow walked down the corridor in a semidaze. In his office he collected his service cap and raincoat and told his aide to suspend moving out. "I'll be away for a few days, Ernie. Call my wife and tell her. After you get me transportation to Andrews."

"Yes, sir. Right away, sir."

On his way out, Barlow stopped at AF Operations Center and checked aircraft availability status at Okie and Luzon. There was no B-1 at Kadena, so he'd head for the Philippines. If he was lucky there wouldn't be a crowd of protesters blocking access to MacArthur Air Force Base.

Funny thing about the Filipinos, he mused as he got into a staff car. We fight for their freedom, hand it to them, and they don't know what the hell to do with it.

AN HOUR LATER, STRAPPED into the rear cockpit of an F-15 Eagle, and buffered from the cold by his pressure suit, General Barlow reviewed the flight plan. Refueling stops at Hamilton AFB, California, and Hickman Field, Hawaii, midair refueling near Johnson Island in the Pacific, then on to Luzon. The trans-polar route was considerably shorter, but could provoke radar tracking near Russian territory, even lock on a SAM. So Barlow had opted for a conventional course to destination.

Already the fighter was far above earth's cloud cover, and Barlow saw the clouds' dark colors lighten below as the Eagle bore westward racing ahead of the pursuing sun.

WASHINGTON

TOMMY GRAY WAS INTERPRETING the latest Gorgon take for Darman Gerold who, he thought, took an unusually keen interest in developments. Gerold slumped in a chair and said, "Looks like the sons of bitches are ready to launch those missiles."

"They're in launch configuration, no question about it."

"And could blast off anytime?"

"With a push of the button."

"Jesus," said Gerold, "if that happens we'll be in a goddam war—unless the President does something damn soon."

"Something may be in the planning stage," Tommy remarked. "Sending the Blackbird on that photo run didn't just happen. And the Chinese had the balls to shoot it down." He shook his head. "That's being kept under wraps officially, but if the pilots' wives start yelling, there'll be no hushing them up. Can you imagine the headlines?"

"I can," Gerold said dolefully. "A real disaster. I wish I knew what was going on at the NSC and the White House. The DCI attended two morning meetings there but not a whisper has trickled down. Then State's travel telegram appears, and no one seems to know why." He tugged the lobe of his right ear. "There's a circumstantial connection."

"Could be, but I doubt there'll be reprisal action over the Blackbird. Technically, I suppose, the plane shouldn't have been there."

"Yeah. Print those last few photos and I'll take them to the DCI. Maybe he'll loosen up and tell me what's going on."

"Don't count on it," Tommy advised, and printed the photos for him.

INSTEAD OF RETURNING DIRECTLY to Langley, Gerold drove to Georgetown and made three phone calls from his study. To Paul Wembley he said, "I think it's not too early to make that move we discussed over lunch."

"Really? Sure of that?"

"Paul, listen to me. My profession deals in possibilities and probabilities, not absolute certainties. No one thought the USSR was going to collapse, but it did. Now, from what I've been seeing and hearing I think it's time you reviewed your situation abroad."

After a pause, Wembley said, "Let me ask you this: If our positions were reversed, you being me and vice versa, what would you do?"

"I would act on the best available advice."

"Okay, all right, I'll do it. But I feel like I'm bungee-jumping without a cord."

"Up to you, Paul, hope things go well for you."

"Jesus, me, too. I've never taken a massive risk like this before. Uh—how long before—you know what I mean."

"Could be a day, a week, a month, but I'd say sooner than later."

"Good enough, Darman. Thanks so much for the call—I'll get busy now."

Gerold's calls to Fred Postlewaite and Darcy Whiting covered the same ground and discussion. Both friends wanted ultimate assurance that now was the time to liquidate and pull out, but Gerold refrained from predicting a certainty. In the end, they said they'd act on his information and thanked him for what he'd done.

Hanging up, Gerold thought, I've done my part, they still have to do theirs.

Before leaving the house he went up to the second floor and walked around the guest room. After it was painted and attractively redecorated it would be Doreen's room. The bathroom needed modern fixtures including a bidet, and an enclosed Jacuzzi tub. He'd never dealt with decorators but he remembered an upscale fixtures shop on lower Wisconsin Avenue that could probably redo the bathroom in pastel shades. Along M Street there were plenty of interior decorators to choose from. He'd visit one or two and describe what he had in mind: a modern bedroom for a very modern young woman.

DEPLANING AT DULLES INTERNATIONAL, Brand and Peter went through Immigration formalities, and as they waited for baggage at the carousel three men approached them. One asked, "Mr. Brand?"

"Yes."

"And son Peter?"

Peter nodded.

"We have transportation for you, sir. Give me your claim checks, and we'll get your baggage through Customs, no delay."

"Sounds good," Brand remarked. "Who are you?"

"Director's office," a second man replied. "A courtesy, sir."

"How about some ID?"

"You know we don't carry buzzers like the Bureau does."

Brand glanced at Peter. "Thanks, anyway. My respects to the Director, but we'll find our own way home."

The first man spoke. "Mr. Brand, that's not the drill. Give me your claim checks and come along." He paused. "We're armed."

"And you're not going to shoot in a crowded airport."

"That depends." His fist shot out and hit Brand's left arm near the bandage. Brand yelped, gripped his arm, and bent over, feeling faint. The other two men grabbed Peter's arms and held him.

As Brand straightened up he sucked in breath and expelled it. "We'll go," he said hoarsely. "Don't hurt my son." Peter turned over the claim checks and walked with Brand and the men who had restrained him outside to where a stretch Lincoln was parked in a space whose curb was stenciled: U.S. GOVERNMENT VEHICLES ONLY. As Brand got onto the rear seat he said, "Hell of a reception," and sat back while an escort sat beside him. Peter and his escort were on facing jump seats. They waited in silence until the apparent leader appeared with their three suitcases. He loaded them on the passenger side of the driver's seat and got behind the wheel.

"How far we going?" Brand asked, taking advantage of the car's lurch forward to press against his escort and feel a shoulder holster.

"Not far, and if you cooperate, you won't be there long."

"Welcome news," Brand responded. "Never felt more cooperative." He gazed steadily at Peter.

The Lincoln was leaving the airport area and approaching the highway. The driver stopped for the intersection red light, and over the idling engine Brand said, "I'd really like to know who you fellows are. Imagine, being so close to the Director you're chosen for a delicate mission like this. Boggles the mind." The car bucked forward and squealed around the turn. "Temper, temper," Brand chided. "You won't reveal your names, so for our civil suit you'll be known initially as the Pep Boys, Manny, Moe, and Jack."

"Civil suit? What the hell you talkin' about?" the man beside him growled.

"Manny Doe, Moe Doe, and Jack Doe defendants, with the Director of the Central Intelligence Agency. Shall I go on?"

"Yeah," Peter's escort snorted, "give us the big picture."

Brand nodded slowly. "The big picture is ten million dollars for unlawful deprivation of liberty, threatening with a deadly weapon, and bodily assault." He rubbed his sore arm. "The criminal charges come later. And it's a federal case because Dulles Airport is federal property. Like the big picture now?"

"Lissen," Brand's seat companion said, "you done something wrong, so you're being taken where you can make explanations. That's all I know."

"Remember those words, Peter," Brand said. "These mooks are digging it deeper every minute."

"Right, Dad, I'll remember."

Brand recognized the highway. It led to Leesburg and south. "Now I get it," he said to Peter. "Remember those papers Briggs Dockerty wanted us to sign?"

"Sure do."

"Well, apparently someone got the bright idea of snatching and holding us until we do. That it, boys? Hear talk of oaths to sign?"

"Heard nothing but what I said."

"Okay, I believe you, and this can be straightened out pretty easily. Our accuser confronts us, we sign papers, and you take us home, right?"

"Something like that," Brand's escort muttered.

The car was going about seventy. At the next hard turn the wheels skidded momentarily, and Brand pushed hard against his seat companion while his hand snaked under his coat and snatched out a small automatic. He slid into the seat corner and covered both escorts. "Take his piece, Peter," he snapped, "and let the driver feel it on his neck."

"Yes, *sir!*" Peter fished out the pistol and pushed it against the driver's head.

"Slow the car," Brand ordered, "and stop on the shoulder."

He saw the driver's right hand drop from the wheel, and realized he was going for his gun. So he fired twice into the back of the seat close to the driver's body. "Take his piece, Peter. Show's over."

The driver steered the Lincoln onto the shoulder and braked.

"Everyone out," Brand ordered, and doors opened. The three kidnappers got out and stood by the roadside. "I'll take your wallets now, no more anonymity. Well, hand them over, goddammit!"

Slowly they handed their wallets to Peter. Brand stepped close to the driver and slashed the pistol muzzle against his temple, then struck the cheekbone, and the man howled. Even in the poor light Brand could see blood trickling down the side of his head. "You punched my arm, I gave you some pain to remember. Down on your bellies, lads, and if you're entertaining courageous ideas, forget them. I won't kill you, just cripple you for life."

They knelt, then sprawled forward. Brand covered them while Peter got behind the wheel. As he got in beside Peter, Brand fired a round near the former driver, slammed the door, and said, "Hit the pedal, make a fast U-turn, and head back to Washington." He chuckled. "I told them we'd find our own way home, and by God we're doing just that."

"What about—them?" Peter asked as the Lincoln accelerated.

"Oh, they'll have to walk." He threw two pistols out the window, keeping an unfired H&K .38 for his pocket. "Next gas station, pull over by a pay phone and call La-li."

"Sure. What will I tell her?"

"Say you'll be there in, oh, forty minutes."

"That all?"

"They know about her. Less said by phone, the better."

After a while Peter said, "So, what are we going to do?"

"First, we pick up my car. I'll drive it. You follow me to the Lincoln Memorial and park this impressive official vehicle. Lock it and throw away the keys. Then we'll collect your fiancée."

Peter nodded. "What's the program?"

"We need to get out of Washington until I can find out what's going on."

"Where will we go?"

"Your grandfather hasn't met La-li, and it's time he did. So we'll spend a week or so with Dr. Simon Brand enjoying a family reunion."

Brand ripped out the car phone and threw it from the window. "There's a gas station ahead. Get ready to stop and make your call."

"You were great back there, Dad," Peter said admiringly. "I had no idea what to do."

Brand smiled. "Lull your enemy, strike when it's least expected."

His arm throbbed; tension had drained energy. He closed his eyes and tried to get comfortable. There was a long drive ahead before his father could see to his wound. Through half-closed eyes he saw Peter steer into the station, park by the pay phones. While Peter was talking, Brand fell asleep.

MacArthur Air Base, Luzon, Philippines

In green flight coverall General Barlow stood in the base control tower and watched three Stealth fighter-bombers slide into the approach pattern, then touch down on the runway simultaneously. Turning to the Base Commander, he said, "I requested two F-117s, Colonel."

"Sir, Kadena Fighter TacWing thought by sending a redundant Stealth you would be able to count on two for your mission." Whatever that is, he mused.

General Barlow nodded and gazed across the end of the airstrip at the hangar where the Rockwell B-1's open bomb bay was being loaded with cruise missiles. It was a beautiful aircraft, he thought, with its long conical nose, swept-back wings, and black radar-absorbent coating. Inboard, technicians were checking and readying the Offensive Avionics System for a mission that might never come.

"I'll want the F-117s armed with Walleye glide bombs, CBU fuel-air explosive weapons, Rockeye cluster bombs, and a pair of Sidewinders apiece. In case," he added, "we encounter opposition."

"May I ask flight distance to target, sir?"

"Primary target is roughly six hundred miles. Secondary targets are double that from here. After I meet the Stealth pilots we'll huddle with your strike navigator and get details. The avionics officer, pilot, and copilot should be there, too."

"Yes, sir." The Base Commander looked down and saw the three Stealth pilots coming by jeep toward the briefing room.

"After the mission's laid on," Barlow said, "I want the crews fed and rested. Assign space in transient officers' quarters, isolated from noise and loose talk."

"Yes, General, I'll see to it, sir."

The Colonel relayed instructions to an operations officer, who saluted and left the control area. Barlow sat down and shaded his eyes against the glare of the midday sun. He had slept only a few hours since arrival, and he knew the order to execute might come at any time. It would be best, he reflected, to accomplish the over-water part of the mission in daylight, crossing the China coast after dark. They could take off in late evening, when the air was cooler and wing-lift enhanced.

He was enthusiastic about the mission, and eager for it to begin. He was also grateful to Chairman Sosnowski for the chance to redeem himself by commanding a mission he was in a large way responsible for having instigated. Fate acts in strange ways, he mused, and I'm going to make the most of this, my last combat run.

When the operations officer returned to report to the Colonel that his orders were being carried out, he glanced at General Barlow and saw that he was asleep in his chair.

Thirty-Six

THE OVAL OFFICE, THE WHITE HOUSE, WASHINGTON

THE PRESIDENT SAID, "I apologize for the late hour, gentlemen, but having reached a decision concerning the China problem I felt the national interest could not wait until morning."

His auditors were the Vice President, the Secretary of Defense, the National Security Adviser, the Director of Central Intelligence, and the Chairman of the Joint Chiefs of Staff.

"You'll take note," the President continued, "that the Secretary of State is not among us. In view of the action I propose to take I decided to allow him the luxury of deniability. As for the rest of you, what I am going to tell you remains within the confines of this room. No notes, nothing for your memoirs, no hints to wives and families. Is that clearly understood?"

All nodded understanding.

"Good. You're familiar with the gas-missile threat to Taiwan, how it developed, the unfortunate loss of our Blackbird, and the launch-readiness of Chinese missiles. Under those circumstances, and lacking viable alternatives to ending the threat to Taiwan, I have decided to authorize a covert air strike to take out the missiles and destroy the chemical warfare plant and warhead factory. It may be that the Chinese will rebuild those facilities over time, but I hope this object lesson will persuade them that this nation will not permit the destruction of a friendly ally."

"But," Vance Jordan interjected, "I don't believe you've considered utilizing the good offices of the Russians to persuade the Chinese to back down."

"I considered it. Bad idea, because the Russians could warn the Chinese, and in my judgment the effort would be useless. Furthermore, I'm not open to argument. I've made a decision, and here and now I order General Sosnowski to execute it."

The Veep said, "I remain concerned about Chinese reactions, re-prisal, trade rupture, the effect on our economy—loss of employment"—he waved a hand distractedly—"and so on."

"I share those concerns," the President said, an edge to his voice, "which is why I chose covert means to eliminate the problem. Assuming the air strikes vaporize their targets, there'll be nothing remaining to argue about, no casus belli. Along with the Chinese we can take the tacit position that a warlike situation never existed, and consequently nothing happened. No face is lost, and my action doesn't distress the national economy. Everyone wins—especially the Taiwanese, who will never know how close they came to extinction." He breathed deeply and addressed General Sosnowski. "I base that scenario on your assumption that after the strikes are accomplished the Chinese will have no proof of our involvement. That right, General?"

"Yes, Mr. President. Our supersonic Stealth aircraft should be undetectable by hostile radar. No identifying markings. In and out in a couple of hours." He looked at his wristwatch. "If I may be excused, sir?"

"By all means, General. You'll keep me informed?"

"Yes, sir." He got up and left the room. In his car he picked up the

telephone and called his aide-de-camp. "Open a channel to Luzon," he
ordered. "I'll be there in fifteen minutes."

So, he thought, it's finally going to happen, and with Bruce Barlow
in charge it's going to be done right. He looked back at the illuminated
facade of the White House and smiled. When the going gets tough, he
thought, the President *is* capable of reaching a decision, though I wonder what the fallout will be.

"ONE FINAL THING," the President said, and turned to the Vice President.
"Security continues absolute? No loose ends or cracks unsealed?"

"No, sir."

"Excellent. You're commended on a first-rate job."

The Veep smiled glowingly—until the DCI held up one hand.
"There *is* one exception, Mr. President, but I'm not really concerned
about it in the overall context."

"Oh? And what's the exception?"

"Well, there were two U.S. civilians in the Beijing area who had
personal knowledge of the train collision and the emission of deadly gas.
They reported it to our Beijing Station."

"Well?"

"They're back now." He cleared his throat. "When they arrived at
Dulles we attempted to detain them, but they eluded our representatives
and vanished."

"Was force employed?"

"Yes, sir, but it proved insufficient." He swallowed. "Efforts to
locate them and ensure their silence are continuing."

"Damn!" the President said loudly. "If they weren't likely to talk
before, they're probably pissed off now. And nothing's to keep them
from spilling to the *Post* or the *Times*, right?"

"Afraid so, sir."

The President grunted. "Who *are* these Johnnies-on-the-spot?
They have names?"

"Yes, sir. Mark Brand, a former Agency employee who's been
working for a proprietary called GlobEco. His son, Peter, got arrested in
Canton and jailed in Beijing. The father, Mark, went there to free him."

"And apparently succeeded. Well, all I can do is pray they'll keep
quiet until after the strike. By the way, who's in charge of the mission?"

The DCI said, "Lieutenant General Bruce Barlow."

"Barlow?" the Veep exploded. "He was the son of a bitch responsible for that unauthorized Blackbird mission. He withheld the surveillance tape. And now he's in charge of the strike? Jesus Christ, how could that be?"

The DCI said, "Apparently General Sosnowski chose him because he was familiar with the targets, and decided to rehabilitate him, as it were."

"Actually," said the President, "it sounds like not a bad idea. If the strike accomplishes its objectives, so be it, all's forgiven. Meanwhile, aside from the strike, we have the Brands to worry about. No, I'm not going to worry about them—that's *your* problem. See if you can do it right this time." He looked at his desk clock. "Late, gentlemen. By morning I want to hear the China problem has ceased to exist. Thanks for coming. Good night, all."

MacArthur Air Base, Luzon, Philippines

THE BASE COMMANDER KNOCKED on the door of General Barlow's quarters; hearing no response, he entered and turned on the overhead light. "General," he said loudly, "call for you. From Washington."

Barlow opened his eyes and stared at the Colonel. He was disoriented from a dream that had him chained, beaten, and bloody in a Vietcong tiger cage. It was a familiar dream that left him shaking, body clammy with cold perspiration. Swallowing, he said, "Washington?"

"Yes, sir. Satellite link." He gestured at the telephone on the night table. "You can take it here." He went out and closed the door.

Barlow swung his legs over the bedside and hesitated before reaching for the phone. Go or No Go? Now he'd find out. Picking up the receiver, he said, "Bruce Barlow here."

"Bruce—remember what we talked about a couple of days ago—that forestry question?"

"Yes, sir, I remember well." He was alert now, mind fully functional.

"If a tree falls in a forest and there's no one around to hear it, does it make a sound?"

"Yes, that was the question." He tensed, waiting.

"Well, the tree fell, and someone was listening, so sound *was* created. Even echoes. Satisfied?"

"Very."

"How are you?"

"Couldn't be better. Everything's A-okay and I'm anxious to get going and head home."

"Do that, and we'll talk again." The transmission ended, and Barlow got to his feet. He opened the door and spoke to the Air Police guard beside his door. "Ask the Colonel to come in, please."

When the Colonel arrived, Barlow said, "Tell my crews to meet me in the officers' mess. We'll need a hot meal and plenty of coffee. From there, final briefing, weather, the works. Mission aircraft fully fueled and on the flight line."

"Yes, sir, right away, sir." He paused. "The third Stealth pilot?"

"Glad you queried that. I've decided we'll fly diamond formation—he gets to cover our tails."

"Yes, sir."

In the bathroom, Barlow submerged his face in cool water, urinated, and flushed the toilet. There was a relief facility on the big bomber, but using one always made his pecker cold, so it was better to board with an empty bladder.

No personalia to take along. He turned off room lights and closed the door behind him. The AP snapped to attention. Barlow said, "You're relieved, son, I won't be back for a while." Or maybe never, he thought as he left transient quarters and headed for the mess hall. Local time fifteen twenty-three. The timeline was about right. They could eat together without urgency, have the final briefing, and be airborne by seventeen hundred. Sosnowski had come through, he reflected, a man of considerable influence with the President. But the mission rationale was unassailable: do it quick and clean and go home. No publicity, so the Chinese could pretend it never happened, and not lose face.

The mess was air-conditioned, but ceiling fans turned lazily overhead. At his entrance, the SOP barked, "Ten-*hut*," and his men snapped to attention.

"At ease," Barlow said, "what's for dinner?"

"Steak, mashed potatoes, and peas. Dessert—ice cream, Jell-O, or yogurt."

He nodded and took his seat at the head of the long table. Filipino waiters came in from the kitchen bearing trays of T-bones and bowls of mashed potatoes, gravy, and peas. "Looks good," Barlow said, "and I'm hungry. Gentlemen, let's eat."

FIVE MINUTES BEFORE the formation reached the China coast, the B-1 bomb bay doors opened and two cruise missiles dropped from their rotary launchers and disappeared in the blackness below. Programmed to strike the missile-launch area of the Leping military base, they slanted downward at six hundred knots, and the avionics officer reported their course steady, their heading true. Moments later General Barlow heard him alert Tail End Charlie—the third Stealth fighter—to a pair of Chinese fighters rising to intercept the formation. The pilot acknowledged, said he'd take care of them, and Barlow could visualize him breaking off, acquiring the targets on target radar, and firing a Sidewinder at each fighter.

The OAS officer reported cruise missiles impacting on target.

The B-1 lifted slightly, then steadied, as two fuel-air explosive bombs dropped into the night. Each of the five-hundred-pound weapons contained three canisters of fuel set to ignite three hundred feet above the ground. They would produce a high blast overpressure and horrific fireball on exploding. Barlow included them in the weapons array to cook any remaining warheads and carbonize whatever might be left of the cruise missiles.

"One down," Tail End Charlie reported laconically. "Oops, there goes the other. Returning to formation."

Thirty thousand feet below, the fireballs illuminated the B-1's interior, and Barlow was glad not to have to see the full extent of destruction around the missile base. He assumed satellite imagery would confirm Leping's total destruction.

As the B-1 and its escort fighters swerved left to take the next target heading, Barlow reflected that had all three targets been of equal value he would have commenced the strike run from the north, taking out Zhuolu and Yangyuan before heading south to Leping, thence out over the China Sea and home. Instead, the primary critical target was— had been—the missile base and its launchers. Ahead of them was a six hundred-mile northward run over Chinese territory defended by China's Air Defense Command with its interceptors, SAMs, and air-to-air missiles. So, he thought, we're not out of it yet, not by a long shot. Still, we're carrying ECM gear, and by flying Mach 1.5 at ninety thousand feet there's not a hell of a lot in the Chinese defense arsenal that can reach and damage us.

He heard the OAS officer say, "Radar's lighting up all over the place."

As expected, Barlow thought, and unscrewed the cap of his coffee Thermos. The B-1 gained altitude and speed and by the time Barlow finished a cup of coffee the bomber was flying level on a computer-guided course.

When a heat-seeking missile rose to meet them, the OAS deflected it with flares. After-scan radar showed the missile vanish from the screen.

To avoid Chinese fears of an air raid on Beijing, Barlow had projected a course two hundred miles west of the city. From there, turning east, the plan was to attack the two factories and head out to the Yellow Sea.

At intervals during the next hour sixteen interceptors tried to reach the strike formation, failing because of its speed and altitude. Their window of opportunity would come when the formation descended to bombing altitude, and Barlow was depending on Tail End Charlie for defense during the attack run.

"Coming in range," the OAS reported as the B-1 descended steeply and its bomb bays opened. A cruise missile and a package of cluster bombs departed through the darkness for the warhead factory, while two F-117s released under-wing missiles for mop-up. The third Stealth was engaging two interceptors with Sparrow and Sidewinder missiles, and presently reported all clear.

Next target, the Zhuolu gas plant. Another cruise missile and two CBU fuel-air bombs leveled it without an F-117 attack. The formation climbed steeply and headed for the coast. Suddenly the OAS yelled a warning, and moments later the aircraft shuddered from an enormous blow. A Stealth pilot's excited voice said, "Missile took away part of your right wing, didn't detonate . . . you're losing fuel."

And altitude, Barlow realized, as the bomber canted to the right. Two of the four GE turbofans were going to flame out any second. He made his way to the flight deck and asked, "Can we make it to the coast?"

"Yes, sir—unless the rest of the wing drops off. But we're never going to get it home."

"Okay. Get MacArthur on the horn and tell them we anticipate ditching fairly soon. Jettison remaining weapons and let's see how long we can stay airborne."

"Yes, sir."

Barlow heard the drone of the bomb bay doors opening, felt the slight upward lift as bombs and missiles dropped away.

He went over to the OAS officer and said, "What the hell happened?"

"It never showed on forward radar," the officer replied. "Must have had radar-absorbing coating. We're just lucky it didn't explode."

"You're right about that. Okay, son, get on a life jacket and get ready to swim."

"Yes, sir. We've got three inflatable rafts. With beacons."

"I guess we all took the survival course at Eglin," he said reflectively. "Now we get a chance to pass." He moved to the flight deck and saw the pilot was fighting the wings' unequal lift with left full aileron. "We can't expect help from Luzon," he said, "but maybe Seoul and Sasebo will pitch in."

"I like the idea," the pilot said. "I'll pray for it."

The copilot/navigator said, "We'll leave the coast in about three minutes, sir. Open water after that. What are your orders?"

"See how close you can get to Korea before we have to ditch." He remembered the F-117s, and called them on the radio link. "How're you boys fixed for fuel?"

"Pretty well, sir."

"Good. I'd like you to cover us while we ditch, hang around long enough to see how many of us get out, and keep those Chink whoremasters from strafing us." He paused. "If you can."

"With respect, sir," the leader responded, "we'll cover as long as we can."

"Don't want you ditching, too. Losing one aircraft per mission is enough. Four would raise eyebrows. Okay?"

"Yes, sir. I'll report ditching and, ah, survival to MacArthur."

"Good man. Hope we'll share steaks and mashed potatoes again."

"Look forward to it, sir. Out."

General Barlow donned a life jacket and passed jackets to the pilot and copilot. In 'Nam he'd ejected and dropped into the jungle where a Cong patrol was waiting. A water landing would have given him a better chance of rescue. He wondered how long the B-1 could float after impact. The damaged wing would fill first and pull the aircraft on its side. Meaning, they'd make a left-side exit to the rafts. Assuming the rafts got free.

The copilot said, "We're at eleven thousand, sir, and over water. Losing a thousand a minute."

Eleven minutes to ditch time, he thought. "Did MacArthur acknowledge?"

"Yes, sir. Relaying situation to the nearest bases with air-sea rescue capability."

The pilot said, "Might as well burn remaining fuel, General. I'm putting left engines on full burners. We'll fly a little farther and float a little longer."

"Concur." General Barlow strapped himself into his check-seat near the OAS. "Enemy air activity?"

"None visible, sir. Could be they think the missile got us."

"Don't bet on it." He looked at his watch. Nine minutes to ditching. At eight hundred miles an hour—estimated—they'd gain a hundred twenty miles before water impact. Mentally he reviewed ditching procedures as the wounded bomber slanted downward toward the sea.

Thirty-Seven

WASHINGTON

PICKING UP THE SECURE NRO telephone, Tom Gray heard the duty officer's excited voice. "I'm transmitting a series of images we haven't had time to evaluate. But it's ground activity you ought to be aware of."

"Dragon Teeth area?"

"Right. Maybe you can shed light on what's happening. Let me know, will you?"

"Sure, start sending." He put down the receiver and stood by the linked printer. As sequential Gorgon photo images slid out of the printer he carried them to the illuminated magnifier and stared in disbelief. Seconds apart, two large explosions erupted from the Leping missile base, then a pair of enormous fireballs rose and spread across the entire base area. Three frames later the fireballs had vanished and all he could see of the base were ground fires among the debris. Jesus, he thought, the missiles are gone, the launchers are gone, and so is the base. His hands trembled with excitement. More photos were arriving, but before Tommy examined them, he got out his desk bottle and swallowed four bracing ounces of Early Times. He looked at the Leping photos again and decided a launch-ready missile had exploded and detonated all the others. Damn!

Checking coordinates, he realized that the next series covered the Yangyuan and Zhuolu factory areas. As at Leping, brilliant explosions erupted followed by immense fireballs. Same at Zhuolu. The repetition couldn't be coincidental, he thought. Ground agents must have sabotaged and destroyed all three targets. Did that mean the Dragon Teeth crisis was over? He studied the complete series again and decided the missile threat no longer existed. Incredible. He collected the photos and spread them across his desk, then called the NRO officer. "My preliminary thought is those three installations were sabotaged and destroyed. Probably by some dissident action group."

"My first reaction was air-ground bombing, but, shit, no aircraft showed up before or after the explosions." He paused. "We'll get another look under daylight conditions but from the magnitude of those explosions I'd say there won't be much to see."

"The fireballs resembled atomic explosions minus mushroom clouds."

"Thought so myself, but it'll probably be a week before upper altitude winds carry debris close enough we can send up Sniffer balloons. If atomic particles register, the International Atomic Energy watchdogs will have to be informed."

Gray sighed. The liquor was giving him a relaxed sense of euphoria. "Okay," he said, "I'll brief my bosses and they'll decide how far the information is to go."

"Meaning, you'll copy Langley?"

"Yeah, but you better copy them now. I imagine the Director will want to know."

"Roger that," he said, and hung up.

When Gray got Darman Gerold on the phone he said, "I need to show you a series of, ah, unusual developments."

"Concerning what?" Gerold said testily. "I've got a meeting going on."

"Concerning that toothy legendary animal we've been concerned about."

"Okay, Tom, I'll be there in an hour."

"Anytime," Gray said and hung up. By then, he thought, the DCI would have seen the photos through normal channels, and Gray expected him to end-run the NSC and show the take directly to the President.

Whoever was responsible for knocking out those installations, he thought, did a damn good thorough job.

APPALACHIAN FOOTHILLS, PENNSYLVANIA

LA-LI WAS CHARMED by Dr. Simon Brand's rustic lodge, had never seen its like before, and marveled at its construction from native stone and timber. During the drive from Washington she had shared the rear seat with Peter and slept most of the way in his arms.

Dr. Brand accepted their unannounced arrival with equanimity, assigned sleeping areas, and busied himself heating a pot of venison stew. He prepared an herbal poultice for his son's wound, and said it would heal rapidly with the products of nature. He asked no questions about the wound or their flight from Washington, but after breakfast the following morning Peter and Brand told him the full story, La-li listening open-eyed.

"So," Dr. Brand said, "you're finally going to marry Chen Mei-ling."

Brand nodded. "I was going to bring them to Washington for a double ceremony, but under present circumstances I think not."

"Hong Kong, then?"

"Or Taiwan. I'll let Mary decide."

Dr. Brand added wild honey to his coffee, stirred, and said, "I think our friend Irving Chenow ought to be informed what's been going on."

"Not a good idea to phone from here," Brand said. "No telling if his phone is tapped—or yours. Anyway, I'm going back to Washington and get to the bottom of things. Alone."

Peter said, "Is that wise, Dad?"

"Probably not, but necessary. And with the three of you safe here I won't be worrying about you. Yeah, there's a couple of people I need to see. Including Irv Chenow."

Dr. Brand said, "Your arm could use more rest, so I recommend you not leave until tomorrow—if you're determined to go."

"Grandpa," Peter said, "I want to make myself useful around here, but I don't want to be in your way. Just tell me what to do."

"Well, there's wood and kindling to be chopped," the doctor said, "fish to be caught, and berries to be picked. And I've been watching the burrow of a fat woodchuck."

La-li said, "I can pick berries, peel vegetables, and wash dishes. Just because I'm pregnant doesn't mean I'm crippled."

"True," the doctor said, "and you're a very welcome addition to our family group."

Peter had been checking objects on the cabin walls and said, "How do we bag the chuck? Not with that shotgun."

"No, that's for the occasional trespassing pheasant or partridge." He gestured at a slim six-foot PVC tube on the wall. "Blowpipe," he said. "I use darts tipped with a sticky mess of copperhead and rattler venom. Got that bearskin on the shed wall with one puff."

To Peter, Brand said, "Taiwanese aborigines tip their darts with *habu* venom."

"*Habu?*"

"A little viper deadlier than the cobra." He smiled. "I learned about things like that when I was a kid in Taipei, but you were too young for matters of life and death."

La-li took Peter's hand, squeezed it, and smiled. "I'm so happy," she said shyly, "and I was sick with worry and fear while you were gone."

"There were times I was worried and scared myself," he responded and pressed her stomach lightly. Observing the motion, Dr. Brand said, "Patience, Peter, takes a while for the baby to quicken, and then it will make itself known unmistakably." He looked at his watch. "I'll show you the woodpile and the berry patches, then I'm off to see a patient with the flu."

"And the woodchuck?"

"He comes out and looks around toward sundown. We'll take him then."

Brand drank more chicory-flavored coffee and heard his father's pickup start, roll down the rocky access road. It might be a good idea, he thought, to leave his BMW hidden in the woods and drive the pickup as far as some parking garage in the District. Taxis from there on.

He'd start with a pay phone call to Irv Chenow, arrange a meeting with Tommy Gray away from GlobEco, and surprise Darman Gerold when he least expected it.

That much decided, Brand opened his suitcases and hung up the bespoke clothing tailored for him by the estimable Jamie McPherson of McIntosh, Queen's Road, Hong Kong.

Thirty-Eight

37° NORTH LATITUDE, 123° EAST LONGITUDE

WHEN THE EIGHTY-TON BOMBER hit the water, the impact slammed Barlow forward against restraining straps and he felt as though his chest was crushed. For a hundred yards more the B-1 hydroplaned forward until the shattered wingtip dug in and spun the plane around.

The OAS officer popped rafts free from the overhead and guided

Barlow toward the emergency exit door. Separation charges blew it outward, and as interior lights dimmed and faded, Barlow saw the rafts floating nearby. Pilot and copilot had exited from their hatch, and were crawling along the up-slanting left wing toward the nearest raft. From overhead came the whistle of Stealth engines. They sped low over the scene, banked away, and gained altitude to orbit above the sinking plane.

Even with bomb bay doors closed the plane took water faster than Barlow expected. Per standard ditch procedure the pilot had approached the surface at stalling speed and brought up the nose so that the tail broke water first before dragging down the forward fuselage. He did a hell of a good job, Barlow thought, turned on the flashlight secured around his wrist by a lanyard, and dropped into the water. He submerged a few feet before the life jacket brought him to the surface, and began stroking to the nearest raft. Drogues kept them from drifting in the light chop so he had only twenty or thirty feet to swim before reaching the raft's handholds. He steadied the raft while the OAS bellied over the tubular side, and was helped aboard in turn. The water was cool but not frigid, it was the breeze that prickled his exposed flesh. His chest ached as he lay back, head against the inflated rim, and watched the OAS unpack the raft's emergency gear. The signal balloon went up first, and the OAS activated the beacon. Barlow saw the same procedure in the pilots' raft and said, "We'll take the third raft in tow, in case we need it."

"Yes, sir." He mounted two short oars in oarlocks and rowed until he could fish the drogue line from the water. The pilots' raft was rowing toward them, and they lashed on a drogue-length away.

"That was excellent flying, Captain," Barlow said. "Any damage to either of you?"

"Two sprained wrists and a sprained shoulder, sir. Nothing major."

"For now," Barlow said, "I don't think we ought to transmit by radio. The Chinese could be monitoring emergency channels."

The copilot nodded. "The beacon will bring friendlies," he said, "and we've got enough drinking water and sealed rations to last until they come."

Barlow looked up at the distant sound of fighter engines. The aircraft were invisible, as they should be. He looked at his watch. The timeline would be important when he made out his crash report.

By now, the B-1's fuselage was below the surface, the empennage, too. All that remained was the undamaged wing sticking upright from the water like the monstrous fin of a whale.

After gazing at it, the OAS said, "We lost a plane but I think we did a pretty thorough job."

"Absolutely," Barlow responded. "Mission accomplished. Now let's make ourselves comfortable. If Chinese radar followed us down they probably won't send aircraft until daylight—and that's a few hours away." He looked up at the two signal balloons and their electronic beacon boxes silently calling for help. The F-117s would cover them for maybe two hours, then fly over to Seoul or Taegu. By then, significant help should be on the way.

"Candy, General? We've got some Tootsie Rolls here."

"Any medicinal alcohol?"

"Pint bottle of Canadian Club—if you like rye."

"Ordinarily no, but I'd drink panther piss to get warm." He undid the metal cap and swallowed a long slug. The OAS drank from the bottle and recapped it. "We've got everything but a charcoal fire to toast weenies, this is the life."

"And we're living," Barlow said jocularly, then heard a far-off sound that made him stiffen. "Lights out," he snapped, "everyone down on your bellies."

The others had heard oncoming jets, but the copilot said, "Could be friendlies, sir."

"Not from the west," he contradicted, and looked upward, hoping the F-117s were alerted.

Two minutes later a pair of Chinese jets flashed low overhead, engine blasts shaking the rafts like toys. Both jets headed skyward, he followed their exhaust rings as they leveled off for a strafing run. Must have spotted the projecting wing on radar, but they've seen us now. And as he watched, he saw a Sidewinder streak across the dark sky toward the leading jet. It impacted in a burst of flame whose concussion waves made the raft shudder. One down, he thought, one to go, then saw a second Sidewinder destroy the other jet. Our shepherds of the sky, he thought in relief, and watched the aircraft's wreckage fall burning and twisting into the sea.

They'll send more, he thought, they don't give up easily. Over Korea they fought like mad dogs and I hoped never to see the bastards aloft again.

Was anyone receiving the beacon signals? Had the Chinese locked on them? By now their air controllers knew two jets had splashed, wouldn't be long before more arrived.

Well, he mused, what will be will be. If they send four, one could get through and finish us, and I don't want to die in the empty blackness of the Yellow Sea.

Twelve minutes later he heard oncoming jet engines, more volume this time, more jets on the way in reprisal for Leping, Yangyuan, and Zhuolu. I'd guess we killed a hundred, mostly military, so if they manage to kill the four of us, the ratio is one even old Westmoreland could boast about.

Cold comfort on a cold, dark sea.

Looking up he saw the Stealth's exhaust rings changing formation, one aircraft above the other, spaced for attack and mutual defense. Then four Chinese fighters swept toward them, outlined by moonlight, and Barlow watched Sidewinders streak toward them. Three explosions followed before a Chinese missile sped toward an invisible Stealth. The fourth Chinese fighter detonated, but its missile hit the Stealth in a blast of red and white fire. Barlow covered his eyes and wept. He was no stranger to losing buddies in combat, but he was shaken by the death of a pilot who had saved the lives of the helpless rafters.

The OAS said, "Sir, sir—look over there—"

Barlow saw a parachute descending. "Alive or dead, we're going for him," he yelled, "now *row!*"

Slowly the rafts moved toward the downed pilot, hidden by two-foot waves, and when Barlow stood up, steadied by the OAS, he saw the orange raft, a pilot in it.

When the Stealth pilot saw them he yelled and sculled toward them. Barlow pulled him into his raft and the OAS stowed the pilot's seat ejection raft in their empty one. "God, am I glad to see you!" the pilot exulted. "First I thought I was dead, then when the blast ejected me I thought the chute might have been destroyed. But no. Goddammit, this is my lucky night!" He punched the chute release, and waves tugged the shroud lines free.

Barlow gave him the bottle and said, "All three of you did incredible things tonight, from takeoff on. You okay?"

"Bruised chest, sore crotch, and the ejection blast probably compressed my spine two inches." He drank again. "But I'm lucky to be alive." He returned the bottle to Barlow. "When I saw you guys ditch I thought, Jesus, they'll go down like a stone. But on the next pass I saw the rafts deployed and you guys getting in them. That was one hell of a splash you made."

"I know," the OAS told him, "we felt it."

"We'll total your kills later," Barlow said, "but what were the Chinese flying?"

"The last four were MIG 23 Floggers. The pair before them were Fishbeds, which is what came up over the Mainland. Old Russian shit— excuse me, General—aircraft, I meant to say."

"Hell, let's be informal while we can. You were saying?"

"I think I spotted a couple of Saab Viggens after Leping, but I'm not sure. Basically we had considerable technical advantage—until I got knocked down."

Waves lapped at the side of the raft. Silently, Barlow thought, we can expect more visitors, with only two fighters to defend us.

They heard more incoming aircraft from the west, and Barlow saw the F-117s climb high to get on top of them. By now, he thought, they must be running low on air-to-air missiles, but maybe they can still splash these MIGs.

It was a formation of four Russian fighters that flashed overhead at about three thousand feet. Barlow watched four Sidewinders slam downward and impact as the fighters turned. "Four for four," he said admiringly, "pretty damn good shooting."

The Stealth pilot said, "They can't see us visually or on radar, so it's not like the air combat you went through, General."

"Risks are the same. Look at you. Where's your aircraft, mister?" he joked. "And who authorized you to go swimming in uniform?"

"No excuse, sir." The pilot grinned. "Mind if I have another sip of that life-giving beverage?"

While they were talking, the bomber pilots were sitting back to back, watching the sea. Suddenly, one of them yelled, "Look! Look at it. Jesus, just *look!*"

At first, Barlow thought a whale was breaching, then he saw a long black body emerge, and then a conning tower. "Show 'em our lights," he snapped, and they waved and blinked their flashlights until answering lights shined back from the submarine. "Let's row now, lads, row like hell before some Chinese cocksucker starts dropping bombs."

The submarine turned toward them, slowly closing the gap until the rafts bumped its bulge and half a dozen rope ladders unrolled to help them up. "Bring your ration packs aboard," Barlow ordered, "and say nothing about why we're here. Not a word. I'll do any talking." As he stepped on the steel deck he saluted astern. "Permission to come aboard, sir."

The Lieutenant Commander saluted and said, "Welcome, aboard, General. Let's get you all stowed below so we can dive. Doesn't look like we're in very friendly waters."

Barlow smiled. "Putting it mildly. Anyway, we appreciate your timely arrival—but then I guess that's the Navy way."

Thirty-Nine

Washington

Darman Gerold stared incredulously at the Gorgon photos. "My God, it looks like a total wipeout!"

"Sure does," Tommy said happily. There was more bourbon in his stomach than in his bottle, and he felt better than he had in weeks.

"But—how?" Gerold mumbled. "Who could have done it?"

"Brave bands of dissident saboteurs, more'n likely, but, hey, let's celebrate freedom from fear. And tonight I get to go home early and get a good night's sleep. That's the beauty part." He grinned at Gerold, wondering why his ex-college mate wasn't happy, too.

Gerold took a chair and sat back, staring at the ceiling. The timing was incredible—incredibly bad. His impulse was to phone his three friends and tell them to suspend liquidations; then it occurred to him that there could still be trouble on the Mainland. Beijing wouldn't want to admit that the destruction of a missile base and two military factories could be accomplished by antiregime activists. That would give international stature to a dissident movement that was supposed to be suppressed. So Deng, like Stalin before him, would blame it on foreign enemies and suppress the people even more.

So there was no urgency about calling Paul, Fred, and Darcy. His working assumption would continue to revolve around disruption on the Mainland. Sucking in a deep breath, Gerold asked, "NRO has seen this?"

"Hell, yes, sent it to me."

"Any speculation on the source of the explosions?"

"Said they'd get a better look by daylight, might be some clues lying around. But so far it appears a domestic happening. Chinese reaction, if any, should suggest something plausible."

Gerold nodded, stood up, and stretched. Tommy said, "I figured Mark would be back by now. Any word on him?"

Yes, Gerold said silently, and all bad. Aloud, he said, "He may have decided to take a Caribbean holiday with his son. He and Peter have gone through some difficult times."

"I'm sure, and I'm looking forward to hearing what they have to say." He gestured at the photos. "You can take these with you, but NRO's already sent them to the DCI."

"I'll take them," Gerold said dully, "keep them for the record."

"Closing the file on Dragon Teeth," Tommy told him cheerfully. "That was the last chapter, end of story."

Gerold opened his mouth, decided against saying anything, and left the office.

Driving back to Langley, Gerold reflected that the unexpected, the totally unanticipated, had happened: underground Chinese elements had eliminated the threat to Taiwan. Consequently there would be no U.S. executive action, no commercial or military threats issued to the Chinese leadership. The menace had simply ceased to exist.

He wondered how badly his friends would be hit by summary liquidation. They'd suffer, no doubt of it, and they'd blame him if things stayed tranquil in China. Brand and his whelp could still do plenty of damage to the Administration if they talked to the media. And after the incredibly slipshod attempt to detain them by Security cretins they had plenty to be mad about.

So they had to be squelched one way or another.

His radio was set to the AM band for news—early warning of China trouble, he'd thought—but now some Southern station drifted in with country music. He was about to shift settings when the talk host began taking calls. Gerold heard a woman talking with a problem. Apparently she had phoned the station before because the talk-show host called her Frog Lady and they chatted familiarly:

"Ah'm still afeard to go out in the yard."

"Because of this frog—that it?"

"Yeah. And Ah don' know what to do."

"Won't neighbors help?"

"Ah tol' you before, got no neighbors aroun'. They too far away. Today the frog was in a tree."

"What did he do?"

"He looked at me." There was fear in her voice and Gerold felt his own neck prickle.

"Well, ma'am, *looking* at you isn't *hurting* you."

"But Ah'm afeard to go out."

"That's not a reasonable fear, ma'am. Maybe you could make a friend of the frog."

"Friend? How's that?"

"I mean, pet him, feed him. Show him you mean no harm and maybe he'll go away."

"Ah'd be afeard to do that. Frogs got poison sacs. He could kill me."

The conversation was becoming increasingly bizarre but Gerold did not change the dial. It came to him that under certain circumstances *he* could fear a frog.

"Ma'am, it's *toads* that have poison sacs, not frogs."

"Maybe this frog is a toad."

"Could be. Now, let's hear from you listeners. Friends, call in your thoughts and suggestions; let's help the Frog Lady, hey? She's got a problem, a frog-size problem." He chuckled. "Let's help her out. The number is . . ."

Gerold clicked off the radio wishing he could help the woman, the Frog Lady, wherever she was.

Is that all these bumpkins have to talk about on their yokel stations? he wondered irritably. A frog in some fucking tree frightening some old farmhouse drudge? The whole context seemed preposterous. First, frogs don't climb trees—the host had nailed that absurdity solid, then he'd done right encouraging her to get out, confront the frog/toad, and overcome her irrational fears. Paranoia, nothing less. The county's rural health officer should check her out and prescribe medication and treatment immediately. Pitiful case, but Gerold felt she could be helped, just as Doreen was being helped by competent practitioners.

Unwillingly, Gerold was reminded of son Fitzhugh, whose adolescent mindset opened him to frauds, schemers, and deceptive practices of all kinds. There was Fitzhugh's Aliens-Killed-Kennedy phase, a summer on peyote, a consuming interest in Armageddon and Edgar Cayce, the inner-world theories of Velikovsky, and sporadic bouts with LSD. Fitzhugh would identify promptly with the maunderings of the Frog Lady, Gerold mused, perhaps embark on a pilgrimage to save her and improve her quality of life. So it was better for all concerned that his son was not around. And with the proximate restructuring of his own living arrangements, Fitzhugh's reappearance would be undesirable to say the least.

He turned into the familiar access road and saw Agency guard stations ahead. At least, he thought, this is Reality, and prepared to reenter a different world.

SSN *SUSQUEHANNA*, YELLOW SEA

WHILE THE ATTACK SUBMARINE submerged to running depth, its Captain, a three-striper, turned over his cabin to General Barlow and told the rescued pilots they were to sleep in Gold Crew cabins, while Gold Crew officers were on watch. The boat's supply CPO brought an issue of dry clothing for each of the five new passengers, and promised to return their own clean uniforms the following day. Hearing a knock on his door, Barlow called, "Come in," and the Captain entered.

"Sir," he said, "I'd better list all your names, if you don't mind."

"Actually," Barlow said, "that's not feasible, given the nature of our mission. How about calling us five shipwrecked supernumeraries and letting it go at that?"

"Well, it's not reg, sir, but as SOP you're calling the shots."

"Thank you, Captain, I appreciate it. Now, if security permits, I'd like to call the Chairman of the Joint Chiefs, General Sosnowski."

The Captain's eyebrows lifted, and he glanced at bulkhead chronometers that showed local and Washington time. "As you can see, it's about nine P.M. there, but I'd guess we can connect you with his office in, say, ten minutes."

"Without surfacing?"

"Yes, sir, not necessary." He paused. "If you're hungry and thirsty like most survivors, the wardroom's available to all of you. And the doctor would like to check you over at your convenience."

General Barlow nodded. "We don't want to inconvenience you any more than absolutely necessary. Where are we headed now?"

"Moving out of international waters bound for Inchon, South Korea."

"I've been there before," he told the Captain, "in a long-ago war. Flown over it anyway. Now, I don't want a lot of fuss over our arrival, but I'm going to need transport aircraft from Seoul to take us to our various destinations. Can that be laid on?"

"Not a problem, sir. Shall I proceed with scrambler linkage to the Chairman?"

"Please do."

"Uh—sir, who shall I identify as the caller?"

Barlow thought for a moment before it came to him. "A Mr. Forester," he replied.

"Forester?"

"He'll understand."

"Very good, sir." He gestured at the telephone on his desk. "You can talk from here."

"Thank you, ah—you said ten minutes?"

"About that, sir."

"Then if I can have coffee now, I'll wait here."

"Aye, sir." The Captain closed the door and General Barlow saw himself in the mirror. Starched, pressed khakis without rank indicators looked strange, he thought, but right now anonymity is a good idea, serving everyone concerned.

Presently a mess steward brought in a silver coffee service: pot, cream, sugar, spoon, and a blue-and-gold china cup and saucer. The Navy does things right, he thought, and while he was sipping coffee the desk telephone rang. Picking up the receiver, Barlow said, "Forester here."

"One moment, sir." Then he heard Sosnowski saying, "Hello there, wherever you are. Understand you're in a cruise mode, so to speak."

"Yes, sir. I believe all objectives were accomplished."

"I can confirm that—saw some late photos. You okay?"

"Yes, sir, but we lost a couple of birds, my big one and a small one. However, everyone's okay, I'm happy to say."

"And I'm glad to hear. Ah—will I be seeing you soon?"

"Can't tell from this remote, ah, location, but I'll keep you informed."

"Do that, Forester, and congratulations on an excellent tree-cutting expedition. The big boss is highly pleased."

"Thank you, sir." He heard the transmission end and the carrier hum cut in. Barlow replaced the telephone, finished his coffee, and went out to the wardroom to join his men at mess.

WASHINGTON

IN THE LIVING ROOM of his Potomac Falls home Irving Chenow was enjoying after-dinner cognac with his wife. "Honey," he said, "if you'll return that envelope to me I'm going to destroy it."

"Oh? Are you sure it won't be needed?"

"Positive," he replied. "I was shown a series of photographs that indicated an end to the Chinese attack posture."

"That's wonderful. I'm so relieved you won't have to use whatever the envelope contains."

"So am I."

"I was a bit afraid our Washington days were coming to an end prematurely. They would have, Irving, wouldn't they?"

"They would, dear, but that's no longer likely."

"Umm. Did some dramatic event take place that changed everything?"

"Must have, but I don't know what it was."

"Maybe the President got some spine-stiffening."

He shrugged. "More cognac?"

"No, and I'll get that envelope right now. Having it worried me obsessively." She left the room and he heard her go upstairs. After a while she came back and handed him the unopened envelope.

"Where did you hide it?" he asked.

She smiled. "That would be telling, wouldn't it? I don't want to lose my little hiding place for gifts and such." She came around behind and circled his neck with her arms, kissed the top of his thinning hair. "You're a great man," she said softly, "and I love you very much."

His throat felt constricted. He found one of her hands and pressed it. After a while he got up and went out to the patio with the envelope, laid it on the charcoal grill, and doused it with starter fluid. After lighting it, he stepped back and watched it burn.

Tom Gray had brought him satellite images that showed flames and destruction at the three Mainland sites. Gray theorized bands of antiregime saboteurs were responsible, but Chenow considered an alternate explanation. Calling General Barlow's office, he had been told that Barlow was away for a few days, and Chenow had not pursued his inquiry. He felt it was no coincidence that Barlow was away at the time the three sites were destroyed, but he proposed to let it rest at that. If and when Bruce returned, he could tell him in his own good time.

Chenow watched disk and cassette melt and burn, sparks rising in the night's cool air. He realized he was largely responsible for ending the threat to Taiwan, but neither Vivian nor the President was ever going to know.

Forty

TWO DAYS AFTER ARRIVING at his father's retreat, Mark Brand drove off in his father's ancient pickup, leaving his BMW stashed in the woods.

It was night. Peter, La-li, and Dr. Brand were in the living room watching a late program on the old black-and-white television set the doctor declined to upgrade. The doctor had told stories of wartime China and postwar Taiwan, and La-li had described her childhood and adolescence in Nanjing. Speaking of her father and mother, she became tearful, and Dr. Brand said, "Now, now, I'm sure they're quite all right. No harm will come to them. And one day you'll be reunited."

"Oh, I hope so," she said, drying her cheeks. "If we live in Hong Kong it will be easier to get information about them."

Peter smiled. "My father and I have influential friends who can help with that very thing."

"Undoubtedly," said Dr. Brand, "if you're thinking of our Fang-tse clan."

Peter nodded and saw his grandfather yawn. "You two get to bed," the doctor said, "and I'll see you in the morning. Sleep as late as you like, I'm up and about pretty early."

The young couple got up from the sofa, kissed his cheek, and disappeared into their bedroom. Dr. Brand drank a final cup of coffee and decided to take a stroll through the woods around his cabin. Whatever Mark was doing in Washington, he felt was the right thing to do. He had more confidence than ever in his son, and he reflected that his flight from Beijing must have been a hair-raising experience. He recalled Cheong Wing-dah's father with distaste; another of Chiang's corrupt looters, whose excesses had, in effect, delivered China to Mao's Yenan bandits. That the son had turned out badly was no surprise, and he was prayerfully grateful that Cheong's bullet had not killed Mark as intended.

After turning out lights he took his blowpipe and a small pocket quiver of poison-tipped darts from the wall and left the cabin. The night was quiet and cool, and he planned to check a stand of cherry trees, where droppings told him wild turkeys were wont to roost at night. He was glad to have his family under his roof, and he thought soberly that God had watched over them all at every turn. With the exception of his wife's death so long ago, a loss he could neither understand nor accept. Not God but Satan had to be responsible for that.

In deerskin moccasins, Dr. Brand moved quietly away from the cabin intending to approach the cherry trees from upwind. Then he heard the sound of an approaching car. It wasn't his pickup, he knew its groans and rattles all too well. No, a much newer car with a smooth-running engine. Dr. Brand assumed it was bringing him a patient when he heard the engine cut off at the bottom of the curving inclined road. The sound of a closing door followed, and the doctor wondered if what his friends called "Revenooers" had come searching for an illicit still.

His nearest neighbor lived more than a quarter of a mile away, so the doctor assumed that the caller or callers were interested in *his* cabin and it angered him. Ever since the Koresh compound debacle, the ATF was viewed with fear and contempt by the mountain folk Dr. Brand served. He found a place from where he had an unobstructed view of the cabin and the access road, sat down, blowpipe beside him, and waited.

Presently he heard the crunch of pebbles underfoot and realized the intruder was coming up the stony road. Peering through the darkness, Dr. Brand saw a man cross a moonlit patch, and caught his breath. For the man had a short automatic weapon slung from his shoulder, and as he neared the wide turnaround, he veered close to the shadowed edge and unslung his weapon.

Blowpipe in one hand, Dr. Brand crawled toward him and heard the snick of the cocking lever. The sound chilled him and he saw the man stop, move deeper into shadows, and look around, listening.

The front door was unlocked, it was never locked, and neither was the back kitchen door. Gripping his weapon with both hands, the gunman moved along the side of the cabin, nearing the owner with every step. The man paused to peer through a dark window, grunted, and moved on. Dr. Brand fitted a dart into the blowpipe and waited. Seeing the man's profile, he realized the left side of his face was bandaged, and something stirred his memory. So as the man put a foot on the rear steps Dr. Brand filled his lungs and bayed like a wolf. The man froze, then turned to face the source of the sound. Dr. Brand sighted along the tube and puffed out a dart, reloaded and launched a second as the first dart struck the man's unprotected throat. He yelped, dropped his gun, and plucked out the darts, bent down to grasp the gun, wobbled, and lurched forward. From thirty feet away Dr. Brand could hear his stertorous breathing as he gasped and fought for breath. The fallen man's body arched and convulsed, fingers clawing the loose soil. Dr. Brand sat back on his haunches and waited for the man to die.

Habu venom was quicker acting, he knew, but the combination of rattler and copperhead venom was equally deadly. So when the body had not moved for five minutes, Dr. Brand left his hiding place and approached cautiously. The bandaged side of the man's face was up, and his left eye stared stonily ahead. No pulse in the carotid. Dr. Brand turned the body over on its back and extracted a wallet from the inside coat pocket. It was a new wallet, he saw, with nothing in it but some currency and a blue temporary carnet identifying Samuel T. Peloso as a civilian employee of the Department of the Army. "Well, Sam," he muttered, "you should have kept to the PX instead of wandering around the woods with your shooter." Peloso was the name in one of the three forfeited wallets Mark had shown him, so the black-hearted scoundrel was trying again.

He was grateful that he had been able to protect his family from this assassin, but Peter and La-li must never know. Guilty knowledge was to be his alone, though he might tell Mark when his son got back from Washington.

For a while he sat beside the corpse, his mind working out details of an arranged scene that would implicate no one.

An owl hooted in the woods. He heard a raccoon rustling downward toward the trout stream. Nocturnal creatures were seeking their prey. And the man who had approached his cabin with deadly intent lay dead beside him.

The first thing to do, the doctor thought, was determine if Peloso came alone. He replaced the wallet and felt other pockets for car keys. None.

Carefully he picked up the spent darts, broken by the dead man's frantic hands, and pocketed them. Then he began walking quietly down the dark edge of his road, and after the curve, where it leveled off, he saw a car parked in roadside grass.

From behind a tree trunk Dr. Brand gazed at the car, looking for the flare of a match, the sound of a radio, but the car was dark and still. Satisfied it was unoccupied, he approached it from the field and saw ignition keys dangling below the wheel. He got in, started the engine, and drove back up to the cabin without headlights. Engine running, he went to the corpse and lifted it in his arms, carried it to the car, and laid it across the rear seat. He put the automatic weapon on the floor. Then he drove partway back to the main road, made a U-turn, and steered the car onto the shoulder. He lifted Peloso off the seat and carried him a short distance into the bracken, where he laid the dead man carefully on his back. He pulled down the trouser zipper and drew up the left trouser leg. Then, holding the darts like chopsticks, their tips a fang's width apart, he punctured the leg skin twice and replaced the trouser.

Standing, he looked around visualizing the scene by daylight. A driver had stopped to relieve his bladder, been bitten by a poisonous snake, died on the spot.

It wasn't a perfect mise-en-scène but perfection could raise questions. And questions about the car's automatic weapon would naturally arise. Let them be answered by those who could, he thought, as he wiped his finger- and handprints from the car door handle, sill, and keys.

Had Peloso been dispatched by his principals? he wondered as he began walking back toward the cabin. Or had he come on his own to avenge his damaged face? In Washington, Mark might find answers, he mused, but meanwhile he was responsible for the care and feeding of his family.

The girl was young and healthy, and the doctor felt she could deliver at term without difficulty. When broken to new responsibilities Peter would make a good and caring father and husband, he told himself, but Mark was quite right: for safety's sake all three should go back to Taiwan or Hong Kong—where Chen Mei-ling awaited his return.

A raccoon scuttled across the road ahead of him. A bat flashed across the sky. Dr. Brand smiled as he trod the rising road back to his silent cabin. He was the nearest physician for miles around, and so authorities often solicited his opinion concerning the deaths of traffic and roadside victims. In the case of Samuel Peloso Dr. Brand's opinion was already formed.

Washington

Pauline Frances Gerold tapped a manicured fingernail impatiently as she waited for Darman to come to the phone. When he answered, she said, "What on earth is going *on* in Georgetown? What are you *doing* to the house?"

"You noticed."

"Impossible not to, with those plumbing and painters' trucks parked in front."

"Touching up the guest room, dear, no big deal."

"I see. Any particular reason?"

He wet his lips. "The clinic psychiatrist wants Doreen in a home atmosphere for a while—experimentally. Redoing her room more attractively might persuade her to stay and not run off again."

"You didn't consult *me.*"

"You seldom stay there—what difference could it make to you?"

"Darman, I'm not talking about the painting, I mean having Doreen there. You know how I feel about her, and she about me."

"Yes, but that could all be changed. In fact, Dr. Hempill predicts it. This time she feels rehabilitation is really working."

His wife snorted. "I'll believe that when I see it. By the way, when is your daughter being paroled?" She smiled at her choice of words.

"Not sure, but soon. And she's not a criminal, Pauline."

"Just criminal tendencies." She sighed. "Oh, Darman. Very well, I'm sending the gala invitations today, and I've booked the caterer and a dance band."

"Thank you so much," he said, relieved she hadn't further questioned Doreen's homecoming, "I know it will be a great success."

"We'll see," she responded, and hung up.

Gerold replaced the telephone receiver and glanced around his office. His In box held intelligence reports, dispatches, and cables to be released. To his surprise a State telegram to Taipei and Beijing lifted the travel ban, and Gerold related it to the puzzling disappearance of the missile threat. His position vis-à-vis his three friends was deteriorating, and it would be only a matter of time before one or all of them began asking questions. Well, it wasn't as though he'd *told* them to liquidate, the option had been theirs all along. He'd tried to do a financially significant favor based on the best information he had at the time. Who could have predicted sabotage to all three sites?

Mark Brand and his son were still on the loose and capable of doing great damage to the Administration. But, he mused, if they go public about the gas missiles, would that be bad for me?

Perhaps not, he said to himself. Darcy, Paul, and Freddy would understand what he'd been concerned about, and his initiative would be validated. So, he thought, I'd be in the clear, let come what may.

IT WAS AFTER MIDNIGHT when Mark Brand left the taxi two blocks from Tom Gray's Cleveland Park home. It was an old, two-story wooden house set back from the street and partly obscured by maple trees in the front yard. As he went up the laid-brick walk he saw no lights on the second floor, but dim light showed through inside curtains of a porch window. Up three steps to the porch, where an old wooden swing hung from chain supports. Brand breathed deeply before pressing the bell button, heard chimes from somewhere within the house. After waiting, he rang again, and after a third try saw a shadow cross the window, heard Tommy's voice. "Who's there? Whatcha want at this ungodly hour?"

"Mark Brand. Let me in, Tom."

"Mark? Hey, sure thing." The snub chain rattled and the dead bolt slid back. The door opened, and Mark saw a disheveled Tommy in blue pajamas. "Mark, Christ, glad to see you! Jesus, we been worried." His words slurred and Mark realized he'd been drinking. He stepped in and closed the door.

"Come in, come in, seems like you've been gone forever."

"Couple of times I could have been, Tom, and that's why I'm here."

"Mark, if we're gonna talk, le's have a drink. I've been working like you wouldn't believe, and I need relief." He gestured at a closed door off the living room. "Lila's sleeping—at last—let's not wake her."

"We won't, and a glass of scotch will be welcome."

"Coming up." He went to the dining-room sideboard and poured liquor in two tumblers, added a few cubes of ice. "Sit ye down, and tell me what's been going on." He gulped from his glass and shook himself. "But first, your son's safe and sound—right?"

"Fortunately." He drank slowly.

"How long you been back?"

"A few days. Long enough to find out I'm on a hit list."

"*Hit* list? Mark, you gotta be kidding."

"Wish I were. So you don't know anything about it?"

Tommy's forehead furrowed. "Only list I know about is the Dragon Teeth Bigot List."

"What's Dragon Teeth?"

"Oh, all that stuff about missiles and gas warheads—the Gorgon take."

"I see. Well, in Hong Kong Dockerty wanted us to sign a secrecy commitment and I declined." He sipped again. "I didn't think it was important, now I'm beginning to."

"Guess I'm not connecting, Mark, but maybe I shouldn't. Not if you're in deep guano. My main interest is having you back in your office so I can ease back—it's been rough, I tell you, with Darman on my ass all the time, Irv Chenow calling for information I can't give him because Darman said no . . ." His voice trailed away.

"So Darman's been on top of things."

"Guess so—acts that way." He grinned. "Anyway, Dragon Teeth's over with. Plants and missiles destroyed."

Brand sat forward. "How? When?"

"How? I've been speculating sabotage. Gorgon showed everything exploding couple days ago—nights, their time. Impressive show, believe me. You'll see it in the office."

"Maybe not, Tom. I sense a growing incompatibility between myself and GlobEco and the Agency. And my clearances will probably be canceled—I went to the Mainland, you know."

"Yeah, but who could blame you? Had to find your son."

"Yes, I had to. Now, what I'm going to tell you has to be secret between us—in fact, I'm not here, haven't been here."

Suddenly sober-faced, Gray said, "I understand, sure. Go on, Mark."

Brand drank and took a deep breath. "When Peter and I got to Dulles there was a three-man reception committee—courteous and friendly at first, but the attitude changed when I asked for ID and they declined to produce. Said they were from the Director's office which, I guess, is possible, but they seemed like low-level Security creeps to me."

"Director's office? Wow!"

"Yeah. Anyway, Peter and I resisted, took over their car, and left them stranded at roadside. And we took their firearms."

"Jesus, Mark, this is getting really strange. What's behind it?"

"Your Dragon Teeth is all I can figure. The Administration doesn't want us talking about what we know—the gas warheads, the gassed bodies Peter saw. When Peter and I declined to sign the special secrecy agreement someone back here went bananas and figured we were going to tell some tabloid, so heavies were dispatched to kidnap us." He shook his head. "None of that was necessary, Tom. Peter and I weren't going to talk about our experiences except in an Agency debriefing. But we're in hiding now, with Peter's fiancée, at least until I find out who set us up."

"Whole thing sounds incredible."

"Doesn't it, though? But the Agency was never renowned for tact or soft glove diplomacy. The three strongarms had Pentagon ID cards, indicating a remote possibility they were sent, maybe, by DIA. But having had a close working knowledge of domestic covers, I'd say the malefactors were from Agency Security—with or without the Director's knowledge."

"Yeah, more likely. Ah—build you another drink?"

"Thanks, no. I'd fall asleep in the chair."

"Well, I can do something about that. There's three empty bedrooms upstairs, or you can couch it here if you like. You look pretty tired."

"Thanks, I'll accept. Just don't let it be known I'm here. I need to see a couple more people before I get a handle on the situation. After that . . . ?" He shrugged. "One day at a time."

Gray looked over at his wife's room. "The only way to live through it," he said soberly. "One day at a time."

Forty-One

It was dusk when Irving Chenow turned into his driveway and saw someone sitting on his front steps. Slowing, he peered at the man and recognized Mark Brand. He braked quickly and got out. "Mark!" he called. "Damn, it's good to see you!"

Brand got up and waited while Chenow jogged toward him. "Why didn't you go in?" Chenow asked. "Nobody home?"

"Didn't ring," he said, shaking Chenow's hand. "As you may know, I'm not in awfully good odor around the Beltway, so I—"

"Not in—? What the hell you talking about? Come in, let's have a welcoming drink." He unlocked the door and opened it for Brand.

As he led the way through the foyer into the living room, he said, "Can't tell you how relieved I was to get that Beijing message saying you and Peter were together. I imagine you both went through quite an ordeal. But what's this about bad odor and such?" He went to the cellarette and opened it. "Scotch?"

"Please. Ice, some water."

After fixing their drinks, Chenow handed one to Brand and said, "I hope you're here to say you'll take the China Desk, Mark."

"Irving," he replied, "I appreciate you holding it open for me, but you'd better find someone else to fill it." He touched his glass to Chenow's and said, *"Jing bao."*

"L'chayim," Chenow responded, and they drank together.

Brand said, "I won't beat about the bush, there's no way I can take the Desk. The main reason is I'm on a hit list, and that's—"

"What? Are you serious?"

"I am, Irving, and I want to know if you know anything about it."

Chenow shook his head. "Never heard of anything so preposterous, Mark, even in this crazy town. Maybe you'd better tell me whereof you speak."

He listened attentively while Brand related most of what he'd told Tom Gray the night before, and when Brand stopped and finished his drink, Chenow said, "Shocking. Absolutely shocking. And you think the Director's behind it?"

"His name was used, and the three would-be kidnappers carried Army Civilian Employee carnets. But, no, I doubt the DCI would authorize physical force on his own. More likely he passed along an order from some higher-up."

"Give me your glass, we both need a refill." That done, Chenow returned and sat facing Brand. "I don't want you to have any doubts about me, Mark, so I'll tell you this. After I saw the first series of satellite photos, my access to satellite information was cut off. Tom Gray told me he couldn't talk with me, and I assumed Darman Gerold told him not to. Then Darman phoned for information but I reminded him I was out of the loop. He implied he was, too, but swore he hadn't been behind isolating me." Chenow shrugged. "Should I believe him?"

Brand sipped his drink and lowered it. "Hard to say. I've known Darman a long time, maybe too long, and he can be very pliable and cooperative with superiors. He'd go a long way to please them, but in this case, I don't know." He grunted. "Before I left for Hong Kong I heard a low-grade rumor he was angling for the directorship."

Chenow nodded. "He was, even asked me to put in a good word for him with the President. I half said I would if the occasion arose, but in view of questions you've raised, I definitely would not. That satisfy you?"

Brand nodded.

"Meanwhile," said Chenow, "I guess you know the gas missile threat to Taiwan no longer exists."

"So I've heard. Plus speculation about sabotage by antiregime activists."

"I've heard the same speculation, and as far as I'm concerned it's plausible."

Brand smiled. "I suspect you may know more than you're telling, but that's okay, I won't press a crafty defense lawyer to come clean."

Chenow smiled slightly but said nothing.

Brand said, "I'm not returning to GlobEco, either. Gerold controls it and I don't want to work for him again. Besides, I think Tom's done a good job in my absence."

"He has," Chenow agreed, "but I hate the thought of you not being around and available. Win Hilyard left as scheduled, so I've been filling in—but I understand your reasoning, Mark, and I won't argue against it."

"Still, I'm flattered you offered me the Desk. And there's another factor. In Hong Kong I encountered my Taiwan sweetheart, now a widow with a daughter about Peter's age. We're going to marry." His throat got tight and he gulped down more scotch.

"Then, congratulations. You not only found Peter, you found a wife."

"Yes. Peter's also getting married, and we'll go into business together in Hong Kong or Taiwan."

Chenow smiled. "Hong Kong's prospects aren't rosy, but you know all that. What about your father? Talked with him?"

"Yes. In Taipei he knew my future wife's father, the late Museum Director Chen, and heartily approves our plans."

"Always good to have a parent's blessing," Chenow said. "I married out of my faith, but my father stayed on my side, and my mother eventually came around. How about you and your bride—Buddhist wedding? Christian?"

"Maybe both—or just the Crown Colony Registrar." He smiled. "Whatever Mary prefers."

"Yes, marriage is for the ladies. Incidentally, Vivian is in St. Louis visiting a sick brother, so I'm alone here. But I've got steaks we can toss on the grill if I can persuade you to stay."

"Glad to."

"Never liked dining alone. I'll make a salad and you pick the wine, okay?"

"Okay."

After dinner Brand gratefully accepted a ride from Chenow to the Hay-Adams, where he took a taxi out to Gray's house. He had a door key, so he didn't have to wake his host, made a nightcap for himself, and went upstairs to his bedroom.

It was obvious that Irv Chenow had nothing to do with the three kidnappers, and was distressed by what had happened.

So, Brand thought, as he got into bed, it sort of narrows down to Darman Gerold, and for lack of another candidate I'll focus on him.

In the morning, Brand called Gerold's home, gave his name as Gray, and learned from the houseman that Mr. Gerold was in Virginia for the weekend. "A long weekend," Brand remarked, "being only Friday."

"Yes, sir."

"You expect him back on Monday?"

"Probably not until evening, after he comes from the office."

"Thank you," Brand responded, "I'll call his office Monday," and hung up.

There was no real chance of catching Darman until Monday night, so Brand decided to return to his father's place and enjoy quality time with his family.

After thanking Gray for his hospitality, Brand took a taxi to the garage where he'd left the doctor's pickup, and drove back to the cabin. When he turned off onto his father's access road, he saw a police car, an ambulance, and several onlookers gathered around a car parked just off the shoulder. Presently two paramedics brought out a litter with a black body bag and loaded it into the ambulance. Brand took the inclined turn and pulled up in front of the cabin. Hearing the pickup, his father came out, they embraced, and Dr. Brand said, "Well? Find out anything?"

"Yes, mostly negative. What's going on at the foot of the hill?"

"A sheriff's deputy knocked on the door a couple of hours ago, said a body was found in the field near an abandoned car. Asked me to check the corpse for gunshots, knife wounds, or other signs of violence." He smiled. "Apparently the poor bastard got out to relieve himself and took a snake bite." He shook his head. "City folk don't know they shouldn't go tramping around the countryside after dark." He shaded his eyes and looked up. "Might be a trout or two worth catching—feel like it?"

"Absolutely. Where's Peter and La-li?"

"Already there. And you were missed, sonny, don't think you weren't. Grab yourself a rod—your own, come to think of it—and we'll take a slow walk to the stream." His smile was conspiratorial. "I have a couple of things to tell you."

Forty-Two

DARMAN GEROLD LEFT HIS OFFICE an hour early to keep an appointment in Rockville, Maryland, with a psychiatrist he had initially consulted four years ago when pressures threatened to overwhelm him. Among them had been the residue of a humiliating divorce, the disappearance of Doreen, concern over Fitzhugh's whereabouts, and the stress of a new job at the Agency. Since then, Gerold saw Dr. Armand Rothblatt several times a year, always in secret because Rothblatt was not on the Agency's list of cleared psychiatrists, and Gerold assumed such visitations would handicap his career.

The good doctor was expensive, but Gerold paid cheerfully because Rothblatt was nonjudgmental, listened attentively, and seldom interrupted with comment or question. Gerold always left his office in an improved state of mind. In short, feeling good. Today's appointment resulted from Gerold's concern over Doreen's proximate homecoming, his concern over his insider friends' reactions to information he had provided in good faith, and the Agency's failure to muzzle Mark Brand and his son.

No one knew where the Brands were hiding, and it was reasonable to assume they were holed up somewhere with an investigative reporter spilling their guts about the threat to Taiwan and their rough treatment on arriving from the Mainland. He dreaded a confrontation with Brand, who probably held him responsible for much of what had happened. Yet, he thought, I only responded to the Director's concern and relayed it to Security. That Security gumshoes subsequently acted inappropriately is hardly my fault. I was a message channel, nothing more. But will Mark understand my minimal role?

And there was Doreen. Today's call from Dr. Hempill announced her provisional release tomorrow. That was sooner than expected, they agreed, but her bedroom and bath were newly redecorated, and Pauline had accepted his explanation more or less uncritically. Anyway, his wife was busy doing what she loved best after her horses—planning parties—and the estate gala was bound to be super-impressive to all who came.

As he accelerated the Jaguar to pass a slower car he noticed its bumper sticker. IT'S EXCITING TO BE POLISH, it bravely proclaimed, and as he returned to the lane he found it vaguely disturbing.

The statement was nonspecific. It didn't say *where* it's exciting to be Polish. Warsaw? Washington? Pittsburgh? He could demolish the assertion in a dozen ways.

But he wasn't going to sink into the unrewarding rut of graffito analysis, not on such a fine afternoon, with Dr. Rothblatt's supportive session just ahead.

As he drove, Gerold reflected that he had been thinking of Doreen more than was altogether healthy. Even alone in bed at night he could not help fantasizing about her. Had she really changed? Or was she the same tough, brazen kid, defiant and unrepenting? Tomorrow he'd find out.

A Porsche whizzed by and he squinted to read the bumper message: PEACE THROUGH SUPERIOR FIREPOWER. Well, he could deal with that; a reasonable statement, though not everyone would agree.

Then peripherally, his gaze picked up spaced signs in an empty field:

AS YOU GO GLIDING

DOWN THE ROAD

DON'T LET

YOUR WHEELS

DESTROY

A TOAD

His neck craned backward. What the hell was *that?* Nothing but blank paint on the signs' reverse. He swallowed, fixed his gaze on the road ahead. They'd tricked him, letting him think Burma-Shave jingles were back. Instead, some demented farmer had posted a plea for toad conservation.

Toad. Poison toads. The Frog Lady.

Unreal how things reminded him of her predicament. Couldn't be mere coincidence or the maunderings of an aging brain. Symbols abounded, significances were everywhere to be detected, if you were alert enough to recognize occult meanings.

Illuminati. A parallel world. Velikovsky.

Despite the derision accorded the philosopher's apocalyptic assertions, could Velikovsky actually be right? Warm seas at the Poles, a subterranean race . . . ? Fitzhugh thought so.

He needed to investigate thoroughly, perhaps inspire the Geographic Society to mount an unbiased, fact-finding expedition.

Only then can we know, he told himself, but I haven't time right now to get things going. Not until I've solved current problems. Then I need to spend a week or so combing Appalachia for the Frog Lady. Otherwise I'll never be able to concentrate on anything for the constant reminders.

Why couldn't the jasper have put it less wordily, in a more forthright demand: SPARE THE TOAD.

Perfect. On the way back he'd stop in and make the suggestion, pay the farmer for his surplus signs, warn him roadside trickery was not to be countenanced.

He wondered if Doreen in her wanderings and well-established sexual receptivity had contracted the pox. If so, it would have been cured at Arbor Vitae. Ethical physicians wouldn't allow an infected, promiscuous young voluptuary to pass it on to other innocent patients.

But where was innocence?

In a madhouse could it exist?

Which of Adam's sons tupped Eve to produce ensuing generations? The Old Testament was redolent of incest. Lot's family. Lear's daughters (but that was Shakespeare). Point being Bible fundamentalists never dealt with original incest, pretended it hadn't taken place, wasn't there, didn't exist.

But it did.

So let's not hear a lot of pious, self-righteous cant about it, eh? I for one will have closed ears.

He barely glimpsed the turnoff, braked hard and spun the wheel, nearly jamming a trailing car.

Driving slowly, Gerold spotted a parking space near the doctor's office. He eased the Jag into it, fed all his pocket change into the meter, and walked into the medical arts building.

DARMAN GEROLD LAY on the psychiatrist's couch, flexing his hands. The injection was beginning to suffuse his system, bringing a sense of euphoria. The shrink had always been helpful—at least he was someone to confide in—and Dr. Rothblatt was never critical. The couch was a secular confessional, the shrink gave absolution. Even so, Gerold had never confessed his fundamental problem. But now as barriers dissolved he felt able to talk about it. Compelled to.

While waiting for the pentothal to exert its full effect, Dr. Rothblatt said, "Let's see, you were last here four, no, five months ago. Things going well with you?"

"Not really."

"Your wife?"

"She's part of it."

"We'll get to that. How are you feeling?"

"Great. Just great. This is wonderful stuff."

"Why not begin by telling me what you've been thinking about lately? Just start anywhere, okay?"

"Sure. Lately I've been noticing"—he choked back a giggle—"uh, well, things like graffiti. Bumper stickers, you know? I mean bumper stickers *are* a form of graffiti, right."

"I never thought of it."

"For example, only yesterday I saw words sprayed on a wall: FREE FLOYD COLLINS. What do you think of that?"

"What should I think of it?"

"Well, I mean, Floyd Collins died about the time I was born—in that cave, remember? So what kind of statement is that supposed to be, anyway?"

"I suppose it depends on your interpretation; how you relate to its meaning."

"Well, that's just the point—its meaning. Right?"

"So?"

Gerold grinned. "I think it refers to God."

"Interesting idea. How?"

"A plea for Floyd Collins's spiritual freedom in Heaven."

Rothblatt muttered unintelligibly. "You believe in an entity called God?"

"Sometimes yes, sometimes no," Gerold said diffidently. "How about you, Doc?"

"Let's leave my beliefs out of this," said Rothblatt, who attended meetings of the Ethical Cultural Society. "What else?"

"Well, here's another puzzler—this one was scratched into sidewalk cement. Now, pay attention: WITHOUT ICE CREAM, FAME AND LIFE ITSELF HAVE NO MEANING. How's that hit you, Doc?"

"A glancing blow," said Rothblatt, somewhat getting into the spirit of the thing. "Is the statement reasonable?"

"Well, at first glance, no. But I've given thought to it, and the more I consider the implications, the clearer it all becomes."

"Suppose you tell me," said Rothblatt, glancing at his tape recorder to make sure the cassette reels were turning. "What's clear about it?" His patient's problems were far more severe than he had ever imagined. There was reality dissociation plus fantasy syndrome.

"Why, very simple, and I'm surprised and chagrined you don't see it: one must avoid dependence on ice cream if one is to maintain mental balance. What a statement!"

Rothblatt made a note of the patient's grin. Really ought to get to the bottom of all this, plow through these surface manifestations. But he couldn't *force* a prominent man like Gerold to go for deep analysis. "Anything else?"

In a quiet, controlled voice, Darman Gerold said, "You have to understand I've never told anyone this before—admitted even in private. It's very painful, Doctor, and I've struggled with it a long time."

Primly, Rothblatt said, "Your confidences are inviolate and I urge you to speak with total frankness. That way we can shorten an otherwise long and painful road." The recorder was running nicely.

Gerold exhaled a long drawn-out sigh. "To salvation? I've thought of telling you before but always evaded it. Now something's happened to bring it to the fore." One hand lifted, fell back limply.

"And what is that?"

"My daughter, Doreen, has reappeared."

"Well, that *is* good news, eh?"

Gerold considered. The hypnotic had dissolved all barriers to confession. "She ran away, you know."

"I remember. Yes, that was quite a while ago." He consulted his notes. "Six months, was it not?"

"At least," Gerold said tonelessly. "Since then everything's gone wrong for me."

"Well, not everything," said Rothblatt encouragingly. "She's back again. And by the bye, why did she leave?"

The answer, long readied, was on his tongue. "I used to fuck my mother, and my daughter found out. Now, I think she wants to take my mother's place." He swallowed. "As my lover."

When no sounds of remonstrance came from the psychiatrist Gerold looked around to make sure Rothblatt was awake and listening.

"You're not reacting, Doc. Incest is a terrible crime."

"But not unusual," said Rothblatt. "It's found in a high incidence of both upper-class and lower-class families. The middle class seems less interested in its offspring as sexual objects. Where is your daughter now?"

"At Arbor Vitae Clinic—in Alexandria."

"Those quacks!" Dr. Rothblatt snorted.

"For detox and rehabilitation," Gerold said defensively. "And Doreen is doing very well." He sighed. "Tomorrow she's coming home."

"I see."

"Aren't you disgusted with me?"

"I'm a professional man, Darman. I'm here to help you resolve your problem. I neither approve nor disapprove. If it helps, you'd be astonished at the number of upper-class incestual situations I've learned about—here in this room. People you know," he added.

"No kidding? That makes me feel better already. I wish I'd told you before."

"So do I." He cleared his throat, sipped from his glass again.

"Pauline's no good in bed, never has been. But Amy—God, she was something else."

"Hmmm. My notes reflect your previous allusions to a long-term passionate relationship with an older woman. Turns out it was your mother. And now it seems there has been a transference to your daughter."

Gerold shrugged.

"Your mother seduced you, did she not?"

Gerold nodded.

"And now you have in mind seducing your daughter."

"Well, not exactly. I think unconsciously *she* began the process long ago. I mean, she was around in those scanty bikinis that barely covered her pubic hair, and when she'd dive in the pool her bra top often came off." Closing his eyes, he remembered those gorgeous pink nipples. "Sometimes she'd leave the bathroom door open, or go from there to her room in the buff." He opened his eyes and stared at the soundproofed ceiling. "So it's a question who's seducing who—whom."

"How do you feel about it?"

"Well, I'd like it to happen—want it to happen, actually."

"And when did this apparently spontaneous or accidental nudity take place? How old was your daughter?"

"Fourteen, fifteen, I guess. Pretty young."

"Oh, I don't know," he said smoothly, remembering young whores—kids, really—he'd put the blocks to in Saigon long years ago. God, to relive *those* times! Clearing his throat, Rothblatt said, "In life some situations are unavoidable. What troubles you, I sense, is maintaining a clandestine relationship with your daughter, while concealing it from your wife. Is that feasible?"

"I think so. We live separately, have different interests, different lives."

"Can you depend on your daughter concealing the relationship?"

"I hope so. I certainly hope so. Exposure would ruin me."

"Then you better make sure of her total complicity before a relationship begins." The timer sounded and Rothblatt got up. "I'll be most interested to hear how all this comes out, Darman. Suppose I give you an appointment for, oh, a month from now."

"There was something else troubling me I wanted to talk about, but I guess we're out of time."

"Keep it in mind until our next session. See you then."

Gerold went into the reception room and relaxed in an overstuffed recliner until the pentathol metabolized and his head cleared enough to drive.

As he headed back to Georgetown, Gerold regretted not having brought up the Frog Lady. Instead, he'd focused on bumper stickers, irresponsible graffiti, and the potential harm they could cause young, unformed, undiscriminating minds. Well, no present help for that, they were there, publicly, for all to see. But, where was the Frog Lady? Tonight at home, after dark when AM stations reached farther out, he'd search the dial of his bedside radio. Maybe he'd hear her phone in again and if that happened, he'd make a note of the station's call sign and location. She was out there somewhere, needing help as badly as any human being he'd ever heard of.

In Georgetown the refrigerator and freezer were stocked with delicacies. There were cases of Chablis and Chardonnay, malt whiskey, vodka, gin, and mixers. Jacques had been given a week off with pay so he and Doreen would be alone in their home. He wasn't much at cooking, but he could scramble eggs and thaw gourmet meals in the microwave.

And Doreen could apply her talents to his.

Forty-Three

APPALACHIAN FOOTHILLS, PENNSYLVANIA

AROUND THE DINNER TABLE they were enjoying a plump wild turkey hen Dr. Brand had ambushed in a cherry tree. Served with vegetables and applesauce, the roasted turkey was a treat for them all. He asked Mark if family plans were crystallizing, and Brand said, "Hong Kong and/or Taiwan is our goal, but we need time in Washington to wrap things up— or wind them down. I have to sell my apartment, pack contents, and clear out."

Peter said, "I've got a lease to terminate, and I guess we'll just sell the junk we've accumulated, mostly thirdhand stuff anyway." He took

La-li's hand. "We'll be married and La-li will have an American passport to travel on."

Brand nodded. "While we're making preparations I don't want undesirable visitors interfering, so I'll be going back to Washington in a few days. Darman Gerold may be the key; if not, he knows who is."

Peter said, "Mr. Chenow told you there was no longer a missile threat to Taiwan, so why should the Agency or the Administration still be interested in us?"

"Hard to say." Brand shrugged. "Could be as simple as some functionary not canceling orders—oversight. It's happened before. Anyway, I'm going to see Gerold where we can talk privately, find out what he has to say."

La-li said, "Dr. Brand, we hope you'll visit us and stay as long as you like."

"Can't stay long away from my mountain friends, but I'd appreciate being with you when my great-grandchild is born."

"We'll advise likely dates," Peter told him, "and count on your being there."

"Assuming continued good health, I will be." He paused. "Give me a chance to see Hong Kong in its final days—before the Red Sea washes over. It'll never be the same again." He stood up. "More turkey, anyone? Anything?" He brought a cider jug to the table and refilled glasses. La-li hesitated until Dr. Brand said, "It's a natural substance, won't harm you or the baby."

Looking around, Brand said, "I'll miss this place, Dad, and I'll miss you. We all will."

"Praise be the Lord, I can take care of myself pretty well. And when I can't I've got friends to look in, so don't worry about me."

Brand smiled, thinking of the gunman his father had dispatched. Yes, the doctor could take care of himself and, he hoped, for many years.

Outside on the porch, Brand thought of Mary and Chu-li in Hong Kong, awaiting his return. Rather than use a possibly tapped telephone, Brand had written them saying all was going well and he planned to be with them in two or three weeks. He assumed Mary had retained a solicitor to secure Chu-li's rights to Wing-dah's properties, though he expected the process to move slowly through Crown Colony courts. When he got there he'd put a burr under the solicitor's bottom, something Mary was probably too reticent to do.

Joining him on the porch, his father said, "Peloso's taken care of, but I'm concerned about the other two coming here."

"So am I. I want to neutralize them and avoid more night visitors. One way or another I'll put an end to it."

His father smiled. "I'm sure you will."

OFFICE OF THE DIRECTOR OF SECURITY, CENTRAL INTELLIGENCE AGENCY, LANGLEY, VIRGINIA

THE DOS LOOKED UP as two subordinates entered, said "Sit down," opened a file, and scanned it. A retired colonel, he was in his mid-fifties, of florid face and bristle-cut gray hair. "I see you boys need field seasoning, so I'm sending one to Lagos, the other to Mogadishu. Help retirement computation. Any objections?"

They shook their heads. "No, sir."

The DOS leaned back in his cushioned executive chair. "With that out of the way, what can you tell me about Peloso's demise? I don't mean how he got snakebit, but why he was headed for Dr. Brand's cabin. With an assault weapon."

The older man, Helliger, said, "Sam didn't tell me he was going. I didn't know he was gone until I heard he was dead."

"Same for me," the younger man replied. "But Sam was plenty pissed off by what Mark Brand did to his face."

The DOS shrugged. "On that I have a couple of thoughts. One, the three of you shouldn't have tried taking the Brands by force. Two, what Brand did to Peloso was his own damn fault. You underestimated an experienced field officer. Three, when the Inspector General gets around to taking statements, I assume you'll tell him just what you told me. That right?"

"Yes, sir."

"And to avoid any possible misunderstanding, you're to forget the Brands, they're no longer a target. By now they're probably out of the country, anyway—considering the welcome you gave them." He shook his head disgustedly. "It's been suggested I authorize an investigation into Peloso's death but I declined. He went off on his own for reasons that have nothing to do with the Agency, and there the matter rests. And will continue to rest. That clear?"

"Yes, sir," Helliger responded.

"Whatever provoked the Director's interest in the Brands is over and done with. He told me so an hour ago, and that's plenty good enough for me. Where and how Peloso died hasn't been brought to his attention, and it's not going to be." He stared at them fiercely. "Anything else I should know about? Any questions?"

"Sir," Helliger asked, "which of us goes to Lagos and which to Mogadishu?"

"You can flip for it," the DOS said curtly, "and I expect you to be in travel status not later than two weeks from today."

"Two *weeks?*" Helliger exclaimed.

"Or is *one* week more suited to your tastes? Now get out of here. You're both relieved from duty, use the time for packing."

They hesitated, then turned and left the office. When the door closed, the DOS spun around in his chair and gazed out over the green woods bordering the Potomac River. I used to command men, he reflected, disciplined men, who could do a job competently. Now I have assholes like those two who can't find their dicks in the dark.

The phone rang, and he picked it up. Back to business as usual.

OFFICE OF THE SECRETARY OF STATE, DEPARTMENT OF STATE, WASHINGTON

THE SECRETARY OF STATE received Ambassador Pu Jiang-fei of the People's Republic of China and, after a perfunctory handshake, gestured the Ambassador to a low table set with tea service for two. Ambassador Pu glowered at it and shook his head. "No time for tea, Secretary, just business."

"At least be seated," the Secretary suggested and took a nearby chair. "How can I assist you?"

"By surrendering those pilot-bandits who shot down Chinese aircraft over Chinese territory."

"I see," he said thoughtfully. "And who are these so-called bandits?"

"American pilots of the U.S. Air Force."

The Secretary shook his head. "I am not aware of any aerial combat involving our two air forces. Can you be more specific?"

"United States aircraft bombed two civilian factories west of Beijing. They assaulted with air bombs an army base at Leping."

"Interesting," the Secretary said noncommittally, "but may I inquire your reasons for believing the aircraft in question belonged to the United States?"

"Because they were Stealth aircraft, and only your country makes and flies them."

"Oh? In that I think you may be mistaken. To my certain knowledge deliveries of Stealth fighter-bombers have been made to NATO countries, to Kuwait, Israel, Peru, Saudi Arabia, Argentina, the Republic of South Korea . . ." He spread his hands. "And others. Making a rather long list." He filled a cup with tea and added sweetener. "Leping, eh? What was going on there to attract hostile attention?"

"Nothing, nothing of any interest to foreign nations. Routine military exercises were being conducted, as is the right of the People's Republic."

"Unquestionably." The Secretary nodded. "All nations do as they please within their sovereign borders." He sipped from his cup and eyed the Ambassador. "Unless, of course, a country is preparing belligerent activity against another nation. And that is proscribed by the Charter of the United Nations."

Ambassador Pu's face reddened. "I demand those criminal pilots be turned over to Chinese authorities for punishment."

"Ah—without trial? I don't believe a status-of-forces treaty exists between our two countries, but I'm uncertain. I'll ask Assistant Secretary Chenow, a lawyer, to look into it. Meanwhile, I am not accustomed to accepting demands unaccompanied by facts. I don't know what school of diplomacy you attended, but you apparently missed the lecture on preparing and delivering diplomatic notes. You indicated you're short of time, so am I. So let me, in the most delicate way possible, suggest that you prepare a proper note and send it to this office where it will be given the consideration it deserves. Such a note should include the names and ranks of the alleged perpetrators, otherwise it will be consigned to the circular file."

"Circular file?" The Ambassador's brow wrinkled, then he saw the Secretary gesture at a wastebasket.

"There are, after all, Mr. Ambassador, certain norms honored and adhered to by civilized nations. And as long as I hold this office I will insist that they be observed by all diplomats having official business with this office." He set down his cup. "Not long ago I asked about a young American citizen's whereabouts in China. You professed ignorance—and I want to believe you told the truth. However, since that meeting, the young man in question escaped from a special prison for political prisoners—Lingyuan, I believe it's called—and made his way back to this country. In Beijing he was given a lengthy sentence without trial, and—"

"But he *was* tried. Tried, I tell you, and—" The Ambassador broke off, realizing his mistake. Staring down at his hands, he muttered, "I was thinking of another case, a Chinese-American. Not the same person."

"Just a coincidence," the Secretary said, "no doubt. Nevertheless, the young American about whom we made inquiries is recovering from his ordeal, and in due course will have an absorbing story to tell."

"Lies," the Ambassador snapped. "All lies."

"I suggest judgment be reserved until we hear what he has to say. In this country we don't prejudge a witness—you get my meaning?" He rose. "And since we are both busy men, occupied with affairs of state, let me say that I appreciate your visit, and look forward to receiving an embassy note detailing your verbal, ah, concerns." The Ambassador seemed reluctant to leave until the Secretary placed a firm hand on his shoulder. "Do allow me the privilege of escorting you to the door. Your visit has been all too short. I beg you will grant me the pleasing prospect of your early return." The Secretary opened the door. "Good day, sir," he said and closed the door.

Walking back to his desk he allowed himself a brief smile.

Like two other Cabinet members he had fought in Korea, been awarded the Silver Star for valor, and nurtured an unappeasable loathing toward the PRC. Therefore, he was immensely pleased to catch one of the little bastards in a lie, and watch him squirm.

As to the alleged air combat, the Secretary doubted he would ever see or hear another word.

Forty-Four

F<small>OR</small> D<small>ARMAN</small> G<small>EROLD</small>, Doreen's first day home was the most challenging. She arrived after midday in the clinic limousine, accompanied by Dr. Hempill, and they embraced each other tentatively to the doctor's approving gaze. Then Gerold said, "She looks just wonderful, Doctor, a new and very beautiful young lady. Dear, how do you feel?"

"Good," Doreen responded. "Better than I've felt in, oh, I don't know how long." She pivoted, skirt swirling above her knees. "New figure, too, gained ten pounds. What do you think, Father?"

Throat dry, he said, "It becomes you very well. And your new hairstyle is enchanting. I—I can't get over the change." He turned to the psychiatrist. "I'm greatly in your debt, Doctor, for everything you've done for my daughter. It's like—like a resurrection." He wiped moisture from his upper lip. Makeup, eye shading, why she looked like a New York model!

He was eager to—but Dr. Hempill interrupted his thought, saying, "Why not show Doreen what you've done just for her?"

"I—" he began, and searched his mind before saying, "Oh, yes. Doreen, come upstairs with me."

"The driver will bring her bags," Dr. Hempill remarked, and watched them ascend the staircase.

Gerold led his daughter to her room and turned on the lights. For a moment she said nothing, then turned to him. "Oh, God, it's so *gorgeous!* And just for me?"

"Only you."

"Thank you, thank you, Daddy!" She flung her arms around him and wet his face with kisses.

Gerold kissed her cheek and nuzzled an ear. "I want things to be different between us," he said huskily, "and I thought the best place to start was here."

Breaking away, she entered the bathroom and stared at the gleaming pastel fixtures, the Italian tile. "Oh," she exclaimed, "it's too much, really too much, but"—she turned with a sly smile—"since I'm naturally selfish, I accept."

"I'm so glad you're pleased." He sat on the edge of the bed and took her hand. "This is your home, honey, and I want you to be happy here."

"I will, I know I will." She stroked the window drapes. "Did Pauline—?"

"No, she had nothing to do with it, my fault entirely."

"Fault? You've got to be kidding." Impulsively, she kissed him again. "It's all so beautiful, I won't ever want to leave."

"I hope you won't," he told her, and then the driver entered with suitcases, boxes, and bags.

As Gerold surveyed them, she said, "Daddy, you bought me so many lovely things I thought you wouldn't mind if I added a few more."

"Of course not." He realized the driver was waiting, fished in his pocket for a five, and gave it to him. The driver touched his cap brim and went down the hall to the staircase. Gerold said, "I guess we ought to say good-bye to the doctor."

Doreen nodded. "She'll tell you about my medication, stuff like that. I'd really like to unpack and put things where they belong, okay?"

"Anything you want," he said, and joined Dr. Hempill below.

"Well, Mr. Gerold, so far everything seems to be working out nicely."

"So it is. As I said before, I can't thank you enough. My daughter is so changed . . ."

"Inwardly as well. Doreen has come to terms with quite a few things that affect you both, your family life. Oh—recently she's been mentioning her brother, Fitzhugh. Apparently there is, or was, a strong attachment between them, and Doreen has been wondering if you're in touch with him."

"Not for years," he said. "No idea where he might be."

"Well, she'll be disappointed, but not all families stay in intimate touch."

"Mine, least of all."

"Still, you have your daughter, and that's a very good beginning. Now, her medications are in this bag. Methadone therapy is minimum maintenance—one cap morning and night. Some light tranquilizers for sleeplessness, and vitamins. All the bottles are labeled, so there won't be any difficulty." She looked at her small wristwatch. "In case of need, I can be reached through the clinic. I live there so I'm always on duty."

"Thank you."

"After a few days you might want to let me know how Doreen is progressing. If she accommodates well to her home environment, I may want to try out your suggestion with other patients."

He edged her to the door, couldn't wait to get rid of the old bag and be alone with his daughter.

"Bye," she waved, going down the steps. Gerold waved back and shut the door, chained it.

Finally.

He leaned back against the door and felt the pounding of his heart. His hands were clammy, face damp. What stress, Jesus!

Her shower was running. He took the stairs and walked past her open door on the way to the bedroom he occasionally shared with Pauline. But with this gorgeous young blonde in the house, how could he even *think* of his wife? Caviar versus dog food.

He pulled off his damp shirt and rinsed hands and face at the washbowl. Shirtless, he went back to Doreen's room and called, "About dinner, honey. Anything special you'd like?"

From the shower she called, "Rare filet mignon, asparagus, Lyonnaise potatoes, and salad, okay?"

"And maybe a little wine?"

"Super."

From his bedside phone he called Dominique's, where he was favorably known, and repeated Doreen's order. "Only double it. Just send everything and I'll do the serving, no waiter needed."

"Certainly, Mr. Gerold. At what time, sir?"

He looked at his watch. "Seven-thirty, eight?"

"Seven-thirty is better for us—before the crowd arrives."

"Seven-thirty it is." He supplied his address and ended the call.

The shower stopped running, and Gerold went down the hall and called, "Honey, I'm going to have a drink—care to join me?"

"Yeah, I'd love some booze. Couldn't get a drop in that prison. What are you having?"

"Vodka martini."

"Suits me. Oh, mind bringing it up? I'm still unpacking and I love being in this room. It's fab, terrific."

Downstairs he mixed a shaker of marts, carried it up with two deep glasses. He knocked at her open door, went in, and saw her bending over a suitcase. She was wearing a translucent chemise that reached only as far as her thighs, and her butt was bare. Without looking around, she said, "Come in, come in, let's dispense with formality, okay?"

"By all means." He set glasses on a dresser and poured. Doreen straightened up and took a glass. "Mmmm." She licked her lips voluptuously. "That's *good.*" Then she turned slowly around. "Like my figure better now I've gained weight?"

"It's perfect, honey. Don't lose or add a pound." He eyed her small nipples, just as he had remembered and fantasized them. Like little pink gumdrops. His mouth watered, and he drank deeply. The iced Stoli was delicious, and he was getting an erection.

Doreen drank, too, asked, "How are things with Pauline?"

"Same as always."

"Bad, huh?" Her glass touched his. "Bet it's the usual problem."

"Doreen—"

"C'mon, Dad, don't shit me. You've got the old Hawaiian disease, lackanooki. Right?"

"You get right to the bottom of things, don't you?"

"Why not? Life's too short to screw around with pretense and nonessentials." She drank again. "When do we eat?"

"Seven-thirty. It's being delivered."

"Well, great." She dipped into a suitcase, held up a sheer black nightgown, and put it on a closet hanger. "I've never had pretty things like this before. How come you're treating me so nice? If *I'm* changed, man, so are you. Big time."

"Well," he said, choosing words carefully, "during discussions with Dr. Hempill it became clear that I'd been doing everything wrong with you, so I made the decision to try doing things right."

"Meaning what?"

"Treat you as an attractive, intelligent young lady, and not be the stern critical parent I was for so many years."

She considered his explanation, finished her drink, and waited for Gerold to refill it. "That's all? No ulterior motive?"

When he said nothing, Doreen said, "Too bad Gran's not around for you. Bet you miss her."

"I do," he admitted. "Always have." He poured a refill for himself, sensing the exchange was approaching a critical zone.

But she changed the subject. "Ever hear from Fitz? Know where he is?"

"No contact since he went to Alaska. No idea where he is."

The glass revolved slowly in her fingers. Nostalgically she said, "He was a sweet guy, Dad, probably still is. All he wanted from you was love and attention." She paused. "Like me."

"Well, when he shows up I'll supply all his emotional needs, that's a promise."

"And I'll hold you to it." She sat on the bed, and motioned Gerold to sit beside her. "Jacques around?"

"Gave him time off—so we could, as they say, interact without distractions."

"Great idea." She moved over and across his thighs until she was sitting on his lap, her bare bottom warming his loins. After a moment she smiled, then laughed. "Dad, you've got a boner! Naughty, naughty. You planning to fill all *my* emotional needs?"

"I'd certainly like to."

Her hand turned his face to hers and she kissed his mouth, hers was open and her tongue began darting like a velvet snake. Then her lips left his and she said throatily, "You planned this, didn't you? All of it?"

"I did."

She kissed his ear, and fingers trailed down to his zippered fly. "When'd you get the idea?"

"In Hong Kong, I guess."

"Because I blew Mark Brand?"

"Probably." His zipper was open, she groped there and kissed his mouth again.

"I was ready for you years ago," she whispered, "but you, you bastard, never noticed me."

"I did," he admitted, "but I wouldn't let myself think the unthinkable."

"Even though you'd been fucking Gran since—how old were you?"

"Fourteen or so—Jesus, honey, that feels so damn *good!*"

"Take it easy, Dad, lots of time before dinner." She stripped off her chemise and pressed his face to her breasts. Hungrily, Gerold mouthed her nipples. Shivering, she murmured, "Because of what Mom told me I knew you had to be horny, and you sure are. It's just taken so damn long to show it."

His eyes closed, he moaned in ecstasy. Naked, she lay back on the bed, thighs apart. Her arms reached out to take him. "Dr. Hempill thought you maybe wanted to fuck me. Let's see if she was right."

For the next three days they never left the house, seldom left her room.

Forty-Five

WASHINGTON

After returning to Washington in his own car, Mark Brand presented Tommy Gray with a case of Early Times whiskey and took him to dinner at a Chinese restaurant across from the National Zoo.

Back at Tommy's house, Brand accepted cognac from his host and said, "I assume GlobEco's made the correct assumption—that I'm not coming back. You'll have my job if you want it."

"For a while, Mark. I imagine it pays better. But I'll still have Darman to contend with."

"Maybe not. I'm planning a serious talk with him."

"Oh? And when might that be?"

"Later tonight. I've called his office and house for several days, no answer. But his Jag is in the driveway and there are lights in the house."

"Could be at the country estate with wife number two."

"Servants there say no." He sipped from his brandy snifter. "It's as though he were hiding out—like me."

"Strange. Usually he's a high-visibility guy. Power lunches, select dinner parties . . . guess he wants the directorship pretty badly."

"Yeah, but that can't happen."

"No way. You wouldn't have seen it but a gossip column predicted the Director leaving for academia—prexy of some Midwest college not named." He looked at Brand's glass. "Top it off?"

"Thanks, no, I have to drive."

"Stay here tonight if you want to."

"I may but I don't want to impose."

"Hey, that case of good stuff buys you a week's free lodging. Say no more."

AFTER TOMMY WENT UNSTEADILY off to bed Brand made instant coffee, watched midnight TV news, and left the house. He drove over to Georgetown and turned into Gerold's drive, parking behind the Jaguar. His dash clock showed a few minutes before one.

He got out of his car, locked the door, and looked up at the house. No lights but for a window showing a dim orange glow. Brand patted the compact .38 in his pocket that had been Samuel Peloso's. He wasn't going to shoot Gerold but some of Sam's buddies might be around in a vengeful frame of mind.

He went up the walk, climbed the steps, and rang the bell.

No response. He rang again. Waited. Only silence. Rang a third time, keeping his thumb on the button, half persuaded Gerold wasn't home. Then over the bell sound he heard Gerold yelling, "Okay, okay, I hear you. Coming."

Brand stepped away from the eyehole just before Gerold snapped, "Who is it?"

"Tommy," Brand said in a muffled voice, "Tommy Gray. Got a hot one for you."

Snub chain rattled, dead bolt withdrew. The door opened and he saw Darman Gerold barefoot in a navy-blue bathrobe, hair disarrayed. *"Mark!* What the hell . . . ?"

Brand pushed in. "You're hard to find, Darman, and I have questions that need answers." He shut the door behind him as Gerold backed into the shadowed room.

"Questions?" Gerold gulped. "What questions?" He licked his lips. "Know what time it is, for God's sake?"

"Yes, I know the time, and it's time you told my why you sent those Security creeps to kidnap Peter and me. We've been on the run ever since, and I don't like it. Put an end to it, Darman. I'm not kidding." He showed the .38 and put it away. "Then you can tell me the whys of it. Who put us on the hit list, and so on."

"Oh, Jesus, Mark, you think I had something to do with it?"

"You knew about it, ergo you were connected. Your bright idea?"

"I swear it wasn't. It was—" At a sound from the staircase, they turned, and Brand saw Doreen sitting on an upper step. She was wearing an unbuttoned pajama top, nothing more.

"Who's that, Dad?" she called.

"Your old friend Mark," Brand said, and saw Gerold shrink away.

"Doreen, please," Gerold called, "go back to bed. This doesn't concern—"

"Oh, but it does, Daddy. Mark's a very special friend. Hey, Mark, how're they hangin'?" She stood and leaned against the banister. Even in the poor light Brand could see the blond patch of her pubes, and sudden understanding came. They were keeping house together. Gerold was screwing his daughter as he'd screwed his mother. Brand was repelled and fascinated by the situation. Swallowing, he said, "About as usual. How're you doing, Dory?"

"Good, real good, Mark. Dad put me in a clinic and got me out so he could fuck me. Right, Daddy? We've been fucking each other's brains out for three days."

To a cringing Gerold, Brand said, "That explains why you've been hard to find—you were here all along."

"Yes, but—" He stopped at a wave from Brand's hand.

"I don't care about your domestic lifestyle. I want the pressure off, as of now."

Doreen said, "Better do what he wants, Dad." She laughed—a little wildly, Brand thought—and said, "Mark's like part of the family now, and the two men I care for most are under the same roof. What a turn-on!"

Gerold's shoulders were shaking. "Mark, please, I beg you, don't tell anyone."

"Who put out the order?"

"The Director. Said the Vice President ordered it. I was just a channel to Security."

"The Eichmann defense," Brand sneered. "Can't do better than that?"

He noticed Doreen coming slowly down the stairs. She looked different, better, a lot better, really attractive. Nearing Brand, she held out her forearms. "Look. Clean."

"Congratulations."

"I'm being a good girl now. I get everything I want—and I want a lot—because I'm Daddy's whore."

Gerold jerked at the word. Tears welled in his eyes. "Don't, honey, don't say that, it's not so," he pleaded.

She shrugged, the pajama top opened briefly to show a bare breast, and she said, "I think we all ought to have a drink together, sit down, and talk this out. Mark, what's yours?"

"Can't stay," he said, "but thanks anyway." He paused. "If a compliment's not out of order, you look great, Doreen. Quite a change from Hong Kong."

"Right you are," she said airily. "My daddy done right by me."

"Splendid," Brand said. "Gerold, what about it—am I off the list? Free to come and go without interference?"

"Absolutely. No problem. But," he hesitated, "what about, about Doreen and me?"

"I don't gossip, Darman. The private affairs of Darman and Doreen Gerold won't be revealed by me—unless I'm harassed. If that happens . . ."

Doreen smiled—a bit wickedly, Brand thought—and said, "I came into this late, but whatever Daddy's supposed to do, I'll damn well see that he does it." She turned to her father. "Otherwise, no more two-in-a-bed. Understand?"

He licked his lips. "Yes, honey."

She came to Brand, ran fingers down his lapel. "We're equal sinners," she said. "Dad used to ball his mother, so naturally he turned to me. Surprise you?"

He shook his head. "I've known about Amy."

"And kept your mouth shut. See, Daddy, you can trust Mark."

From Gerold came only a long whimpering sigh.

Brand said, "All that aggravation because Peter happened to see some gassed Chinese bodies." He shook his head. "I won't be back at GlobEco, so if you're still around, give the job to Tommy."

"Sure, of course, Mark, anything you say."

"And don't plan on the directorship, Darman. It won't happen."

"Good," said Doreen, "he's needed here at home."

As Brand turned to leave, she said, "If you need a place to stay, there's plenty of room—and we could do threesies. Unless Dad objects."

No sound from Gerold. Brand smiled. "I'm not usually at a loss for words, but 'Have a good day' doesn't do it. How about, 'Have a good time,' and my best to you both?"

"It'll do fine," she said, "and I know you'll think of us from time to time. Will you stay in touch?"

"No," he said, and went out.

At the bottom of the stone steps he stopped and looked up at the house. She was right, of course, he *would* think of them from time to time—how could he not? The spectacle of a cowed Darman Gerold and dominant Doreen was unforgettable. That they'd broken an ancient taboo, a taboo ordained to keep kids from being born with two heads and no legs, was their problem. Darman had always come off as a supercilious but suppressed and disconnected figure. Now in his fright he was pitiable. Doreen had already taken charge, and in their design for living her father was probably better off than before.

She'd said they were equal sinners. Aside from the theological aspect they must be equally complicit, for Darman would hardly have dared approach his daughter unless she appeared receptive. And Brand knew from their Hong Kong hotel room how accessible she could be.

He turned to the sidewalk and went to his car. Now that Doreen was healthy and apparently rehabilitated there could be a new life for her. How much of it she would allow her father to share was an equation to be worked out between them.

And there was Darman's wife. How long before she found out, as her predecessor had?

Problems ahead for all three Gerolds, but Brand counted on Darman's new docility to spare him further persecution.

He got behind the wheel and backed from the drive. He'd stay at Tommy's tonight and leave early for the cabin. In Washington he and Peter had plenty to do before leaving for Hong Kong.

Forty-Six

WASHINGTON

WAKENED BY THE INSISTENT RINGING of the telephone in the master bedroom, Darman Gerold sat up in bed and rubbed his eyes groggily. Beside him, Doreen slept undisturbed—passed out, more than likely, he reflected, for after Mark Brand's departure they had begun drinking French 75s, a mix of iced champagne and brandy. Each of them, he remembered, had consumed a bottle of Cordon Rouge with more than half a bottle of Hine cognac, and collapsed in bed too drunk for sex.

The phone rang as irritatingly as a hornet in his ear, and Gerold got off the bed and lurched down the hall to the offending telephone. Snatching it from the cradle, he bellowed, "Yeah, whatcha want?"

"Darman? Paul Wembley. I've been trying to reach you since yesterday. Don't you ever clear your answering machine?"

"I'm sick," he said, with some truth, for his head pounded and ached abominably, and he felt like throwing up.

"Oh," said Wembley, somewhat mollified. "I've been watching CNN news reports, reading all the papers, and I can't come across anything suggesting trouble on the Mainland." He paused. "Or Taiwan."

"So what?" Gerold challenged. There was too much sunlight in the room. It seared his eyeballs painfully.

"So," Wembley said, "liquidating assets cost me a big bundle, a lot more than I can afford, and if it's all a false alarm I'll have you to thank for a multimillion-dollar loss."

"Take it easy," Gerold responded. "Wait and see."

"I've been waiting, Darman, and I want to know now if the high-grade so-called intelligence you gave me was accurate."

Gerold swallowed. "At the time it was. Things change. Rome wasn't burned in a day."

"You prick," Wembley snarled. "If that's an example of your intelligence insight there's not a hope in hell you'll get the directorship. I'll see to that personally. I'll tell the President you conned me, passed classified information and anything else I can think of."

"Suit yourself, Paul. I was only trying to do you a favor."

"Okay, I believe that. So I'll wait a week before hitting the Oval Office. Meanwhile, you'd better hope for big problems on the Mainland."

Gerold heard Paul's receiver slam down and replaced his own. For a while he sat on the king-size bed, squinting at the sunny window. Then he closed the blinds and went unsteadily back to Doreen's bedroom. She was sleeping facedown, one arm under the pillow. Her left breast bulged invitingly. He looked away and his gaze found the cognac bottle on her night table. Normally he wasn't a heavy drinker, but being caught in flagrante by Brand was a traumatic shock he was unprepared for. God, imagine what the bastard could tell if he decided to! Gerold grasped the open bottle and drank deeply. Coughing, he set the bottle aside and felt the liquor warm his guts. The bastard had interrupted and almost destroyed what Gerold had come to regard as a honeymoon. Brand was a goddam intruder into things that didn't concern him, and Gerold hated him more than ever.

Surprisingly, Doreen hadn't been as stunned and anxious as he'd expected her to be. "Dad, maybe we oughta cool things for a while, know what I mean?" she suggested after Mark's departure.

"Like what?" he demanded.

She said, "Like you stay with Pauline, and I stay here. Until things settle down."

"Settle down how?"

"Well, we've been on a sex binge for days. Suppose Jacques comes back unexpectedly. Or Pauline?"

"Won't happen, honey." He mixed a pitcher of 75s and they began drinking together. After the first one, he kissed her roughly and said, "These things work out. The whole situation will look better in the morning."

But things weren't looking better, they were looking worse, and it wouldn't be long before Freddy and Darcy called in with bitter complaints and threats. Fuck 'em, he thought. Wembley's already destroying my chance for the directorship, so what more can they do to hurt me? If they claim I passed classified info, they'd be confessing insider knowledge, which they're probably too smart to do. Or their lawyers are.

He drank again from the bottle. Doreen stirred and turned her head on the pillow. He wondered if his office had been calling him. Later he'd check the answering machine.

Reaching over, he stroked his daughter's arm, thinking, For every good thing there's a negative, and having Doreen as my sweetheart is worth more than anything I can think of. In Europe they could travel and live together as he and Amy had, no questions asked. Maybe they should plan on that solution. Exposure here would ruin me, he mused. I'd be snickered at in every club, every floor of the Agency, a laughingstock. Pauline would divorce me, and I can't go through that again. The first time, all papers were sealed by the court, but Pauline might not go along with that. She has too much money to compromise, and she's likely to be mean-spirited and vengeful. Sullying the marriage bed with her stepdaughter. Every tabloid in the country would headline the story, and the British and French press doted on scandal and exploited it— especially if it involved rich Americans.

His headache was mostly gone, thanks to the cognac. He considered waking Doreen for a few shots to make her feel better. She had an absolutely gorgeous pear-shaped ass that he could have been fucking for years if he hadn't been so goddam inhibited. Told me so herself. Dr. Rothblatt had it right, that last session. Right on the fucking button. She was trying to seduce me displaying herself and I was too dense to catch the clue. How dumb can you be?

His stomach rolled and he belched. Acid reflux made him grimace. There was more champagne in the kitchen fridge, nicely chilled for mating with cognac. Good to know it was there. Available. Like Doreen.

What was the future? First he ought to give notice at the Agency. Give stress, ill health as the reason. He hated the dronelike hours, the desk job he'd never viewed as more than a stepping-stone to bigger things with more status—like the directorship. That opportunity having vanished, why stay around? He needed freedom to travel, see the world with Doreen, carve out a new life for themselves. He wasn't young, but he wasn't old either. Seasoned was the word. And Doreen proclaimed him a marvelous sexual partner. True, she wasn't as experienced as Amy was—his mother having been a showgirl with multiple lovers—but Doreen could learn. *Was* learning his likes, and her own.

Gerold lay back beside her, pulled the sheet over his naked body. The room was dark, the house silent. He slept.

AT HER UPPERVILLE ESTATE Pauline Gerold was annoyed by her inability to reach Darman. His office said he was on leave but didn't say where. Possibly he was off on some secret CIA assignment, corrupting high-level foreign officials, and she'd hear about it later. The secrecy of his work had always intrigued her, and she knew that some of her equestrian friends envied her inside status. She'd phoned the Georgetown house several times, leaving messages on the machine that went unanswered, so Darman was surely away. Not even Jacques was there to answer, so she assumed Darman had given him vacation time knowing he'd be gone more than a few days. But he should have told me, she thought irritably, and I could have reminded him to be back in time for our gala.

One invitation envelope had been returned to her, and an alternate address was available in the study Rolodex they both used. When I do these things, she reflected, I really ought to have a social secretary for invitations, RSVPs, catering, and so on. Next time I will. Meanwhile, she needed the Senator's residence address, and while at the house she'd look in on what had been done to enhance Doreen's room. It was possible she'd like the improvements even though she detested the room's future occupant. A sneering, defiant, antisocial little dopehead was what Doreen was, and Pauline understood why her father had put her in clinical rehab. There was always hope for a turnaround if the little bitch could stay off drugs.

After stopping at the house she'd lunch at the Washington Club, perhaps encounter a friend or two with whom to share a cocktail.

Leaving her room, Pauline told Benjy, the houseman, she'd be away until late afternoon and to take any messages. If anything important came up, she could be reached in Georgetown or at the club, he should use his judgment.

Outside, the country air was fresh, the sun brilliant in a cloudless sky. As she walked to her Mercedes she gazed at the white-fenced fields where her horses grazed, at the training ring, where a trainer was working the palomino mare. The mount wasn't quite ready for showing, but the trainer anticipated that in another three weeks or so she could be. A proud, beautiful horse, really, almost pure white with the breed's distinctive golden mane. Tomorrow she might saddle up and canter the palomino around the ring, see how responsive she was.

Before getting into her car, Pauline paused a few moments to scan her outlying property and possessions. Oaktree Farms.

In addition to a long, fourteen-stable building, there was a large feed barn, tack room, and a separate building for tractors and other heavy equipment necessary to a working farm. Somewhat to the south of it, concealed behind a protective berm, was a trap and skeet range. Pauline had been raised with three brothers, and their father decided they should all learn shooting together. Pauline was proficient at trap, less so at skeet, and maintained the range largely for the enjoyment of county friends and the occasional visits of her brothers, Darman having shown himself uninterested in the sport. She herself had not shouldered her custom-fitted Greener twelve-bore in several months. Cleaned and oiled, the trap gun was kept in an upper hallway gun cabinet beside a twelve double and two twenty semi-autos of different makes. Pauline was not a gun nut or even a member of the NRA, but she enjoyed an occasional round of trap with friends at day's end, when the sun was right.

Later she might invite a few riding companions and shooting enthusiasts for cocktails, snacks, and a few rounds of skeet, the weather being so fine. And with that thought in her mind Pauline started the engine and drove out toward Washington.

APPALACHIAN FOOTHILLS, PENNSYLVANIA

THEY HADN'T BROUGHT MUCH with them in their hurried departure from Washington, so Peter, La-li, and Brand had little to take back.

After saying good-bye to Dr. Brand, they got into Brand's BMW, knowing they'd return a final time when everything was taken care of, and foreign travel arranged.

As he drove, Brand thought back to the night before and considered the enormity of what Gerold had done. Bad enough that Gerold had concurred in hunting down Peter and himself, but to make his daughter his whore—as Doreen put it—was incredible.

And if I'd even suspected that Gerold wanted his daughter found so he could seduce her I wouldn't have had my brothers look for her. And find her. But I did it in good faith because I was searching for my son and empathized with Darman, assuming he wanted only to straighten out her life. How wrong I was.

What kind of life can they possibly have? It's not just a husband seeking to conceal an affair from his wife, it's a thousand times worse because the woman is his daughter, his own flesh and blood.

To put it in the best possible light, Gerold was corrupted by his mother, crippling his ability to discriminate between female lovers. He wanted Doreen, she looked good, was available, and so they got together.

Now that they know I know will they stay together? Common sense says no. But Darman was never noted for that particular quality, lived in an insulated, protected world where wrongdoing is seldom punished. Assumed he could do what he wanted, with impunity. And for all I know, he will.

AFTER LETTING OFF PETER and La-li at their place, Brand drove to his apartment and went in, the door pushing aside thirty or forty pieces of mail dropped through the slot. Ignoring them, he turned on the air-conditioning and went to his desk. The long distance operator put him through to the Celestial Galleries, and even though it was late night in Hong Kong, he heard Mary's answering voice.

"Darling," he said, "I haven't been able to call for reasons I'll explain when I see you. Did you get my letter?"

"Yes, Mark, yesterday. And it meant so much to me. Forgive me, but I'd begun having doubts—"

"Never," he said sternly, "never doubt me. I think I can be with you in between two or three weeks, just as soon as I can get out of here. Peter will be with me, La-li, too, and they'll need a place to live."

"Of course. I'll ask our daughter to start looking—for her brother and sister-in-law."

Her words thrilled him and he thought, I've got to start thinking of our new relationships in just those terms. "How is Chu-li?"

"Anxious to see you—as am I. Dear, there is so much to do—disposing of assets, deciding the future of our galleries—I really need you here."

"I know," he said, "and there's our wedding to plan."

She hesitated before saying, "I've not been a good Buddhist, and I feel you've not been an enthusiastic Christian despite being a missionary's son."

"Medical missionary. So?"

"So, I thought we might have a simple civil wedding. My solicitor can arrange all details with the Registrar before you arrive. Is—is that agreeable?"

"Absolutely. Oh, my father, who knew your father, sends his most affectionate regards and wishes. He'll visit us when Peter's child is born."

"Wonderful. Is there anything else, dear?"

"A great deal," he told her, "but it has to wait. Oh, here's my apartment telephone number," recited it and said, "I love you both," before hanging up.

He would never, he thought, looking around at all the chinoiserie he'd accumulated, ever leave her again.

Forty-Seven

WASHINGTON

WHEN PAULINE GEROLD REACHED their P Street house she was surprised to see Darman's Jaguar parked in the driveway. She pulled up behind it and turned off the ignition, wondering if he could possibly be home.

Then she discarded the notion, remembering that Agency cars took him to and from airports when he was traveling on official business.

After locking her Mercedes she went up the steps, taking the door key from her purse. She unlocked the door, went in and closed it, then walked to the study, where she consulted the Rolodex and found the Senator's home address—on Woodley Road, not Kalorama where the invitation had been sent. She copied the address on a blank card and put it in her purse, remembered the sub-purpose of her visit, and went up the carpeted staircase. Reaching the top of the stairs, she looked down the corridor and saw that the master bedroom bed was properly made up, Jacques having straightened the room after Darman's departure. The guest room Darman was having redecorated was only a few steps away, the door partly open, so she went to it and looked in. New curtains and carpeting, but the blinds were closed and the room dark. Wanting to see the wall color, she reached for the switch and turned on the ceiling lights. And froze.

Darman was in bed asleep on his back, mouth open the way he always slept but—there beside him was another person, blond hair on the pillow. Pauline shrieked and jerked down the sheet to reveal two naked bodies, her husband and—his daughter. Pauline felt faint, nauseated. Darman sat up and stared at her. "Pauline," he said idiotically, "didn't know you were coming."

Throat so tight she could hardly force out the words, she grated, "Obviously not. Wake her. I don't want her to miss this."

The scent of rut was in the air. She saw her husband lift Doreen's arm, hold it upright until the girl said, "Ouch, don't *do* that, I'm—" She broke off as her eyes opened and she saw what her father was pointing at. "Oh," she said, and sat up. "Hello, Pauline. Daddy and I have been having a ball." She reached for the cognac bottle.

Pauline swallowed. Brazen as ever. "That what you call an incestuous orgy? My God, to find you together—like *this*. I can hardly believe it. It's like a ghastly dream. Pull up the sheet, Doreen. Your nudity disgusts me."

After a long swallow, Doreen said, "Doesn't disgust Daddy, does it, old dear?" She handed him the bottle. "Have a drink, I think you're going to need it." Slowly, she drew the sheet over her legs and thighs. "That better, stepmother?"

Pauline snorted. She felt like vomiting, but held back. Her son-of-a-bitch husband wasn't even *trying* to offer explanations. He was there in bed with his daughter, and he was caught. *Caught*, damn him. She closed her eyes; maybe the nightmare would vanish. But when she opened them again the scene was as before.

With a lewd smile Doreen said, "So we've been getting it on for—days, I guess, and nights. What are you going to do about it?"

"Plenty," she snapped. "I'll disgrace you both."

"Pauline, you shouldn't have come snooping around. Bad form. Daddy's a real stud—if you didn't know—and not to be trusted out of sight." She stroked her father's near arm. "Tell her, Dad."

Darman ran his tongue over dry lips. "I don't know what to say."

Pauline stared at him. "You could say she seduced you, how's that sound?"

"Unrealistic," Doreen replied with that same lascivious smile. "We seduced each other. I wanted him a lot longer than he wanted me. Now you've seen the situation, why don't you get out?"

"You slut!" Pauline screamed. "Despicable little drughead slut!"

Doreen jerked as though struck. "That's what I am, Daddy's little slut. Okay? Now get out of here, you dried-up old bag. You have no feelings, don't know what it is to be a real woman. Well, I do, and your husband appreciates it. You weren't laying him, treated him like furniture. Well, I'm the opposite of you."

"You certainly are," Pauline retorted in controlled rage. "You're everything I never wanted to be, could never be. Whore!"

Turning, she went quickly from the room, but not before she heard Doreen's final yell: *"Get fucked, bitch!"*

She stumbled on the stairs, clutched the banister, and steadied herself. No wonder Darman hadn't answered the phone; he was conducting their debauched bacchanal. Oh, God, she thought imploringly as she reached the floor, what am I to do?

In the bedroom they heard the screech of Pauline's tires as her car backed out of the drive. Doreen yawned, stretched, and left the bed for the bathroom. Gerold heard the rustling of her stream striking bowl water. He felt almost too paralyzed to move, overwhelmed by events, Pauline's discovery, her threat to disgrace him. For one of the few times in his life he felt powerless.

The toilet flushed. Doreen came back into the bedroom and gazed at him. "Well, Dad, you didn't have much to say."

He sighed. "What could I say?"

"What did you say when Mother caught you humping Gran—on your honeymoon?"

"I don't remember and I don't want to talk about it." He glared at her resentfully.

"Well, the cat's out of the bag, as the saying goes, and the old bag caught us. Only way it could have been worse was if we were actually fucking."

"Would you have cared?"

"Not really. Not unless she came in with a gun."

"Honey," he said, "you were pretty cool through that whole awful scene, and—"

"Someone had to be. Pauline was poised like a fucking panther and I didn't want my face clawed." She smiled. "Or your balls." Pulling down the sheet she fondled his crotch. "Family jewels have taken on new meaning in the Gerold family."

"God, you can find humor in anything."

"Better than weeping, dear." She handed him the nearly empty bottle. "Finish it off, Dad, might as well."

He drank then, and after the last drops slid down his gullet he tossed the bottle toward a wastebasket. It missed and rolled on the floor. "What are we going to do?" he wondered aloud.

"What do you want to do?"

"Shut her mouth, kill her." The intensity of his voice startled him. Would he really murder Pauline? For a few moments he pondered the question, concluding that he would—if he thought he could get away with it. The frigid bitch was useless; worse, she was an immediate threat to his reputation, persona, way of life, everything. He didn't care about the money she could suck from him. Money was replaceable; reputation was not. How could he silence her? He looked at Doreen's placid face, the slope and curve of breasts he had come so well to cherish, and decided that if he took the lethal option, his daughter must never know. Doreen might shrink from the idea, begin to distrust him. And knowledge of his act would give her a powerful lever for possible future use. Already she had suggested he buy her a Ferrari or Lotus roadster. But with her own car she could tool around the countryside collecting pot-smoking, needle-sharing friends, taking them to Wolf Trap concerts, and *that* he didn't want. Having drawn her into his own adult world, he couldn't have her slipping back into old, disreputable adolescent ways. A sure way to lose her. So foreign roadsters would stay on the back burner for a while.

"Dad, what's on your mind?"

"Well," he lied, "I was thinking of a long cruise. One of those long, multiport voyages to Rio or B.A. We could leave the ship and never come back. What do you think?"

"Oh, if we're going to run away from Pauline it's a good idea—only I wouldn't want to stay away forever."

"Wouldn't have to." He was feeling better; that cognac dividend had done the trick. "Feel like champagne?"

"Sure, why not? Stay there, I'll get it. *And* more brandy."

"Perfect." And after they'd shared a few swigs he'd part her legs and go at it again. He'd never known such vibrant lust before, felt insatiable, and she was insatiable, too, like Amy, a perfectly satisfying partner.

As she went lithely past the bed he watched her cheeks dimple, the small hip loveholds, and then she was gone. No better way to get the witch Pauline out of his mind than sex plus French 75s. A marvelous, therapeutic combination. If he felt up to it—which he didn't—he'd phone Rothblatt and recommend the combination as a sovereign remedy for—what? Guilt? No, he wasn't letting guilt creep in. He'd suppressed guilt before laying plans to bring Doreen home. Distress was the better word. Distress over being caught in flagrante, even though at the time he wasn't actually humping his child. Pauline hadn't needed a video to comprehend the situation—one glance was enough. And she was vengeful, humiliated by a younger woman she couldn't compare with in any way—least of all in bed. So she'd strike back with all her force, all her female guile. Disgusting. His hatred ballooned. His fingers itched for her throat.

Doreen returned with champers and cognac, and he admired the way her young breasts jostled as she moved. God, she was desirable. He absolutely *had* to have her. For now, forget Pauline. He'd deal with his wife later.

From Georgetown Pauline Gerold drove toward the Washington Club, inwardly shaking. Tears were making her makeup run, she couldn't enter the club looking like that . . . couldn't have a drink there and encounter friends. Whatever she did about Darman and that sexy snake he lived with wasn't to be revealed now. There had to be some clever way of destroying him without humiliating herself forever in the process.

Half rounding the circle, Pauline pulled into the club parking area and activated her mobile phone. She dialed her lawyer's office, knew the number by heart from frequent conferences about horse sales and estate matters, and asked to speak with Warren Bass.

"Sorry, ma'am, Mr. Bass is in conference."

"*Shit,*" she said, the unintended exclamation surprising her. After apologizing, she said she needed an immediate appointment. Gave her name and waited.

Warren's secretary came on the line. "Sorry, Mrs. Gerold, but Mr. Bass is having a partners' business lunch, then he'll be in court the rest of the day."

"Ummm. Tomorrow?"

"That's bad, too. Day after?"

"If that's the best you can do. What time?"

"Have to be toward day's end. Four o'clock?"

"I'll be there." She replaced the phone, saw ladies entering the club, among them two she recognized. No, couldn't go in, feeling too distraught. Better go back home—*her* home—where she could have privacy. In her room. To cry her heart out. Oh, that bastard! she thought, half aloud, to violate our vows with his own daughter. The sordid scene was still unbelievable. Who could imagine it? Darman Gerold, of all people. It was like coming unexpectedly on a set for a dirty movie. At least he hadn't sullied their actual bed—Doreen's was there to share— so he didn't win points for that. But they'd probably coupled all over the living room, every chair, sofa, and rug. She closed her eyes in anguish, gripped the wheel.

She couldn't bear thinking of it.

Starting the engine, she backed around, nearly smashing a parked car, straightened out, and drove slowly from the club.

Another time, she told herself, when I can face people. Now I want to get home, and if I don't have lunch—and I know I'd vomit the first bite—I'll have a drink to soothe my nerves. Darman and his baby-bitch were drinking, stench of liquor all over the place. Probably drinking for days, in addition to the other thing they were doing. Animals in rut.

She took Whitehurst Freeway across Key Bridge into Virginia, turned onto Route 66, and followed it almost all the rest of the way, guided by habit and instinct, so full were her eyes of self-pitying tears.

OAKTREE FARMS, FAQUIER COUNTRY, VIRGINIA

PAULINE FRANCES GEROLD née Imhoff was a product of Milwaukee Country Day School, Mary Baldwin College, and all the advantages her wealthy brewing family could bestow on their only daughter.

Wearing bra and teddies, she sat at her vanity table in a large, well-lighted dressing room off the master bedroom, and stared at her reflection in the four-by-six-foot mirror. She was still a good-looking woman, she decided, but her marriages had been unfortunate.

Her first husband, Charles, was a law student at the University of Virginia when they met at a college dance. They dated occasionally until his graduation, when he returned to San Francisco to take the California Bar. For generations, Charles's family had owned a private utility company in Orange County and generously supported San Francisco cultural institutions and civic associations. A year after passing the Bar examination, Charles ran for Congress, was easily elected, and took up bachelor residence in suburban Washington. During his absence, he and Pauline had written occasionally, and on his return they began dating. Though Charles kept a much larger racing yawl at the San Francisco Yacht Club, he had a thirty-foot ketch at Washington's Corinthian Yacht Club, and during a Sunday afternoon sail on the bay Charles proposed marriage and Pauline accepted.

During their three-month engagement Pauline visited his family and he hers—happy occasions, she recalled, though she virtuously refused his demands for premarital sex. Thus, she was a virgin on her wedding night, Charles was lustfully rough, and her introduction to coitus distasteful.

After the pain and trauma of an ectopic pregnancy Pauline never conceived again, so they were childless at the time of her husband's death during a cup race to Hawaii. His yawl foundered in high seas, and Charles and his three-man crew were lost and presumed drowned. No bodies were ever found. Pauline attended a symbolic funeral off the Golden Gate, strewing flowers over the waters, and returned to managing

Oaktree Farms and riding with the Faquier and other hunts. Three years into widowhood she met Darman Gerold at the Governor's Ball, decided he was a suitable successor to Charles—despite certain rumors about his divorce—and married him six months later.

I suppose, she mused, if I'd been sexually liberated like his daughter—and perhaps his mother as well, if those old rumors were true—he would really have loved and cared for me, not debauched Doreen.

She closed her eyes, opened them, and stared again at her face. Her dark hair had not begun to gray, her tan skin was unlined, and under-eye pouches had barely begun. Never having nursed, her breasts were firm and small-nippled. Riding kept her abdomen flat and her haunches trim, and she thought herself in excellent physical condition. She conceded she had some psychological problems involving sex that a good therapist could probably eliminate, and she would see to that before dating men who were husband candidates. Among equestrian friends were several well-to-do widowers, and other divorced or unattached acquaintances.

Her eyes widened, and she realized that in her mind Darman no longer existed, he was gone like Charles, never to be seen again.

Well, that forethought would become legal reality after her consultation with Warren Bass day after tomorrow. It would be an easy divorce, she told herself, Darman would not contest it in return for her silence on the proximate cause of alienation. Warren would choose the best, most discreet venue for divorce, perhaps the Virgin Islands, Lichtenstein, or some other place where she could enjoy whatever waiting period there was.

She was simply not going to think of Darman anymore, much less his slutty daughter. Jacques could remove Darman's clothing and other possessions, whose presence would be a grating reminder. And having considered the recent past and her coming future, Pauline went to the bedroom cellarette and poured a tumbler of vodka, iced it, and turned on the bathtub taps. While the tub filled she added foaming bath pearls and drank vodka, finishing the tumbler when she was in the tub, chin-high in scented foam.

The liquor buoyed her spirits, and as hot water eased tenseness from neck and back muscles, she began to feel liberated from a rotten, unrewarding marriage. Soon, she would be herself again, Pauline Frances Imhoff, heiress to Imhoff Breweries, and a renewed woman, who deserved and would find seasoned happiness in years ahead.

But for today's nauseatingly erotic discovery, she thought, I'd have followed my same drab, unexciting life to the grave. There's more to living than horses and estate management, and I suppose I owe Darman for finding it out.

After an hour's soaking, and two more tumblers of vodka, Pauline went to bed and slept deeply until evening.

PART
FIVE

Forty-Eight

By NIGHTFALL DARMAN GEROLD had formulated his plans.

Unnoticed by Doreen, he abstained from swallowing liquor while plying her with drinks. In her last coup of champagne he had dissolved two sleeping capsules supplied by Dr. Hempill, and as she snored on the rumpled bed, he felt sure that she would remain there until morning. She lay on her back, thighs slightly apart, blond muff showing impudently. But Gerold was sexually exhausted and felt he needed the night off, before resuming intercourse in the morning.

In the closet of the master bedroom Gerold got out black warm-up pants and a black turtleneck he seldom wore. He dressed in them, put on comfortable black shoes, and got a woolen ski mask from his athletic drawer. He noticed fingered ski gloves and stuck them in his waistband. He was ready to go.

Down the corridor he paused at Doreen's open doorway and saw her position had not changed. He went to the bedside and listened to her regular breathing, confident he hadn't administered too heavy a dose. Losing his daughter was a thought he couldn't bear to contemplate. So he bent over, kissed her forehead lightly, murmured, "Good night, sweetheart," and left the room.

To avoid being seen by passersby, Gerold went out the back kitchen door and came around through the alley to his driveway. He got quickly into the Jaguar, looked around before starting the engine. No headlights from either direction, no dog-walkers or university students strolling by. He turned west, drove to Wisconsin Avenue, and turned south to Key Bridge.

With the ignition on, the AM band came to life, and as he drove across the Potomac, he heard snatches of country music and the moronic drolleries of a far-off deejay. Maybe, he thought, the hillbilly station would come in; he hadn't changed the setting since hearing the Frog Lady fearfully expound her problem. Maybe she'd call again tonight.

The dash clock showed ten twenty-two. Take him an hour to get there, half an hour to make his approach, and a few minutes to do the job. He'd be back in bed beside Doreen no later than two o'clock. Then, sometime before noon he'd get a call from police telling him his wife had been shot by a burglar.

Pauline was usually asleep by ten. She was probably asleep now, and the house had no alarm system or pet dog. Servants' quarters were on the third floor with a rear staircase down to the kitchen. He opened the glove compartment and drew out the nickel-plated .38 revolver he kept there to ward off carjackers and other troublemakers. The revolver had no serial number, and a silencer tube was screwed onto the barrel. Someone had left it at the Farm's pistol range, where Gerold pocketed it unseen. The hammer rested on a fired casing, leaving five jacketed bullets in the cylinder. Two quiet shots should terminate his marriage and end her threat to his existence.

On TV, he remembered, hit men usually fired through a pillow to muffle their shots, and doing so tonight would lend a touch of professional realism to her murder. Jewels that weren't in a safe deposit box were usually on her vanity, so he must remember to pocket whatever was available. He slid the revolver under his seat and locked cruise control at fifty-two, just under the highway limit.

Tonight's timing was crucial and circumstances were ideal. He had to neutralize Pauline before she saw a lawyer and exposed him. To kill her afterward would suggest motive, and as matters stood, there was no motive linking him to her death. The sole risk concerned the possibility that Pauline had seen a lawyer after leaving Georgetown, but Gerold appraised her parting mood as too distraught to think rationally and logically.

On the high plus side was having Doreen as an alibi witness. She could definitely swear that he had not left the house the night of Pauline's murder, and she would believe it. Of course, she wouldn't say they'd *slept* together, just that she hadn't heard him leave or return to his bedroom. Against that, no one could say that he had.

In fact, he mused, I'll stay in bed beside her until she wakes me in the morning. That'll convince her completely.

A pickup zoomed around him, and Gerold's headlights illuminated a bumper sticker reading:

HELP STAMP OUT MENTAL HEALTH
OR I'LL KILL YOU

My God, was it possible people were allowed to display such cruel, insensitive messages? Who conceived, printed, and distributed those malicious threats? If there was no law against them, Congress should act speedily to cleanse the highways. The President should be aware of madness lurking behind the wheel, and use his considerable influence to end it. Life in America was becoming too disorganized to tolerate that kind of arrant irrationality.

A truck whizzed past, a huge twelve-wheeler, its only rear sticker reading:

IF YOU DON'T LIKE MY DRIVING
CALL 1-800-EAT SHIT

What insanity! The arrogant challenge ought to be dealt with at the next truck stop. He wasn't going to threaten the driver, just shoot out a pair of tires.

Leaving three bullets for Pauline.

No, the truck was going too fast, at least seventy-five. Another defiant lawbreaker who ought to be behind bars.

His fingers carefully edged the AM dial to each side of the setting, then back to where it had been. No Frog Lady talk-show host's voice came through the speaker, but perhaps when he was farther into the countryside the station would come in.

Only the talk-show host could lead him to the Frog Lady, and Gerold felt strong compulsion to help the poor soul, guide her away from superstition and fear into the restorative light of mental health.

Too bad his limited session with Rothblatt hadn't allowed him to bring up the Frog Lady. Undoubtedly the psychiatrist would have had suggestions, guidance in the matter, but he'd be seeing his favorite shrink in another few weeks. Somewhere he had the appointment card.

No, he reflected, Rothblatt isn't my favorite shrink; that honor belongs to Dr. Hempill who, wittingly or not, allowed me access to my beloved Doreen and delivered her in an entirely new semblance of female beauty and desirability. Skinny, dirty, and addicted no more. For that, I will be forever grateful. Her youth makes her body even more exciting than Amy's had been—though at the time she was everything to me.

The dash clock showed he had driven nearly an hour, ought to be nearing Oaktree land. He watched route signs carefully, and at 17 made the turn. Only a few miles to go. He wanted to see the big house dark, nobody stirring. He had a key, but a true burglar would have to pry a door open to get in. There were crowbars in the tractor shed; he'd pick one up as he approached the house.

With gloves on. So many details to remember. But this crime had to be perfect. And it was justifiable. One had to be sacrificed so that two could live. Majority rule no less. He hoped Pauline was sleeping as soundly as Doreen, and tried to remember why he had ever decided to marry her. Hadn't been on impulse, either. Divorced and unattached, he needed a companion of his own social and economic class to confer a status cachet on his career, his unspoken ambitions.

Their encounter at the ball had seemed at first fortuitous, then foreordained. The widow Pauline had been physically attractive, wealthy, and well known as an active equestrienne. Well, he'd exploited almost all of those qualities, and what remained had to end. The big tented gala he'd been counting on to cement his nomination for the directorship was never going to take place. And he wasn't going to be Director, anyway. Not when a new life with Doreen was beginning.

He inclined more and more to the concept of a lengthy cruise to exciting destinations: Rio, Hong Kong, Tokyo—maybe not Hong Kong, though, Doreen was familiar with Hong Kong and might hold residual memories of Mark Brand's staff. Jesus, how he hated Brand. After finishing off Pauline, why not take a short side trip and blow out Brand's brains as well? Then no one alive would know about him and his daughter. Think about it, he told himself. Blast the know-it-all bastard and eliminate the final witness. Take maybe half an hour, forty-five minutes. Be in bed by three, well before Doreen wakens.

Hadn't considered eliminating Brand before, because his mind had been too deeply involved working out his Pauline plan. Now he had time to decide how best to get face-to-face with Mark.

Unsuspectingly, Mark would let him into the building, open the door, and *pow!* His hand clenched. *Pow, pow!* Two for the missionary's son, the big Taiwan-China expert. Two down. Pauline and Brand. This was twofer night. He grinned in the darkness, saw the whitewashed fencing of an estate adjoining Oaktree. Slowed on the two-lane asphalt road and turned headlights off. The estate frontage was somewhere around four hundred yards, beyond the property vacant field waiting for a buyer. In from the road was a stand of trees, some bushes. Leave the Jag there, put on mask and gloves, take the revolver, and follow the fencing back beyond the barn.

Crowbar there.

Scant moonlight showed him the property's terminus, a little farther on the bushes and trees. Not quite midnight, he'd wait a bit to make sure. Turned off the shoulder and bucked down into the field. Plowed through tall grass to reach concealment, and killed the engine.

His heart was pounding, his whole body felt wet with perspiration. Excitement. Contemplating her killing *was* exciting; he could summon a hard-on just envisioning it. Jesus, did *all* killers feel the same way when they put it to an enemy? He sucked in a series of deep breaths to calm his nerves, reversed the ignition key, and saw the AM dial light up. Good. Now he could kill time searching for the talk host and his bizarre caller, the Frog Lady. Nothing Gerold had ever heard before so combined sheer menace and absurdity.

If she was making up the story—as callers sometimes did—she needed professional help. But where in the outland would she get it? He felt compelled to offer assistance—if only he could find that same damn station again. And while conversing with the talk host, bring up graffiti—the menace of bumper stickers that flaunted irrational things. On that score Rothblatt hadn't been very helpful even though the problem was ever-present in his thoughts.

He moved the dial very slightly left, then right. What was *that?* The talk host's jarring voice? Yep, same man! Gerold felt his body trembling in anticipation. This was the night for great things happening: two enemies dispatched, and the poor old Frog Lady succored and sustained. Excitedly, he listened, and when the station's call-in number was given, Gerold snatched up the cellular phone and demanded the operator put him through to the station. Emergency, life-threatening situation. He closed his eyes, breathed deeply to calm himself, and waited for the host man to come through. Two minutes later, during a commercial break, Gerold heard the fellow say, "Hi, there. Off the air, so tell me what your emergency is. Life threatening? Whose life?"

Gerold swallowed. "The—the Frog Lady's."

"The—*who?* This some kind of put-on joke?"

"No, serious, dammit. I heard her call in twice, and I want to help her if I can. Just put me in touch with her, will you? Thank you very much."

The host chuckled. *"Now* I remember, that was a while back, right? Listen, fella, appreciate your offer, but there's no problem."

"No problem? What—?"

"Because there's no Frog Lady. Lissen, phone action was slow so my old aunt called in, put that tree-frog bullshit on the air. We had a good laugh afterward. Must have got ten, twelve calls like yours offering advice." He laughed loudly. "Thanks, anyway, I'll tell auntie you called, appreciate it. Night, fella, back to the mike."

Click.

Gerold yelled, threatened, jiggled the phone, but the host was on-air again still chuckling over his little fraud. Gerold cut off the radio, the cellular was silent. Shakily, Gerold put it away. He'd been suckered by a goddam country jasper and his moronic aunt. How could he have been so credulous? But, was the story pure bullshit, or somewhere within it was there a germ of truth? He stretched out on the seat, exhausted from stress.

Whatever the true story he had neither strength nor will to pursue it. If the neurotic caller—aunt or not—got poisoned by frog or toad, so be it, she'd brought death on herself through calculated deception.

Like Puritanical Pauline was bringing death on *her*self.

Gerold looked around, scanned outside. Less moonlight now. Twelve-eighteen. Time to go. As Doreen counseled, Just Do It.

For a few moments he reviewed actions ahead, drew on the ski mask, pulled on gloves, and stuck the revolver in his waistband.

Then he got out of the car, quietly closed the door, and walked into the night.

IN BED AT TEN, Pauline Gerold had tried sleeping with the night-light on, tried for an hour before turning it off. In the dark she felt dreadfully alone, like a child abandoned in her nursery, and scenes from her awful day ran through her mind like frames from a manic projector.

Her recent life—as she saw it now—had been a disaster. She'd had no love, no caring, no real attention from her second husband, and she'd made the mistake of compensating by focusing on the estate, her horses, her hunt club friends. On the other hand, Darman was an unworthy mate, and their stale marriage was almost entirely his fault. Of course, it made no difference now, but she resented those wasted, useless years when he was nominally the husband to whom she owed fealty and devotion.

Well, it was over now, and for the better. Warren Bass would sink a deep harpoon, and Darman would never forget the wife he had so recklessly betrayed.

She rolled over on her back, stared at the ceiling, where moonlight reflected from the windowpane lightened a patch of shadows. She'd let herself be put off too easily by Warren's secretary, should have insisted on meeting him tomorrow. Oh, there were country lawyers in Middleburg, Warrenton, and Upperville, but they were for real estate transactions, lacked Warren's courtroom skills. Definitely she'd call Warren in the morning. At home.

She wanted a better, more enjoyable life. She could afford travel anywhere, but fashionable watering spots abounded in con men and mountebanks—men not unlike Darman Gerold, whose life was a hollow fraud. Only now did she realize how deeply she hated him.

Let him keep the Georgetown house. After what she'd seen there she would never enter it again. He must be mad to think he could keep their secret long concealed. So intimate a relationship was sure to be noticed and commented on—to his detriment, if not to his daughter's.

She, Doreen, was beyond redemption.

Pauline heard a stable dog bark, horses began nickering. She left the bed and looked down toward the moonlit stables. A fox or wild dog could be there, most likely only a possum or raccoon searching for grains of feed. The stable dog kept yapping, horses neighed. She lifted the window and heard the crack of breaking wood. Someone was out there trying to steal a horse.

Pulling on a robe, she went to the gun cabinet, got out her shotgun, and loaded it with two double-ought high-base shells. Then she returned to the window and knelt, resting the twin barrels on the sill. No time to alert Benjy, the houseman; he wouldn't know what to do, anyway, and trainers, grooms, stable boys, and field hands came by the day. If she was to prevent horse theft she'd have to do it alone.

Then, eyes fully adjusted to darkness, she saw a black-clad figure loping from the barn. There was a long bar in one hand, something glinting in the other. She started to call out a warning, but her throat was too dry, and she realized the intruder was headed for the house.

For *her*.

Carrying weapons!

Couldn't let him get inside to rob and kill her. Had to stop him now.

Sighting down the Greener, she led the oncoming figure, and when it was less than fifty yards from the house she aimed at his thighs and fired.

Flame blanked him out, she heard him yell, and fired again.

Breeze drifted gunsmoke back into her nostrils. She saw him lying in the moonlight, unmoving.

Benjy burst into the room. "What is it, ma'am? What's happening?"

She pointed down at the still body. "Not just a horse thief," she said tremulously, went to the hall, and reloaded her shotgun. "Take a flashlight and go down there," she told him. "I'll cover you from here."

"Yes, ma'am." He left the room, she heard his footsteps on the staircase.

Again she knelt by the window, resting the Greener on the sill, her mind a jumble of thoughts and apprehensions. Police questions, publicity, notoriety, possible lawsuits.

Benjy could call the police, while she called Warren Bass, damn him, he'd have to come *now*—even though it was the middle of the night.

She saw the cone of Benjy's light moving toward the black-clad man. The light traveled from feet to masked face. A glinting handgun lay where it had fallen from his hand, the other hand still clutched a long black bar.

"Is—is he dead?" she called.

"Think so. Not moving, lots of blood."

She closed her eyes, clenched her teeth, and withdrew her shotgun. Then she called, "Pull off the mask, Benjy, I want to see who it is."

"Yes, ma'am." Obediently he knelt, worked the mask up and off the shattered face. For a few moments he said nothing, then stood and cupped his hands to call, "You won't like this, ma'am, but it looks like Mr. Gerold."

Pauline fainted. Her shotgun clattered to the floor.

Forty-Nine

"MRS. GEROLD, I'm Deputy County Sheriff Giles Burden. I have a very few questions to ask, and I wonder if you feel up to them?"

Midmorning, and Pauline looked around her living room, still feeling dazed by the events of yesterday and last night. Benjy had brought a tray of coffee, and cook had prepared small sandwiches for visitors.

Deputy Burden looked at the man standing beside Mrs. Gerold and asked, "Sir, are you here in an official capacity?"

"My name is Warren Bass. My law offices are in the District. However, I also practice in Maryland and Virginia."

"Then you represent Mrs. Gerold?"

"I do, of course, but I am here more as a supportive friend than as legal counsel. However, I believe I can say that Mrs. Gerold will willingly cooperate with you or any duly constituted authorities in the course of your investigation. But may I suggest you consider the trauma Mrs. Gerold has suffered and make your questions as brief as possible?"

"I will, sir, I surely will." Deputy Burden was a clean-shaven man of thirty-two with an associate's certificate in criminal justice from Virginia Commonwealth University. Seated across from Pauline, he said, "You gave a statement to deputies who arrived here at—I believe one-fifteen this morning?"

"About then, I guess." She looked up at Bass. "I was too distraught to really notice the time."

"Ah—your houseman Benjamin Hamilton gave us an approximate time." He cleared his throat. "Is there anything you care to add to your initial statement at this time?"

"I—I don't think so."

Bass said, "I assume a copy of that statement will be made available to us?"

"Yes, sir."

Bass said, "The whole thing is a tragedy, an unbelievable tragedy. No one, least of all Mrs. Gerold, understands it at all."

"Yes, sir, and that's why we would like to make some sense of it. The decedent's car was found nearby, where he apparently left it. A few minutes after midnight Mr. Gerold placed an operator-assisted call on his cellular phone to a radio station in Front Royal. Do you know why he might have done that?"

Pauline said, "How did you know about the call?"

"By redialing his phone."

She smiled wanly. "Very clever, I would never have thought of that. Warren, may I have more coffee?"

"Of course."

"The call, Mrs. Gerold, any idea—?"

"None at all. Unless it was a talk program and Darman wanted to broadcast an opinion."

"We'll talk with the talk-show host later today. Now, I understand your stepdaughter—Mr. Gerold's daughter by a previous marriage—has been living with him at the Georgetown residence?"

Pauline accepted coffee from Bass before saying, "Doreen was a patient at a clinic in, oh, Arlington, someplace in northern Virginia. Her father arranged her release to his care in a family home environment." She sipped from her cup. "The clinic people could tell you more about the background—if that is important."

"Mrs. Gerold, when was the last time you saw your husband alive?"

Her face set. "When he was running toward me with weapons in his hands. He was going to kill me, murder me." She began to cry, tears welled and rolled down her cheeks.

Warren Bass stood up. "I think that's enough for now, Deputy. Neither Mrs. Gerold nor I has any idea why her husband would try to kill her. It's not our obligation to hypothesize, either. That's for you people."

Rather doggedly the Deputy asked, "Mrs. Gerold, do you know your late husband was seeing a psychiatrist?"

"No," she said, "but I'm not surprised. I've felt for some time that he was losing touch with reality." She paused. "A CIA psychiatrist? That's where Darman worked, you know."

"No, ma'am. A Dr. Armand Rothblatt in Rockville, Maryland. This appointment card was in your husband's Jaguar."

Looking up, she said, "Think of that, Warren. Darman must have felt the need of counseling, but apparently he was either too late, or therapy was inadequate."

"Or inappropriate. We may have cause for a malpractice action against Dr. Rothblatt, but we'll get to that later. Anything else, Deputy? Mrs. Gerold is obviously quite exhausted."

"I understand. We're taking the shotgun—matter of routine—and will return it in a day or so. Here's a receipt for it, ma'am."

Pauline pushed it aside. "Keep the damn gun, for God's sake. Think I want it around reminding me it killed my husband?" She began to cry again. Deputy Burden took leave of them and walked outside.

When they were alone together Bass said, "Darman planned a premeditated murder, Pauline. Unless he was insane, what possible motive could he have had? Not money, surely."

"No. I really don't know. And I don't want to think about it. I killed him. I didn't know it was him, just a threatening figure running at me." She wiped her cheeks, sniffled, and blew her nose. Doreen was a drug addict—maybe he was on drugs, too. "Am I under some sort of suspicion?"

"No, no, of course not. But the authorities would like to make sense of why he was there—outside, I mean." He swallowed. "Motive."

She shrugged. "Unless he left a note of some kind—which seems equally irrational—how will we ever know?"

Bass patted her shoulder. "Is there anyone I should notify?"

"My parents in Milwaukee. They can tell you where to reach my brothers."

He hesitated. "Darman's relatives?"

"Except for Doreen I don't know of any. Wait—a son named Fitzhugh, but there's been no contact between them for years. He was not around when I married Darman." She looked up at him. "Funeral arrangements—I don't know what to do." She hugged herself tightly. "Does a widow who killed her husband go to his funeral?"

"That's not within my experience, Pauline. You'll have to make that decision yourself." He got up and looked outside, at the yellow crime scene ribbon marking the place where Darman died.

"Something you may be asked—is why, when you saw the man fall after firing once, you fired a second time."

"The muzzle blast blinded me. I thought he might be running away. Pulling the other trigger was automatic. At least for someone accustomed to shooting clay pigeons it is."

"Quite understandable," he said, "and you were very brave."

"I was trying to protect my life."

"Nevertheless—" he began, and broke off. "If you'll allow me I'll begin notifying your family, make funeral arrangements. Ah—is there a preferred cemetery?"

"I suppose the old Oak Hill in Georgetown." A nerve in her cheek twitched. "If there's no room, let them dig a hole and bury him in the Harvard Yard."

"I'll make suitable arrangements. Pauline, I have a suggestion: Given your and Darman's prominence, reporters and TV cameramen are going to be all over the place. So far the deputies are keeping them out, but I strongly suggest I arrange with a security firm to maintain your privacy."

"Please do, Warren. I welcome all your suggestions." She shook her head. "I seem unable to do the simplest things for myself."

Except for last night, he thought, in the darkness, you did very damn well for yourself and everyone in the house. That crazy bastard could have killed them all. You're one hell of a woman, Pauline.

"May I use your telephone?"

"Of course, just take over the study, Warren. I need you to get some sort of order back into my life."

He poured another cup of coffee and carried it into the study, closed the door. Benjy came in from the kitchen and asked, "Anything I can do, ma'am?"

"No, Benjy, thank you for everything. Now I think I'll go back to my room."

She took the stairs slowly, and when she was there, she poured vodka in a tumbler and drank it down unhesitatingly. *His* closet was there, filled with *his* apparel, have to get rid of it. Some charitable institution—Benjy will know.

She added more vodka to her glass and went to a chair that faced away from the window where she'd knelt last night. The horses must be fed and groomed, trained. This part of my life has to go on—for a while. I won't be at the funeral—Doreen can go as his last survivor. Daddy's daughter-lover. She drank slowly and stared at the bed where she'd lain until roused by the barking and neighing. Cancel the gala, though invitees will have enough sense to realize it won't be held. The caterer . . . so many things to deal with, and I can accomplish only a few . . . From below, the sound of vehicles driving away. How long would the yellow band stay there? She'd have the gardener remove the blood-soaked soil, replace it with sod.

I wonder if Doreen knew he planned to kill me? If not before his death, by now she'll have put two and two together, realize he thought he had to silence me. With him gone, only she and I know what happened yesterday at the house, and I think it would be prudent to make some gesture toward her. Before the funeral. If she thinks anything at all of herself—and that's debatable—she'll preserve their secret and keep ridicule from my door. Yes, a gesture appropriate from a bereaved widow to an orphaned child . . .

Another vehicle drove away and Pauline finished her drink. A hot tub was in order. It would relax her, enable her to think.

WASHINGTON

AT HIS APARTMENT DESK Mark Brand had been going through accumulated mail. One plain envelope postmarked Washington, D.C., contained a Xeroxed copy of a Hong Kong obituary notice: Nina Kenton's death of natural causes. Clipped to it was the Bureau card of Special Agent Kevin Hoffman, and on a separate note-sized sheet of plain paper Hoffman had scrawled: *Her controller poisoned her, but we caught him. End of story.*

Caught him, and . . . Hoffman didn't say. End of whose story?

Poor Nina, Brand mused, he'd enjoyed their relationship until Peter disappeared; after that she became an irritant, and dangerous. It was her love of luxury that killed her, Tarnovski was only the means.

He crumpled the message and tossed it into a filling wastebasket, thought of her for a few moments, and resumed opening envelopes. Bills on top of bills. The real estate agent would be there in a few minutes to appraise the place for sale. Furnished properties sold better than vacant ones, she said, many buyers couldn't visualize how an empty room would look when there was furniture and pictures. So Brand hoped for a quick sale—before the packers came.

Not until he watched the midday news did Brand learn of Gerold's death. Details were few, but Brand surmised that Pauline had discovered Gerold and Doreen together, and Gerold had gone out to the estate to reason with his wife—or kill her.

Instead, he had been killed by Pauline.

Ending Gerold's aspirations, and drawing to a close a life warped by the errors and excesses of blind ambition.

The phone rang, Brand answered, and began talking with his son.

Postlude

DURING THE YEAR FOLLOWING THE DEATH OF DARMAN GEROLD:

Mark and Mary, Peter and La-li, were married in Hong Kong. Dr. Brand arrived for the birth of great-grandson Simon Mark, and stayed two weeks before returning to his medical practice.

Mary and Chu-li removed smuggled Chinese artifacts from their galleries and presented them to the Taipei Museum that Director Chen had founded and supervised until his death.

Mark and Peter formed a company to assist Hong Kong business firms to relocate to Taiwan. While in Taipei, Peter Brand was inducted into the Fang-tse society for courage and fortitude, qualities his father and grandfather had earlier displayed.

And through their Fang-tse brothers, La-li's parents were brought to Hong Kong, thence to Taiwan, where Brand bought them a house, land, and a tailoring shop catering to foreigners. They were industrious managers and business flourished.

Chu-li departed for a month's spring skiing in Bariloche, Argentina, her companion an Anglo-Chinese lung surgeon she had dated at Cambridge. After a month-long engagement, during which their families were visited and consulted, the wedding was celebrated in Hong Kong. The surgeon husband bought a practice in Harley Street, and a house in Mayfair, where they live.

Tommy Gray's wife died and was buried in the family plot near Portland. Tommy sold their Cleveland Park home and its contents, and moved to Taos, New Mexico, where he financed a bed-and-breakfast enterprise for his son and daughter-in-law, and worked as bookkeeper and bartender.

Ah-peng received the yuan equivalent of ten thousand U.S. dollars from an anonymous messenger she never saw again. She returned to Nanjing and established a restaurant open round-the-clock for night workers and others. The restaurant offered rice, noodles, pork, chicken, and seafood at affordable prices, and was never without customers.

In a corner of her upstairs apartment, Ah-peng set up a shrine to the Holy Mother, and her son Peter Brand, and worshiped there in secret.

Nina Kenton's son, Gareth, was located in a Miami hospice where he was dying of AIDS. Investigators from the court-appointed conservator of Nina's small estate left him a check for thirteen hundred dollars, net proceeds from the sale of her personal effects.

Oleg V. Tarnovski worked seven months for his FBI controllers after a lengthy FBI/CIA debriefing. He cooperated in identifying arriving agents of the revived Russian Intelligence Service, and worked as a double agent in ongoing cases. Then he disappeared.

A CIA report from Paris suggested that Tarnovski had surfaced there as Yuri Chesnikov, a clandestine vendor of surplus Red Army weapons and matériel. Before a joint decision was made concerning Tarnovski/Chesnikov's future, the Russian disappeared and was never seen again.

Lieutenant General Bruce Barlow, USAF, did not receive the fourth star of a full general before retirement. Joint Chiefs Chairman Sosnowski told him, confidentially, that influential elements within the Defense establishment opposed the promotion, and Defense Secretary Billings bowed to them.

Barlow retired then and was honored by well-attended ceremonies at Fort Myers and Andrews Air Force Base. During the latter, the President awarded Barlow a fifth Legion of Merit and the Distinguished Service Medal. Among friends present were Vivian and Irving Chenow. Following the ceremony the President took Barlow aside and asked if he would be willing to continue serving his country. "Of course, sir," Barlow replied, and the President grasped his hand.

"Consider yourself the new Director of the CIA."

Barlow's nomination was unopposed in the Senate, and before he took office the President ordered his promotion to four-star rank.

Also before leaving the Pentagon, General Barlow paid private visits to the widows of Blackbird pilots McAwley and Sampas. He gave each widow a posthumous DSC and a government check for half a million dollars. "Their sacrifice must never be known," he told them, "and the President's and my hope is that this will, at least in a small way, compensate for the honors and distinctions they would have gained in a longer career."

The Government of the People's Republic of China constructed new chemical warfare plants in hardened underground caverns, according to plans provided by Iraqi engineers.

The Chinese Ambassador to Washington was summoned to Beijing "for consultations" and did not return.

Irving Chenow left the Department of State and resumed the practice of law in Chicago. He declined to engage in raising funds for the President's reelection campaign.

The President was renominated by a divided convention, and failed of reelection by seventy-two electoral votes. After leaving the White House, the ex-President took to the lecture platform to acquire funds for a library to house his presidential papers and personalia.

The former Director of Central Intelligence accepted the presidency of a small college in New Hampshire.

Doreen Gerold had her father cremated and kept his ashes in a bronze urn on the living-room mantel. Half a dozen former colleagues of her father's gathered in the CIA headquarters chapel for a private ceremony that Doreen attended.

She was given six months' notice to leave the Georgetown pied-à-terre by Warren Bass, who was arranging its sale.

While a patient at Arbor Vitae Clinic, Doreen had become friendly with a female literary agent hooked on cocaine. When the agent was released she looked up Doreen and persuaded her to write a book about her worldwide experiences with drug addiction.

The agent supplied a word processor for Doreen's outpourings, and visited twice weekly to check on progress made. The agent was enthusiastic about Doreen's memoir, and called it a firm statement for feminism and a powerfully unique exposure of parental sexual abuse.

Sample chapters circulated by the agent brought Doreen a publishing advance of eight hundred thousand dollars.

While overseeing final editing of the memoir the agent moved in with Doreen, and they became lovers.

During the ensuing book promotion tour of twenty-two cities, the agent was Doreen's PR adviser and constant companion.

Doreen hired international investigative agencies to locate her brother Fitzhugh, and publicized a reward of a hundred thousand dollars for his return. Fitz had been her first lover and she loved him still. Over seven months she paid investigators two hundred thousand dollars for fruitless searches, and told them to press on. She had to know if Fitzhugh was dead or alive before she could find spiritual peace.

Pauline Frances Imhoff Gerold was cleared of any and all possible responsibility for the death of her husband. Nevertheless, she sensed a coolness among erstwhile friends and left Oaktree Farms in charge of Warren Bass's equestrienne sister, while she took a long restorative cruise on a new Holland-America Line vessel.

Among bridge-playing passengers, Pauline met a fifty-two-year-old widower, graduate of Amherst College and Yale Law School. They became inseparable partners for bridge, shore sight-seeing, and nocturnal lovemaking. In him, Pauline found the gentle, sensitive lover she had sought all her life, and a month after the cruise ended they were married in Milwaukee at her parent's Episcopal church, and took up residence in St. Louis, where he practiced law. His sister, Vivian, Pauline learned, was the wife of Irving Chenow, a Chicago lawyer, whose name she had heard Darman mention in the past.

Warren Bass handled the sale of Oaktree Farms, and Pauline never saw it again.

EPILOGUE

SKULL SHAVEN, BAREFOOT, SINEWY BODY clad in saffron robe, a monk sat cross-legged on an outcropping beside the Nepalese mountain trail. He was known as Marachandra and this was his place to sit, beggar's bowl in hand, seeking the alms of travelers and pilgrims who passed.

Through the gorge below rushed the clear, snow-fed waters of the Bheri River where twice each day he bathed and quenched his thirst.

He had come, the monk remembered dimly, through Turkey, Iran, and India, following with others the Trail to Self-Knowledge and Spiritual Truth. He had been ill for a time, he knew, and kindly monks had nursed him whole, believing through his fevered ravings that he was God-touched, a holy man. And so they satisfied his cravings while teaching him the True Way. His mother, the monk now knew, was the silver moon; his father, the sun toward whom he turned each day his nearly sightless eyes. Beside him lay the gnarled staff that symbolized his piety and helped him walk each day from temple cave to begging place.

Ganja is God, he often husked aloud; Ganja is Our Father, without remembering where first he had heard whispered the secret truth. But that had been long ago in another life, and its meaning was lost to him as so many other things were lost, dissolved in mists that often filled the gorge and overflowed across the rocky trail. With the taking of his name he had been reborn, come unencumbered into a new and worthy life. His books were the trees, his music the wind. He ate what was offered in his bowl remembering to set aside for the temple those coins that now and then appeared among the scraps.

Sometimes, asleep, he would dream of other places, other times, then waking know them as no more than dreams, illusions, or perhaps remembrances from some existence long ago. Often there floated through his imaginings the hair-framed face of a young white woman who seemed to speak to him though he could never understand. She had no name, merely features, a presence; perhaps, he once decided, she was a sister from another life; of women he had no need: his vows were celibacy and poverty, of service to the Infinite Master, and Marachandra was faithful to his vows.

A porter trudged along the trail, burden high-set on shafts and thongs. A coin of zinc clattered into the beggar's wooden bowl and the monk uttered a benison to the shadow that moved on.

Wind stirred the prayer wheel at his side, tinkling and chiming the prayer glass, and Marachandra became aware that it was evening breeze, cooler and from behind him rather than the river gorge. Soon his father, the sun, would give way to his mother, the moon. By then he would have taken his staff and made his way to the temple caves for evening orisons in the ritual of fellowship shared by Fitzhugh Gerold with his brethren in Eternal Light.